His Final Deal

His Final Deal

Theresa A. Campbell

www.urbanbooks.net

Urban Books, LLC
300 Farmingdale Road, NY-Route 109
Farmingdale, NY 11735

His Final Deal Copyright © 2020 Theresa A. Campbell

ISBN 13: 978-1-64556-198-9
ISBN 10: 1-64556-198-4

First Mass Market Printing June 2021
First Trade Paperback Printing July 2020
Printed in the United States of America

10 9 8 7 6 5 4 3 2 1

*This is a work of fiction. Any references or similarities
to actual events, real people, living or dead, or to real
locales are intended to give the novel a sense of reality.
Any similarity in other names, characters, places, and
incidents is entirely coincidental.*

Distributed by Kensington Publishing Corp.
Submit Orders to:
Customer Service
400 Hahn Road
Westminster, MD 21157-4627
Phone: 1-800-733-3000
Fax: 1-800-659-2436

His Final Deal

by

Theresa A. Campbell

Dedication

This book is dedicated to anyone who has ever been abused—physically, emotionally, verbally, sexually, or mentally.

Please remember . . . with God by your side, you'll be fine.

"I'll Be Fine," by Theresa A. Campbell

You play with my mind
Using your fists to knock me blind
Thinking you've got me in a bind
But with God by my side . . . I'll be fine

Groping, fondling, squeezing, and probing
You took from me what's mine
And you didn't even do any time for your crime
But with God by my side . . . I'll be fine

You promise me forever, only to find out it's never
Instead of a kiss, I get a kick

Dedication

Instead of a touch, I get a punch
But with God by my side . . . I'll be fine

Trapped by a wall, darkness is my call
Voices in my head telling me I'm better dead
Use this razor blade to make the pain fade
Swallow these pills to ease the chills
But with God by my side . . . I'll be fine

Calling me names was one of your games
You nagging, jeering, laughing, and rejoicing
Me crying, begging, pleading, and hurting
But with God by my side . . . I'll be fine

Betrayed, beaten, and mocked. I feel like I'm living
by the clock
Enslave my mind, rape my body, and hurt my pride
For you this is just a jolly ol' ride
But with God by my side . . . I'll be fine

I may be tired and weary, fumbling and stumbling
But on wings like an eagle, one day I'll soar away and
leave you
Victory will be mine, in hell you'll do your time
But with God by my side . . . I'll be fine

With a Heart of Thanksgiving

All that I am and all that I'll ever be is because of you,
Lord. . . . Thank you!

Dedication

To my family and friends who support me (you know who you are) . . . Thank you!

To my readers who enjoy my soul-fulfilling, entertaining books and take the time to share them with others . . . Thank you!

Prologue

Kingston, Jamaica, West Indies, 1976

His long legs eating up the dark, cracked, narrow road, the fourteen-year-old boy bolted down South Cochburn Road, zigzagging from one side to the other, his heart somersaulting in his chest.

Ziiing! The bullet snapped at Suave's right ear, and he ducked his head, his feet picking up even more speed as he ran for his life. Perspiration poured down his face with the black, damp T-shirt clinging to his body. The big backpack containing the reason for the attack still on his back, Suave sprinted toward Spanish Town Road.

Pow! Another bullet crackled at Suave's foot, followed by a muzzled blast as the clapping of hurried feet behind him got closer and closer.

The small boarded and zinced houses and dilapidated buildings along the street were eerily quiet in the night. But Suave wasn't fooled. He knew unseen eyes were watching him, so he kept running, jumping over potholes, stepping on loose stones, and leaping over the litter-strewn street.

"Stop right there!" commanded a deep, winded voice some distance behind Suave, shattering the silence. A warning shot then exploded into the air.

"Drop the bag now," roared another breathless voice. "We don't want to kill you."

But Suave ignored both men.

"Don't put up a fight if you're getting robbed," his boss had told him a few months after he had started his job. *"Trust me, I'll find the culprit, and you can be sure they'll pay one way or another. I don't want you to get hurt."*

Suave had nodded in agreement but was now doing the opposite. He sucked oxygen into his burning lungs, breathing heavily through his mouth as he zoomed around a corner with the bag still secure on his back.

The black car seemed to have fishtailed out of nowhere into the narrow three-road intersection. Its tires shrieked as it spun around in the middle of the road before stopping a few feet in front of Suave, blocking his escape to freedom.

Suave stumbled when he screeched to a sudden halt. His eyes bugged, and his mouth popped wide open in alarm.

"Don't move!" yelled the short, stocky man who hopped out of the driver's seat. The gun in his hand was raised and pointed at Suave.

His chest rising and falling rhythmically, Suave peered over his shoulder at the two men trotting toward him. He turned back to the front and saw the other man was almost upon him. He was trapped.

"All right. You win." Suave raised both hands in the air while taking a few slow, calculated steps to the right where a low, rusty zinc fence was wrapped around an abandoned house that was gutted by fire a few months before.

"I said, don't move," the man from the car shouted again as he wobbled over to stand in front of Suave, his finger on the trigger of the gun. With his head tilted back, he stared up at the tall, lanky boy and spat, "Are you deaf, boy?"

Suave looked down at the little man without fear. For some reason, an image of a pit bull popped into his mind. But he dare not say a word. This pit bull had a gun trained on him.

Soon, the other two men joined them, huffing and puffing from running after the boy.

"I told you to drop the bag." The light-skinned Michael Manley look-alike slapped Suave hard across his face.

Suave's face was on fire. Tears welled up in eyes, but he blinked rapidly, refusing to cry.

"This is for not listening when a big man talks to you." The other man who was running after Suave delivered an upper cut to the boy's stomach in true Muhammad Ali style.

Suave doubled over in the middle of the street, screaming in pain. He was retching and coughing, his mouth filled with bile, and the tears now seeped down his face.

"Now I take the bag the hard way," said the same man. He gave Suave a sharp kick in his bottom, sending the boy flying into the zinc fence, before landing hard facedown.

Suave sprawled out on the road, motionless. His head was bent at an unusual angle, and blood poured from his mouth.

"You killed him?" Michael Manley look-alike asked in disbelief.

"He . . . He's not dead." The man's voice was laced with fear.

"Look at him. He's—"

"Shut up!" Mr. Pit Bull, the leader of the group, barked. "We had him cornered, so that wasn't necessary. Do you know what's going to happen if his boss finds out we killed him?" He glared at the two men.

"It's his fault."

"You hit him first."

As the men argued over who was responsible for Suave's demise, his backpack forgotten for the moment, Suave took a tiny peek from under an almost closed eye. Agonizing pain pierced his body from head to toe, but he played possum, barely breathing.

They're going to kill me once they realize I'm not dead, Suave thought. *I have to get away or at least die trying.*

"Go get the bag, and let's go," the leader instructed one of the men. "We need to get out of here now."

That's all Suave needed to hear to make a move. He dug deep down inside and found the strength to leap to his feet. Biting his lips against the excruciating pain, he threw himself over the short fence into the tall, wild grasses and bushes.

"What the . . .?"

"He wasn't dead?"

For a few seconds, the three men stared with open mouths at the place where Suave disappeared.

"He's getting away!" The boss opened fire in the yard as he moved closer to the broken-down fence. His two accomplices joined in, spraying the area with bullets.

Suave lay on his belly, eyes closed, with bullets flying all around him. His heart hammering in his chest, he waited for a bullet to penetrate his body.

"Cease fire," the leader shouted, and the other two men complied. "Do you see anything?" He leaned forward, squinting as he peered into the dark.

"It's too dark in there," one man replied. "Let's go and look. I'm sure we hit him." He hopped over the fence.

"Follow him," the boss commanded the other man. "Hurry. With all those shots we fired, I'm sure someone must have called the cops by now."

Suave, who wasn't too far away, overheard the conversation. He began crawling away as fast as he could through the grass, ignoring the pain. Luckily for him, it was dark, and he was wearing all black. This would work to his advantage.

"He couldn't have gone far." The man used his leg to move the grass as they searched for Suave. "He should be hurt."

"I see him!" the other man exclaimed, pointing. "See? That's the backpack."

"Now we got you, little bugger."

The men hastened their steps, their prey within sight.

Suave heard them and forced himself to his feet. He wanted to run, but his aching body wouldn't cooperate, and his right leg felt as if it had died. So, he staggered along, knowing he would be caught soon. "This is it for me, huh?" Suave whispered under his breath, looking up into the sky. "Why am I not surprised, God? You're never there for me."

Eeeeee, weeeooee, wooo! The police sirens reverberated in the night air, getting louder and louder with each passing second.

"Police! Let's go!" The leader took off toward the car, leaving his two men to follow.

The men didn't need to be told twice. They turned around, plowing through the tall grass and bushes, and raced back to the road. The car's engine was running when they jumped into the backseat, their boss flooring the gas pedal as they made a quick getaway.

Suave went the opposite direction, dragging himself through the back of people's houses until he saw the busy main road up ahead. Only then did he lower himself onto a rock under a big mango tree. He took off his backpack and unzipped it. Reaching inside, he pulled out a handful of high-grade Jamaican marijuana. He brought it to his bloody nose and sucked in the aroma, his eyes closed as if in ecstasy. "Safe and sound," he muttered, a big grin on his bruised face.

Part One

Chapter One

Kingston, Jamaica, West Indies, 2003

"*Psssst.* Hey, baby girl. Hold up." Raymond "Suave" Brown hopped out of his brand-spanking-new, cherry-red Cadillac Escalade that was parked alongside the curb on Hope Road. With his long dreads hanging down his back, he swaggered over to the blushing young woman, a big smile on his face.

Like a laser beam, Suave's eyes scoped out the tight, super minidress that hugged the voluptuous body like a second layer of skin. Big, firm breasts strained against the restricted material as the woman stuck her chest out, with her huge behind pointing in the opposite direction.

Suave noticed how she nervously shifted from one foot to the other, her index finger twirling around a long strand of her blond weave as she watched him approach her.

"Hello, beautiful. How is it going?" Suave gave her a wink and licked his lips in a LL Cool J kind of way.

"I'm . . . I'm fine," she said in a small voice, looking down at the ground.

The dimples deepened in Suave's cheeks. He was used to this type of reaction from the ladies. After all, he was "Smooth Suave"—six foot one with silky, chocolate skin wearing a tan Armani suit and a Rolex on his wrist. When money talked, everyone walked were the words he lived by.

"What's your name, honey bunch?" Suave was laying it on real thick.

"Hmmm, Bubbles."

"That's a very pretty name for a very pretty lady." He reached out and ran his index finger down her cheek.

Bubbles glanced up at him and smiled before looking away. "Thank you."

"So, Bubbles, where am I dropping you off?" Suave grinned at her when she raised puzzled eyes to look at him. "I'm offering you a ride home, baby." He spread his arms wide open as if to say, *I'm all yours*.

Bubbles's eyes widened in excitement as the impact of Suave's words hit her. She was just on her way to the bus stop. Glancing over at the Escalade, Bubbles felt her heartbeat speed up.

"I'm going home." Bubbles gasped in delight. "I live in Pembroke Hall."

"Pembroke Hall, it is." Suave strolled over to the passenger-side door and opened it. His grin widened as he watched her rush over and hop into the truck without any hesitation. As she nestled back into the rich leather seat, glancing around wide-eyed, he closed her door.

Suave strutted around the car to take his seat behind the steering wheel. He glanced down at his watch and nodded his head. He had an hour before he had to pick up his main girl, Monica, from the hairdressing salon.

Monica Lambert was the mother of two of Suave's eight children and was now five months pregnant with the third. She was the "wifey" and lived with their children in his big house in the affluent neighborhood of Jacks Hill, St. Andrew.

"Everything good, baby?" Suave's eyes locked on Bubbles's soft, brown, exposed thighs. The minidress had ridden farther up, exposing her thong. "You are one sexy woman."

Bubbles giggled and glanced out the car window.

Suave started the car and drove off. "How old are you?"

"I'll be nineteen in six days." She beamed at him. Just the thought of spending her birthday with him was surreal.

"Cool. A grown woman who I'm sure knows how to handle a grown man." Suave threw a sly smile at her before turning his attention back to the road. He was a lot of things, but a pedophile wasn't one of them. He made it a rule never to get sexually involved with any girl under eighteen years old. Of course, if they lied about their age, it wasn't his fault.

"Where are we going?" Bubbles asked a few minutes later, peering through the window as Suave took a turn off Waterloo Road into the parking lot of the Hide Away Motel and parked. "What's going on?"

Suave turned sideways in his seat to face Bubbles, impatience splashed across his face. "I was thinking we would get a room and get to know each other some more. You have a problem with that?"

Bubbles looked at him with uncertainty for just a few seconds. Not because she hadn't done this before. She had had her fair share of men, especially if they had lots of money. She just never expected him to move so fast. But as the bright, warm sun shone through the opened car window and the huge diamond cross pendant around Suave's neck and the big rock in his ear sparkled, Bubbles felt a burst of excitement wash over her. *Money,*

money, money. "I would like that." She blushed and looked down at her bare lap.

"Cool." Suave leaned back in his seat, reached into his pants pocket, and took out a wad of money.

Bubbles's eyes grew large.

"Here, go get us a room." He placed a thick bundle in her trembling hand.

After Bubbles hurried over to the small office, Suave drove around to the back of the building and parked behind a huge dumpster. This was one of his regular motels where he took his women for a little rendezvous, so he had to be careful. Who knew. . . . Maybe Monica was playing detective again. A few days ago, Suave pulled into another hotel to meet one of his women, and Monica drove in and parked right beside him. She was always driving around town trying to catch him in the act of cheating . . . as if the six other kids he had outside their relationship weren't enough evidence of that. Shaking his head, Suave pressed his key fob, locking the doors behind him, and walked around to the front. He saw Bubbles coming toward him, waving her hand in the air.

"I got it." Bubbles handed him the room key. "We're in Room 303."

How coincidental. Yesterday he had the same room.

Suave had gone to Sovereign Center to handle some business. As he was walking to the parking lot, deep in thoughts, he collided with a soft body.

"My bad." Suave's eyes lit up when he saw the beautiful woman standing before him. "I wasn't paying attention." He smiled broadly.

"No, you weren't, Smooth Suave," she replied softly and teasingly. "You almost knocked me over."

Suave looked at her, trying to remember if he knew her, but drew a blank. Obviously, she knew him. "I'm sorry, but—"

"We never met," the woman responded. "But I know who you are. I've seen you around and sometimes in the club. I'm Georgia."

Suave's grin got wider. His reputation preceded him. "Hi, Georgia, let me make it up to you," he said quickly. "Why don't we go back inside, and I'll buy you lunch?"

Georgia didn't hesitate. She happily took Suave's hand in hers, and they walked back inside to the restaurant.

Suave enjoyed a lunch of steamed fish and bammy, and Georgia for dessert, at the same motel in Room 303.

"Hello?" Bubbles had a puzzled look on her face.

Suave enfolded her hand in his, and they took the stairs to the third floor. With a final look at his watch, Suave entered the motel room with Bubbles to get better "acquainted."

Bubbles was thrilled to become Suave's girl, and Suave was psyched to satisfy his lustful appetite. Any woman Smooth Suave wanted, Smooth Suave got.

"Li'l mama, you ain't no joke." Suave winked at Bubbles as he pulled up his pants almost an hour later. The encounter he had in mind wasn't as brief as he had thought it would be. Bubbles showed him some moves and took him on a sexual journey so intense he had to savor the moment. Now, he was late to pick up Monica.

"So, when will I see you again?" Bubbles asked as she slipped the little dress over her head.

An awkward silence crept into the room as Suave contemplated his situation. This was the part he hated. He really had no intention of seeing her again, but after her raving performance in bed, he knew he needed more. "How about we decide on that after I drop you off at home?" This was another first for Suave. Usually, he would give the women some money to catch a cab with plenty left over, but he was breaking his rules for the queen of the bedroom . . . Bubbles.

"That sounds good to me." Bubbles's grin stretched from ear to ear as she bent down to slip the platform sandals on her feet. Inside, she rejoiced.

Fully dressed, Suave and Bubbles left the room and headed around to the back of the motel where he parked. Bubbles noticed how the car was hidden, but she never said a word. It was all good. He loved the women, and the women loved him . . . as long as she got her fair share.

Suave's cell phone rang nonstop. A few of the calls he answered with an, "I'll hit you back in a minute," and others he ignored altogether.

Soon, Suave was navigating his Escalade down the narrow road to Bubbles's house, creeping over potholes and loose stones. Passing small houses on both sides of the street, he became apprehensive as he looked around. Children ran around outside playing, while grown folks sat on their verandas or leaned up outside their gates, chatting and laughing. He was in unknown territory without any of his soldiers for backup. Due to Suave's line of business, he had made enemies all over Jamaica, with competitors just itching for the opportunity to catch him vulnerable. His 9 mm Glock was hidden under his seat with a loaded semiautomatic rifle under the spare tire in the trunk, but what if there were a few of them? Suave said a few choice curse words under his breath. *A woman has me slipping,* he thought nervously.

"Over there." Bubbles pointed to a small, pink house at the end of the street. The truck rolled forward. Faces were staring through opened windows and doors at the expensive truck in the neighborhood. Bubbles beamed with pride. She wished she could see the look on her haters' faces when she hopped out.

Suave pulled up in front of her house, the engine running, the car still in drive.

"Are you coming in?" Bubbles asked hopefully, although she lived with her mother, stepfather, two brothers, and three sisters in the small, three-bedroom house. She hoped her sisters were out, and the room she shared with them was empty.

"Nah." Suave shook his head. "I have some business to take care of, beautiful." He reached in his pocket and took out some money, which he placed in her hand. "Why don't you take my digits and hit me up later?"

Bubbles nodded with great anticipation. She stuffed the money in the small purse on her lap before she dug inside for her cell phone to add Suave's number. After repeating the number back to him, she kissed him on the cheek before she alighted. As if in slow motion, Bubbles shut the car door, flung her long weave over her shoulder with an attitude, and struck a pose for all eyes to gaze upon her.

Suave ignored her antics and took his foot off the brake. He then pressed the gas and made a U-turn in the middle of the street before he sped off down the road as if demons were chasing him.

He never saw the flowery white curtain that slipped back into place as the man turned away from the window, a big joker grin plastered on his face. *Well, well, look at this now. The big man all by himself in my neighborhood . . .* It looked as if he didn't have to go to the mountain after all—it just came right to him. Was it luck or destiny? Whatever it was, thank you, Bubbles.

Chapter Two

"Where are you, Suave?"

"Suave, I'm waiting on you. Hurry up!"

"I'm still waiting on you!"

Suave was listening to his messages after dropping off Bubbles. As he expected, most were from Monica.

"One hour! You have me waiting one hour!"

"That's it! I'm going home! Wait until I see you!"

Suave groaned loudly. He had told Monica he would pick her up from the hairdressing salon in an hour. Then he saw Bubbles. She had called a few times when he was with Bubbles, but he ignored the calls. Now, it was almost two hours later.

"Where were you, Suave?" Monica stood at the front door of their house with her hand on her hip. "Do you know how long I waited for you?" She pointed her finger in Suave's face as her enormous stomach created a much-needed barrier between them. "Which one of your whores were you with this time?"

"I had to take care of some urgent business," Suave lied.

"So why didn't you answer any of my calls and tell me that? Huh?"

Suave tried to maneuver around Monica to get inside the house, but she shoved him back out to the veranda. "Answer me, Suave. Where were you?" At five foot eight, with a pregnancy weight of about 170 pounds, Monica wasn't a lightweight.

Suave took a deep breath, his chest rising and falling as anger crept up on him. "I'm a grown man and don't need to report my every move to you. Now, can I get into my house?"

"You are not going anywhere until you tell me why you left me stranded." Monica shoved him again in the chest, this time much harder.

Suave stumbled back a little. His nostrils flared as he glared at her. "Don't you have money to take a cab? As a matter of fact, why can't you drive one of the cars in the garage?" he asked her.

"I can't drive because I'm five months pregnant with your child, and my feet hurt," she yelled. "I don't want to take a cab when my no-good baby daddy has a car and can pick me up."

Suave looked at her and shook his head. She was really pushing his buttons today, and he wasn't in the mood to deal with her foolishness. "You know what? I'm—"

The cell phone in Suave's hand rang. He glanced at it and saw that it was an important business contact in Westmoreland. He answered the call. "What's up, my brother?" Turning his back on Monica, he strolled over to one of the veranda's side chairs and sat down.

As Suave was engrossed in his conversation, Monica hurried inside the house. She returned and stood in the middle of the doorway, her hands behind her back.

Suave concluded his call. He looked up and noticed that Monica was still blocking the door. "I can't deal with this right now." Suave sucked his teeth and stood up.

"I'm not done talking to you, Suave," Monica hissed.

"I'm outta here." He turned around and walked away. As he descended the few steps into the yard, Suave felt a cool breeze fan his ear as a plate flew by his head, smashing into pieces at his feet. He spun around to see something flying in the air toward his head. He ducked.

"You think you can treat me any kind of way?" Monica screamed as another plate flew out of her hand into the yard. "I'm the mother of your children!" Another plate went sailing through the air. "I gave you ten years of my life, and you treat me like trash." Two more plates landed at Suave's feet as he jumped, ducked, dodged, and slipped.

"You are one crazy . . . Hey!" Suave dodged a plate as he inched closer to the gate.

"Say it, you nasty whoremonger." Monica fired off another plate.

Suave completed the sentence under his breath as he ran through the gate toward his truck parked on the road.

"Peace out!" Suave hopped into his truck. He looked through the tinted window and saw his seven-year-old son, Rayden, and four-year-old daughter, Raven, hiding behind their furious mother, tears running down their faces. Shame and guilt swept over him. He wasn't sure why he continued to hurt Monica and his children. He loved his family, but, unfortunately, they weren't enough.

Suave drove away from his house with a heavy heart. *"Destiny, Mama look from when you calling,"* Buju Banton's raspy voice blared from the car speakers. *"I wanna rule my destiny."* Suave bobbed his head as he maneuvered the truck along Barbican Road, over to Hope Road, onto East Road, turning onto Waltham Park Road. Moments later, he pulled up in front of a small, two-bedroom house and parked.

"Daddy!" The little girl threw down the ball she was bouncing off the outside wall, opened the gate, and ran into Suave's waiting arms. "I see your big truck coming down the road," four-year-old Alissa informed her father, giggling as he placed little kisses all over her face.

"I can't hide from you, huh?" Suave smiled as he held his daughter. "Where's your mama?"

"Inside cooking dinner."

Suave's stomach growled at the mention of food. He intended to go home, shower, have dinner, and spend some time with Monica and the kids, but that didn't work out too well. "Come on, let's see what's for dinner." Suave walked up to the house with Alissa held in the crook of his arm.

"Daddy, you don't see me too?" said a small voice from the adjoining house next door.

Suave's hand paused on the doorknob as he turned to see his other daughter, Janelle, staring at him with a big frown on her face. "Hey, baby. Daddy didn't see you. Come here and give me some love."

Four-year-old Janelle smiled with happiness as she ran through her gate, over to her father at her aunt's house.

Suave took care as he bent down with Alissa and scooped up Janelle in his other arm. He then stood up, balancing the two girls in each arm.

"Did you bring me something nice?" Janelle wrapped her little hand tighter around her father's neck. "You promised me ice cream."

Suave beamed with pride as he looked down at his two beautiful daughters. Both girls were not only sisters, but they were cousins too. Alissa's mother, Charlene, and Janelle's mother, Darlene, were identical twins who lived beside each other for years. Suave got both sisters and Monica pregnant just about the same time, with all three women giving birth to daughters within days of each other.

The nurses and doctors in Mona University Hospital maternity ward watched in amazement when Suave, the dedicated father, came in three times within a week, coaching his baby mommas through the births and cutting the umbilical cords. The proud papa also named his three daughters, who were small replicas of him—Raven, Alissa, and Janelle.

"Wow, look at these beautiful little girls. Are they triplets?" a woman asked Suave one day when he took his three daughters to Hope Gardens. Everyone who saw the girls always assumed they were because of their strong resemblance to each other, and they looked to be the same age.

"Thank you. Yes, they are my triplets." Suave glowed with pride. He never mentioned his triplets were from triple births with triple mothers.

"Ahem." Suave's head snapped up to see Janelle's mother, Darlene, standing on her veranda next door. "You are here to see Charlene but not me, huh?" Darlene walked closer to the short, wired fence that separated the houses. Her pretty face was screwed up with a cigarette dangling from the corner of her mouth.

Suave's eyes lit up as he stared at Darlene. Her long, straight "Indian" hair fell down her back. Big, brown breasts were popping out of the midriff tank top, exposing tight, flat abs. Smooth, high butt cheeks peeked out from the booty shorts she wore. "Baby, you know I wouldn't come in the place and not see you." Suave lowered the two girls to the ground. "Both of you go inside. I'll be right there."

After the girls ran into the house, Suave walked out the gate and over to meet Darlene in her yard. "What's up, sexy mama?" He slapped her on her behind.

Darlene rolled her eyes. She dropped the half-burning cigarette to the ground and crushed it with her slippers. "Don't try to sweet-talk me, Suave. You came, and the first place you headed was over to Charlene's house. What am I, huh? Chop liver?" Darlene was angry. She folded her arms across her chest, pushing her boobs higher up.

Suave licked his lips, overcome with lust. "Girl, you know I was saving the best for last. I was just going to grab a bite by Charlene because Alissa said she was making dinner. But trust and believe, Smooth Suave was coming next door for dessert." He leaned in closer to Darlene and nibbled on her bottom lip.

"Behave yourself, man." Darlene playfully shoved at him but was now grinning.

The two sisters spent their whole lives competing. If Charlene dated a guy in high school, Darlene never stopped until she slept with him. Darlene got pregnant when she was nineteen years old; Charlene was pregnant weeks later. Charlene became an exotic dancer; Darlene began dancing at the Gentleman's Club across the street. Darlene rented a house on Waltham Park Road; Charlene moved into the house next door within a few weeks. Charlene met and slept with Suave one night when he came to the club with his boys; the following week, Darlene had Suave in her bed.

"Suave and I are having a baby," Charlene had bragged to Darlene almost five years ago, a satisfied

smirk on her face. "We may be sharing him, but I'm his baby momma now."

Darlene threw her head back and laughed. "For your information, Suave just brought me home from the doctor." She rubbed her small baby bump, her smile growing bigger at the shocked expression on Charlene's face. "I am Suave's baby momma too. You better come correct."

"Let's go inside." Suave reached out and lightly touched one of Darlene's breasts.

Darlene laughed, turned around, and walked back to her house.

Suave was right on her heels. Darlene's backside was the best real estate on her body. She had the shape of a Coca-Cola bottle with curves that made his blood rush like a raging river.

"Mama, I'm hungry," remarked Darlene's three-year-old son as he wandered out of a side room. He was wearing white briefs with his thumb in his mouth. "I want fry chicken."

"Your aunt is cooking next door. Go tell her to give you some dinner."

"Yay!" The boy raced past his mother and Suave.

"Little Mr. Chin looks more like his father each day." Suave looked at Darlene with a frown on his face. "And you tried to plant that baby on me, huh?"

Suave was right. When Darlene got pregnant with her son, she told him the baby was his. Suave was known to take care of all his kids, so he stuck by her, even though Charlene warned him the child wasn't his.

"The baby's father is Mr. Chin, the Chinese man, who owns the bakery in Downtown Kingston," Charlene had informed Suave. "He's afraid of his wife finding out, so he doesn't claim the child. Trust me, Darlene is giving you 'jacket.'" "Jacket" was a Jamaican term for a child that was raised by a man who didn't know that he wasn't the biological father.

"Well, none of my kids can hide," Suave had replied. "All my children favor me. I'll find out when the baby is born." And he did. The little boy was born light skinned with small, slanted eyes and a head full of straight, black hair. Suave didn't speak to Darlene for months.

"I said I was sorry," Darlene mumbled, rolling her eyes. "It was an honest mistake." She strolled off down the hall and into her bedroom, leaving the door open.

Suave shook his head, followed her into her room, and closed the door behind him. It had been almost four years since the deception, but he still got upset whenever he saw the boy. Even so, he found it hard to stop messing with Darlene.

If a woman was skilled in the bedroom, Suave was hooked. Women were his weakness . . . a fact that was well known to everyone—which, unfortunately, included his enemies.

Chapter Three

Darlene knew she had to get Suave back in a good mood really quickly. She couldn't afford for him to change his mind and head back over to Charlene's house. Her rent, electricity, and water were due, and she also needed groceries. Things weren't the same at the club anymore. After giving birth to four children, Darlene still looked good, but she was no competition for the eighteen- and nineteen-year-old strippers. Her regular customer pool was dwindling, and she got no help from her other kids' fathers. There was only Suave, who made sure his daughter had everything she needed.

Darlene provocatively pulled the blouse over her head, baring her breasts.

Suave swallowed hard as he went and sat down on the edge of the bed, his eyes glued on Darlene. His heart rate went up as she took her time easing the little shorts over her ample hips, down to her ankles. With her back now to Suave, Darlene bent over as she stepped out of the shorts. She wasn't wearing any underwear.

"Lord, have mercy." Suave swallowed hard and jumped to his feet. He couldn't take off his shirt fast enough and dropped it on the hardwood floor.

"No, let me." Darlene placed her hands over Suave's hands as he was getting ready to unzip his pants. Without a word, she took over the task, her eyes locked on his dilated pupils.

In record time, Suave was butt naked again, for the third time that day. Monica was for breakfast, Bubbles was lunch, and now Darlene for dinner. Suave pulled Darlene down on the bed, his earlier resentment replaced by lust.

Minutes later, loud knocks came from the door. "Open this door right now!" Charlene screamed as she pounded on Darlene's bedroom door. "Suave, get your nasty behind out here now."

Inside the room, Suave and Darlene ignored Charlene as they continued their sexual dance. The louder Charlene beat on the door, the more Darlene's groans escalated. Suave, used to the twins' antics, ignored both as he got his fill of Darlene.

Suddenly, a loud noise exploded in the room as the door slammed against the wall. Suave leapt off the bed to face Charlene as she stepped into the room, raving mad. With big rollers in her hair, streaks of flour on her forehead and nose, her hands balled into fists, he watched Charlene's wild eyes go back and forth between them. Suave knew things just took a turn for the worst.

Darlene, not the least bit fazed by Charlene's entrance, rolled over on her stomach, her big, naked buttocks in the air, and an amused grin on her face. It was such a pleasure to see Charlene this angry. "You are too late for the party, sis," Darlene mocked her sister.

Charlene was on Darlene like a hungry lion. She leaped on Darlene's back, wrapped a handful of her long hair around one hand as the other punched Darlene repeatedly in the back of her head.

Darlene twisted and turned on the bed, shouting expletives as she tried to shake Charlene off her back. She crawled to the edge of the bed and threw herself over, landing on her back on the floor with Charlene on hers a few inches away. "I'm going to kill you now," Darlene yelled before she sprang to her feet, her heavy, exposed breasts swinging from side to side.

Charlene, still winded from the fall, tried to get up but wasn't fast enough. Darlene was soon sitting on her stomach, raining punches all over her face.

As the two women rolled around on the floor, scratching, punching, kicking, and screaming, Suave found his clothes and got dressed. He went and stood calmly at the door and watched as perfume bottles, flower vases, photo frames, and other items fell to the floor.

"Mommy? Daddy?" Janelle called out as she entered the house. Fear splashed across her face at the commotion coming from her mother's room.

It was then that Suave sprang into action. "Janelle, go back outside," he shouted. "You and the kids stay out there." Suave heard the door shut as Janelle did as he instructed. He walked over to the fighting women, reached down, and wrapped his arms around Charlene, who was now on top of Darlene. With all his might, Suave pulled her off and onto her feet. Pushing her behind him, he used his body to create a barrier between the sisters.

Charlene was breathing heavily, her hair flying around her scratched up face, yelling and swearing as she tried to get around Suave to pound her sister.

Darlene, now on her feet, with blood running down her nose and one eye swollen, threw herself at Suave in an attempt to get to Charlene.

"Enough!" Suave screamed and pushed back Darlene with force. She stumbled but grabbed on to the bed to break her fall. "That goes for you too," Suave yelled as he turned to face Charlene. "Stop it now." The veins in

Suave's neck stood up, his nostrils flared, and his eyes widened in fury. "What's the matter with you two?"

The women rolled eyes at each other but remained silent.

"Go home. I'll be over in a minute." Suave glared at Charlene.

Charlene flipped the bird at Darlene before she walked out of the room without a word. She dared not disobey Suave.

"And you, go clean up yourself and put on some clothes," Suave instructed Darlene. "I hate to see grown women acting like children."

Darlene rolled her eyes, walked out of the room and into the bathroom across the hall. She hoped Suave would still give her some money. If that skank Charlene let Suave leave without giving her anything, another fight was about to take place.

Suave went and sat on the couch in Darlene's living room as he waited for her. He took out a joint and a lighter from his pants pocket. He lit the joint and sucked the drug deeply into his lungs. With his head raised, his eyes closed contentedly, Suave blew the smoke into the air before he took another hit.

"Sorry." Minutes later, he opened his eyes to see Darlene standing before him, a puppy dog look on her face. She was wearing a maxidress with her hair pulled back in a ponytail. Her left eye was almost swollen shut.

"Look at your face. Was all that necessary?" he asked her. He was still angry.

"Why you blaming me? She came over here to *my* house."

"Well, you shouldn't have egged her on," Suave replied, refusing to take any responsibility. "You know how crazy Charlene can get."

Darlene opened her mouth to reply but stopped herself. She needed some money, and arguing with Suave wasn't the way to get it. She sat beside him on the couch, her leg brushing against his. "Sorry," she repeated in a low voice.

Suave looked at her, shook his head, and took another drag on the joint.

"Suave, can I please get some money for the rent?" Darlene stared at him. "The light and water bills are also due."

Suave stood to his feet. He leaned over and stubbed out the joint in an overflowing ashtray that sat on the coffee table. "Follow me outside." He walked out with Darlene behind him toward his truck. He pressed his key fob and opened the doors, then reached into the glove compartment and took out two padded envelopes.

"Here, this should take care of it." Suave handed Darlene an envelope filled with money. As Darlene knew, Suave would make sure his daughter had a roof over her head, food to eat, and all the basic necessities required. "I'll catch you later."

"So, are you going over there after what she did?" Darlene asked as Suave headed toward Charlene's house.

Suave paused and glared at her. "Shut up! Go inside and go take care of your business." He pointed toward Darlene's house. "I've had enough of your foolishness for one day."

Suave watched Darlene storm through her gate, into her house, slamming the door shut. He took a deep breath before he strolled up to Charlene's door. It opened as soon as he reached it with Charlene smiling innocently at him. She had on a pair of tight jeans and a small, low cut tank top. Her long hair was hanging straight down her back, her lips were glossed, and her beautiful, lined eyes held seduction. Except for a small bump on her forehead, the scratches were covered up by flawless makeup.

Charlene had been peeping through the front window and saw the exchange between Suave and Darlene. "Serves that heifer right," she had whispered under her breath with a satisfied grin.

"Here." Suave handed Charlene the other envelope filled with money. "I'll call Janelle and Alissa later. I'm out." With that, he strolled out to his truck, clicked it open, then hopped inside and drove off.

It was getting dark outside as night rolled in. Suave was feeling hungry and tired—physically and mentally. He needed some rest. But he was about to find out that wouldn't be happening anytime soon. His stress level was about to skyrocket to a whole 'nother level.

Chapter Four

Suave's personal cell phone on the passenger seat began ringing. He reached for the phone and glanced at it before focusing his attention back on the road. It was Barbara, one of his baby mommas. He sucked his teeth and threw the phone back on the seat. He'd had enough baby momma drama for one day.

Immediately, his business cell phone, which was also on the seat, rang. He had a phone for business and another for personal use. He answered that phone.

"Yo, Cobra, what's up, bro?" Suave greeted his top lieutenant and good friend.

"You tell me, Boss," Josh Blank, a.k.a. Cobra, replied. "I've been calling and paging you all day but can't hear a word from you."

Suave had indeed neglected business this day. He had men working for him all over Jamaica and knew they had things under control, but he was still the boss. "My bad, partner. I got caught up in some personal stuff."

Cobra didn't have to ask what that was. He had been rolling with Suave for many years and knew of his drama-filled life. "I need to see you as soon as possible. My finger got burned with the lighter."

Tires screeched as Suave cut around a minibus to pull over to the side of the road. "What! How bad did you get burned?" he screamed into the phone.

"Bad enough that I need medical attention," Cobra continued to speak in their code. "Like right now."

Suave pounded his fists on the steering wheel, shouting expletives. Cobra just informed him that they got robbed again. This was the third time in less than a month. Just last week, one of Suave's runners was held at gunpoint, robbed of a large quantity of marijuana and cocaine and thousands of dollars. The teenager was beaten almost to a pulp, and a letter to Suave was left on his battered body, saying, *There is only room for one.*

"You and Daddy Lizard meet me at the hut in thirty." Suave clicked off the phone and threw it down on the seat. He took deep breaths as he stared off into the distance, his mind racing. Someone was out to get him. This wasn't anything unusual or unexpected, but the method was new. Robbing Suave's workers and beating them down was total disrespect. Who would be so brazen to do something like that?

He took a deep breath before he put the truck in drive. Glancing up and down the busy street, he then eased into traffic. He was pissed.

Suave raced toward the "hut," speeding through red lights, cutting off vehicles left and right. He climbed the hill of the prestigious neighborhood of Belgrade Heights, St. Andrew, and drove up in front of a beautiful minimansion. Once he pressed the garage door button above the sun visor, Suave drove in and parked in one of the four parking spots. He pressed the garage button again to close it, grabbed his phones, and walked into the house.

The hut was nestled in a corner of one of the most attractive, tree-lined streets in the area. The light-filled home emanated charm and appeal, with its five bedrooms overlooking the beautifully landscaped tropical yard. The four bathrooms were fully renovated with a water heater system, and the huge living room with its floor-to-ceiling windows was elegantly furnished with expensive furniture and paintings. The kitchen had custom cabinetry and top-of-the-line appliances, while a carved extendable dining table sat on a large, rich oriental rug in the dining room, with a huge chandelier hanging above.

This was Suave's safe haven away from the streets. Only a handful of people knew about the house. Not even Monica and his other baby mommas knew.

Suave went into his bathroom, undressed, and took a quick shower. After getting dressed in a white Nike sweat suit with his long dreads pulled back in a ponytail, he marched barefoot into the kitchen and got a cold Red Stripe from the refrigerator. A horn honked outside as soon as he took the first sip.

Suave looked through the window and saw the familiar black Range Rover in front of the house. In a few quick strides, he was at the door entrance to the garage, pressing it open.

The truck pulled in beside the Cadillac, and two tall men alighted from the vehicle and marched toward Suave with solemn expressions on their faces.

"Paulie is at Public in critical condition," Samuel Briscoe, a.k.a. Daddy Lizard, greeted Suave. He was referring to the Kingston Public Hospital in downtown Kingston.

Suave took a big gulp of his beer, then fired off a few curse words before he turned and marched back inside. Cobra and Daddy Lizard followed him.

"How much they got?" Suave sat on the leather couch facing the two men who were sitting across from him on a matching couch.

"Our entire shipment from Westmoreland and all the payments that Paulie collected from his runners." Cobra took two joints out of his pocket and lit one before he passed the other and a lighter to Suave.

"We took a big loss, Boss." Daddy Lizard sucked hard on the spliff he had just lit. "They are not only robbing us, but they are hurting our workers too. We have to find out who it is and hit them back hard."

Suave remained silent as he drank his beer and smoked the weed. "There's beer in the fridge," he said moments later.

Cobra jumped up and went to get two for him and Daddy Lizard.

"What's the word on the street?" Suave asked when Cobra returned and sat down.

"My source claims it's Queen Bee." Daddy Lizard's eyes blazed with anger.

"Word is that it's King Kong," Cobra added in a low and dangerous voice. King Kong was one of Suave's main competitors in the Kingston area. Both men knew each other since they were children and had a personal vendetta against each other going back many years.

"So . . . Three robberies—and we don't know for sure?" Suave stared at his two top men. "Is *that* what you're telling me?" His nostrils flared. "All those fools we have on payroll and *nobody* can tell me who's disrespecting me?" By now, Suave was shouting. "They hurt my people, steal my money, and nobody knows nothing!" He threw the joint in an ashtray sitting on a glass coffee table between the two couches.

"We're working on it, Suave," Cobra was quick to assure him. "You know Queen Bee and King Kong are very powerful in the business. People are afraid to talk, but we'll find out."

"It's not Queen Bee." Suave stood to his feet and paced the carpeted floor. "We've been doing business with her for years. She was the one who gave me a start."

"Well, that leaves King Kong." Cobra stood and looked at Suave. "Say the word, and we can hit a few of his spots tonight."

Suave looked back and forth between Cobra and Daddy Lizard as a plan began to form in his mind. "I think I have an idea." A sinister smile spread across his lips. "My brothers, King Kong ain't got nothing on me."

Cobra and Daddy Lizard stared at him, puzzled.

"I'm starved." Suave sat down, settled back on the couch, and crossed his legs. "What do you say we order some food and I'll tell you all about my plan?"

Chapter Five

Danny Moore, King Kong's best friend and second in command, whistled a tune as he walked from his mistress's house toward his car parked in her driveway on Mountain View Avenue. It was 5:00 a.m., and he needed to head home. His wife was going to raise hell that he never came home last night. After spending the night with freaky Bambi, Danny was exhausted but content. Bambi was like a tranquilizer. Even if taken in small doses, she still knocked a brother out.

Danny clicked his key fob to unlock the car and pulled open the door. He was about to slide behind the wheel when he heard a click, followed by the feel of cold metal pressing into the back of his head. His hand flew to his hip where his gun was but paused when he heard two other guns click, one after the other.

"Reach for it, and you're a dead man," said an unfamiliar deep voice in Danny's ear.

Danny held up his hands in the air, his back still facing the men. He knew he was outnumbered. "Do you know who I am?" Danny was angry. "You are dead men walking."

The blow to his right ear temple caused Danny to see bright colored lights flashing before his eyes as he was thrown up against his car. His head began to throb with pain.

"Threats, Dan?" said another muffled voice. "You are about to die, and you are making threats?"

"O . . . O . . . Okay, take it easy." Danny blinked rapidly to regain his focus. "Take what you want and go. No hard feelings."

The men laughed out loud.

"We have what we want, Danny boy," came a disguised voice before a blindfold was slid over Danny's eyes.

"Wait a minute. What the—" Duct tape was snapped over Danny's mouth. His hands were handcuffed behind his back.

The three men dragged Danny to an old Honda Civic parked a few feet away from Bambi's house. Danny struggled to no avail as they opened the trunk and stuffed him in. In the tight, confined space, he felt the car start and drive off. His heart was pounding in his chest. He had a sickening feeling who the men were, although he never saw their faces.

That idiot, King Kong, Danny thought in anger. *I told him not to do it, but he wouldn't listen to me. Now* I'm *the one about to pay the price.*

The car drove for what seemed like hours to Danny before it came to a stop, and the engine was cut. His sweat-drenched shirt clung to his body. He was in trouble. Just then, the trunk popped open, and Danny's nostrils greedily sucked in the fresh air.

"Okay, Dan, let's go." Rough hands lifted him over a strong shoulder.

Danny tried to talk, but his words were smothered. He twisted and turned his body, kicking like a young goat about to be castrated.

But Danny was ignored. The man carrying him continued on his journey as if Danny were a mere handbag.

"Here you go." The man lowered Danny on to a hard, metal chair.

Danny jumped to his feet but was roughly shoved back down.

"Do that again, and this will be over before it even begins. *Capish?*"

Danny nodded his head. He made muffled sounds, hoping someone would take off the gag so he could plead his case. He didn't want to die for King Kong's ignorance.

King Kong alighted from the backseat of the Lincoln Town Car, the door held opened by his driver. He was a dark-complected man, standing at six foot four, weighing almost 300 pounds. Huge diamonds adorned his ears, neck, and wrist. He straightened the jacket of his white pin-striped suit, with his white Kangol hat perched on top of his bald head. His white Stacy Adams shoes tapped the ground as he swaggered into his bar located in Arnett Gardens, the community also known as Concrete Jungle.

Concrete Jungle, which was often shortened to simply "Jungle," was on the edge of West Kingston's Trench Town ghetto, a deprived area on the outskirts of town consisting of large numbers of crude buildings. It was a poverty-stricken community that was one of the most frequent locations for political violence in Jamaica.

King Kong was born Mason Dyke Jr. and was known as Junior when he was young. But as he got bigger in the drug trade, it wasn't long before he became known as King Kong for two reasons—his gigantic ego and his strong resemblance to the big gorilla. The nickname was given to him by Suave when they were children.

"Here's your coffee, Boss." A worker handed King Kong a huge cup of black, steaming Blue Mountain coffee. "I know you are not used to waking up so early."

King Kong grunted and snatched the cup. He just went to bed a few hours ago but had to get up early to meet a big potential customer. The man was coming from Clarendon and insisted on conducting business at this ungodly hour. With a lot of dollars on the line, King Kong had no choice but to make the deal himself.

"Where's Danny?" King Kong yelled as he walked toward the back of the restaurant where business was conducted. He took a sip of his coffee. "I know he's here. If I'm here, he better be here too."

"I think he's running a little late, King," the restaurant manager informed King Kong. "I also found it strange that he's not here yet. He knew this deal was a big one."

Just then, King Kong's cell phone blasted a reggae song from his pants pocket. He took it out, flipped it open, and put it to his ear. "Speak."

"King, they took Danny!" Bambi's voice was filled with panic.

"What? Who took Danny?"

"I don't know. It was three men wearing black clothes and hoodies over their faces. They cuffed and blind-folded him, then took him away." Bambi began to sob.

"Bambi, stop the bawling," King Kong yelled, "and tell me when they took him. Where did they take him?" In rapid succession, he fired off one question after another.

"I ran outside just in time to see a Honda Civic driving away," Bambi said in between sobs. "They're going to kill Danny boo!"

King Kong snapped his phone shut. "Phil! Saddam!"

Two rough-looking men ran from a side room into the back. They were King Kong's top trigger hands. "Yes, King?"

"Get over to Bambi now and see what's going on. She just called to say three men kidnapped Danny."

Phil and Saddam ran from the room as if their lives depended on it.

King Kong threw the cup of coffee against the wall, shattering it and splashing brown liquid all over the tiled floor. "Who would dare do something like this?" But deep down in his gut, King Kong knew. It seemed like a good plan at the time. Robbing Suave's workers and giving them a good beat down was supposed to send a strong message. Suave needed to know that King Kong was the head of the drug game, and the King didn't want to share it with anyone—*especially* Suave. King Kong hated Suave and vowed to ruin him at all costs.

It looked as if his plan had backfired.

"King, we are—"

"Get out!" King Kong pulled his Glock from his waist and waved it around the room like a madman. He felt as if his head were about to explode. Danny was like a brother to him. For most of King Kong's life, Danny was there for him. Now, Suave had taken Danny and was about to do God knows what.

King Kong, feeling weak and suddenly looking older than he was, went and sat down on the black leather couch, deep in thought. Would Suave really kill Danny? Would Danny betray him to save his own life? After all, Danny had warned him more than once not to mess with Suave.

***

"King, there's enough business for all of us. Please don't start any war with Suave," Danny had begged him. "He will not take it lying down."

"Suave is a fool. He can't test the King," King Kong said arrogantly. "Soon, I'll put a bullet in that clown's head. You watch and see."

"You have to go through Cobra and Daddy Lizard first. You know those two are crazy. King, stop this now."

King Kong laughed at Danny. "Man, you getting soft on me? I'm not stopping until I ruin or kill that punk, Suave!"

"Now, look where we are, Danny." King Kong nibbled on his thumb, a sign that he was very nervous. "What are you going to tell Suave, Danny?" This was eating away at King Kong. He knew that Danny was aware of the operation inside out—every supplier, customer, worker, stash house, and business venture. Danny knew where King Kong lived with his wife and four children. He knew his mistresses and outside kids. Danny knew King Kong like the back of his hand, and this bothered the King. Was Danny going to turn him over to his nemesis to save his own life? King Kong felt sick to his stomach.

Chapter Six

"We're going to ask you some questions, and we need the truth. Got it?"

Danny was slapped hard across his face, and tears sprang to his eyes behind the blindfold. He nodded. *Please help me out of this one, Lord.*

"I'm removing the gag, but don't even think about screaming, or we *will* kill you."

A hopeful feeling washed over Danny. He was getting a chance to beg for mercy. The duct tape was ripped off, setting Danny's mouth on fire. The handcuffs were removed, and shackles were placed on his legs.

"Thank you," Danny muttered in a hoarse voice, rubbing his numb hands together. "Please don't kill me. I'll tell you whatever you want to know."

"That's all we ask of you, Danny. Play by the rules, and you just may live to play another day. Cool?"

"Yeah, man." Danny got more hopeful that he could get out of this alive. "I told King Kong not to mess with Suave," he blurted out. "But he refused to listen to me."

The room went silent. Fear began to sneak up on Danny again. "Hello?" Danny turned his head to the left, then the right, the blindfold making everything black. "Anyone there?"

"Danny, we don't know what you're talking about with this Suave business, but it's good to know," the man said in a very deep, disguised voice. "We just want some information on King Kong's operation."

Danny knew what the man just said about Suave was a lie, but he played along. "Oh, my bad. I thought this had something to do with King Kong robbing Suave. What do you want to know? I'll tell you everything."

Phil and Saddam returned about two hours later, bearing bad news.

"Nobody saw or heard anything, King," Phil reported to his boss. "Bambi only saw an old Honda driving away. No license plate number or nothing."

"We went around and talked to some people, but they are all closed mouth." Saddam made eye contact with King Kong. "But we know who has Danny. I say we go over to his headquarters and light it up with bullets. This will let him know we mean business."

King Kong shot up from the couch. "We can't make assumptions, Saddam." He went over to a small, dirty window and looked outside. He saw the dilapidated, abandoned house with missing windows and doors directly across the street. It was home to a few of his customers. "Also, we have to get Danny back before we take action. To act prematurely will end his life."

The men nodded their heads in agreement.

"You're right, King. Suave will kill Danny if he hears that we attacked his place. We have to plan this right."

King Kong turned around and looked at the two men. "We'll wait awhile and watch Suave's next move." Then he stormed out of the back room into the restaurant. "Give me a scotch," he said to the manager sitting behind the counter. The restaurant, which was a front for King Kong's drug business, wasn't open for business yet.

"King Kong! King Kong!" someone shouted from outside. "Come here, quick."

King Kong ran outside with Phil and Saddam on his heels. His eyes widened when he saw a man trying to pull Danny out of the front seat of a car parked in front of the restaurant. King Kong pulled his gun as did Phil and Saddam.

"Hey! Wait a minute." The man let go of Danny and raised his hands high in the air. "It's me, Boogie. I didn't do anything." Fear filled Boogie's eyes. "You know I run my little taxi, King. I was driving down Slipe Pen Road and saw someone staggering. It was Danny. He was blindfolded and shackled."

King Kong stared coldly at Boogie for a few seconds before he walked over to the car and looked inside. A semiconscious Danny was slouched back in the passenger seat with his eyes swollen shut, his face covered in blood, and his lips were busted.

"I took off the blindfold, but I couldn't get the shackles off," Boogie said behind King Kong. "They beat him up bad."

"Saddam!" King Kong roared, his eyes burning with rage.

Saddam reached into the car and pulled out Danny. He threw him over his shoulder and rushed into the restaurant to the back room. Saddam took care lowering a groaning Danny onto the black couch.

"Get them shackles off." King Kong entered the room. "Phil, go get Miss Gala."

As Saddam cut away the shackles with a small ax saw that they kept in the back room, King Kong looked down at Danny with concern.

"You want me, King?" Miss Gala came into the room with a black bag. She looked down at Danny and shook her head. "Poor Danny." Miss Gala was a retired registered nurse who now worked solely for King Kong. It was her job to patch up his workers when they were injured. The more severe cases were sent to Kingston Public Hospital.

"Take care of him." King Kong went to stare out the window, deep in thought.

Miss Gala worked on cleaning up Danny without delay. "Dear God, what is this?"

"What?" King Kong walked back over to Miss Gala. "What is what?" King Kong felt like someone kicked him in the gut when he saw what Miss Gala was pointing to. Bitter bile filled his mouth. Danny's jawbone was opened up with a long cut running from his right ear to his mouth.

"It's a very deep cut. We need to take him to Public." Miss Gala stared up at King Kong who looked like he was about to throw up.

King Kong took deep breaths and forced himself not to be sick. "No Public. This will get the cops involved, and most of them know Danny. It will come right back to me. I don't need that right now. *You* deal with it."

"Okay. I'll stitch it up, but he'll be scarred for life." Miss Gala continued to work.

"Danny? Danny, can you hear me?" King Kong asked as he bent over the couch, gazing down at his man.

Danny groaned and mumbled incoherently. Phil and Saddam stood by silently.

"King, look." Miss Gala had her hands on Danny's lips. "They glued his mouth shut."

King Kong let off some curse words that caused the few strands of hair on Miss Gala's head to stand straight up. "Those fools are dead!" He spat an expletive between each word.

"We're lucky. It looks like superglue." Miss Gala went into her bag of tricks and took out a bottle of nail polish remover. She used it to wet a cotton swab and applied it right on the glue covering Danny's lips.

Danny groaned in pain when the acetone hit his injured lips.

"There's something in his mouth," Miss Gala said a few minutes later after freeing Danny's lips. She used her fingers to take out a piece of paper and held it up to King.

King Kong grabbed the note. *"There is only room for one,"* he read aloud. His eyes flew to Phil and Saddam. "I guess Smooth Suave solved the puzzle."

"So, the question is, what will he do next?" Phil had a big frown on his face. "You can bet Suave, Cobra, and Daddy Lizard won't let this go. They didn't kill Danny, which means they have something else up their sleeves. But what exactly?"

Chapter Seven

"Man, you are a genius." Cobra slapped Suave on the back enthusiastically. "I couldn't believe Danny spilled the beans like that."

Suave grinned and shifted positions in his lawn chair. He crossed his legs and took a sip of his beer. "I knew Danny since we were kids. He was a coward then, and he's a coward now. All of Danny's power comes from the gorilla."

Suave, Cobra, and Daddy Lizard laughed as they drank beers and smoked weed. They now had all the information they needed to bring King Kong to his knees.

"I still think we should have put out Danny's lights." Daddy Lizard's face now held some concern. He wanted Suave to kill Danny when he was kidnapped. "He could be a problem later."

"The man didn't see our faces. We're good." Suave puffed on the spliff and blew smoke in the air. "Plus, I'm not scared of those fools," he said, firing off a few F-bombs.

"Please don't kill me. I'll tell you everything you want to know," Cobra mimicked Danny in a squeaky voice, his body trembling as if he had the chills.

Daddy Lizard spat out his drink as he roared with laughter, tears running down his face.

Cobra's face became serious moments later. Fun time was over. It was time to talk business. "We need to put some men on the bar," he remarked, referring to their headquarters where they conducted business. "That message to King Kong will no doubt reveal we knew he robbed us, and we had taken Danny. That idiot may try to hit some of our spots."

"Get some workers on it now." Suave nodded in agreement. "Tell them to shoot first and ask questions later."

Cobra took his cell phone out of his pants pocket and proceeded to make the calls.

"Danny, how are you feeling, my brother?" King Kong took a seat in the white, padded accent chair by Danny's bed. It was three days after the kidnapping, and King Kong stopped by Danny's house to see how he was doing.

Danny's face was still bandaged up like the Mummy. He groaned. "A lot of pain, man. But Miss Gala gave the wife some strong pain medication, and that's helping a little." Danny's voice was very low, with his eyes shut tight as he lay propped up on two fluffy pillows in his king-sized bed. "I took a bad beating, King."

King Kong nodded his head as if Danny could see him. Anxiety filled his eyes. What did Danny tell Suave? "So, did you see who took you?"

"Nah. Those cowards attacked me from the back, and then blindfolded me."

"What did they want? Why did they say they grabbed you? What did you tell them, Danny?" King Kong jumped to his feet and began pacing.

Danny shifted restlessly on the bed and groaned as pain washed over his bruised body. "I didn't tell them anything, King." Danny opened his eyes and stared up at the ceiling, avoiding eye contact with King Kong. "You think I would do something like that?" Danny began a coughing fit.

King Kong waited until Danny settled down. He could tell Danny was as nervous as a hen in a cockfight. The question was . . . Why? "You do know it was Suave, right? He sent us the same message we sent him."

"I thought so at first. But when they didn't ask me anything about the robbery, I figured I was wrong." Danny glanced quickly at King Kong before looking away.

"See, what I can't figure out is why these men kidnapped and beat you for nothing," King Kong replied as he sat down again, pulling the chair closer to the bed. "Who knew about that message we planted on Suave's men that we robbed, except Suave and his people?" King Kong leaned over the bed, his ugly face all twisted up in anger. "I am going to ask you again, *what* did you tell them, Danny?"

Danny swallowed hard. "They asked about our operation, but I didn't tell them anything. Why do you think they beat me up and glued my mouth shut?" Danny was desperate for King Kong to believe him. If not, he knew King Kong wouldn't hesitate to do what Suave and his men didn't do. Danny and King Kong may be like brothers, but money was the only thing that King Kong loved. Anyone or anything that threatened his drug empire had to go—including his beloved brother, Danny.

"One of them said, 'Oh, your mouth is sealed? Okay, we're going to make sure it stays that way,'" Danny informed King Kong. "You see my face, man? You think they would cut me up if I had said anything?" Danny forced himself to lock eyes with the gorilla's dark, infuriated ones.

King Kong held Danny's stare for a few seconds, then responded, "Maybe you held out until they beat you so badly you couldn't stand it anymore, so you talked. Is that what you did, Danny?"

"Shame on you, King!" Danny struggled to sit up straighter but whimpered in pain and slumped back down on the bed.

King Kong inhaled deeply, exhaling loudly as he reclined back in the chair. "Sorry, man. You know you're my right hand. I had to know if they pressured you into telling them anything that could come back to haunt me. You do know I would understand if you had to talk to save your life, right?" King Kong's eyes held faked compassion. He looked point-blank at Danny as if he were trying to hypnotize him to reveal the secret.

Danny wanted to roll his eyes. *Yeah, right. You would put a bullet in my head right now, and then do the same to my wife and three kids to eliminate all the witnesses.* He moaned and groaned as he slowly and deliberately raised himself a little. He looked King Kong straight in the face. "I. Did. Not. Say. Anything." He placed his hand over his heart. "We're in this for life, King. It's you and me all the way, brother."

Danny wondered if he had managed to fool King Kong, and King Kong wondered if Danny was full of crap.

King Kong's face broke out in a wide grin. "My bad." He reached over and took Danny's hand into his. "I apologize for doubting you. You know I get a little anxious sometimes, especially when dealing with that snake, Suave. I'm happy he didn't get the info he wanted. Next time I hit him, it's not only business, but it's also personal."

Danny tried to smile but grimaced at the pain that shot through his jaw. "We're going to take care of him, King. Just wait until I get back on my feet."

"That's the plan, baby." King Kong released Danny's hand and stood to his feet. "I have some business to take care of, but I'll stop by later. Call me if you need anything. Cool?"

"Thanks, man. Hold it down out there until I get back."

"You got it, Danny. I'm out." With that, King Kong walked toward the door.

Danny closed his eyes and breathed a sigh of relief as he slowly and painfully lowered himself down on the bed. Good God, he pulled it off. King Kong bought the story as he hoped he would.

"You have to rough me up a little bit, so King Kong doesn't suspect anything," Danny had said to the men who kidnapped him after he had told them all they wanted to hear. "I need him to believe me when I tell him I didn't say a word." Danny was sure they would go easy because he had cooperated.

"No problem, Danny. I think we can do that for you."

The men laughed. Danny didn't know he was going to get the whooping of his life, whether or not he asked for it. It was just GP—General Principle. He helped King Kong rob and disrespect Suave, and he had to pay for that. Danny talking saved his life . . . for now but didn't prevent the beating.

Danny was gagged and beaten within an inch of his life. His muffled screams went unnoticed. He wiggled, twisted, and turned but couldn't escape the kicks and blows. Danny could have sworn he saw stars behind the blindfold when the knife cut into his jawbone. His body couldn't handle the intense pain, and mercifully, he slipped away into a black, pain-free darkness. Danny came around when his body was thrown out of the moving car into the middle of a busy street. The blaring of horns, squealing tires, and curse words brought him to his staggering feet as he tried to peek through the blindfold.

Danny has a vague recollection of being led into a car and taken to King Kong's headquarters. Everything and everyone was a blur until the next day when he woke up in his bed with his wife's anxious face hovering above him.

"You weren't supposed to beat me that bad," Danny muttered under his breath. "I snitched on my partner, but yet, you disfigured me for life." He reached up and gently touched the bandage over his injured jaw. "What else did you want?" Tears seeped out of Danny's eyes and ran down his bruised cheeks. He never saw King Kong tiptoeing away from the doorway, where he stood all this time watching him in silence.

Chapter Eight

"Respect, Boss."

"Big up, Godfather."

"What's good, player?"

"You the man, Suave."

"Blessed, my Lord. Good to see you in the place."

Suave pounded fists and exchanged man hugs and high fives as he strutted toward his bar, a front for his headquarters, in Wilton Gardens, better known as Rema.

Rema was a crime-infested, inner-city community in Western Kingston. Often, unstable and dangerous, it was plagued by rival gangs who wreaked havoc on the residents and war against law enforcement. Rema and Jungle were neighboring rival communities. Suave was from Rema, and King Kong was, appropriately, from the Jungle—two fierce rivals.

Suave had just parked his Mercedes-Benz in front of his bar and hopped out to see a bunch of men waiting for him. Most of them were his workers. Others were just waiting for a handout, which Suave would do on a regular basis.

A rich man by illegal means, Suave was considered very generous by some of the residents in the community. He often helped single mothers pay tuition, bought uniforms, books, and school supplies for dozens of children. The elders often received money for food and their medications, while many of the men were added to his payroll in various capacities.

Very few people were concerned about the little boys who dropped out of school to run drugs for Suave. They didn't see the dope fiends who were strung out on the drugs Suave supplied or the "soldiers" who got killed or locked away like animals in a jail cell for a very long time. It was Suave's world, and they just existed in it.

"What's up, hot stuff?" Suave said as he entered the bar, slapping the booty of the voluptuous bar manager who was bent over the counter that she was wiping down.

The woman turned and blushed. "What's good, daddy?"

Been there and done that. Suave ignored the open invitation. On occasion, he slept with the manager, especially if he had to work late, but for the most part, she was for business purposes only. "Cobra and Daddy Lizard here?"

"They're upstairs getting payroll ready. You want me to bring up breakfast now?"

It was a two-story building. The bar was on the first floor and the executive offices of Suave's empire on the second.

"Yeah, do that. And make sure the coffee is—"

"Good morning, Brother Suave," came a deep, strong voice from behind Suave.

Suave fired off a few curse words before turning around to face the owner of the voice. "Rev, how many times have I told you not to come into my place of business?" Suave took a few steps to bridge the small gap between them until they were standing nose to nose. "Why don't you leave me alone, man?" Suave's nostrils opened and closed in anger, his fists balled at his sides.

"I'm not here to cause trouble, Brother Suave." Reverend Stanford was very calm. "I have a message for you from the Lord."

The curse words thrown at the reverend had no impact on him. Reverend Stanford wasn't the least bit fazed by Suave's disrespect. He had a job to do, and he was going to do it until the breath left his body.

"Take your message and your Lord and get out now!" Suave barked, raining spit all over the reverend's face. "Go back over to your little church while you can," he warned, pointing outside.

The Kingdom Church of God was a small, brick building located right across the street from Suave's headquarters. Except for the headquarters, it was one of the few buildings without graffiti. Headed by the young, handsome Reverend Stanford, the church was determined to convert every sinner in Jamaica, by the blood of Jesus Christ, starting with the residents of Rema. So far, the only blood that seemed to be running was those of murdered citizens on a regular basis. However, Reverend Stanford and his few church members refused to give up the fight.

"Matthew 19:26 says, '*But Jesus beheld them, said unto them, with men this is impossible; but with God all things are possible.*'" Reverend Stanford always reminded his church, "We won't stop until the residents of Rema turn their lives over to the Lord. Murderers, drug dealers, and gang members must come to God!"

Reverend Stanford returned Suave's glare with a look of compassion. "You are supposed to be saving lives, not taking them with that poison. God wants to use you for His kingdom, my brother." He placed a hand on Suave's shoulder.

In a flash, Suave knocked the offensive hand off, pulled his gun from his waistband, and rested it on the reverend's temple. "Don't ever talk to me about your idiot God again, or I swear you are going to get a bullet in your head. I don't do the God thing. Got it?"

"No, you get this." Reverend Stanford didn't even flinch. "God won't stop until you succumb to Him. This is not what He wants for you, my friend. One day, you will have to stop running."

Suave cocked the gun. "Get out of here now! I swear I'm—"

"Wow! Hold it, Boss." Cobra ran up to Suave and held on to the hand with the gun. "Don't do anything stupid now." He and Daddy Lizard were upstairs and heard Suave yelling. Sensing trouble, Cobra left the pile of money they were counting and ran down the stairs to find Reverend Stanford visiting again.

Suave shook off Cobra's hand but lowered the gun to his side. "Get this fool out of here before I kill him." Suave stepped even closer to Reverend Stanford, his warm, furious breath fanning the reverend's face.

Cobra moved closer to Reverend Stanford. "Why do you keep coming over here and creating problems, man?"

Reverend Stanford turned his head to lock eyes with Cobra. "Because I have to do as the Lord bids me to. I'm not afraid of anyone or anything when I'm on a mission for God."

"When you get two copper shots in your skull, you'll see if you're not afraid," Suave remarked, recapturing the reverend and Cobra's attention. "Keep messing with me and see something." With that, he turned and walked away toward the stairs.

"Proverbs 29:25 says, '*The fear of man bringeth a snare: but whoso putteth his trust in the Lord shall be safe,*'" Reverend Stanford shouted at Suave's back.

Suave paused at the bottom of the stairs, turned around, and waved goodbye to the reverend with his middle finger before he jogged up the stairs.

Cobra chuckled and said to Reverend Stanford, "Now, see what you let the man do, huh?"

Reverend Stanford looked at Cobra and smiled. "I'm sorry I upset Brother Suave. Well, now that I have you here, I just—"

"Bye, Rev. I don't have time for your rubbish myself. Sorry." Cobra ran up the stairs, leaving Reverend Stanford staring at his back.

With a deep sigh, Reverend Stanford walked out of the bar. As soon as he got outside, the group of men scattered in every direction like ants. It was as if the Word of the Lord were a contagious disease, and no one wanted to catch it. But the reverend crossed the street to his church, humming a song of praise. It was all in God's hands.

Chapter Nine

"Things have been quiet so far." King Kong's cold eyes glanced over at Danny, who was sitting beside him on the couch. They were in the back room of their headquarters located in the Jungle. "It's been a month since that fool found out I was robbing him and kidnapped you. Yet he has done nothing."

Danny turned his disfigured face toward his partner. The deep cut didn't heal well, as Miss Gala had predicted. A thick, angry, ugly scar that seemed to be pulling the right side of his mouth toward his ear left Danny with a permanent lopsided grin on his once handsome face. "I told you I didn't say anything," Danny replied, rejoicing to himself that Suave hadn't used the information he'd given them. "Don't you think he would have tried something by now?"

King Kong had ramped up security at his houses, his businesses, and made sure all his workers were armed. But the days ran into weeks, and he heard nothing from his nemesis. "Appreciate the lookout, my friend." His smile didn't reach his eyes.

King Kong raised his fist, and Danny bumped it with his own. "We're in this together, partner," King Kong said. "Don't worry yourself. We're going to get them for what they did to you." He glanced at Danny's marred face and quickly looked away.

"Oh, they *will* pay." Danny rubbed the hideous scar. His eyebrows almost met in the middle of his forehead in fury. "I know in my heart that it was Suave, Cobra, and Daddy Lizard who did this to me. If it's the last thing I do, they'll live to regret it." Now that he was back with his sidekick, Danny's bravado had returned. He was now carrying two guns—one in his waistband and another strapped to his right leg. Danny vowed not to go down again without a fight.

"You know I'm with you. We are—"

"Soon and very soon, we are going to see the King!" Loud singing, clapping, and chanting made its way into the back room where the men sat.

Danny closed his eyes in frustration, muttering a few curse words. "I wonder why that bootleg pastor can't leave us alone."

"Only a bullet is going to shut him up." King Kong was furious as he stood to his feet. He marched through the restaurant and stepped outside, with Danny on his heels. Right in front of the restaurant stood Reverend Stanford and ten of his church members, singing and clapping.

When Reverend Stanford saw King Kong, he held up his hand, and the singing stopped. "God gave me a message for you, my brother." He walked closer to the sidewalk where King Kong stood fuming, his fists folded. "God wants you to turn away from this life of sin and come to Him. If you don't, you are going to find yourself six feet under or in prison for a very long time."

"Are you threatening me, pastor boy?" King Kong spat, moving closer to invade Reverend Stanford's personal space, his big ugly face flushed with rage. "You want to bet you leave Jungle today in a body bag?"

A few of the church members gasped loudly; others started to pray aloud.

"You think you can disrespect the king and get away with it?" King Kong pulled two guns from either side of his waist and held both to the reverend's head. Most of it now was for show for the small crowd that was gathering.

"Give him a copper shot, King," Danny egged him on. "He just said you are a dead man."

Reverend Stanford was a well-known and respected pastor in Jamaica with strong ties to Kingston, where he was born and raised. He was well acquainted with the prime minister, many politicians, high officials, and wealthy businessmen. Since the age of nineteen, Reverend Stanford had been working hard to better the inner-city communities in Kingston. As such, he was loved by many but despised by the criminals he was trying to reform.

"I meant no disrespect, my friend." Reverend Stanford stared into King Kong's red eyes, his face void of fear. "I have known you for years, and you know I am a man of God. I go where He leads and do as He instructs. You need to turn away from your sinful ways and seek God before it's too late."

King Kong replied, "I am going to count to three, and you and these religious fools with you better be gone by then. One . . . Two—"

"We are not going anywhere until I have preached God's message to the people and visit a few sick folks we came to see. This is God's work, not mine." Reverend Stanford turned and walked a few steps away.

Some onlookers shifted uncomfortably, others trembled with fear, while a few exchanged nervous glances as they began to pray. The reverend just defied King Kong's order, and he wasn't going to take it just like that. His huge ego and pride ruled King Kong.

"Oh, so you are a bad man now, huh?" King Kong fired a shot in the air, and the crowd quickly dispersed. Some people screamed and fell to the dirty ground with their hands over their heads, a few jumped over short zinc fences, and others ran away to avoid catching a stray bullet. Fear for Reverend Stanford held the area captive. Was King Kong going to kill the reverend?

"Take another step, and you're a dead man," King Kong roared at Reverend Stanford's back, halting his steps. "You better recognize when the king speaks." As King Kong rushed to catch up to Reverend Stanford, he tucked one of the guns in his waist.

Reverend Stanford slowly turned around to face King Kong. They were standing so close that he felt King Kong's warm, sour, marijuana breath on his face. "I don't want any problems with you. I'm walking—"

King Kong grabbed the reverend by his shirt collar, choking him as if he were a little boy.

Reverend Stanford's church members prayed louder and harder.

"Please take your hands off me, my brother," Reverend Stanford said through clenched teeth. "I can assure you that you don't want a fight with God." He reached up and tried to pry King Kong's hand loose, but the gorilla held on even tighter. A tall, strong man himself, Reverend Stanford took deep, calculated breaths, silently asking the Lord to intervene. "I plead the blood of Jesus against you right now!"

King Kong threw his head back and laughed. "I'm going to make sure you never mess with the king again."

As he held on to Reverend Stanford, glaring at him, his eyes began to widen in alarm. The hand that gripped the shirt began to tremble, with the gun shivering a little in the other hand. King Kong quickly let go of the reverend's shirt and took a step back. "Wha . . . wha . . . what the . . .?"

Reverend Stanford continued to lock eyes with King Kong without saying a word, while Danny and the people who were present went quiet, with puzzled expressions on their faces.

King Kong tried to move again, but his feet felt like they were planted in wet cement. His body began to shiver as if he were having a seizure. Almost robotically, King Kong's head tilted up, his eyes staring up to the sky in horror. He blinked over and over, shaking his head to regain his senses. Right before his eyes, Reverend Stanford grew to over eight feet tall and was still growing, his body expanding like the Incredible Hulk.

"What's the matter, King?" Danny asked as he moved closer. "Man, you feeling all right?"

King Kong pointed up to the reverend high in the sky that only his eyes could behold. "Pastor. Pastor." The gun fell from his shaky hand to the ground.

Everyone looked up except Reverend Stanford but saw nothing.

"Lord have mercy, King Kong done lost his mind," someone whispered under their breath.

"That's what happens when you mess with God's people. How can he disrespect the reverend like that?" someone uttered.

Reverend Stanford was looking at King Kong with a smirk on his face. He didn't know what was going on as it was between King Kong and God. But he had a strong feeling the king was beholding the power of the *real* King.

King Kong's eyes stayed fixed up to the heavens, his hands wrapped around his body, whimpering as if in pain.

Danny picked up King Kong's gun and looked at him, unsure of what he should do.

Suddenly, a loud horn resounded in the air. Everyone jumped out of the way of the speeding motorcycle that came to a stop at King Kong's feet. "What's going on here?" Saddam asked, jumping off the bike to stand in front of his boss.

"He got into it with the reverend, and then he started to act weird," Danny informed him. "I don't know what he's looking up at because I can't see a thing."

Saddam followed King Kong's gaze, and he didn't see anything either. "Come on, King. Let's get you inside." He placed one hand on King Kong's shoulder.

"Pastor . . . up in the sky. Do you see him?" King Kong mumbled some more mumbo jumbo before Saddam and Danny led him back toward the restaurant.

At the restaurant entrance, Danny turned around. "Obeah man," he screamed, referring to a person who practiced witchcraft. "Get out of here before I finish what King Kong started." But even his voice faltered a little. Danny glanced up into the beautiful blue sky before slamming the restaurant door shut.

Reverend Stanford and the people stared at the closed door for a few seconds. Many were wondering what in heaven's name just happened to the big bad gorilla.

"Okay, everyone. I apologize for that little misunderstanding." Reverend Stanford smiled at the people. "You see now why I have to serve the Lord? Psalm 105:15

says, '*Saying, Touch not mine anointed, and do my prophets no harm.*' No enemy is too bad for God to handle! Hallelujah!"

Hallelujahs and amens rang out. The unbelievers were in wonder and the believers in praise.

Chapter Ten

"Old dog like me, we haffi have dem inna twos an three . . ." Dance hall king Beenie Man proclaimed with no shame to his game. Loud, rhythmic reggae music blared through loudspeakers as the crowd made the moves to the popular fun dances. Boisterous laughter and animated chatter, induced by the rapid flow of alcohol and the power of marijuana, reverberated around the club. Scantily clad women wearing miniskirts, short shorts, skintight pants, halter tops, and supershort dresses moved their hips to the beat of the music. The lustful men in their baggy jeans, name brand T-shirts and sneakers, silk shirts, and tailored pants watched in appreciation.

As couples grinded on each other, pumping and salivating in musical bliss, Suave watched in amusement. Leaning against the wall in a dark corner reserved for him and his crew, he puffed away on a spliff before taking a sip from the glass of Hennessey. Clad in black from head to toe, he blended in with the dark venue as intended.

It was Queen Bee's annual birthday bash at the Asylum Club in New Kingston. Many said she was turning sixty, but Queen Bee got stuck at thirty years old many moons ago.

"You okay, Boss? Want me to refresh that for you?" one of Suave's soldiers inquired of him, his hand outstretched for the glass.

Suave gave it to him and watched as he reached into a big bucket on the ground that was filled with bottles of Hennessey. The young man took out a new bottle and popped opened the cork. He refilled Suave's glass and handed it back to him.

"Yo, hit me up again too," Daddy Lizard said as he rocked his hips from side to side to the music, blowing weed smoke in the air.

Suave, Cobra, Daddy Lizard, and about ten of their soldiers were in the house. A supposedly gun-free venue, Suave and his men paid a hefty price for the bouncers at the door to look the other way. Needless to say, the men were heavily armed.

"Now, *this* is what I call a party." Suave bobbed his head up and down to the beat of the music, the rest of his body as stiff as a corpse. He looked across the room and made eye contact with a young, dark-skinned woman. She was wearing a pair of shorts that exposed her big buttocks leaving little to the imagination. Unconcerned about a wardrobe malfunction, the woman bent over with her head almost touching her ankles, her huge breasts fighting hard to stay in the low cut blouse, her booty jiggling in the air.

Suave began to perspire, and it wasn't because of the warm, close quarters of the club. He gobbled down the rest of his Hennessy and handed the glass to a worker for a refill.

"You see how little mama is watching you?" Daddy Lizard whispered in Suave's ear. "You want me to call her over?"

"Nah, maybe later." Suave was aware of many of the women scoping him out. A few were exes, and others were prospects. A player to the end, he didn't want to single out any one woman in public, so he kept everything neutral and partied with his crew.

"It's almost time," Cobra muttered in Suave's ear. "I just got a text message that everything's in place, and it's a go when you say so."

Suave nodded his head. "Do it."

Cobra stepped away to make a call with Suave's instruction. A minute later, he returned and winked at both Suave and Daddy Lizard. The deed was done.

The door almost kicked off its hinges and exploded against the wall. Screams echoed from the living room as three armed, masked men rushed in with guns drawn.

"Hands in the air!"

"Nobody move, nobody gets hurt!"

Mother Bloom stood to her trembling, arthritic feet, her aged back bent, with her hands in the air. Tears ran down her weathered face as she stared at the intruders in her home. "Wha . . . What do you want?" her voice shook.

They ignored her. One of the gunmen turned to the old man sitting on the couch, watching the late-night news without concern. "Old man, get to your feet now," the gunman yelled.

Elder Bloom turned his droopy face to look at him. Without saying a word, he nestled farther back into the couch and crossed his legs in defiance. "You don't break into my house and give me orders."

"Elder, please do as he says," Mother Bloom begged her stubborn husband. "I don't want any problems."

But Elder Bloom sucked his teeth and folded his arms. He wasn't moving.

The gunman said, "You hear what—"

"Let's just get the stuff and get out of here," another gunman remarked. "I'll watch these two while you go take care of business." He pointed his gun at Mother Bloom, his eyes going back and forth between her and Elder Bloom.

"Where are you going?" Elder Bloom screamed at the backs of the other two gunmen as they exited the living room. "Get your sorry behinds back here." He jumped to his feet, took a step, but stopped when the gun was turned on him.

"Don't move another step," the gunman who remained behind warned. "We don't want to hurt you, Grandpa. Relax."

"I'm not your grandpa!" Elder Bloom stomped his feet in anger.

Elder Bloom was Saddam's grandpa, one of King Kong's main soldiers. He and his wife of sixty years, Mother Bloom, raised Saddam after his parents were killed in a car accident when he was only ten years old.

The couple lived in Ensom City, Spanish Town, in the same house they bought over forty years ago. They were active members of their church and well known to everyone in their community. However, they harbored one deep, dark secret that placed them in the situation they were now in. In the kitchen, under the big six-burner cooking stove, was a deep cellar filled with tons of marijuana, cocaine, and bundles of money. This was King Kong's biggest stash.

After waiting two months, Suave was now using the information he got from Danny. He knew this financial loss would bring King Kong to his knees while keeping Suave at the top of the game where he currently sat. Suave also chose this night because he, Cobra, and Daddy Lizard had perfect alibis.

It was payback time.

"Got it!" one of the gunmen stuck his head into the living room and shouted, his yellow teeth flashing through the mask. Over his shoulder were two large flour bags. He hurried off to put the loot in the stolen car parked in the Blooms' driveway.

Elder Bloom dragged himself back over to the couch and gingerly lowered himself into it.

"Go and sit down, Grandma," the gunman said to Mother Bloom, who gladly accepted. Her back and legs were aching like crazy.

"About three more trips to the car and we got everything," a gunman updated his colleague standing watch in the living room.

"You're going to pay for this," Elder Bloom warned. "Mark my words, you are all going to pay."

The masked gunman chuckled. "Oh, I'm going to get paid all right."

Elder Bloom replied, "You think—"

"Shut up!" a gunman hissed in a much-lower tone so as not to alert the neighbors. "Keep threatening me, and I'll make you pay, old man."

Mother Bloom reached over and patted her husband's leg, willing him to keep his mouth shut. Getting killed over Saddam and King Kong's drugs and money wasn't the way Mother Bloom wanted to go and meet her maker. Mark you, King Kong did take good care of them for using their house, and the balance in Bloom's retirement bank account was a testimony to that. But it wasn't their fault they got robbed. Who told these thugs about the stash anyway?

"Okay, player. Let's roll." The other two gunmen returned to the living room after emptying the cellar.

"Cut the phone line," the watchman instructed in order to delay the call to Saddam and King Kong. He wasn't worried about the Blooms calling the police. After all, what were they going to report? My grandson's drugs and money were just stolen from our house?

After the phone line was cut, the men headed toward the front door.

"Stay where you are," one of the gunmen warned. "See? We're leaving now."

Two gunmen marched out, while the third one with the gun backed out slowly, his gun still pointed at the Blooms. Once he was out in the hallway where he could no longer see the couple, he stuck his gun in his waist, turned around, and walked to the opened door to exit the house.

"Don't move!" Elder Bloom appeared in the hallway like Houdini, a long shotgun in his feeble hands.

The gunman spun around, his eyes opening wide behind the mask when he saw the gun that was now turned on him. "Now wait a minute, Gran . . . sir. We don't want anyone to get hurt here." He put a hand to the gun on his waist, the other outstretched toward Elder Bloom.

"I said don't move." Elder Bloom cocked the gun and took another step closer to the intruder.

The gunman dropped the hand that was reaching for the gun. He glanced over his shoulder to see if any of his partners in crime were coming to his aid. "Listen to me. You don't want to do—hey!"

A loud boom rang out into the night as Elder Bloom fired a shot over the gunman's head, solidifying that he wasn't joking around. "I said bring back the stuff in the house."

Mother Bloom appeared behind her husband, pleading with him to come back into the living room and let the gunmen go. "Sweetheart, please don't let things get worse."

Elder Bloom ignored her and cocked the gun again, leveling it. This time, he was going to make sure he hit someone. "I'm going to show you some—"

Pow! Pow! Two shots rang out.

Elder Bloom's eyes and mouth popped open in surprise. The shotgun fell out of his hand before his body followed it to the ground with a bullet hole in his forehead and another in his neck. His body twitched in the throes of death before it stilled. His eyes stared lifelessly up into the ceiling.

One of the gunmen ran over, grabbed the shotgun, and took off.

Mother Bloom screamed. She wobbled over to Elder Bloom and, with some difficulty, lowered herself beside him. She lifted his head onto her lap, and her husband's blood soaked through her nightgown. A small river of snot seeped down Mother Bloom's face as she rocked the body of the man she had spent most of her life with.

The gunmen ran to the car, started it up, and backed out of the Blooms' driveway with the tires squealing as they made their escape.

Lights came on in neighboring houses as calls poured in to Jamaica's 119 emergency number switchboard.

The plan to rob King Kong's drugs and money didn't go as anticipated, and Saddam's beloved grandfather was dead. Everything was about to turn upside down!

Chapter Eleven

The phone vibrated in Cobra's pocket. With a smirk on his face, he moved away from the crowd to a corner of the club to read the good news.

"What the . . .?" Cobra felt as if he were about to wet himself. He flipped the phone closed and rushed past a baffled Suave and Daddy Lizard. Pushing his way through the jam-packed club, Cobra dashed into the men's room. He looked to see that the bathroom was empty, then quickly dialed a number.

"You better tell me it's not true!" Cobra shrieked when the call was answered. "Please, tell me it's not so."

Little Bimbee, one of the gunmen, said, "He took us by surprise, Godfather. He was going to ghost my brother and left me with no choice."

Cobra bellowed a few more expletives as he paced the men's room. His head was pounding. "Where's the baby?" he asked of the drugs and money.

"Sleeping safe and sound."

"All right, I want everyone to take that vacation." Cobra instructed the men to disappear with the stash as planned. He disconnected the call, cursed some more, and kicked the wall in anger. How in heaven's name was he going to tell Suave?

"Yo, the boss wants to know if everything is cool," Daddy Lizard remarked as he entered the men's room, closing the door behind him. He took one look at Cobra's face, and his heart fell. "What happened?" He glanced toward the closed bathroom door before moving closer to Cobra. "No dice?" His eyebrows rose and fell.

Cobra took a deep breath. "They killed Elder Bloom," he whispered.

"They did *what?*" Daddy Lizard screamed. "What do you mean—?"

The men's room door opened, filtering loud music inside, as two men staggered in and made their way to the urinals.

Daddy Lizard marched out of the men's room with Cobra on his heels. They made their way through the sweaty, moving bodies over to Suave.

Suave took one look at their faces and fired off a few F bombs. "What happened?" He looked at Cobra, who oversaw the operation.

Cobra moved near to him and whispered the bad news in his ear.

Suave closed his eyes in frustration. "You mean to tell me the three jackasses didn't check the house for weapons?" he said through gritted teeth for Cobra's ears.

"The man is about eighty years old and is an elder at his church. Who would expect that from him?"

"The man is crazy Saddam's grandfather! He raised a lunatic, so what did you expect, huh?" Suave took deep breaths as he tried to think. No doubt Saddam and King Kong had heard the news by now. "Let's get out of here."

"No." Cobra laid a hand on Suave's arm. "If we leave now, people will be suspicious. We have to chill for another hour or so."

Suave nodded his aching head in agreement. The game just took a dangerous turn.

***

"Speak to me!" Saddam shouted into his cell phone above the noise in the bar. He took a sip of his whiskey.

"Saddam, it's me, Brother Jones."

Saddam paused, his heart racing in his chest. Brother Jones was one of his grandparents' neighbors. He had given the man his number a few years back in case of an emergency. "What's the matter?" The ice cubes rattled against the glass as Saddam's hand began to tremble.

"There was a shooting over at your grandparents' house. We called the police, and they're over there now. My wife just told me that they took Mother Bloom away in an ambulance but . . . hmmm, well, we don't know exactly what happened to Elder Bloom. You should come now."

Without a word, Saddam threw his drinking glass against the wall, sending crystal shrapnel flying. A few curious customers turned to look at him as he stormed out of the bar without paying his tab. Saddam hopped on his motorcycle that was parked in front and peeled off toward Ensom City.

Luckily for Saddam, he was just a few miles away in Central Village, Spanish Town. With his motorcycle eating up the road, Saddam zoomed into Ensom City in less than twenty minutes after he got the call.

Red, white, and blue flashing lights from police cars lit up the block. The crowd parted as Saddam slowly rode up to his home, a look of disbelief on his face. He'd had his own house since he was twenty years old, but this was home for him. As if in a trance, he parked the motorcycle on the street and walked toward the house.

"Stop right there." A policeman planted himself in front of Saddam. "Who are you, sir?"

"My-my-my grandparents." Saddam pointed toward the house. The tears escaped down his face. "Where are they?"

The policeman's eyes were filled with sympathy. "Well, your grandmother was taken to Spanish Town Hospital for observation. She fainted, and we wanted to make sure she was okay." He paused and took a deep breath. "Mmmm, there was a little—"

"Where is Dadda?" Saddam snapped, his chest rising and falling, his breathing labored.

"I'm sorry to tell you, but your grandfather was killed." The officer reached out and grabbed Saddam's arm when he stumbled backward.

"Let me go," Saddam barked and rushed toward the house. But at least five police officers blocked his entrance.

"You can't go in there, sir," one policeman stated.

"This is now a crime scene, sir," a kind-looking policewoman added. "We can't allow you inside until we have completed our investigation."

Saddam kicked and screamed, trying to force his way through the barricade of officers. It took four policemen to hold him down until King Kong drove up. A few whispered words from his boss calmed Saddam . . . somewhat. The anger then gave way to despair as Saddam mourned the man who had raised him.

"Dadda! They killed Dadda!" Saddam marched up and down the driveway of his grandparents' house, bawling unashamedly. "Woieeee."

Soon, Saddam crumbled to the ground, his feet no longer able to hold up his huge body. The police and onlookers stared at the grown man weeping like a child. Most of them knew Saddam the thug and were surprised at the display of his vulnerability.

"Saddam, what's the news, man?" King Kong asked. "What happened to the stuff?" he whispered in Saddam's ear. His concern was for his drugs and money, not the murdered old man.

"Come on, let me help you up." Phil ignored King Kong, reached down, and grabbed his friend's arm. "Take it slow. Here you go." He pulled Saddam to his feet and gave him a brief hug before pulling back. The two men had been partners in crime since their early teens.

"Dadda. They killed Dadda," Saddam cried, the mucus and salty mixture gushing down his face. "Dadda is gone, Phil."

"I'm sorry, man." Phil handed Saddam his handkerchief. "Where's Mother Bloom?"

"The hospital. They said she fainted." Saddam ran the handkerchief one time down his wet face, leaving some residue behind, his crying tapering off to sniffles.

Phil replied, "We'll go—"

"Ahem."

Phil and Saddam turned their heads to see King Kong's ugly face bent out of shape.

"Look, Saddam. I feel for you, my brother." King Kong stepped closer to the two men. "Elder Bloom was a nice man, and we'll get his killer. But right now, I want to know where my stuff is."

Saddam hung his head, his fists folded, breathing in and out through his mouth. He was close to beating down his insensitive boss like he was the one who killed his grandfather. Huffing and puffing, Saddam trudged off toward the house again.

Phil shot King Kong an "I can't believe you" look, which he ignored. "King, let's deal with that later. Our people are inside, and we should get some word soon."

He nodded toward a detective who was on King Kong's payroll.

Earlier, King Kong was home relaxing when the detective called to tell him about the shooting. Part of the detective's job was to patrol the Blooms' neighborhood to keep an eye on things.

"What?" King Kong had screamed into the phone. "Who? When? Did they take anything? Where are you?" He was flabbergasted.

"I was working a homicide in Eltham Park," the detective informed King Kong. "I'm en route now, but other cops are already there."

King Kong fired off a slew of curse words. "Keep close and find out what happened!" He pressed the *end* button on his cell phone before dialing another number. "Come get me now," King Kong yelled when Phil answered. "Shooting went down in Spain."

Phil was there in fifteen minutes, and half an hour later, the men pulled up and parked across the street from the Blooms' residence.

King Kong's heart fell as he walked toward the house and saw the number of police scurrying around. He wouldn't get a chance anytime soon to check for his drugs and money. In his mind, King Kong felt they were gone, but he still held out hope. After all, only a few people knew about his stash. If Elder Bloom got killed, it was safe to assume he put up a fight to prevent the robbers from getting access to the stuff.

"My goods better be in there," King Kong complained to Phil after Saddam left. "You know if we lose this, we're in big trouble."

Phil nodded and replied, "I know, but it's not the right time to hassle Saddam. His grandfather was just killed."

King Kong sucked his teeth without sympathy. Fear and anxiety filled his eyes. "I owe people a lot of money for that shipment. The money from the last six months is in that house. I cannot lose that," he hissed. He turned to stare at the action a few feet away.

The house was taped off as detectives from the Spanish Town Police Station went in and out, searching for clues to the murder of the gentle, kindhearted, Christian man. The couple lived in a very nice house, but they didn't have anything worth killing for.

"I bet it's some crackhead who knew that they lived alone," King Kong lied to the police when questioned.

Detective Stone frowned. "From what we can see so far, nothing obvious was taken. The television and other electronics are here. Mother Bloom's jewelry box with a few nice gold pieces is still on her dresser. Of course, we're not finished yet." He ran a hand over his smooth bald head.

"Nothing was taken?" King Kong's eyes lit up. "No furniture—"

"Maybe Elder Bloom prevented them from robbing the house," Phil remarked, discreetly stepping on King Kong's toe. "That would explain why they killed him."

Detective Stone bobbed his head and said, "You could be right. This could be a random burglary that went wrong." He was young and just became a detective a few months earlier. "But I'm going to solve this one." The hunger showed in his eyes. Detective Stone had to prove himself worthy of this position. "Whatever happened here tonight, I'll find out." He turned on his heels and marched back to the house.

"Anything new?" Detective Stone asked as he walked into the kitchen where two officers were.

"No, we haven't found a thing," one answered. "We searched the entire house."

"But do you know what you're looking for?" asked a gravelly voice from the doorway.

The three men turned to see Detective Bird leaning against the door, a toothpick dangling from the corner of his mouth.

"We're looking for clues to a murder." Detective Stone's voice held resentment at the insult. He frowned at the older detective.

Detective Bird said, "I bet you think this was a normal burglary gone wrong." His voice was grainy from years of smoking and drinking. Gray hair sprinkled all over his head and in the thick beard he sported.

"As a matter of fact, I do," Detective Stone snapped. He was an admirer of the veteran detective, who had been on the police force for almost forty years. However, he didn't like the way Detective Bird was trying to undermine his investigation. "Why are *you* here, Detective?"

Detective Bird peered at him through slanted eyes. "Watch your tone, son." His droopy face had a hard look. "*I'm* taking over the investigation."

"No, you're not!" Detective Stone was appalled. "The lieutenant sent me over here."

"Why don't you give him a call? He'll explain everything to you."

"Explain what?"

Detective Bird sighed aloud. He walked over to the kitchen counter and rested his hip against it. "Can you give us a minute?" he said to the other two officers. "Do you know who that is outside there?" He pointed toward the door that the officers just exited through. "That's King Kong and one of his right-hand men, Phil."

Detective Stone looked puzzled.

"Do you know who the victim's grandson is? Saddam." He answered his own question. "He is King Kong's *other* right-hand man."

"And who is King Kong, and why should I care?"

Detective Bird threw his head back and laughed out loud before dissolving in a whooping cough. After composing himself, he replied, "That's why the lieutenant reassigned the case to me. The three biggest drug dealers in Jamaica are King Kong, Suave, and Queen Bee. While their headquarters are in Kingston, they operate in all fourteen parishes. I've been after King Kong for years, but he's always one step ahead of me. Yes, he owns legal businesses to justify his wealth. But trust me, most of that comes from the cocaine and marijuana that he deals. Weeks ago, my informant told me that King Kong was robbing his rival, Suave."

Detective Bird continued. "Suave is even bigger than King Kong in the drug business. I've been working with some detectives in Kingston to get him too, but nothing ever sticks. Rumor has it that Suave had kidnapped King Kong's partner, Danny, in retaliation of the robberies. Danny was badly beaten and released. Now Saddam's grandfather is dead."

"So, you think it's all related?" the younger detective asked the veteran. "All of this is about drugs?"

Detective Bird pointed at him. "*Now,* you get it. Elder Bloom didn't deserve to be killed, but this just might be the way for me to finally get those two criminals. Cross my heart and tell no lie, I'm going to get them one day soon."

Stone saw the determination in Detective Bird's eyes. It looked as if King Kong and Suave's days as free men were numbered.

Chapter Twelve

"I'm out," Suave barked after exiting the club. He threw a cold look at Cobra before storming off toward his Benz. It was 1:00 a.m.

"Suave. Wait." Daddy Lizard ran up to the car as Suave slipped behind the steering wheel, slamming the car door shut. He started the car and rolled down the window.

"At least take two soldiers with you," Daddy Lizard implored his boss, his head hanging inside the car through the opened window. "Things are going to get rough. You can't take any chances."

Suave replied, "I'm good. You know I don't leave my piece. Plus, where I'm going, King Kong won't venture."

"Are you sure? I know you're pissed at what went down tonight, but you have to be careful."

Suave said through clinched teeth, "Now I'll not only have King Kong and crazy Saddam on my behind but the police as well. I don't need this right now."

"I know. Let's sleep on it, and tomorrow, we'll come up with a plan." Daddy Lizard pulled back from the car.

Suave peeled off without a response. He drove with one hand on the steering, the other reached for his cell phone and dialed a number. He held the phone to his ear.

"Hey," Pat answered Suave's call on the first ring. "My mind just ran on you."

"I'll be there in twenty minutes." Suave's voice was very cold. "Get some food ready because I'm starved."

"You know I got you, Big Daddy." Pat's voice held a mixture of fear and excitement. "It'll be ready when you get here."

Suave clicked off the phone. With a mean, hard look on his face, he pressed a little harder on the gas. He needed to get to Pat's fast so that he could get away from all the craziness that had gone down tonight.

True to his word, twenty minutes later, Suave pulled up in front of Pat's house in Havendale, Kingston. The garage door was up, so Suave drove in and parked beside a white convertible BMW. He exited the car, hurried over to the garage door opener mounted on the wall, and pressed it. The door made a low grinding sound as it rolled down.

"Where are you?" Suave yelled when he entered the living room through the side door from the garage. "Yo, Pat?"

"I'm right here." Pat glided from the bedroom into the living room, wearing a short, sheer, red bathrobe with nothing under it and struck a pose in front of him. "Hey." Pat stared at Suave's face intently, trying to gauge his mood.

Suave swallowed loudly, his face set in stone. "Where's my food?" The grumbling of his stomach seemed to agree.

Pat took a step back and laughed. "Someone is hungry. Come on, I heated up some chicken soup for you." Pat walked into the kitchen with Suave a step behind.

"So, how was the club?" Pat asked with caution as they sat around the dining table. "How many hoochie mamas gave you their number?"

Suave took a sip of his soup before he looked up. "How many times I told you not to question me?"

Pat frowned. "Sorry. I was just making conversation."

Suave drank some more of the delicious soup before saying, "Do I look like I need conversation to you? Just sit and keep your mouth shut."

Pat's lips pouted like a spoiled child but didn't speak again. Except for the slurping of the soup as Suave ate, no sound was heard.

Moments later, Suave said, "So, how was your day?" He placed the spoon into the almost empty soup bowl and leaned back against the chair. Pat now had his undivided attention. It was time to converse for a while.

"Same ole, same ole. I helped Queen Bee and the girls take care of some business. Queen Bee got into it with a few workers, so I had to break up some fights . . ."

Suave laughed out loud.

Pat stared at him for a few seconds before joining in.

"That Queen Bee is something else. In fact, all of you are a piece of work," Suave remarked when the laughter ceased.

Pat smiled. "That we are. What can I say?"

"So, where were you guys taking care of business and behaving like gangsters?" Suave was cunning in extracting as much information from Pat as possible. This was something he would do every time he and Pat were together. He asked questions about Queen Bee's operation, and Pat, who was so infatuated with him, provided all the answers without even realizing it.

"Over in Spanish Town. Central Village, to be exact." Pat smiled, happy that he was conversing. It was all about pleasing Suave. "We have a new supplier who just came in from Haiti."

"Go, Queen Bee. You all are doing it, huh?" An idea began to form in Suave's head. Queen Bee did business in Spanish Town today. The same day that someone robbed King Kong and killed Saddam's grandfather. What a coincidence.

"Yup, we are doing it," Chatty Mouth continued. "We just got a huge shipment that will give even you, Big Shot, a run for your money." Pat laughed out loud.

Suave's dimples flashed in his cheeks, his eyes as cold as icebergs. "Be careful where you keep this huge shipment."

"Oh yes. Queen Bee stored it at Lizzie's house. You know not even the devil himself would dare to set foot in Lizzie's place."

Lizzie was like a sister to Queen Bee and her right-hand woman.

Suave threw his head back and roared with laughter. It was a performance worthy of an Academy nomination. "Don't mess with Lizzie."

"You right about that." Pat was happy. It was great to get Suave talking like this. It meant the rest of the night, or morning as it was then, might go smoothly.

Suave gave Pat a big, fake smile. "Lizzie still rests up in Norbrook, right?" Norbrook was an upscale neighborhood in Kingston, Jamaica.

Pat felt giddy from the power of Smooth Suave's smile. "Yeah, you know how Lizzie is rolling."

Suave nodded. "That's what's up." *A huge shipment just came in from Haiti. Wow.*

"You good, daddy? The soup was okay?" Pat leaned over and touched Suave's hand that was resting on the table.

Like a bipolar bear, Suave's face became ugly as he pulled his hand away. Now that he got the information he wanted, his fury returned. Sometimes he couldn't stand the sight of Pat, but he just couldn't stay away.

"Get up," Suave commanded, pushing his chair away from the table, hatred now shimmering in his eyes. The fierce look that was meant to scare Pat was more like a turn-on.

Like a snake, Pat slithered out of the chair and locked eyes on Suave. Understanding their usual routine by now, Pat strolled out of the kitchen toward the bedroom.

Suave followed. Slow music greeted him when he entered the semidark bedroom, illuminated only by one lit candle.

"I hear you callin', here I come, baby, to save you . . ." R. Kelly's sexy voice echoed around the room.

In a flash, Suave strode over to the small CD player on the nightstand and whacked the *off* button. R. Kelly disappeared, and then Suave marched over to the candle and blew it out like the big bad wolf. There was nothing romantic about this hookup. There never was.

The full moon that night peeped into the solemn bedroom.

"Get on the bed," Suave snapped.

Pat obeyed, dropping the bathrobe to the hardwood floor and went to lie on the bed, facedown.

Suave walked over to a closet and pulled it open. He reached inside and took out a long, thick, rubber belt, resembling a piece of truck tire.

At five foot nine, Pat's long, smooth legs stretched out on the king-sized bed, with that cute buttock in the air. She began to tremble.

Suave approached the bed with blood in his eyes. His nostrils flared like a bull, his chest rising and falling as he breathed deeply.

"You disgusting piece of—!" Suave brought the belt down hard on Pat's bottom. One lash right after the other, over and over.

Pat's screams were muffled in the pillow, tears leaking out. There was a lot of pain, but for Pat, there was also that titillated rush. Being whipped by a tall, strong, sexy man was a perverted bliss.

"I told you to leave me alone." Suave was now sweating, huffing and puffing as he whipped Pat's behind. "Didn't I? Okay, I'm going to show you not to mess with me." *Whip! Whip!*

It was really hurting now. Nothing was exciting about this anymore. Pat was getting scared. The blows were now raining down on Pat's back, legs, and buttocks. "*Woieeee,*" Pat yelled out after receiving a sharp whack across the head.

"Shut up!" Suave was leaning over the bed, beating Pat as if his life depended on it. In a way, it really did.

"No. Please, wait a minute." Pat rolled over and scurried away from Suave.

Suave had a disgusted expression on his face as his eyes ran over Pat like an x-ray machine. He scanned the thick, curly Afro, gazed over the lovely, chiseled face, his eyes passed over a taut, smooth chest, and moved down to settle on the erected penis.

Patrick Walters, a.k.a. Pat, looked up at Suave in anguish and said, "The beatings are getting too bad. This is no longer fun. Please—"

"Shut up!" Suave's face was ugly with rage, his tall, muscled body shaking at the furnace boiling up inside him. "Turn over, and don't look at me! I don't want to see your disgusting face." Suave was no longer talking to Pat but a ghost that had been haunting him for years from the grave. The same ghost that kept on leading him to this house against his will, over and over again.

As Suave called Pat every derogatory name under the sun, Pat rolled over onto his tummy, trembling, his body aching. He knew deep down inside that it would only get worse unless he could once again tame the demon that was now rearing its ugly head in Suave.

"I hate you," Suave yelled before he lunged himself on top of Pat on the bed. "I'm going to kill you again. This time, you'll stay dead."

Part Two

Chapter Thirteen

Kingston, Jamaica, West Indies, 1974

"Good morning, Pastor Ralph," twelve-year-old Suave mumbled in a hoarse voice, his red, puffy eyes fixed on his feet.

Pastor Ralph stood in his doorway, looking at his nephew, his eyes filled with concern. "Good morning, son." Everyone called him Pastor Ralph, including his family members.

"Good morning, Pastor," Sister Winnie said from behind Suave. She shoved Suave a little closer to the front door and went to stand beside him. "I know you heard what took place last night." She tsked her teeth, shaking her head. "What a tragedy."

"Can't say I'm surprised." Pastor Ralph reached out and briefly touched Suave's shoulder. "I'm sorry for your loss. How are you holding up, son?"

Tears sprang to Suave's eyes. He used the back of his hand to wipe his face, his eyes still planted on the ground.

"The poor child is still in shock," Sister Winnie replied. "I let him spend the night with us, but you know I can't keep him. I already have nine mouths to feed, and I can't take on another. So, I took a bus to bring him to you."

Pastor Ralph replied, "You did the right thing, Sister Winnie. I just finished breakfast and was coming to see about him. I'm all the family Suave has left now. Come in and tell me what exactly happened." Pastor Ralph moved aside and allowed Suave and Sister Winnie to enter the dingy living room of the small, dilapidated, two-bedroom house. The house leaned a little to the left as if it were in pain.

"Suave, you go and lie down in the back bedroom. You hungry?" Pastor Ralph asked.

Sister Winnie answered, "I gave him some fried dumplings and salt fish this morning, but he hardly touched it. I don't think he wants any food right now. Poor child."

"Well, he has to eat. Go and get some rest, son." Pastor Ralph pointed down the narrow hallway.

With his head still hanging low, Suave shuffled away.

"I'll fry some fritters for him in a few minutes." Pastor Ralph walked over to a lumpy couch and sat. "Sit and take the load off, Sister Winnie." He patted the space beside him on the couch.

Sister Winnie groaned as she lowered herself onto the couch. "This arthritis is giving me a hard time." She rubbed her knees. "But anyway, George done lost his mind and killed Gloria last night. Then the old fool turned the gun on himself and put a bullet in his own head," she said of Suave's parents. "Can you believe it?"

Pastor Ralph sighed loudly and stared off into space. "I have been telling Gloria to leave that man," he said of his sister. "George was always beating on her. But as soon as she left, he came crying and begging for forgiveness, and back she went. Now see what happened."

"It was a good thing Suave was hanging out up the street when it happened. Who knows, George would've probably killed him too." Sister Winnie leaned back on the couch.

Gloria Wilkins and George Brown lived in Vineyard Town, Kingston, with their son, Suave. The two had been together since they were teenagers, but it was a volatile relationship that only intensified as they got older. George was possessive and jealous of the beautiful Gloria. If a man so as much as said "hi" to her, then she was having an affair with him. Gloria paid dearly for this jealousy with beatings, day after day, year after year. But for some strange reason, she refused to leave her man.

"I love him," Gloria often told the people who asked why she stayed. "George is just a little jealous, but he won't do it again." She would smile, showing the few teeth George hadn't knocked out yet. "Plus, Suave needs his father. He needs a man in his life."

Gloria was only eighteen years old when she got pregnant with Suave. George, only a teenager himself, nineteen years old, turned to selling marijuana to take care of his family. A small-time dealer, he barely made enough to pay the rent for the two-bedroom house they lived in and to put a little food on the table.

But last night, at only thirty years old, Gloria got the last beating of her life. The argument started the same . . . George accusing her of sleeping with the neighbor across the street.

"I saw you coming from over there!" George had barked, spit flying from his mouth. "You think I'm a fool?"

"I just went to borrow some sugar," Gloria explained fearfully. Her body was still aching from the beating the night before. "I was going to sweeten the little cornmeal porridge for dinner."

George pulled a gun from his waist and said, "I'm tired of you disrespecting me. You have people whispering behind my back and laughing at me." He pointed the gun at Gloria's chest.

Gloria's eyes bugged. She was used to George's fists and feet but not a gun. Where did he get it?

"George, listen to me. Please put the gun away," she begged, backing away into a corner of the tiny kitchen. "I love you."

George laughed crazily. "Love me? I bet you love the joker across the street too, huh?"

"Please think of Suave." Gloria continued to plead for her life. She glanced at the door, praying Suave would not come through it. "He's just a child. He needs his mother and father."

"I'll take care of my son after I kill your behind," George replied, waving the gun at her.

A loud noise reverberated throughout the house. Gloria stared at George in disbelief, a hand over her chest. "You . . . shot . . ." she said before falling to the ground. Blood poured out of the bullet hole in her chest.

The gun fell out of George's hand, sounding like a bomb in the now quiet room when it landed on the hardwood floor. Standing as stiff as ply board, George stared wide-eyed down at the body of the woman he loved. What had happened? He didn't pull the trigger. . . . Did he? He was only waving the gun around to scare her. Gloria wasn't dead. . . . Was she? She was just faking.

As if in a trance, George knelt beside her. "Glo', wake up, baby. You know I was only playing with you. I didn't mean to shoot you." He gently slapped Gloria's cheek.

"Come on, Glo'. I'm going to take you to the hospital, and they'll fix you up. I won't do it again, I promise."

It was the first time George would get to keep that promise because Gloria never responded. She was dead.

"Oh Lord, I killed Glo'." George dropped down on his bottom and sat on something hard. Sliding over a little, he looked down and saw it was the gun. Mindlessly, he picked it up and peered at it for a few seconds. Without thinking, he put the gun to his head, and this time, he intentionally pulled the trigger. Brain matter splashed against the wall as he fell beside Gloria. Suave's parents were gone.

The shots alerted the neighbors next door. Upon arrival, the police saw the two bodies and called for a hearse. It was clearly a case of murder-suicide. No investigation was necessary.

"Mommy! Daddy!" Suave shouted, struggling against Sister Winnie, who held him tightly to her hefty body. "Leave them alone," the little boy yelled to the men who were putting the bodies in the hearse. "Take them out of the black bag. They can't breathe."

"Hush, baby," Sister Winnie whispered to him. "They're gone."

"Noooo!" Suave kicked and flung his hands wildly in the air, trying to get to his parents before the men took them away, but Sister Winnie held on tightly.

The onlookers watched the heartbreaking scene. Their eyes filled with pity for the little orphan.

"Reggie!" Sister Winnie called out to one of her sons standing a few feet away. "Come and take Suave up to the house."

Suave kicked and screamed when Reggie threw him over his shoulder and began to walk to the house. "I want my mommy and daddy!"

It took most of the night before Suave wore himself out. His voice went hoarse, and his eyes were red and swollen when exhaustion finally took over his little body. Suave had locked himself in Sister Winnie's bathroom and fell asleep on the floor. Reggie put his talent to use and picked the lock on the door. Sister Winnie took the sleeping boy off the floor and placed him on the couch, where he slept restlessly.

The next morning after breakfast, Sister Winnie boarded a bus with Suave to Tivoli Gardens, where his only known relative lived—Pastor Ralph.

"And so, here we are," Sister Winnie concluded the story of the demise of Suave's parents. "I know you will take good care of him."

"Of course," Pastor Ralph replied. "He is my only sister's son. I'll take care of him like my own." Pastor Ralph being Gloria's only living relative, was left to take care of the child.

Pastor Ralph, at sixty years old, had never been married and had no children of his own. He had a little storefront church in Tivoli Gardens with twelve members on a good Sunday. A "fire and brimstone" preacher, he was always informing the residents of the community that they were all going to hell.

"Well, I better be going now." Sister Winnie groaned and gingerly rose to her feet. "I'll be stopping by to visit with Suave, if that's okay." She looked at Pastor Ralph, who had also stood to his feet.

"That will be fine, my sister. I know you have known him since he was born. Please stop by anytime you want."

Sister Winnie smiled in appreciation. "Let me go and say goodbye—"

Pastor Ralph said quickly, "That's probably not a good idea."

Sister Winnie looked at him with a frown. "I just want to tell him I'm leaving."

Pastor Ralph explained, "It will just make it harder for him when you leave. Remember, Suave doesn't know me too well. I don't want him to start fussing because you're leaving."

Sister Winnie gave him a sympathetic look. "You're right. Sorry, I wasn't thinking about that. I'll be back in a few days to see him."

"Okay." Pastor Ralph walked Sister Winnie to the door. "See you soon." He waved and watched from the doorway until she disappeared . . . a sinister grin on his face.

Chapter Fourteen

"I'm not hungry." Suave rolled over to the far corner of the small, metal twin bed. With his back to Pastor Ralph, he stared at the dirty, chipped wallpaper on the wall without seeing it.

"You have to eat something, boy." Pastor Ralph stood looking down on Suave, a plate of white rice and tin mackerel in his hand. "You are already too skinny as it is."

Suave ignored his uncle, his mind consumed with his deceased parents. The tears trickled down his face. "I want my mommy and daddy," he mumbled.

Pastor Ralph heard and replied in an icy voice, "They're dead. Your worthless daddy killed your stupid mommy, and both are now in hell."

Like a rabid cat, Suave spun around, leaped off the bed onto Pastor Ralph's chest, scratching and kicking at the much-bigger man. "Don't talk about my mommy and daddy!"

Pastor Ralph plucked the boy off him like a tick and threw him across the room. "If you ever do that again, I'll snap your scrawny neck."

Suave whimpered in pain after bouncing off the wall and curled his little body into a ball. The boy felt as if he had just been run over by a trailer.

"Now you get nothing to eat, you bastard. Not even a scrap ever in this house." Pastor Ralph walked to the door with the plate of food. "You should be glad I'm taking your homeless behind into my home. You just like your no-good daddy." He walked over to the light switch by the door and plunged the room into darkness. Livid, he exited the room, slamming the door shut behind him.

Left alone, Suave sobbed loudly. He was hurting so much—mentally and physically. That night he cried himself to sleep on the filthy floorboard.

Early the next morning, Pastor Ralph asked, "You okay in there?" He pulled the door open and stepped into the still dark, windowless bedroom. Shock flashed across his face after he switched on the light and saw Suave lying on the floor. The boy was stretched out flat on his back, his legs straight, and his hands by his sides with his eyes closed. He wasn't moving. "Good God, did I kill him?"

Pastor Ralph tiptoed over to Suave, a feeling of dread in his gut. He used his feet to poke him in the side. Suave didn't move. A little bit harder now, he kicked Suave again, but he remained still. With a much-stronger force this time, Pastor Ralph's foot slammed into Suave's side, and the boy screamed out in agony.

"Now, you're back from the dead." Pastor Ralph snapped and kicked him again. "What you trying to do, huh? Give me a heart attack?" He lifted his foot to strike Suave again, but the boy jumped to his feet, slipped around him, and ran out the door.

"Come back here!" Pastor Ralph went after him. He walked through the living room and hurried to the door. He quickly glanced down the street in time to see Suave sprinting around the corner before disappearing.

Suave ran and ran until he knew he was a good distance away from his uncle's house. With his hands resting on his knees, he bent over in the narrow road, sucking air into his burning lungs. Still panting, he began to walk down the street looking around at the little houses and shops along the roadside. Soon, Suave came upon a group of men sitting under a grocery shop piazza.

It was early morning, but they were drinking rum and smoking marijuana for breakfast. Suave was familiar with the menu because it was one of his father's favorites. Like a little mouse, he approached the men.

"I hope you get my money today from Ramsey," Suave heard the man dressed in full white say as he got closer to the men. "If he gives you any trouble, put a bullet in his skull. I don't give—Who are you?"

Suave felt nine pairs of eyes piercing through him and said, "Suave."

"What the heck are you doing listening to grown folks' conversation?" the leader asked.

Suave shook his head, confused. What had he done wrong? "I was just wondering if someone can please give me a dollar to buy a bulla cake and a bag juice." The boy was now feeling hunger. He hadn't eaten since his parents died two days ago.

Mason Dyke Senior's eyes ran over the strange, lanky boy while his men looked on. He noticed a large bump above Suave's eye and a big bruise on his arm. "Where do you live, son?" He knew everyone in Tivoli Gardens, and he had never seen Suave before.

"My daddy killed my mommy, and then himself, so I have to stay with Pastor Ralph."

Sympathy filled Mason's eyes. "Oh, sorry about your folks."

Unshed tears danced in Suave's eyes, but he refused to cry in front of these men. He replied, "Thank you, sir."

"Did Pastor Ralph do that to your face?" one of the men asked in a rough voice. "Did he beat on you?"

Suave's eyes opened wide in fear. "No, I . . . uh, slipped and fell on the floor."

Mason leaned back on the bench he sat on and folded his arms across his chest. He didn't like Pastor Ralph. For years, the old fool had been condemning him to hell for "poisoning the minds and bodies of God's wonderful people." Pastor Ralph claimed Mason was the devil's advocate for selling drugs to innocent folks. "Go down to that green house," Mason pointed down the street, and Suave looked in that direction, "and ask for Miss Pam. Tell her Mason says to give you some breakfast."

Suave looked at him in dumbfounded silence.

"Go on now," Mason said. "After you eat, come back here."

Suave stared at him for a few seconds longer before he headed off toward the house. He pushed the metal gate open, then walked up the walkway to the veranda. "Miss Pam?" he called out in a tiny voice. "Hello? Miss Pam?"

The door opened, and a young boy around Suave's age stuck his head out. "What do you want?" Mason Dyke Junior, a.k.a. Junior, asked Suave. "What're you calling my mother for?" His eyes were very cold for someone so young.

"Mr. . . . Mr. Mason sent me to Miss Pam." Suave looked down at his feet, now ashamed. "But don't bother." He turned around and began walking toward the gate.

"Young man, were you calling me?"

Suave spun around to see a plump, smiling woman standing beside the sulking boy. "Yes, ma'am."

"Well, come here, son."

"He was leaving, Mommy," Junior said. "Let the little fool go on his way."

"Shut up, Junior, and go back inside the house." Miss Pam glared at the boy.

Junior shot Suave a nasty look, then stomped back into the house. It was the beginning of his hatred for Suave.

Suave saw the look and hesitated once again. His stomach rumbled, and he soon forgot his little pride. "Mr. Mason says to please give me some breakfast, ma'am. I'm hungry."

Miss Pam held out her hand to Suave, smiling. "You are just in time because we are about to eat. What's your name, baby?"

"Suave." He placed his hand in Miss Pam's and allowed her to lead him inside the house. They walked through a beautifully furnished living room to a kitchen in the back of the house. Junior was sitting around the dining table with a huge plate of fried dumplings, boiled bananas, salt mackerel, and hot chocolate in front of him. His face twisted up when he saw Suave approaching with his mother.

"Go and have a seat, sweetie." Miss Pam pointed to an empty chair around the table, facing Junior. "I'll be right there with your breakfast."

Suave jumped into his seat, ignoring Junior. His main concern right then was to get some food in his empty stomach. "Thank you, Miss Pam," he said when a plate piled high with sweet-smelling food was placed in front of him.

"You are welcome, baby." Miss Pam cautiously put a big mug of hot chocolate in front of him. "Be careful, this is hot."

"Yes, ma'am," Suave mumbled through a mouth already filled with fried dumplings. He began to eat as if he hadn't eaten in years.

Miss Pam came and took her seat around the table. "Junior, why aren't you eating?"

"Because his nasty face makes me lose my appetite." Junior rested back in his chair, folded his arms, and his lips pouted out.

"Boy, shush your mouth, and don't ever say that again. You better start eating this food." Miss Pam glared at Junior until he began to nibble on his food. "You watch yourself, boy."

Suave paused to watch the exchange between mother and son.

"Eat up, Suave. Don't listen to Junior," Miss Pam said.

During breakfast, Miss Pam asked Suave about himself, and he told her about his parents' demise. Her heart broke for the little orphan. "I'm sorry, baby. I want you to know you are always welcome to come and eat with us."

Junior snorted but quickly looked away from his mother's stern look.

After breakfast, Suave turned down Miss Pam's invitation to stay and watch a little television. Although he wanted to, he just didn't want to be around Junior any longer than necessary. He thanked Miss Pam for the delicious food and strolled out on a full tummy back up the road to where Mr. Mason and his men were still laughing and talking.

"I hope you left a little for me," Mason joked when Suave approached.

"Yes, sir." Suave's handsome face broke out in a big grin. "Miss Pam gave me a big plate of food."

The men laughed, and Suave joined in as he took a seat beside his new savior.

"That's good, son." Mason lightly tapped Suave on the back. "Hang with me, and I'll make sure you never go hungry again."

Suave's grateful eyes lit up in gratitude. "I will, Mr. Mason," he replied, his young, impressive, immature mind not comprehending that he was making a deal with the devil.

Chapter Fifteen

Mason handed Suave a small package. "Here, Suave. I want you to take this to Mackie." The two were in the supply room at the back of Mason's little grocery shop run by Miss Pam. "He's waiting for you at the usual location."

"Okay, Mr. Mason." Suave stuffed the drugs into his knapsack and threw the bag over his shoulders. He then walked outside to retrieve his bicycle, compliments of Mason, that was leaning up against the wall. He hopped on the bike and took off at a fast speed down the lane, headed to Mackie's spot on Spanish Town Road.

Mason watched until Suave disappeared around the corner, a proud smile on his face. It had been a little over a year since Mason met the boy, and he had taken Suave under his wings. Although Suave continued to live with Pastor Ralph, who ranted and raved about the boy's association with the community's drug kingpin, Suave spent most of his free time with Mason and his men.

Now a student at Kingston Technical High School in the eighth grade, Suave spent his days in school and evenings doing drug runs for Mason. His main duty was to make sure all Mason's men around the area always had a full supply of marijuana. On a few occasions, he delivered the merchandise to customers in the neighborhood. These tasks were shared with Junior and two other young boys—Josh, nicknamed Cobra, and Samuel, known as Daddy Lizard. Suave remained aloof from Junior, whose hatred for him only intensified as Suave's relationship grew with his father. However, he became best friends with Cobra and Daddy Lizard in no time.

"Anything else, Mr. Mason?" Suave asked his mentor later that evening as night was falling. "You want me to do that pickup on Keith Avenue?"

Mason was perched on a stool under the shop. He took a sip of the beer in his hand and said, "Nay, that's it for tonight, young gun. You did a good job, as usual."

"Are you sure? It's still early. I don't mind, sir." Suave was almost begging Mason to give him something else to do.

Mason frowned. "Every night, it seems as if you don't want to go home. What's going on?"

"No . . . Nothing, Mr. Mason," Suave stammered, his eyes widened in fear. "I'm just not ready to go home. That's all."

"Suave, you do know if that old fool is mistreating you in any way, I need to know," Mason said in reference to Pastor Ralph. "It would take nothing for me to fix his business. You know that, right?"

Suave nodded, his eyes looking everywhere but at Mason. "Well, I'll see you tomorrow. Good night, Mr. Mason." He hurried away before Mason decided to probe a little deeper.

Fear filled Suave's gut as he approached the house. He hated going home, but he had no choice. He knocked a few times on the door and waited for Pastor Ralph to come and open it. The man refused to give him a key.

"This is my *house, and you will not come and go as you please," Pastor Ralph had told him. "I am the man up in here, not you."*

It took Pastor Ralph ten minutes to open the door. Suave knew it was a deliberate ploy to show his displeasure of him.

"Well, well, he remembers where he lives." Pastor Ralph sneered at Suave. "I have a good mind to leave you outside."

Suave wished he would. This way, he would have an excuse to tell Mason, who just might allow him to stay with him. Although he hated Junior and the thought of living with him, Suave hated Pastor Ralph more.

"Get your butt inside," Pastor Ralph barked. He stood to the side.

Suave kicked off his sneakers and left them on the veranda. As he passed his uncle into the living room, he felt a sharp blow to the back of his head. Suave shrieked and spun around to a fist that smashed into his gut. The boy doubled over in pain, crying.

"How many times I told you to stop running around with that devil and his followers, huh?" Pastor Ralph kicked the boy in his bottom, sending him to the floor, howling in agony. "I should just twist your neck right now." But Pastor Ralph knew he couldn't. If he killed Suave, Mason would make sure he was dead in seconds. So, he did the next best thing. Pastor Ralph abused the young boy and threatened him into silence.

"And remember, if you ever say a word to that drug dealer, I'll make sure everyone knows. Both of us will pay the price." His nasty grin didn't reach his bloodshot eyes.

Suave whimpered, not from the pain but from the shame. It was the reason why he came home to a beating almost every night. He would rather kill himself than let anyone know about his ignominy.

Pastor Ralph knelt beside Suave and whispered in his ear, "You won't say a word to anyone, will you?" His breath stank of the Johnnie Walker he often laced his coffee with. "Will you?" he shouted when Suave didn't respond, his hand squeezing the back of the boy's neck.

Suave shook his head, wincing at the sharp pain. "No."

"I can't hear you!"

"No, Pastor Ralph," Suave said louder this time. "I won't tell anyone."

Pastor Ralph squeezed harder on Suave's neck for a few seconds before he let go. He rose with some difficulty due to his arthritic feet, stared down at Suave before striding away to his bedroom, and slammed the door shut.

Suddenly, gospel music from Pastor Ralph's records filled the house, washing over Suave on the floor like a bucket of ice-cold water. He jumped to his feet, ignoring the pain that flooded his body, ran to his bedroom, and shut the door, unable to lock it. Pastor Ralph had removed the lock days after Suave moved in. This way, Pastor Ralph could come and go as he pleased.

Suave sat down on the edge of the bed, nibbling nervously on his lips. *Run out. Go on and get out now before he comes.* He got to his feet and moved toward the door before stopping short.

"I'll make sure everyone knows," Pastor Ralph's words rang in Suave's head. *"Both of us will pay the price."*

On heavy feet, Suave walked back over to the bed and sat down. Tears ran down his face as he reminisced about his parents. It didn't matter what anyone said about Gloria and George. They loved their only child and showed it.

***

"Wake up, sleepyhead," Gloria whispered in Suave's ear, tickling him until he woke up giggling.

"Mommy, behave yourself." Four-year-old Suave squealed with laughter. He laughed even harder when Gloria rained little kisses all over his face.

"I got something for you." Gloria sat on the bed beside her son, wearing a big grin. *"It's under your pillow."*

Suave's eyes got big. His tiny hands reached under his pillow and pulled out a little red car. *"Wow. It's my sports car."* The little boy hugged the car tightly to his chest, his eyes sparkling.

A week before, Gloria took Suave with her to Cross Roads to get away from George for a while. The two spent most of the day window-shopping. When they got to a toy store, Suave stared in awe at the little red sports car on display.

"Mommy, can you buy that for me?" Suave's eyes pleaded with his mother.

"I don't have any money today, baby." Gloria looked down at her son with regret. *"But as soon as I get some, I'll come back and buy it for you,"* she added quickly after seeing the disappointment on his little face.

And she did. That night the family had hard dough bread with sugar and water for dinner. Gloria had used the little money George gave her for food to buy the toy car her son wanted. Even the beating she got that night from George was worth it. After all, her son deserved nice things.

"Here you are," Pastor Ralph's loud voice interrupted Suave's thoughts.

Suave's mouth opened wide when Pastor Ralph entered the bedroom wearing a short, white, frilly negligee. His big gut made him look like he was eight months pregnant. His thick, cracked lips were smeared with bright red lipstick, while mascara and eyeliner were smeared all over his face. Pastor Ralph's feet strapped in the high heel shoes rocked unsteadily as he moved toward the boy.

Suave stared at him flabbergasted.

Pastor Ralph went and sat on the bed beside the boy, his thick, naked thigh pressed against Suave's leg.

Suave moved down a little on the bed, creating some space between them. Helplessness washed over him from head to toe.

"You know I don't like to hurt you," Pastor Ralph said loud enough to be heard above the music that was turned up louder before he came to the boy's room as he massaged Suave's back.

Suave flinched at the unwelcomed touch and jumped to his feet, away from his uncle.

"Get back here!" Pastor Ralph demanded.

The tears poured down Suave's face like a stream. "No. Please, Pastor Ralph," Suave begged, backing away from the man. "Please leave me alone."

Pastor Ralph angrily stood to his feet and approached Suave. He grabbed the boy's arm, dragged him back over to the bed, and threw him onto it. "Take it like a man, boy. You know you like it."

Suave lay on his back weeping. He cried even harder when he felt his shorts pulled down over his legs, followed by his briefs. In no time at all, Suave was naked from the waist down. *Mommy and Daddy, please help me.*

Pastor Ralph knelt on the floor between Suave's legs and began performing oral sex on the boy while masturbating. Suave closed his eyes as if to shut out the whole ugly incident. His shame only intensified when his body responded to the sexual act, his erection betraying him.

The melodious voices of the Mighty Clouds of Joy clashed with the slurping sounds from Pastor Ralph as they informed Suave that "God's still on the throne."

"Please help me, God," the terrified boy prayed silently. "Please come down off your throne and take me away from Pastor Ralph." But God never came; not then, nor over the last few months that Suave had been begging Him for help. In Suave's mind, God stayed on His throne and watched him being abused without helping. What kind of God would do something like that?

Suave's resentment for the God he felt failed him continued to grow.

Chapter Sixteen

The abuse started a few weeks after Suave moved in with his uncle. First, it was a pat here and there on the boy's behind, then an "accidental" touch on his penis, soon to be elevated to fondling, and then the oral sex. At first, Suave fought his uncle, but after the beatings in places on his body unseen by others and the many threats, Suave knew he was no match for the beast. His shame only intensified when he listened to Mason and his men admonish one another about homosexuality.

"Copper shots for all gays," Mason had said, his ignorance on full display. "Anyone of them I catch, they are dead." He detailed how he could kill a gay man. His men agreeing with their boss, laughed as they too took part in the gay bashing.

"I shot the gayyyys," Mason sang in glee, putting a spin on Bob Marley's popular song, "I Shot the Sheriff."

Suave laughed out loud with the men to hide his despair. *Am I gay because of what Pastor Ralph is doing to me? Is this all he plans on doing, or is there more to come? I must find a way to stop him before everyone finds out.*

"Yo, Suave," Mason said. "Any man who even look at you funny, kill that. You hear me, son?"

"Yes, sir," Suave replied. "No man can mess with me like that. I'm all about the ladies."

Mason hollered with laughter and high-fived his student. "This boy right here is going to be a lady's man like me. I love this boy."

And that was the hold Pastor Ralph had on Suave. There was no way Suave could let Mason and the other people in the community find out what was going on. Pastor Ralph was right. Surely Mason would kill them both.

I'm not gay, Suave chanted over and over in his head. *I don't want Pastor Ralph to do this to me.*

But stopping was the last thing on Pastor Ralph's mind. He had hidden his secret desires for years, waiting and yearning for the opportunity when he would get a chance to fulfill them. His sister left him his little nephew that he had been eyeing, and if this wasn't destiny, Pastor Ralph didn't know what it was.

"I think you are now ready for the next step," Pastor Ralph informed Suave a few nights later after he finished the despicable act on the boy. "It took awhile to prep you, but it's time for the home run." The pervert grabbed his groin, beaming down at Suave, who was curled up on the bed. "Yup, you're indeed ready for the Chief." Pastor Ralph slapped Suave on the behind to make his intention known, laughing when Suave whimpered. Whistling a tune, Pastor Ralph exited the bedroom fully satisfied with himself.

Suave didn't sleep that night. It was just as he thought. Pastor Ralph was going to rape him. It was obvious Pastor Ralph didn't plan on stopping at oral sex. He wanted more. Pastor Ralph wanted to turn him into a homosexual, and Suave could not allow that. But what could he do to stop the man? Suave knew he couldn't fight off Pastor Ralph. God knows he had tried. And he certainly couldn't ask anyone for help. What would he say? *My uncle is molesting me, and I need your help?* He might as well just shout it from the rooftop because everyone would know. He had to stop Pastor Ralph by himself . . . but how?

The next day, Suave had to make a delivery for Mason to a customer who lived on Dike Road, a few miles away from Tivoli Gardens. It was his first time at this location. When he got to the house, he repeatedly knocked on the gate, but no one came out. Just then, he heard laughter coming from the back of the house. Curious now, Suave lifted the latch off the gate and pushed his bicycle into the yard. He leaned his bike against the wall, then made his way around the side of the house to the back.

He stopped short when he saw four men forming a circle around two other men trying to hold down a pig. One of the men held a big butcher knife in his hand, with another firmly grasping the thick rope around the pig's neck.

"Yo, stop the laughing and come help hold down the pig," the man with the knife said, perspiration pouring down his face.

Suave edged closer, his eyes fixed on the scene playing out in front of him. He loved pork—jerked, stewed, or boiled, he didn't care. But he had never seen a pig butchered before.

The men were so involved in their task that no one paid any attention to the boy standing behind them, peering at what was going on.

Suave noticed a huge pot of boiling water sitting on three big stones, a roaring fire under it from the lit pieces of wood. The hair on his head stood up when the pig squealed, flopping around wildly as it tried to escape the men holding it captive.

With one guy sitting on pig's back, another guy pulled its head back and plunged the butcher knife deep into its throat, again and again. The pig squealed louder, flapping around as blood gushed out all over the ground. Soon it grunted, its movements slowed, and the pig fell to its belly. The man then used the big knife and sliced the pig's throat from ear to ear, killing it.

Suave peered at the dead pig, and right before his eyes, it changed into Pastor Ralph. Gasping loudly, he stepped back, his hand covering his mouth.

The sound caused the men to turn around.

"Who are you?" one man asked.

"I-I have a delivery for Dusty," Suave said, still a little shaken up at the disturbing image. He took off his knapsack and took out the package.

"Okay. That's for me," said the same man. He took the package Suave handed him. "Tell your boss I'll pass through later this week."

Suave nodded and looked over to see boiling water being poured over the dead pig, while the hair was scraped off. Bile filled his mouth. One thing was for sure . . . Suave wouldn't be eating pork ever again.

It was a horrible scene to watch, but it just might be what he needed to see. A big butcher knife could do so much damage. Bidding goodbye to the men, Suave hurried to get his bike and rode off.

He was sweating when he got on Spanish Town Road. Pedaling fast, he got to the hardware store in record time. He left his bicycle outside and hurried into the store.

"Can I help you, young man?" a pleasant, silver-haired man asked Suave.

"Yes. My mother asked me to buy a very large butcher knife. Where can I find it, please?"

"Right this way. Follow me." The man led Suave down a few aisles until they came to the knives. "Pick the one you want. As you can see, we have various sizes."

Suave looked through the array of knives, his eyes settling on one that looked like a small machete. "I'll take that one," he said, pointing at the knife.

"Great choice." The man reached up to take down the knife. "Would you like to also buy a whetstone to sharpen it?"

"Yes, sir. I would like that. I mean, my mother would like that," Suave lied. The sharper, the better. "I would also like some rope."

Minutes later, Suave left the store with his purchases neatly tucked away in his knapsack. He had a few more runs to do before he headed home. Luckily for him, Pastor Ralph had a revival meeting that night at church with his few members and wouldn't be home for a while. This would allow him some time to put his plan into place before the monster tried to make good on his threat to rape him.

"Why don't you just disappear?" Junior asked Suave when he entered the shop looking for Mason. The shop was empty except for Junior.

"Where's Mason?" Suave ignored the bait.

"My father is not here," Junior replied, emphasizing the word "father."

Suave let out a long, deep breath. "Fine. I'll go see if he's at the house." He turned around to walk away when he felt a sharp pain shoot up his leg. Raging, Suave rushed Junior and punched him in the mouth when he realized Junior had kicked him.

The two boys exchanged blows before Suave got the upper hand and flung Junior to the ground. He sat on Junior's chest, raining blows all over his face. Unfortunately for Junior, he messed with someone who had a lot of anger buried deep inside, and Suave was letting him get a dose of it.

"What's going on here?" Mason rushed in and hauled Suave off Junior. "Relax!" he screamed when Suave tried to get around him to take another go at his son. "You too," he yelled at Junior who had jumped to his feet, blood running from his busted lip, trying to get to Suave.

"I have a strong mind to whip both of your rumps." Mason glared at the two boys.

"He started it." Suave pointed at Junior. "I only came to get the rest of my deliveries, and he kicked me."

"That's a lie, Daddy," Junior replied. "He just punched me in the mouth for no reason." He wiped his busted mouth with the edge of his white T-shirt, smearing it with blood. Turning pleading eyes to his father, Junior begged for Mason to believe him.

"Suave, don't go around attacking people." Then Mason glared at Junior. "I *know* you're the one who started it and have the nerve to be lying to me. Go home and stay there until I say otherwise."

Junior shot Suave a look that would have killed him if it could before he marched away, mumbling threats under his breath.

"I'm sorry, Mason," Suave said to his mentor after Junior left. "I should have walked away from him."

"Someone hit you, and you walk away?" Mason peered at Suave through squinted eyes. "Listen, Suave, Junior is my son, and I love you like a son as well, but don't ever let anyone take advantage of you. You must nip it in the bud. You understand me?"

"Yes, sir. I'll never let anyone take me for a punk again." Pastor Ralph popped up in Suave's mind.

Mason remarked, "If you cut off the head of the snake, you kill the body. Always remember that."

Suave nodded his head, a fierce look on his face. "I hate snakes."

Chapter Seventeen

"Oh, how I love Jesus . . ." Pastor Ralph sang merrily as he sprawled out on the couch in the living room. He took a sip of his black coffee laced with white rum, then belched loudly, the rum burning his throat a little. He looked at his big mug, puzzled. He tasted more rum than coffee. Hmmm, guess his hand was a little heavier on the rum than usual.

Taking another sip, he glanced over his shoulder toward the back room and yelled, "Suave, I'll be there in a moment." Pastor Ralph giggled. "Set yourself up, boy." He roared with laughter, his head feeling a little light. "Tonight, I'm going to make you a man. Hahaha."

Suave felt goose bumps wash over him at Pastor Ralph's sinister laugh. But instead of the usual fear, fury swam through his veins, his heart hammering in his chest. "You cut off the head of the snake, you kill the body," Suave muttered softly. "You hate snakes. You kill snakes. If not, the snake will bite you."

He got off the bed, knelt, and looked under it. Just for reassurance. His eyes fell on the big, sharpened butcher knife and the coil of rope.

Earlier that evening, after he completed his runs for Mason, Suave went home to put his plan into action. He entered the empty house through the back door he had unlocked that morning. He closed his bedroom door and sat on the bed sharpening the knife on the whetstone. Back and forth, Suave's hand moved, over and over, until the blade of the big knife glistened.

After he hid the knife and rope under his bed, Suave then strolled into the kitchen. Pastor Ralph's thermos with his spiked coffee was sitting on the kitchen counter. He reached under the cupboard where he knew the rum was and emptied the contents into the coffee. Using a match to light the small two-burner gas stove, Suave reheated the coffee in a pot before pouring it back in the thermos, nice and hot.

Too hyped to lie down or sit, Suave was nervous as he paced the house. Tonight, he would stop Pastor Ralph's sexual abuse. Tonight, he was going to prevent the monster from raping him and turning him into a punk.

Tonight was the night.

Later that night, Suave was peeping out of the front window when he saw Pastor Ralph heading toward the house. He ran to his bedroom and closed the door, unable to lock it. He knew it was only a matter of time before it was opened again by Pastor Ralph.

And he was right.

"Ready or not, here I come." Pastor Ralph's words were slurred as he opened the door and staggered into Suave's bedroom. The loud music filtered in with him. Pastor Ralph's eyes were glazed over when he saw the figure hidden under the sheet in the middle of the bed. "Trying to hide from me, Suave?" he slurred and hiccupped.

Pastor Ralph stumbled toward the bed, leaning over it, and slapped what was supposed to be Suave's rump, but his hand connected with a soft pillow. Suave had used the pillows to form a figure on the bed. "What the—"

"I hate you!" Suave screamed from where he was hiding behind the door and shoved Pastor Ralph hard. Pastor Ralph went flying onto the bed, facedown.

"Hey, what—" The rope was now around Pastor Ralph's neck, tightening by the second, biting into his neck. Pastor Ralph grabbed at the rope and weakly tried to pry it from his neck, but he had no strength. He stumbled to his feet, the rope now choking him, and spun around to face Suave, still clawing at his neck. But in his drunken state, Pastor Ralph was no match for the raging boy.

The veins in Suave's neck stood up as he held on to the rope, tightening it as he bit his lips. Face-to-face, he looked into the bulging eyes of the man who had been molesting him. Pastor Ralph's eyes were filled with fear, while Suave's were filled with hatred.

In a flash, Suave kicked at Pastor Ralph's legs, and the man landed on his back on the bed like a bag of yellow yams. Froth bubbled up at Pastor Ralph's mouth, his eyes rolling in his head.

Suave raced to wrap the rope around the metal headboard, around and around, he knotted it. In a flash, he reached down for the butcher knife under the bed and stood over the man lying on it. "Hello, Pastor Ralph," Suave mocked as he looked down on him, the rays of the light dancing off the deadly looking knife in his hand. "Ready or not, here I come."

Pastor Ralph kicked his feet like a jackass in a wire trap, his arms weakly flying around, but this only tightened the rope more around his neck. He tried to speak, but gibberish came out. His windpipe was being crushed.

"*If you wonder where help has gone . . .*" It was that annoying song again. One of Pastor Ralph's favorites. If only the Mighty Clouds of Joy could just shut up.

"Oh, I know where help has gone!" Suave yelled and punched Pastor Ralph in the mouth. "Away from here! That's where." He punched Pastor Ralph in the stomach. "Where was help when I begged God to save me? Huh? Where was help when this pig was molesting me?"

Suave jumped on the bed and straddled Pastor Ralph, the knife firmly gripped in his hand.

"Ple . . . please," Pastor Ralph tried to beg but was unable to get the words out. He was now slipping in and out of consciousness, slowly choking to death.

"Maybe your God will come off His throne and help you." Suave had a nasty grin on his face. "After all, He didn't help me." Without another word, Suave plunged the knife into Pastor Ralph's throat. Blood spurted out like a water sprinkler all over Suave's face and upper body, soaking into the bed.

With the strength of a bull powered by his hatred and anger, Suave sliced the knife across Pastor's Ralph's throat like he saw the guy do earlier that day with the pig—from one ear to the other.

Finished, Suave bolted off the bed, covered in blood, and looked down at Pastor Ralph as he twitched in the throes of death. "What's the matter, Pastor Ralph?" Suave asked, his head leaned to the side as he peered at the dying man. "You're dying. Take it like a man."

Soon, the twitching stopped, and Pastor Ralph's body stilled for the last time. Death had won. Pastor Ralph stared up at Suave with his long tongue hanging out of his mouth, his lifeless eyes wide open. He did turn the boy into a man, but not the way he envisioned it. It was his slaughtering at Suave's hands that did the trick.

Suave untied the rope from Pastor Ralph's neck. Reaching under the bed again, he took out a garbage bag and put the rope and bloodied knife in it.

Next, he stripped out of his bloodstained clothes and dumped his shorts into the garbage bag as well. Barefoot, Suave tiptoed backward toward the door. He made his way down the hallway and into the bathroom, bending down along the way to smear his bloodied footprints with his T-shirt.

After placing the shirt in the bag, he left it by the bathtub and stepped under the shower. As the cool water ran over Suave's body, with Pastor Ralph's blood trickling down the drain, Suave smiled. Pastor Ralph was dead. Holy cow, he had pulled it off. Suave had cut the head off the snake!

Chapter Eighteen

Suave looked up and down the dark streets, cautiously glancing around him before he knelt and stuffed the garbage bag with the bloodied rope, knife, and clothes into one of the deep drains along the street. No one would think to look there. And after a hard rain, the bag would wash away unnoticed into the sewage with the other trash.

Now wearing a clean pair of jeans and a black T-shirt, Suave walked down the street, his head held low until he reached Cobra's house. Cobra lived with his mother. Just as Suave thought, Cobra, Daddy Lizard, and two other boys were sitting on stools around a small wooden table in the yard, playing cards.

"Man, where were you?" Cobra asked Suave when he opened the gate and entered the yard.

"I had to go back down to Three Mile to take care of something," Suave lied. "The man wasn't home earlier today."

Cobra nodded. He and Daddy Lizard also worked for Mason. "Well, come and join the game. I'm beating these fools like they done stole my money."

Suave laughed along with the others. He joined the game, and the boys played cards into the wee hours of the morning. It was a Friday night, so there was no school the next day. However, they still had runs to make for Mason.

"That's it for me." Daddy Lizard yawned and stood up.

"Me too," said the other boys, and they too rose to their feet.

Suave reluctantly stood up. He now had to go back home to the corpse he left, and he wasn't looking forward to it. But he had no choice.

"Suave, you look like you can't take another step," Cobra joked. "You can crash on the couch in the living room if you want."

Suave was so relieved he could have hugged Cobra but restrained himself. "I think I'll do that." He followed Cobra inside the house as the other boys went home.

"Suave! Wake up!" Cobra shook Suave's shoulder until he groggily opened his eyes. It was late the next morning, and Suave was still asleep on the couch.

"What's going on?" Suave yawned as he sat up, rubbing his eyes. He looked at Cobra and saw the sick look on his face. "Cobra, what's wrong?" But Suave knew. It looked as if Pastor Ralph's body was discovered. "What's going on?" he asked again.

"It's Pastor Ralph," Cobra said a little above a whisper. "He's dead."

"Dead? Dead? What do you mean he's dead?" Suave jumped to his feet, shaking his head. "No, my uncle can't be dead."

Cobra's mother walked into the room, her eyes filled with sympathy. "I'm so sorry, baby," she said to Suave. "One of his church members just found him."

Suave fell to his knees, wailing as he pounded his fists on the hardwood floor. "No no no! Not again." With his face almost touching the ground, Suave wept, forcing himself to shed tears.

"Shush, my dear." Cobra's mother bent over and rubbed his back. "To lose another loved one again must be so hard for you."

It took a few minutes for Suave's crying to taper off. Using his T-shirt to wipe the tears from his face, he staggered to his feet. "How . . . How . . . How did he die?" he stammered.

Cobra looked away, and his mother looked down at her feet.

"Can someone please tell me how my uncle died?" Suave's voice cracked as if he were going to burst out in tears again.

"He was murdered," Cobra's mother replied in a low voice. "Someone cut his throat like a pig."

Because that's what he was, Suave thought but said, "My poor uncle. Oh, Pastor Ralph." He wrapped his arms around himself, shivering as if he had the chills. "I want to see my uncle."

"No, Suave. I don't think that's a good idea." Cobra's eyes pleaded with his friend. "I heard it's not a pretty sight, man."

But Suave grabbed his sneakers off the floor, slipped them on his feet, then stormed out the door. Cobra ran after him, begging him to stop, but Suave ignored his friend.

Suave allowed the tears to run down his face again as he passed people along the street. Everyone stared sympathetically at the unlucky boy. First, he lost his mother and father, and now his uncle, the only living relative he had left.

When Suave got to Pastor Ralph's house, a large crowd was gathered outside. Two of Pastor Ralph's church members were crying loudly at the demise of their beloved pastor. Suave wished he could give each one a hard slap in the face that would make them see the monster that Pastor Ralph was. But instead, Suave joined in the crying.

"You can't come in here, young man." A police officer stopped Suave on the veranda. "A terrible crime was committed inside, and the police are investigating it."

"But it's my uncle. Who killed my uncle?" Suave bent over with his hands resting on his knees, gasping for breath.

"You okay, son?" The police officer touched his shoulder.

Suave managed to squeeze out a few more drops from his eyes. He had to wrap this up soon. He was running out of tears. "I . . . I . . . I don't feel too well."

"Suave, come here, son." Mason reached down and pulled up the boy he now considered a son. "Let's get you down to the house. You shouldn't be here." Mason put his arm around Suave's shoulder and led him out to the street.

"Here, take him down to the house and see about him," Mason instructed Miss Pam. "I'll stay here until everything is settled."

Miss Pam nodded and took Suave's hand into hers, pity splashed across her face. As they walked down the street, everyone offered Suave their condolences. Once they arrived at the house, Miss Pam led Suave to a bedroom in the back. Junior was nowhere in sight, and Suave was happy about that. He was probably at the crime scene trying to get a glimpse of the dead pig.

Suave's blood ran cold when he entered the room. It was a nice room but reminded him of the little back room where he had killed Pastor Ralph.

"Go lie down, sweetie," Miss Pam said to Suave. "You want some breakfast?"

Suave shook his head and walked over to the bed, sitting on the edge of it. "I just want to fall asleep and wake up to find out this is all a bad dream. I can't believe someone killed my uncle. Who would do something like that?"

Miss Pam said, "I don't want to speak ill of the dead, but I never really liked that man. He walked around here, condemning everyone to hell, but I couldn't help feeling like he was the devil."

Suave lowered his head toward the floor so Miss Pam wouldn't see the smirk on his face.

"Oh, I'm sorry," Miss Pam said quickly, misinterpreting Suave's action. "I shouldn't have said that. He was still your uncle. He took you into his home and helped you when you needed him."

You mean he helped himself. Suave looked up at her through sad eyes and said, "Yes, my uncle was really something." *I hope you rot in hell, Pastor Ralph. Bye-bye.*

"Okay. I'll come back and check on you later." Miss Pam exited the room, pulling the door closed behind her.

Alone in the room, Suave kicked off his sneakers. He lay down on the bed, his legs crossed, and his hands under his head as he stared up at the ceiling. Soon a smile spread across his face. Suave chuckled softly. "I think I want to be an actor when I grow up."

Chapter Nineteen

Five years later, Suave, now eighteen years old, was one of Mason's right-hand men. After Pastor Ralph was killed, Mason insisted that Suave live with him, Miss Pam, and Junior, against Junior's protests. Mason sold Pastor Ralph's house that was now Suave's as his only surviving relative and put the money in an account for Suave.

Suave wanted to drop out of high school to hustle full-time, but Mason wouldn't hear of it. "Education is very important, my son," he told Suave. "I dropped out of school to run the streets, and while I'm doing okay, I know you can do so much more. No dummy can build or run an empire. Do you want to depend on another man to run your business? No. You need street *and* book smarts to take on the world."

And that was what it took for Suave to stay in school. He had already built his drug empire in his mind and wanted all the resources to make his dream come true. So, he continued to work for Mason while he finished high school.

"Hey, Mason, can I talk to you for a minute?" Suave asked as he entered the living room where Mason and Junior sat on couches facing each other.

"Can't you see my father and I are busy?" Junior sneered at Suave. He still hated Suave, and over the last few years, the two fought day and night. "Why don't you pack up your little bundle and get out of our house?"

"Junior!" Mason glared at his son, and Junior quickly looked away, his face filled with contempt for the young man who had been sharing his father. "Go and open the shop until your mother comes."

Junior stood to his feet, muttering curse words under his breath as he walked toward the door.

"Yes, go open the shop, King Kong," Suave mocked. His laughter grew louder when Junior flipped him the bird and stormed out of the house.

Over the years, as Suave and Junior's hostility toward each other grew, Suave nicknamed Junior "King Kong." "You're ugly like the big gorilla," he had told Junior. "That's why none of the girls want you." While Suave's good looks made him very popular with the girls, Junior was the opposite. He did get a few dates now and then on his father's reputation in the community, but Suave was the one in demand. His charismatic personality and handsome face made him a chick magnet.

"How many times have I told you to stop calling him that?" Mason asked as Suave took the seat that Junior vacated. "The two of you are my sons. I want you to be close as brothers and have each other's back."

Yeah, when hell freezes over. Suave grinned at Mason. "Don't worry about Junior and me. You know we have a love-hate relationship. But that's not what I want to talk to you about. I'm eighteen years old now, and in the eyes of the law, I'm a grown man."

Mason leaned back into the couch and stared at Suave. "That you are."

"I was thinking that it's time for me to launch out on my own. I've learned a lot from you over the years, helping you to run your business, but I need to start building my own."

Mason bobbed his head. "Uh-huh. So, you don't want to work for me anymore. Is that what you're saying?"

"I'm saying I need to do *me*," Suave noted. "You know I'll never leave you, Mason. You are like a father to me, and I love you like one. I just want to follow my dreams. That's all."

"Follow your dreams, huh?" Mason looked at Suave, anger flashing in his eyes. "After everything I've done for you, you want to compete against *me*?" His voice was getting louder. "I fed you, gave you a job, took you into my home, and treated you like a son. And now you want to *betray* me?" Mason jumped to his feet and closed the distance between him and Suave. "I deserve better from you!" He leaned over Suave, who was still sitting on the couch. "And you should be loyal to me." He pointed his finger in Suave's face. "But no, now you're getting greedy."

Suave took his time rising to his feet and came face-to-face with his mentor. He was a tall young man. "As I said before, I won't be competing with you. I'll find my own spot and do my own business. I'll continue to help you with yours, but I want to do my own too." He locked eyes with Mason, refusing to back off.

After taking the life of his molester, Pastor Ralph, Suave became a fierce young man. He feared nothing or no one, and his hard reputation was becoming well known in his community and surrounding areas as he climbed the ranks in Mason's operation.

"I have the money from the sale of my uncle's house," Suave continued in a hard tone. "I'll buy my first supply from you and do my thing." It was a statement, not a question.

"Go to hell." Mason's spit sprayed Suave's face. "I don't want your money, nor do I need you in my business. You're fired!"

Suave stared at Mason for a moment. The man's words hurt him to the core, but he refused to show his emotions. Suave's vulnerability died with Pastor Ralph. "I'm sorry you feel that way. I was hoping you'd support me as you've always done."

"Support you? Support a *traitor?* I don't think so." Mason glared at Suave. "Get out of my house and never come back. Now I see why Junior hates you so much."

"Your son hates me because he's a coward. I'm everything that Junior will *never* be."

"Get out!" Mason yelled. "My son will take over my business one day, and you'll be sorry that you walked away from it."

Suave gave Mason another long look. *I guess this is it. I'm once again on my own.* He walked out of Mason's door for the last time, leaving his clothes and personal belongings behind.

Mason burned everything a few minutes later.

Suave was furious as he walked up the street toward the bus station. "I'm a traitor because I want to do my own business. Right, Mason? I'm supposed to work for you forever?" Suave talked to himself, pissed, and hurt at the same time. He loved Mason and Miss Pam.

"Yo, Suave. Wait up," Cobra shouted from behind as he hurried to catch up with him.

Suave stopped and turned around to face Cobra, his nostrils opening and closing like the mouth of a fish on dry land. "What do you want?" he asked when Cobra caught up with him.

"Hey, why are you angry with me? What did I do?" Cobra was puzzled as he stared at his furious friend. "What happened?"

Suave took a deep breath before saying, "Mason. He just fired me."

"He did *what*? When? Why?"

"Just now. I told him I wanted to start my own business, and he flipped out. Said I'm betraying him, and I should get out of his house and never come back." Suave struggled to keep the tears at bay. He felt like he had lost his parents all over again.

"Oh man! What are you going to do now?" Cobra stared at Suave in concern. "Maybe you can stay with Mama and me for a little while."

"Thanks, man, but I'm out," Suave replied. "I'm leaving Tivoli Gardens and have no intention of coming back."

Cobra pleaded with Suave some more. "I know you're mad now, but think about this, Suave. You don't know anyone out there. It's dangerous, especially in our business."

"You cut off the head of the snake and the body dies, Cobra." Suave had a cold, hard, determined look on his face. "I dare *anyone* to try to stop me from doing me. I'll link you." He bumped fists with Cobra. Then Suave walked off with his head held high to catch a bus to an unknown place with an uncertain destiny.

Chapter Twenty

The next morning Suave awoke. "Ouch. Aaah, man."
He twisted his neck around and around, trying to ease the
crick in it. He looked down at the piece of a cardboard
box on the concrete floor where he had slept in front of a
Court's furniture store. It was now daybreak, and the sun
was rising. Soon, it would be time for business in the
busy, commercial Cross Roads, the center of Kingston.

I need to find somewhere to sleep, Suave pondered
as he crossed the street to a wooden bench. *I don't want
anything too expensive because the little money in my
bank account is for my business. I'll show Mason that
I can make it on my own.* He lowered himself onto the
bench, staring off into space.

The thought of Mason caused an ache in Suave's heart.
Yesterday morning, he woke up in a nice, warm bed, and
this morning, it was on a cardboard box on the streets.
"Maybe I should go back and apologize to Mason," Suave
muttered. "I'll tell him that I changed my mind about doing my own business, and I'll continue to work for him."
But just as soon as the words left his mouth, he shook his
head. He was born to be his own boss and run his own
business. If Mason couldn't understand that, then so be it.

At 9:00 a.m., Suave was in line at the bank to get some
of his money from the sale of Pastor Ralph's house.

"Here, put this up carefully," Mason had said and handed Suave the bankbook. "By the time you're ready for this money, it will have grown some interest."

Suave had grinned as he looked at the bankbook in his hand. Killing Pastor Ralph had definitely paid off in more ways than one. He then hid the bankbook under his bed, where he left it when Mason kicked him out of his house.

"Hello, beautiful." Suave smiled at the pretty bank teller when he got to the counter.

"Good morning." The teller blushed before looking away from him. "How may I help you, sir?"

Suave handed her his driver's license that he had gotten just two weeks prior. He had begged Mason to teach him to drive when he turned fifteen years old. And although he never owned a car, he often practiced when Mason or one of his men allowed him to drive. Everything was in preparation for his milestone eighteenth birthday. "Well, I forgot my bankbook, but I would like to withdraw some money from my account."

"Here, please fill this out and sign the bottom." The teller gave Suave a withdrawal slip, a smile flirting at the corners of her mouth. "I'll use your name to locate your account."

"I appreciate it very much, gorgeous." Suave's dimples winked at her, and she giggled before glancing around for her supervisor.

After receiving the money, Suave tucked the envelope in his pocket, his eyes locked on the teller. "What's your name, baby?"

"Nadine."

"Nadine, can I take you out to dinner later?" Suave didn't even have a roof over his head, but that didn't stop his game. He was a player for life.

"Huh? I . . . I don't think so, but thanks." Nadine's mouth was saying no, but her eyes were saying yes.

"Why don't you take the day and think about it?" Suave wasn't giving up. "I'll be outside the bank at five o'clock. If you still say no, I'll go away, and you won't see me again. Fair enough?"

Nadine chuckled lightly before stopping abruptly when her supervisor appeared at her side, sporting a big frown. "Well, have a great day, sir," she said quickly.

Suave smiled and swaggered out of the bank as if he didn't have a care in the world. With money in tow, he was able to rent an inexpensive, furnished room off Old Hope Road. After he showered in the dingy, stained bathroom that he shared with five other tenants, he slipped on his new blue and white sweat suit with white sneakers. It was time to make some links.

"I can be there in an hour," Suave said into the pay phone moments later. "Cool?" He hung up the phone, a big grin on his face. He was about to make his first big marijuana purchase to kick off his business.

Suave kept information on Mason's connections over the years. Mason might have put him out, but his money gave him an in with other drug dealers. For them, it wasn't personal . . . just business.

"I can't believe you're here." Nadine's eyes opened wide in surprise that evening when she exited the bank and found Suave waiting for her at the bottom of the steps. "I thought you were joking."

"Suave Brown doesn't joke about important things and important people." The words gushed from his mouth like smooth molasses. "I'm a man of my word. So here I am, darling." He opened his arms wide, his eyes twinkling and dimples flashing in his handsome face.

Nadine rolled her eyes teasingly. "I don't even know you."

"That's why I'm inviting you to dinner, baby. So, we can get to know each other." Suave stared at her, a puppy dog look on his face. "Come on. There's a restaurant right around the corner. We can have an early dinner."

Nadine nibbled on her bottom lip before nodding her head. "Okay. I guess dinner won't hurt."

Suave took her hand in his as if they were longtime friends. They walked to the restaurant, laughing and chatting along the way.

During dinner, Suave had Nadine in stitches, sharing one joke after another. He found out that Nadine was nineteen years old and a full-time student at the University of the West Indies. She was working at the bank for the summer. Also, her parents owned a supermarket chain in all fourteen parishes in Jamaica.

"So, I'm having dinner with a rich, uptown girl?" Suave leaned back in his chair, smiling at Nadine.

"My parents are rich. I'm just a student currently working as a bank teller." Nadine was getting embarrassed. She was the only child of wealthy Jamaican socialites and lived in Cherry Gardens, home to many of the movers and shakers in Jamaica.

Suave had told her that he was an orphan and was working as a sales representative. "Hey, I'm cool with that. I don't want anything from you except your company," Suave told her. "You can trust and believe that I'll get mine soon."

Nadine looked at him. He was a thug through and through with a bad boy persona. Her parents would have a heart attack if they saw her with him. But there was just something about Suave that intrigued her. "Do you plan on going to college?" she asked him.

Suave chuckled lightly. "I have all the education I need, babes. Right now, I'm all about making money."

"Well, okay, then, big shot," Nadine replied and laughed out loud, Suave joining in.

The dinner went very well, and it was much later that evening that Suave walked Nadine to her Lexus convertible parked in the bank's parking lot.

"Can I drop you off somewhere?" Nadine asked him. He had admitted that he didn't have a car.

Suave shuddered at the thought of Nadine seeing the dump that he now lived in. "Nah, I'm good. I have a few stops to make, so I'll catch the bus."

An awkward silence wrapped around them. "Thank you for dinner, Suave. I had a good time," Nadine said, smiling. She knew that this was where she should say goodbye and let the evening be a distant memory. She and Suave were as different as steak and shrimp.

Suave nodded his head. "You're welcome, and thank you for coming. I enjoyed your company." He wouldn't ask for another date. The next move was Nadine's.

"Maybe we can do it again," she blurted out. Well, so much for staying away from the bad boy.

Suave grinned at her. "I'd like that very much." He took Nadine's telephone number as he didn't have one for himself and promised to call her soon. Suave was still grinning and waving as Nadine's car vanished from sight.

The rat was playing around the cat's jaw. Soon, it would end up in the cat's craw.

Chapter Twenty-one

Things quickly heated up between Nadine and Suave. It had been two months since they met, and they saw each other almost daily. During the day, Nadine worked at the bank while Suave hustled in the street, trying to grow his clientele and build his business.

It was a late Friday night, and the two were spooning on Suave's bed in his new apartment on McArthur Avenue. It was a garage converted into a small, furnished, one-bedroom flat by an elderly couple who rented it out to supplement their income. Suave had moved in just a month before, and Nadine was there every night.

"Hello? Anyone home?" Nadine snapped her fingers in front of Suave's face, trying to regain his attention.

Suave nibbled on her ear, and she giggled. He kissed her neck softly and whispered, "What's up?"

"I was reminding you that today was my last day at the bank."

Suave said, "Oh, trust me, I remember. Now we can spend more time together."

Nadine rolled over so that they were face-to-face. "I'm going to Miami tomorrow with my parents for a week, and when I return, I'll be starting school." She gave Suave a frown. "But I'll try to spend as much—"

"It's all a part of your father's plan, isn't it?" Suave's voice was hard. "He's taking you to Miami to get you away from me, right?"

Nadine nestled her face into Suave's neck, embarrassed. Her parents had just found out she was seeing him. After forbidding her to see him, the next day, Nadine was back in his bed. The two made love as if their lives depended on it. Suave wanted to lay a claim to his girl, and Nadine wanted to show him that she cared and wasn't going anywhere. Her parents could huff and puff, but they couldn't blow away the love that she and Suave shared.

Now, here they were, days later, still going strong, or so Suave had thought . . . until he heard this little news.

"It's just for a week, sweetheart," Nadine assured him. "We're going to see my uncle and cousins and do a little shopping. Before you know it, I'll be back."

Suave frowned. He didn't like it one bit, but there was nothing he could do. Nadine's parents held the handle, and he the blade. Heck, it wasn't like he could take care of Nadine. Her bedroom was probably bigger than his entire apartment. "Fine," Suave mumbled under his breath. "I'll just focus on work until you get back."

Nadine lifted her head to look at him. "Before you know it, I'll be back. Trust me. I won't allow my parents to keep us apart." She kissed Suave with passion. "Nothing will keep us apart."

But that was easier said than done.

Over the next few months, Nadine's parents did everything they could to end her relationship with Suave. They threatened to ban her from their house, to disown her, and take her out of their will.

"You don't even know him," Nadine shouted one day. She was having another argument with her parents about Suave. "If you meet him, you'll see he's a nice guy."

"We don't need to meet that thug," her father snapped. "And if he knows what's good for him, he better not let me see him."

But Nadine continued to see Suave. She mostly drove to meet up with him, and if he were picking her up, it would be at work or some other prearranged location, with him dropping her off at her car. Suave never came to her house nor had any interaction with her parents. It was her way of trying to keep her two worlds apart while seeing the man she loved.

"I'm pregnant." Tears seeped down Nadine's face as she sat hunched over on the edge of Suave's bed, wringing her hands together nervously. "The doctor said I'm about eight weeks along. I'm sorry." She had been dating Suave for almost a year now.

"Sorry? Sorry for what, babes?" Suave knelt before her, his face flushed with happiness. "This is good news." He took her trembling hands into his, tears of joy in his eyes. "We're having a baby!"

Nadine pulled her hands out of Suave's and jumped to her feet. She walked over to the open window that overlooked the backyard and stared out into the night. "I'm in my second year of college," she began. "I want to finish school and pursue my dreams of becoming a teacher. . . ."

Suave was still on his knee, a perplexed look on his face as he listened.

". . . then later, I want to get married and have children. This pregnancy isn't a part of the plan right now."

Suave rose slowly to his feet as he peered at Nadine through squinted eyes. "What are you trying to say?" He swallowed loudly against the big lump that was lodged firmly in his throat.

"My parents almost had a heart attack when I told them."

"You told your parents before me? Why would—"

"They are my parents," Nadine snapped as she turned around and glared at him. "I need them. You don't have any parents, so you wouldn't understand."

Suave winced as if he were sucker punched in the gut. As if they had a mind of their own, the tears leaked down his face.

"I'm sorry. I shouldn't have said that." Nadine looked ashamed. Suave had shared with her how much he loved his parents and the effect their death had on him, and now she had used it to hurt him. "I'm just so angry right now."

Suave didn't answer. He used the back of his hand to wipe his face and walked over to a used ottoman in the corner of the bedroom where he sat down.

"I'm getting an abortion." Nadine dropped another bomb. "I'm leaving for Miami. . . ."

In a flash, Suave had crossed the room and grabbed Nadine by the throat. He pulled the gun from the back of the waist of his pants and rested the muzzle on her temple. "You're going to kill my seed?"

Nadine trembled with fear as she struggled to breathe. "Please," she said a little above a whisper, but Suave's hold on her neck only tightened.

"Your parents told you to kill my child, and you agree?" Suave's eyes blazed with anger. He looked like a savage pit bull.

Nadine slapped at the hand around her throat, kicking at his feet. "Suave, I-I can't breathe." Her eyes were wide open, a small river pouring down her face. "Please, stop."

As if he were coming out of a trance, Suave released her neck, but the gun was still directed at her head. "You are *not* going to have an abortion," he screamed.

Nadine coughed as she took gulps of air into her lungs. She stared at Suave as if she didn't know him. What was he doing with a gun? Where had he gotten it?

"If my baby dies," Suave was yelling in her ringing ears, "I swear you will die along with it." The baby was the only family that Suave had now. Nadine's thinking about taking that away from him was the ultimate betrayal in his mind. "Tell your parents they will die with my child too!"

Nadine saw the look on his face and knew he was serious. Fear filled her heart. "Okay, Suave. I won't get an abortion."

"Don't play with me, Nadine!" Suave rested his nose on hers, his bulging eyes holding her hostage. "I will *not* allow you to kill my child." His nostrils flared; the veins stood up in his neck. He cocked the gun, and Nadine jumped in fright. "I don't want to hurt you. I love you. But you don't love me."

"Yes, I do," Nadine whispered, glancing at the gun through the corner of her eye. "I love—"

"If you love me, then you wouldn't want to kill the baby we made together." Suave was weary. The anger was now giving way to despair. "If you love me, you will cherish our child."

Suave refused to let Nadine leave his apartment. He feared if she left, then she would go and get an abortion. So, he kept her locked up for three days, without allowing her to call her parents.

During this time, Nadine pleaded with him to let her go, promising on everything she loved that she wouldn't get an abortion. "I'm sure my parents have called the cops by now," she told him. "I don't want you to get in trouble. Please, let me go, Suave. Do you want to go to prison and not see your child?"

That touched something in him. Jail was not an option, especially in his line of work. "Remember what I said if my baby dies, Nadine. I'll gladly spend the rest of my life in prison for my child." Finally, he allowed Nadine to leave and go home.

Just as Nadine suspected, her parents had called the cops and reported her missing. Nadine lied and told them that she willingly spent the time with Suave. After apologizing for worrying them, she informed her parents that she wasn't getting an abortion after all.

A week later, Nadine left for Miami to stay with her uncle without seeing or saying a word to Suave. She took a leave from college to prepare herself mentally and physically for motherhood. There were days when Nadine would rub her swollen stomach happily, and others when she wept bitterly. This wasn't the way it was supposed to be.

Chapter Twenty-two

After waiting a few days for Nadine to contact him, Suave began to think the worst. . . . Nadine had gotten an abortion and was avoiding him. He had allowed her to leave his apartment that day because she had promised not to get the abortion and that she would return to him the next day. It had been over a week, and he still hadn't heard from her. To make matters worse, she had disconnected her phone.

"Enough is enough," Suave said aloud as he marched into "Esquire Fine Food Supermarket" on Half Way Tree Road days later, unaware that Nadine was already out of the country. He didn't know exactly where Nadine lived, but he knew that her parents owned the business.

"I would like to speak to Mr. Esquire, please," Suave informed the middle-aged, bald man behind the customer service counter that was stuck in the corner of the huge supermarket. "Tell him it's Suave Brown, and it's very important."

The man looked Suave up and down, a suspicious look on his face. "Mr. Esquire isn't here. Do you want to leave a message?"

"No, I don't want to leave a message!" Suave was losing his cool, although he had promised himself that he wouldn't. "I want to see him now!" He pounded his fists on the counter, and the man backed away in fright. "Tell Mr. Esquire to get down here right now."

A few customers stopped to stare at the angry young man creating a scene in the busy supermarket. But instead of Mr. Esquire coming out to meet Suave, his security came. Three tall, big, burly, muscled men who looked as if they were bodybuilders surrounded Suave in a tight circle.

Suave had his gun in his waist but knew he couldn't take on all three buffaloes. Also, there were a lot of people now gathering around, and he had no doubt the cops were on their way. As upset as he was, Suave had to let a cooler head prevail.

"Look, I don't want any trouble." Suave raised his hand in the air. "I just need to ask Mr. Esquire where Nadine is. I need to know if she's okay."

Upstairs behind a huge hidden glass window that overlooked the store, Mr. Esquire watched the scene, smirking with satisfaction. *You will never see my daughter again, you piece of trash.*

"Mr. Esquire doesn't want to see you," one of the security guards said. "He would like you to leave his place of business right now."

"Oh, so he *is* here. Well, tell Mr. Esquire I am not going anywhere until he tells me where Nadine is." Suave folded his arms across his chest, a determined look on his face. He really had the heart of a lion.

The security guards exchanged amused glances before one grabbed Suave by his shirt collar, lifting him off the ground. Suave kicked and screamed, demanding that they let him go, but he was ignored. As if he were nothing but a little insect, Suave was carried out of the supermarket and dropped on his behind outside.

Humiliated as some onlookers laughed at him, Suave slowly rose to his feet. He shot dirty looks at the three buffaloes that were using their bodies to block the entrance of the supermarket before he spun around on his heels and stormed away. Their laughter followed Suave until he disappeared around a corner.

Upstairs in his office, Mr. Esquire laughed so hard, he began to cough. He drank some water that was on his desk, his eyes twinkling in his head. He wished he had taken some action before Nadine had gotten pregnant. He should have transferred her to a school abroad and had his men take care of Suave. This would have saved him and his family all this heartache.

But his celebration was short-lived.

Two days later, Suave was back. He got thrown out again, but that didn't faze him. Suave was doing this for Nadine and his unborn child.

Day after day, Suave would show up at the supermarket, screaming for Mr. Esquire to tell him where Nadine was. He got roughed up a few times by the security guards but nothing too extreme. Smart guy that he was, Suave made sure he went to the supermarket when it was bursting with customers. Just as he was unable to shoot up the place as much as he wanted to, Mr. Esquire knew he too could not let his men hurt Suave too much. There were too many witnesses around, and he had a reputation to maintain. Therefore, Mr. Esquire did the next best thing. . . . He reported Suave to the police for harassment.

"I need to see Nadine!" Suave shouted one day, standing in the middle of the supermarket. It was his nineteenth birthday, and Nadine had been missing for over a month now. "You can't keep her or my baby away from me, Mr. Esquire."

Soon, the crowd of curious fascinated shoppers that had gathered around Suave parted. Two police officers entered the supermarket and approached Suave, their hands on the guns at their waists. "Sir, we are going to have to ask you to come with us. You are trespassing on private property."

Suave looked at them apprehensively and said, "I didn't do anything wrong. I just want Mr. Esquire to tell me where my girlfriend is."

"Who is your girlfriend, sir?" one officer asked mockingly.

"His daughter, Nadine."

The officers chuckled, and the crowd nearby roared with laughter. The thought of this boy with Mr. Esquire's sophisticated and well-bred daughter was as farfetched as a pig flying in the sky. Impossible.

"Sir, I am going to ask you to please put your hands behind your back," the police officer said. "Mr. Esquire is pressing charges against you for trespassing. Please don't cause any trouble and make this any harder on yourself."

Suave stared at the police officers in shock. "Press charges against me?" He was getting a little nervous now. Not at the bogus charges by Mr. Esquire but the probing that would follow as a result of his arrest. Suave was living on the wrong side of the law. Being interrogated by the police would open a can of worms. He had to find a way out of the situation.

"Okay, I'll leave," Suave said. "There is no need to arrest me."

"Hands behind your back, sir," the police officer's voice held a dangerous tone, his gun was now in his hand and was pointed at Suave. His partner held a similar position.

The crowd gasped and backed farther away. The situation was getting out of control.

Suave looked from one police officer to the other, wild ideas racing through his mind. *You can't afford to go to jail. You know you can take them both. Go on, pull your gun, and shoot your way out.*

"Fine." Suave put his hands behind his back. Again, he had to be smart. Suave flinched when the handcuffs tightened on his wrists. How ironic that he wasn't getting arrested for his drug dealing but for a woman. His anger was again intensifying toward Nadine.

The police officers led Suave out of the supermarket, one on either side of him. Outside, one officer opened the back door of the police car for Suave to get in. Suave slid into the car, wondering how he was going to get out of the jam he was in.

Both officers hopped into the front of the car, leaving Suave by himself in the back. As the driver started the car, a tall, distinguished man hurried out of the supermarket toward them, waving his hand for the police to wait, a security guard on his heels.

This must be the great Mr. Esquire, Suave thought. He could see some of Nadine's features in the man, especially the light brown eyes.

"Hello, Mr. Esquire," one police officer greeted, giving Suave the confirmation he needed. "Is there something wrong?"

Mr. Esquire walked to the back passenger window where Suave sat. He locked eyes with the young man responsible for his daughter's downfall, wondering what Nadine had seen in Suave to throw away her future.

Suave held Mr. Esquire's stare without flinching. The old goat could get him arrested, but he wasn't going to keep him locked up. Suave was going to make sure of that.

"So, we finally meet, Mr. Brown." Mr. Esquire moved closer to the car. "You wanted to know where my daughter is, right?"

Suave didn't respond. If looks could have killed, Mr. Esquire would have been a dead man.

"She is far away from you, and you will never, ever see her again," Mr. Esquire laughed. "Did you know that my Nads has dual citizenship, here and the U.S.?"

Suave's heart fell. Yes, he knew. Nadine had told him that she was born in Miami, Florida. Her parents were students at the University of Miami when they met. Her mother, who was born and raised in the United States, fell in love with the young Jamaican man. Upon their graduation, they got married and eventually moved to Jamaica when Nadine was two years old.

"You can keep her away from me, but you can't change the fact that I'm the father of her child. Nadine and I will always have a bond that you can never break." Suave was speaking as if he knew for a fact that Nadine would have the baby, but deep down inside, he wasn't sure.

The police officers were silent, listening to the incredible exchange between the men.

Mr. Esquire's chest rose and fell in anger. The truth in Suave's words had hit home. This scumbag was going to be the father of his first grandchild, whether or not he liked it. "I'll drop the charges if you promise not to come back here again," Mr. Esquire said to Suave. "Nadine is now living in Miami and has no intention of returning to Jamaica."

Suave gasped loudly. He fell back against the car seat, his mouth wide open. Good God, Nadine had really left the country with his unborn child. "Did . . . Did she . . . I mean, is she going to have the baby?" He stared up at Mr. Esquire through glassy eyes.

Against his better judgment, Mr. Esquire nodded. "Yes, she's keeping the baby."

The water tank burst open, and Suave lowered his head into his lap and sobbed. He may never see his child, but at least he knew there was going to be one.

Mr. Esquire looked at the police officer in the front passenger seat and nodded his head.

The officer got out of the car and walked around to Suave's door. Pulling it open, he said, "You are free to go, Mr. Brown. Please stay away from Mr. Esquire and his business."

Suave didn't need to be told twice. He leaped out of the car. Standing inches away from Mr. Esquire, Suave peered at the older man. "I won't be back," he remarked. "If at all possible, please tell Nadine to take care of herself and the baby. I'll always be here for them both." With his head hanging low, Suave walked away. There was nothing else left for him to do or say.

Time was longer than rope.

Chapter Twenty-three

It had been almost four years since Nadine left, and Suave was on a mission to make a name for himself in the drug business.

"What's good, my brother?" Suave exchanged a man hug with Cobra. "A little birdie told me you ate all the candies last night."

Cobra grinned and pulled back to look Suave in the eye. "You know how I do. I have a very sweet tooth." The men shared a laugh and bumped fists, standing outside in front of Cobra's apartment on Sunshine Avenue.

"That's what I'm talking about." Suave looked at Cobra with maximum respect. Cobra had sold off the big stash of marijuana that Suave had given him the night before. Cobra had proven himself to Suave since he left Mason and came to work with him six months ago.

Suave and Cobra kept in touch over the years, but both were too busy to hang out frequently. Suave was taking care of his business, and Cobra was handling Mason's business.

"I need to talk with you," Cobra had informed Suave. "Let's meet tomorrow."

The next morning over breakfast, Cobra laid it out for Suave. "I want to work with you." He locked eyes with Suave. "I think the two of us together can really make some big moves."

"Did Mason send you?" Suave asked angrily. "Is he trying to set me up?"

Cobra looked hurt and replied, "Really? Is that what you think of me? Of our friendship after all these years?"

Suave stared at him for a while. "In this business, it's hard to trust anyone. And you know Mason won't let you go without a fight."

"Mason doesn't own me, Suave. I've made him a lot of money over the years. I need mines now."

Suave nodded but was still apprehensive. "Let me sleep on it and get back to you."

It took a week for Suave to meet with Cobra again. "All right, I'm going to give you a shot. But if you ever cross me, you'll see a side of me you never knew existed." His dark eyes showed how serious he was.

"I'm with you all the way, my brother," Cobra told him. "Just watch and see."

And Suave did watch Cobra for a few weeks. He gave him only nickel and dime packages to handle, while he kept a close eye on him. But Cobra continued to work and prove his loyalty, and gradually, Suave began to give him more to handle. Now months later, the friendship between the two had not only gotten stronger, but their working relationship as well.

"Cobra, it's workers like you who are going to help me take over Jamaica," Suave said in a serious voice. "I couldn't choose a better person to be my right-hand man."

Suave was moving up in the drug trade. He now had four men working for him, including Cobra. Suave was living in a modest two-bedroom house in Three Oaks Gardens in Kingston and drove a secondhand Toyota Camry. It wasn't where he wanted to be in life, but it was a huge come-up from sleeping on the street. After all, Rome wasn't built in one day.

"What's good for today?" Cobra asked his boss. "You said you were coming to get me so we can roll together."

Suave replied, "We need to stop by Queen Bee for some supplies. Later, I want a meeting with the little soldiers. I have a big order in Portland, and I need at least three people on it."

Cobra bobbed his head. "Let's make this money, man."

The two men walked toward the car parked by the curb. Suave hopped behind the steering wheel, and Cobra climbed in the passenger seat.

"We need to get you a little ride," Suave said to Cobra after he started the car and drove off. "Something inexpensive for now but durable. You know what I mean?"

"Yeah, that would be good. My neighbor is selling his car. It's about ten years old but seems to be in good condition. I could check it out if you want."

"You do that and let me know. In fact—"

Just then, Suave's cell phone rang. "Talk to me," Suave said when he answered the phone, one hand maneuvering the car. "What? Man, stop playing. Hold on."

Cobra turned sideways to peer at Suave. "What's going on?" he whispered.

Suave ignored his question and pulled over to the side of the road. He put the car in park and barked into the cell phone, "Don't joke with me, Daddy Lizard." He listened for a few seconds, different emotions flashing across his face—shock, sadness, and then anger. It wasn't good news.

"What's going on, Suave?" Cobra asked again.

"It's Mason," Suave answered in a somber tone. "Hold on," he said into the phone, then turned back to Cobra. "He was just murdered."

Cobra was rendered speechless. He stared at Suave as if he had two heads. "Murdered? Who did it? Where?"

Suave held up his index finger, signaling Cobra to wait a minute, before returning to his call. "Where's Miss Pam?" He listened for a few minutes while Daddy Lizard updated him on Mason's demise. "Thanks, man. Cobra and I are on our way. I'll see you in a few." He flipped the cell phone closed.

"They killed Mason?" Cobra was still in disbelief. "*Our* Mason?"

Suave rested his throbbing head back against the car seat, his eyes tightly closed as he took deep breaths. The anger fumes were almost visible coming through his pores. "I loved that man like a father. Yes, we parted on bad terms, but Mason will always have my respect for what he did for me. Who had the nerve to disrespect the godfather of the community like that?"

Cobra was shaking his head. "I . . . I . . . I can't believe it," he stammered. "Mason had his enemies because of what he did, but I didn't think anyone would try to take him out."

"I guess I'm going back to Tivoli Gardens after all this time." With a heavy heart, Suave started the car and drove off.

It took almost an hour fighting through traffic before Suave entered Tivoli Gardens. A few miles down the street, his car was stopped by a group of men sporting furious expressions. The bulge at their waists wasn't their belts.

"What are you doing in these parts, man?" A rough voice growled before his stern face appeared at the passenger window of Suave's car.

"Mambo, it's us," Cobra answered, instantly recognizing one of Mason's men. "It's Suave and me."

"We just heard about Mason." Suave peered at Mambo. "I still can't believe that someone would do something like that."

Mambo grunted but didn't respond to Suave. After all, Suave was one of Mason's enemies too. For all he knew, Suave could have hired the hit on his boss.

As if he were reading Mambo's mind, Suave said, "You know I loved Mason like a father, Mambo. You were there when he took me in and cared for me. We had a falling out because I wanted to spread my wings, but I would cut off my right hand before I hurt a strand of hair on Mason's head."

Mambo locked eyes with Suave for a moment. He saw the sincerity in them and relented. "Mason talked about you every day." Mambo mumbled and quoted a few of Mason's words. *My boy is doing big things for himself. Mark my word, one day, Suave is going to be the biggest godfather in Jamaica.*

Suave looked away and stared out his window, blinking rapidly to keep the tears from falling. Mason never forgot about him after all.

"He still loved you," Mambo said, regaining Suave's attention. "He was just too proud to reach out to you after you left. Come on. I'll meet you by the house and tell you how it went down."

As Suave drove down the narrow street toward the house, a large, boisterous crowd was gathered on both sides of the streets, crying and wailing. It was a community in mourning—A very violent and enraged community that wanted justice.

"We want justice for the godfather!"

"Woieeee, they killed Mason!"

"It's kill for kill!"

"Murderers!"

"Blood is on your hands!"

The police were out in even greater force. The killing of a man with Mason's status in the community wouldn't go without retaliation. This type of murder often resulted in other killings in neighboring communities to get revenge. The police were adamant about preventing this from happening.

Suave paused briefly in front of the shop where the murder took place. Yellow and black crime tape blocked it off, and police officers and their cars were blocking any form of entry. The onlookers were here chanting as numerous police went in and out, trying to collect evidence.

"It seems as if they already took the body away," Cobra said as he too stared at the place where they spent so much time with Mason. He could almost see Mason drinking and cracking jokes, enjoying being the center of attention. Now he would be there no more.

Suave parked the car in front of the house and got out, leaving Cobra still sitting inside, deep in his thoughts.

"Get out of our house," Junior yelled as soon as Suave entered the living room. He planted himself in front of Suave, preventing him from taking another step forward. "My father said you weren't welcome here ever again. Get out!" Junior's face was twisted in fury and pain.

It was at that moment Suave knew he got it right with Junior's nickname. Standing in front of him was the real deal King Kong. But Suave still wasn't scared of him.

"I'm not even going to bother with you," Suave replied and gently but forcibly pushed past Junior. "I know you're hurting right now, so I'm going to ignore you." Suave made his way down the hall until he got to the master bedroom. He knocked on the closed door.

"Come in," said an unfamiliar female voice.

Suave turned the doorknob, pushed the door open, and entered the bedroom. He felt the tears well up again in his eyes at the sight of Miss Pam. She was lying across the bed with her head in a woman's lap, crying uncontrollably.

"Miss Pam?" Suave walked over to the bed and sat on the edge of it. "I'm so sorry." He reached over and began rubbing the back of the woman who cared for him like a son.

Miss Pam peeked through one eye before rising and throwing herself in Suave's arms. She sobbed on his shoulder as he whispered words of encouragement in her ear.

"They killed him, baby," Miss Pam muttered. "He was just getting ready to turn the business over to Junior, and they gunned him down like a dog."

Suave looked over Miss Pam's head at the strange woman.

"I'm Celes, her sister," the gentle-looking woman answered Suave's unasked question. "I live over in Jungle and came as soon as I got the news."

"What happened?" Suave asked above Miss Pam's sobbing. "Mambo is to meet me here."

"All I heard is that Mason was getting ready to close the shop, so he paid the men that were there, and they left. Pam wasn't feeling well today, so she never left the house. Thank you, Lord!" Miss Celes raised her hands in the air to give God some more praise. "They would have killed my little sister too, Lord, but you prevented it.

You are a mighty God! A wonderful Savior! A God in our time of need! Lord, you—"

"Miss Celes," Suave interrupted. He had had enough of the foolishness. Why was the woman praising God when Mason was dead? Didn't she know her so-called God don't give a rat's behind about anybody?

"Yes. I have to always give my Lord the praise for being so good to us," Miss Celes said with a smile. "So, anyway, a neighbor said a motorcycle stopped in front of the shop. Two people were on it, a man wearing a helmet and a young boy no more than twelve or thirteen years old. The boy got off the motorcycle and entered the shop. Seconds later, there was a whole heap of shots. The boy ran out with a big gun in his hand, hopped onto the back of the motorcycle, and it peeled off down the road."

Suave looked at her in shock. "A *boy* killed Mason?"

Miss Pam, whose crying had tapered off to hiccups, whimpered in pain as she clung to Suave.

Miss Celes nodded her head. "They knew that a strange man by himself would have caused Mason to be suspicious, and he would be on guard, so they used a child. Mason loved children and wouldn't have thought anything strange when the boy entered the shop. The boy took advantage of that and shot him over ten times."

Suave was floored. He too had killed when he was a boy, but it was because Pastor Ralph had left him no other choice. But this young boy who took Mason's life was a trained, cold-blooded killer. Obviously, snakes came in various sizes and ages. But Mason found out too late.

Chapter Twenty-four

A week after Mason's huge, statelike funeral, Suave was still in a rut. He felt sad that he didn't get a chance to make up with Mason before he died. He kept playing different scenarios in his head on how he could have prevented Mason's death. Maybe he should have stayed with Mason instead of going on his own. If he had gone back and apologized to Mason, then he would have forgiven him. He should have found a way to stay in Mason's life. He would have been there to stop the child killer. Maybe this, maybe that . . . but Mason was still dead.

"You couldn't stop it, you know?" Daddy Lizard's voice snapped Suave's head toward him. "That was Mason's destiny." Daddy Lizard reclined on the couch he sat on in Suave's living room, stretching out his long legs before him. After Mason's death, Daddy Lizard started working for Suave.

"He's right, Suave," Cobra said from his seat beside Daddy Lizard. "Not even you would have suspected a little boy to be a killer. But we will use that to our advantage because they can't try that with us."

Suave looked at his two friends and knew in his heart they were speaking the truth, but he still hated how things ended between him and Mason. "Yeah, now we know not to trust anyone . . . man, woman, child, or animal."

"I heard that Junior and Miss Pam moved to Jungle to live with Miss Pam's sister," Daddy Lizard added. "Miss Pam is selling the house, the shop, the bar on Spanish Town Road, and the other businesses. I guess she just wanted a fresh start."

Suave took a sip of his Red Stripe beer. "I'm glad Miss Pam didn't stay there. Who knows, they might have come back to kill her too."

"Mambo said Junior vowed to carry on his father's business in Jungle," Cobra replied. "So, I guess we have some more competition now."

Suave smirked, a look of disgust on his face. "King Kong doesn't know where his behind starts from where it ends. How is he going to run a drug business?"

Cobra and Daddy Lizard laughed out loud, and Suave joined in. Junior, a.k.a. King Kong, was a joke to them, or so they thought. Little did they know that King Kong was going to become one of their biggest nemeses.

"All right, I'm going to take care of some business," Suave stated when the laughter died down. "Daddy Lizard, ride with Cobra today. You guys collect the money and distribute the work. Also, get the supply from Queen Bee. We'll meet back at your place around six o'clock." Cobra and Daddy Lizard were roommates, sharing an apartment.

After the men left, Suave took a drive and was mentally checking off all the stops he had to make that day. Business was good, and with Daddy Lizard now on board, Suave was ready to take it to another level. He wanted to expand into St. Catherine, focusing on the Spanish Town market. "I'll put Daddy Lizard in charge of that operation," he muttered, making his way down Half Way Tree Road. "I'll let Cobra . . . What the—?"

Tires screeched, horns blared as Suave swerved across two lanes of traffic, narrowly missing a collision with a truck before coming to a grinding halt in front of Esquire Fine Food Supermarket. His breathing labored, Suave leaned over the steering wheel, trembling as if he had hyperthermia. Cold sweat washed over him as his bugged eyes peered at the sight before him—Nadine, draped in a long, tight, floral dress with her gorgeous hair blowing gently in the breeze, was laughing at a little boy who was making funny faces. A little boy who was the spitting image of Suave.

"My son," Suave whispered and allowed the tears to run down his face. "That's . . . That's my son." He rested his head on the steering wheel and wept. He worked hard, day and night, trying to forget Nadine and the baby but had only managed to push it to the back of his mind. There wasn't a time that he hadn't thought about them as the days ran into weeks, weeks into months, and months into years. Suave had kept his promise and never went back to see Mr. Esquire, so he had no idea if Nadine had a boy or girl. He didn't even know if she had the baby. For all he knew, Mr. Esquire could have been lying when he said Nadine was keeping the baby. But he wasn't, because right in front of Suave stood his son.

It took a few minutes for Suave to compose himself. He wiped his wet face with his handkerchief, blew his nose, and took deep breaths to relax his nerves. Then he got out of the car, slammed the door shut, and marched toward Nadine.

Nadine was laughing so hard at her son's antics that her sides were beginning to hurt. Then suddenly, she stopped as a chill ran through her body. Her heart leaped in her throat and before she turned around, she knew who was standing behind her. Only one man had had that effect on her—Suave Brown.

As if in slow motion, Nadine turned, coming face-to-face with her son's father after all these years. Her tear-filled eyes moved over the clean, white sneakers, to the baggy blue jeans, up to the white T-shirt that was molded to a broad chest, exposing muscled arms, and finally landed on the handsome face framed by small dreads. Nadine saw the tears that came back and were once again dancing down Suave's face unashamedly.

The couple lost themselves in each other's eyes, crying from the years of hurt and pain suffered.

Joel, seeing that his mother was crying, ran and wrapped his little arms around her legs. Nadine reached down and lifted him, his face pressed into the crook of her neck.

"I'm sorry," Nadine whispered, her eyes pleading with Suave. "I just had to get away." With one hand still draped around Joel, she reached into the handbag on her shoulder and took out a handkerchief to wipe her face.

Suave's body felt drained by all the emotions running through it. But surprisingly, instead of anger, he felt pain. "You came back." His voice was hoarse as he wiped his face. "I . . . I . . . I never thought I would . . ." His voice broke, and he inhaled and exhaled, trying not to cry again. "I have a son."

"Yes. His name is Joel. Joel Brown." Nadine rocked Joel in her arm.

Suave looked down at his feet before looking back up at Nadine. "You gave him my name?"

"Of course. You're his father."

"Thank you." Suave sniffled. "Thank you for keeping him and giving him my name. That means a lot to me."

Nadine nodded her head. "I know you must be angry with me, but—"

"I'm not," Suave quickly replied. "Well, I was for a long time after you left, and I thought I would always be. But now that you're here, I feel more sad than mad. I'm sad that I didn't know if I had a son or daughter. I'm sad that I wasn't there for you throughout your pregnancy. I'm sad that I missed four years of my son's life. But most importantly, I'm sad about the way I treated you, making you feel you had to run away from me. I'm sorry. I just snapped when you said you were going to have an abortion."

"I know. I did what I thought was best for the baby, and me, Suave," Nadine said sadly. "But after a while, I felt bad for keeping him away from you. I also missed my home."

"Are you back for good?" Fear filled Suave's eyes.

Nadine nodded her head. "We came back a week ago. Daddy was in the hospital, but he's home resting now." Nadine glanced toward the supermarket. "I came here to help Mommy today."

"Were you ever going to let me see him?" Suave glanced at Joel. "Hello, Joel."

Joel raised his head and looked at the strange man. "Hello," he mumbled shyly.

"Can I hold him?" Suave looked at Nadine pleadingly. Before Nadine could respond, Joel was stretching his hands out to his father. Suave reached out and took the child into his arms, pressing him close to his heart. He was holding his son for the first time.

Choked up, Suave rocked Joel from side to side. He felt a love that was fierce and unconditional. "I want to be a part of his life," he whispered over Joel's head, his eyes locked with Nadine. "I want to know him."

"We have to talk. I know what you do for a living, Suave." Nadine stared pointedly at him. "I know the kind of 'sales representative' you are." Her voice was laced with sarcasm.

Suave took a deep breath. "So, you're going to make this about what I do for a living?"

"I'm going to protect my child," Nadine snapped, her maternal instinct in high gear. "Joel comes first," she murmured, glancing at the little boy who had his little arms around Suave's neck, his head resting on his shoulder as if he knew who he were.

Suave looked at Nadine and saw the determination and love for their son in her eyes. Gone was the young, naïve teenager. Suave was looking at a woman who had matured mentally and physically. "Can we talk alone later?" he asked. "I don't want you and me to fight about this. I want us to work together for Joel's sake."

Joel heard his name and raised his head to look up at Suave curiously. He flashed his dimples at his father, who did the same.

Suave kissed Joel on his forehead. "It's so nice to meet you, Joel." Joel giggled and tightened his hold around Suave's neck.

Nadine watched the exchange between father and son. "We'll try to work something out, but I really need to speak with you first." Nadine lowered her voice. "Once we have come to an agreement, I'll tell him who you are."

"How about we meet at my house?" Suave said and quickly added when he saw the frown on Nadine's face, "Just to talk and so you can see where I live. I want you to know that Joel will be safe with me."

"Uh-huh. I guess that's okay." Nadine took a pen from her handbag and jotted down Suave's information. "I'll come around four o'clock tomorrow after church. The supermarket will be closed, so Mommy can watch Joel for me."

Suave nodded reluctantly. He was hoping they could talk later, and maybe he would get Joel for a visit tomorrow. However, he waited all this time. Surely, he could wait another day. "That's fine. Call me if you have trouble finding the place." He gave Joel a tight squeeze and kissed him on the forehead again. "I'll see you soon, Joel. Okay?" Joel nodded, and Suave passed him over.

"I'll see you tomorrow." Nadine was feeling happy that they had gotten through their first meeting after all this time in a civilized manner. "It was good seeing you, Suave."

"Thanks, same here." Suave peered at Joel, who was still looking at him. "It feels so . . . so good. But not just good, much more than good. You know what I mean?"

"Yes, I know. He has that effect on me too." Nadine kissed Joel's cheek.

Joel giggled, and Suave grinned.

Every little thing gonna be all right.

Chapter Twenty-five

"This is a nice place you have here, Suave," Nadine said as she walked through his house. Every room was nicely furnished and immaculately clean. But that was Suave. "It's in a nice neighborhood too."

"It'll do for now. In a few years, I'll be your neighbor up on the hill."

Nadine paused at the door leading to the veranda and looked at him. "That's what I want to talk to you about. Your choice of career." She emphasized the word "career."

"Nadine, I know you don't like what I do," Suave began, "but it's only for a while."

Nadine sucked her teeth, walked out on the veranda, and took a seat in one of the three chairs. "A little while, huh? Until when, Suave? Until you get killed or locked up for the rest of your life?"

Suave sat facing her. "That's not going to happen. I'm very careful, and I know what I'm doing."

"I bet you do." Nadine rolled her eyes. "I can't bring Joel around that life, Suave. People might be after you and get him instead." She trembled at the thought, fear lurking in her eyes.

Suave felt like an eel for the worry he was causing her. "Listen to me." He waited until Nadine locked eyes with him. "No one but Cobra and Daddy Lizard knows where I live."

"Of course not," Nadine replied in a too sweet voice. "Only the animal kingdom knows your whereabouts."

Suave threw his head back and roared with laughter.

Against her better judgment, Nadine laughed too.

"Girl, that's why I love you." Suave took a gulp of breath. "I'll always love you, Nadine." The mood turned serious. The former lovers stared at each other, the atmosphere tainted with their sexual tension.

Nadine shook her head. "It's over, Suave," she said above a whisper. "We are too different in so many ways. That ship has sailed."

Suave stared at her. He knew he could have Nadine in his bed in the blink of an eye, but he would respect her wishes. He didn't want to do anything that would jeopardize his relationship with Joel. Suave had lost them before, and he didn't want that to happen again. "Okay, but I'll always love and respect you," he said. "You are my son's mother, and I'll always be here for you and him."

"I know." Nadine smiled at him.

Over the next few weeks, Nadine allowed Suave to see Joel at least twice per week. Now Suave had unsupervised visits with his son for an entire day, and he hoped soon he would get to keep Joel overnight.

That day, Suave watched Joel ride his tricycle around the yard, and pride filled his being. "Be careful, Joel. You're going too fast."

Joel grinned at his father but continued speeding on the trike. Suave shook his head and smiled. At the rate Joel was going, he would soon need a bicycle. Suave had Joel for the entire day. His mother had dropped him off that morning and would be back to pick him up later.

"Daddy, your phone is ringing." Joel stopped the tricycle in front of his father, staring up at him.

"Hello?" Suave said irritated because Cobra and Daddy Lizard knew he had his son and didn't want to be disturbed.

"Sorry to bother you," Cobra said as if he read Suave's thoughts. "We have a situation and need your permission to handle it."

"Hold a second." Suave looked down. "Joel, go on inside. I'll come and give you your lunch, and then we can watch cartoons, okay?"

"Okay." Joel leaned his trike up against the side of the house before he ran inside.

"What's going on?" Suave asked after Joel disappeared inside the house.

"The store owner in Spain Town refused to sell us any more candy."

Suave's nostrils flared in anger. "What? We don't owe him anything."

"He said King Kong was paying a better price and was ordering many more candies than us. They are now exclusive."

Suave fired off some expletives before he glanced toward the house and lowered his voice. "You know King Kong is just trying to mess with me, right?"

"Yeah, I know. But what are we going to do about it?"

"Nadine is coming for Joel around five o'clock." Suave looked at his wristwatch. It was 12:30 p.m. "I'll meet you and Daddy Lizard at your apartment around six o'clock." Fuming, he flipped the phone closed.

"So, how is little Suave doing?" Daddy Lizard asked Suave when he entered their apartment that evening. Suave had invited him and Cobra over to have lunch with

Joel and Nadine one afternoon. The men had looked from Joel to Suave and from Suave to Joel in amazement.

"Good God, look at little Suave," Cobra had remarked. "I wonder if the world is big enough for two of you."

Nadine and Suave had laughed at Cobra's comment. By the end of lunch, Nadine could not help but like Cobra and Daddy Lizard. She didn't like what they did for a living and told them as much, but she and Joel enjoyed their company.

"That's my little man right there." Suave's eyes twinkled as he talked about his son. "Can you believe he asked me to drive my car?"

Daddy Lizard laughed. "Yup, old before he's young, just like his daddy."

Cobra, who was in the kitchen and heard the comment, roared with laughter. "Like father, like son, right?" he yelled.

Suave chuckled as he and Daddy Lizard walked into the kitchen and took seats around the table. In front of Cobra was a huge pile of marijuana that he was cutting, weighing, and wrapping up in little pieces of plastic paper.

"Why are you doing that?" Suave asked him. This was a job for one of his soldiers.

"Well, since we didn't get any supply today and we already collected all the money, I decided to just go ahead and do it."

Suave's anger returned. "Tell me again what that fool said." His face was bent out of shape as Cobra relayed the conversation he'd had with the supplier earlier that day.

"That's a loss for us because he was giving us a very good price," Daddy Lizard noted.

Suave leaned back and stared up at the ceiling, deep in thought. He didn't want to get into a war with King Kong, but in the same breath, he couldn't allow him to ruin his business. "We fight fire with fire."

Daddy Lizard and Cobra stared at him, waiting for an explanation.

"I know that Queen Bee also supplies King Kong. So, what do you say we make her an offer to cut him off and deal with us exclusively? At least for a while, just to make King Kong sweat a little. You know he can't do much with that fool in Spain Town."

Cobra smiled. "That's why you're the boss."

Daddy Lizard grinned. "Let's do it."

Suave took out his cell phone to call Queen Bee. "I hope he stays in his corner now that he sees he can't beat me," Suave said in reference to King Kong. "There's enough business for everyone, so he better know his place."

But King Kong was just getting started. The big gorilla would roar again . . . and louder than before.

Chapter Twenty-six

Life had been very productive for Suave in more ways than one over the next decade. He had built his drug empire and was the most lucrative drug dealer in Jamaica. He had workers in all fourteen parishes, successful businesses, numerous luxury houses, vehicles, expensive jewelry, and more money than he'd ever spend in a lifetime. Smooth Suave was the man.

Suave was also the father of eight children, and he couldn't have been happier. His live-in girl, Monica, had given him two children, Rayden and Raven. The stripper twins, Charlene and Darlene, each had a daughter with him, Alissa and Janelle. Freaky Abby "accidentally" got pregnant and just gave birth to a baby girl whom she named Angel. The cute, youth church choir director, Carol, fell from glory and gave him his daughter, Tiana. Barbara, the conservative secretary by day but bedroom bully by night, had a daughter for him named Natasaja. And, of course, there was Suave's firstborn, his beloved son Joel.

"Man, don't you think you have enough kids?" Cobra asked Suave one night as they relaxed on his veranda in Belgrade Heights. "What, you won't stop until you get a dozen?"

Daddy Lizard and Suave laughed merrily.

"A man needs his legacy." Suave beamed with happiness. "Who am I going to leave all this to, huh?" He made a wide circle with one hand as he glanced around his posh house sitting on the hill. Suave had moved up to "the hills," as he had told Nadine many years ago. "You know I love all my kids."

Cobra and Daddy Lizard agreed. Suave was a whoremonger, but he took care of all his children. With a busy schedule running his drug empire that was now one of the largest in Jamaica, he still found time for all his children.

"Joel is coming to spend the weekend with us tomorrow," Suave informed his right-hand men. "That boy is so smart that he's making his teachers look like fools." Joel was a student at Jamaica College, a prominent all-male high school, where his mother, Nadine, was also an English teacher.

Cobra and Daddy Lizard chuckled. They knew how much Suave liked to boast about his children, especially Joel.

"Monica really loves Joel," Cobra noted. "She treats him like her own."

Suave nodded in agreement. "Joel even has his own room at the house. Monica also gets along well with Nadine." The house Suave was referring to was the home he shared with Monica and their children in Jacks Hill. The house in Belgrade Heights was called "the hut" and was his secret getaway home. No one except the part-time housekeeper, Cobra, and Daddy Lizard knew about this house.

"That's because Joel and Nadine came before you met Monica." Daddy Lizard winked at Suave. "The other trailerload of kids and baby mommas were during your relationship with her. How do you expect her to like *those* women?"

Suave sucked his teeth loudly and cut his eyes at Daddy Lizard. But Daddy Lizard was right. He had been unfaithful to Monica throughout their entire relationship, begetting one child after the other, but she still stayed with him. Suave loved Monica but not enough to settle down with her. "She treats my children well whenever I bring them to the house, though," Suave noted. "Monica is a good woman. That's my wife."

"Uh-huh, so what are you waiting for to marry her?" Cobra asked Suave.

"As soon as I get out of the game." Suave looked down the hill at the thousands of pecks of flickering lights in Kingston City. "I'm a rich man now. It's almost time to call it quits and go straight. You know what I mean?"

Cobra and Daddy Lizard bobbed their heads in agreement. They too had thought about getting out of the game. Of course, they didn't have Suave's level of wealth, but they had accumulated some money working with him over the years and had families of their own.

"What do you say we take care of loose ends and bow out in a few years?" Cobra looked from Suave to Daddy Lizard. "We just open up some more businesses and live a good life?"

Suave raised his glass with a little leftover rum and Coke in salute. "Sounds like a plan to me."

"All right, we're heading out," Daddy Lizard announced. "We need to collect some money from the soldiers in the field."

"Leave the garage door up. I'm heading over to Queen Bee myself," Suave said. "She just got a supply of the good snow." Suave was distributing cocaine as well as marijuana. The drug was becoming more prevalent in Jamaica, and all the dealers were dabbling in it.

After Cobra and Daddy Lizard left, Suave locked up the house. He walked out to his four-car garage and looked at the brand-new Mercedes-Benz and the BMW convertible parked beside each other. He decided on the BMW, clicked it open, and got in the driver's seat, closing the door.

Traffic was light as Suave made his way to Jones Town, St. Andrew, where Queen Bee headquartered. Before long, he was pulling up in front of a huge, three-story house that was surrounded by small zinc and board houses, graffiti, run-down buildings, and old, abandoned and burnt-out structures. It was like a queen's mansion in the midst of her peasants.

The tall iron gate slowly opened, and Suave knew that one of Queen Bee's girls saw him pull up. He drove in and parked in a vacant parking spot at the side of the house, among the numerous luxury cars already parked there. After locking his car, he made his way to the front door, where a beautiful young lady greeted him. This one was new because Suave knew all of Queen Bee's girls in more ways than one.

"Hello, beautiful. I've never seen your fine self before." Suave flashed the killer dimples.

The girl playfully rolled her eyes. She knew who Suave was, and his reputation was legendary. "That's because I just started to work with Queen Bee a few days ago."

The big house was home to at least fifteen girls who worked for Queen Bee. They were known around Kingston as the "Sinful Angels," but angels they were not. They indulged in devilish acts like prostitution, money laundering, stealing, and dealing drugs. "SA" was tattooed on the girls' right butt cheeks or their ample right breasts. A selected few of the girls were also the madam's, Queen Bee's, lovers.

"We definitely need to get better acquainted." Suave winked at the girl.

The young, sinful angel blushed and laughed. "Come on. Queen Bee is waiting for you upstairs." She moved to the side for Suave to enter the house. After closing the door, she walked ahead so Suave could follow her. They climbed up a flight of stairs to the second floor.

"Wait. I need to use the bathroom really quick," Suave informed the girl.

"Okay. Just go down the—"

"I know where it is," he cut her off. "I also know how to find Queen Bee's office." He pointed to a set of steps that led to the third floor. "I'll see myself up when I'm done."

"Catch you later." Miss Thing turned and walked up the stairs, giving Suave a great view of her big butt cheeks that were peeking out the daisy duke shorts.

"Mercy, mercy," Suave muttered as he stood and stared until the girl was gone. "That's one of the reasons I like to personally handle business with Queen Bee."

Suave shook his head and began strolling down the long corridor past a bedroom but stopped abruptly. With a puzzled look on his face, he slowly turned around and came back to the room. He peeked inside the partially opened door, and his eyes landed on high, smooth, butterscotch buttocks. He gently pushed the door with his hand and as if he were in a trance, he entered the room and came face-to-face with a naked Pat.

The two men stared at each other as if frozen at the moment. Suave's eyes traveled over the thick, curly Afro with spiral curls sprouted in every direction and a smooth face with arched eyebrows and slanted, exotic eyes covered over by naturally long eyelashes. Pat's tall, slender, toned body displayed tight abs and long, clean-shaven legs. Suave glanced at Pat's exposed penis, and rage flooded his body. Right before his eyes, it were as if Pat had changed into Pastor Ralph, smirking as if he didn't have a care in the world.

Suddenly, Suave pounced upon Pat, wrapping his hands around his throat. He squeezed hard. "Why don't you stay dead?" Suave growled and squeezed harder, intending on killing Pastor Ralph again for the last time.

Pat's eyes bulged, and he clawed at the iron grip around his neck, but it only tightened. He kicked at Suave's legs, twisted this way and turned that way, struggling to get free. "Let . . . let . . . me go." Pat sounded like a sick kitten with a sore throat.

"Die, you nasty pig." With eyes shut tight, Suave continued squeezing the slender neck in his hands, feeling the life slipping out of Pastor Ralph. "Yes, you are dying."

Pat felt light-headed. His eyes rolled to the back of his head, but he kept on fighting for his life. With a final surge of strength, he pushed Suave, loosening the grip on his neck. Suave stumbled back and let go of his neck.

Pat sucked some much-needed air into his lungs, inhaling and exhaling heavily.

Suave stared at Pat as if he were an alien. He threw a nasty look at Pat before he turned on his heels and marched out. Suave ran down the flight of stairs and had his hand on the front door when it dawned on him that he was there to see Queen Bee. He leaned his head against the door, his chest rising and falling as he breathed out deeply, willing his body to relax. "Take it easy, man. That wasn't Pastor Ralph," Suave muttered. "You killed him years ago, remember?"

His body still tensed but more under control, Suave turned around and ran up the flight of steps to the third floor. He approached the room that Queen Bee converted to an office and entered through the opened door.

"I was wondering if you were hiding somewhere with one of my girls." Queen Bee's back was turned to Suave. She blew a puff of smoke into the air, then took another hit of the spliff in her hand. "I'm glad you know that it's business before pleasure." She turned to face Suave, an amused expression on her face.

But Suave wasn't in a joking mood. He'd just fought with a ghost from the past and was still a little rattled. Without a response, he leaned back against the wall, arms folded, staring at the obese, elderly woman who dressed and acted like a teenager. Tonight, his usual amusement of Queen Bee was replaced by disgust as he scanned her from head to toe.

Queen Bee had ropes of thick gold chains around her neck and a ring on almost every finger. She was sporting a short, spike "Marilyn Monroe" blond hairstyle; her face was heavily made up with black drawn on eyebrows that clashed against her light complexion. Heavy, thick, black mascara highlighted long eyelashes over hazel contact lenses. Her thick, bright, ruby-red lips parted in a smile, revealing a gold front tooth.

Queen Bee's huge box-shaped body was struggling against the restraint of a tight, supershort, red minidress. Her large, floppy butt cheeks flashed dimples as big as saucers that winked in greeting on every eye that landed on them.

"Cat got your tongue?" Queen Bee walked closer to Suave. The grin fell from her face when she saw the vicious look on his. "Hey, what's wrong, baby?" She peered at Suave with concern. "Can I help with anything?"

Yeah, you can get rid of your sissy brother. Suave closed his eyes and took a deep breath. He had to get it together. Queen Bee wasn't the enemy. Pastor Ralph was. Queen Bee gave him the start he needed when Mason ran him out, and she had been a great help over the years. "Just some things I have to deal with." Suave opened his eyes and looked at her. "More money, more problems, right?" He chuckled a little, shaking his head.

"But you do know I'm here if you need me, right?" Queen Bee was still concerned. She had grown to respect and care for the young hustler who was now her equal in the business. Heck, if Queen Bee were batting on Suave's team, she would have made a move for him a long time ago with his fine self.

"I appreciate it, Queen. But I got this." Suave leaned forward and gave her a brief hug. "Okay, let's do business. You have something I want, and I have something that you need."

They laughed, clearing the air. After taking care of business, Suave couldn't leave the house fast enough. He raced to his car and was out the gate in a flash. Once he was outside on the street, he paused and glanced through the car window to the second-floor bedroom window. His eyes met and held those of a still nude Pat, who was posed as if on exhibition.

Pat winked and blew Suave a kiss. He should be feeling mad that Suave almost killed him, but he wasn't. In fact, Pat had never felt more turned-on than he was right now. There was just something about Suave taking out his anger on him that was exhilarating.

Chapter Twenty-seven

Suave stretched out on the long couch, still fully clothed, staring up at the ceiling until his exhausted eyelids drooped into a restless sleep. In his dream, he saw his live-in woman, Monica, strolling nude down a long, paved road toward him. He watched excitedly as she approached, salivating at her naked beauty. As soon as Monica stood in front of him, Suave pulled her to him for a deep, passionate kiss. Sexual desire flooded his entire being. Suave finally broke the kiss. He smiled and opened his eyes . . . to stare into Pat's amused face.

"What!" Suave jumped back a few steps, using his hand to wipe his mouth. "What . . . What are you doing here?" Puzzled, he glanced around in disbelief, looking for Monica.

Suddenly, loud laughter echoed from behind him. He made a 180-degree turn in the road and saw Pastor Ralph hooting like a hyena on crack.

"You think you can get rid of me, huh?" Pastor Ralph mocked and doubled over in hysterics. Pat joined in.

Suave was shaking like cooked spaghetti. He used his hands to cover his ears as he glanced back and forth between the two laughing men. "Go away!" But the jeering only got louder and louder, ricocheting into the air, hammering away at Suave's aching head.

"Come to Big Daddy, baby." Pat chuckled as he walked closer to Suave. He was coming from one side, and Pastor Ralph the other. "You can't run away from us, Smooth Suave."

Suave was trapped. He tried to move, but his feet felt like they were stuck in a bucket of Krazy Glue. Looking around frantically, he opened his mouth to scream for help, but his tongue wouldn't move. Pat and Pastor Ralph were getting closer and closer.

Then Pastor Ralph and Pat reached out to grab Suave.

"No! No!" Suave jumped up off the couch, swinging his arms wildly. It took him a few seconds to get his bearings, realizing he was at his hideaway home. With his heart flip-flopping in his chest, his breathing sporadic, Suave grabbed his gun that was in the corner of the couch. He walked crazily around the house, looking under the couches, the beds, tables, in the bathroom, kitchen, and closets searching for Pastor Ralph and Pat. The dream felt that real.

"Come on out, you two big sissies," Suave screamed as he marched through the house, waving the gun in the air. "You think I'm scared of you?" He called Pat and Pastor Ralph every derogatory name under the sun as he combed the house from top to bottom without any luck.

"I'll get you next time." Tired, Suave went into the kitchen, opened the fridge, and took out a cold Red Stripe beer. He used his teeth to pop the cap and drank noisily like a parched man coming out of the desert with drips of the beverage escaping out of his mouth.

"Aaah, that was good." Suave stared out the kitchen window at beads of daylight breaking through the dark sky of night, finishing off his beer. He knew he wouldn't be getting any sleep even if he tried, so he went to take a shower.

Less than an hour later, Suave was opening the front door and entering the home he shared with Monica and their kids. As he passed by each child's open bedroom door, he paused and watched them sleep for a minute. "I have to get myself together," he muttered before walking toward the master bedroom.

Suave pushed the bedroom door open, tiptoed in, and saw Monica fast asleep, her face partially covered by the sheet. Just to be sure, he moved the sheet slightly and peered at her beautiful face for a moment.

Suave breathed a sigh of relief and undressed down to his boxers. Careful not to wake Monica, he slipped onto the bed, under the sheet, to cuddle with her. It wasn't long before Suave slipped away into a deep slumber. This time, there was no Pat or Pastor Ralph. At least for now.

"Well well well. Look what the cat dragged in this morning." Monica's voice was laced with sarcasm. Her lips were pouted out, and a scowl smeared her pretty face as she rested her hip against the kitchen sink. "Which one of your whores were you with last night, Suave?"

Suave smiled. Shirtless in black sweatpants, he walked over to Monica and stopped inches in front of her. "Good afternoon, babes."

Monica glared at him. "Don't 'babes' me, Suave. I'm tired of your foolishness. One day soon, I am going to take the kids and go live with my parents in the Bahamas." Monica had been telling him that for a few years now, but Suave knew she wasn't going anywhere.

He leaned over and planted a loud, wet smooch on her lips. "Girl, you know I was doing business last night. Stop tripping."

"You need to spend more time at home with your kids."

"I know, but I'm doing this for all of you." He kissed Monica's neck. "By the way, where are they?"

"My sister took them to National Heroes Park. If you keep your behind at home as you should, you would have known that."

He nibbled on her lips.

"Stop that," Monica said with a smile flirting the corners of her mouth. "You know I'm mad at you."

Suave chuckled. "I know, and I'm sorry. So, how about some lunch? A brother is starved."

Monica rolled her eyes. Now, sporting a big grin, she walked over to the fridge to make him something to eat. Last night was now forgiven, like the many years of unfaithfulness that resulted in the many kids by many other women.

Moments later with a full stomach, wearing a white wife beater, a baggy pair of blue jeans riding his narrow hips, and a new pair of white sneakers, Suave hurried to the Benz parked in the driveway. His long dreads were pulled back in a ponytail, and the huge rock in his ear and around his neck winked at the bright shining sun. Suave had places to go and people to see. But first, he needed to touch base with Cobra and Daddy Lizard to check up on business. He had missed a few of their calls.

Suave's cell phone rang as soon as he got into the car. It was Queen Bee. He peered at the phone. *I think I'm going to let Cobra or Daddy Lizard deal with her from now on,* he thought as he drove off, placing the cell phone on the passenger seat. *I'm not going anywhere near that punk again.*

The phone rang again. With one hand on the steering wheel, Suave reached for the phone. He glanced at it and saw it was Queen Bee again. Something must be wrong. "What's up, Queen?"

"Suave, I'm glad I got you," Queen Bee began. "Listen, I'm on my way to put out a fire."

"What about the—"

"That's what I want to tell you. I left the stuff with my brother, Pat, at the house. Please go and get it now because he has to leave soon."

Suave's hand tightened on the steering wheel, his face twisted in a deep frown. "You know I don't like people handling my business, right?"

"Pat is not people, Suave. He's family."

"I'll take care of it." Suave flipped the phone shut, before opening it again. He glanced back and forth between the road to the phone while dialing a number. "Cobra, where you at?" he asked when Cobra answered.

"I'm in St. Ann with Daddy Lizard."

"What? What are you doing there?"

"We tried calling you last night and this morning, but you never picked up," Cobra explained. "We have some trouble with a few soldiers, so we came down to take care of it."

Suave shook his head. He was too messed up last night to take care of business, and it was all Pat's fault. "I got sidetracked. My bad."

"That's cool, Boss. Just so you know, we're taking care of it and should be back later tonight with an update."

"Okay. Call me if you need me to come down." Suave disconnected the call. He had a problem. With his two right-hand men out of town, he had to go and get the product from Pat himself. The last thing he wanted to do.

"You know what? Business is business," Suave muttered as he steered the car toward Jones Town. "I'm not afraid of no punk or no ghost. I'm Suave Brown." His face was set in stone.

Approximately thirty minutes later, Suave was pulling up in front of Queen Bee's gate. Like the night before, it opened immediately, closing after Suave drove in. *Some of the girls should be at home. I'll get my stuff from the sissy and be on my way,* he thought, patting the gun in the waist of his pants as he walked up to the front door that was left open.

"Hello?" Suave peered down the hallway but saw no one. He took a few steps inside the quiet house. Puzzled, he glanced around before closing the door. Where was everyone? "Anyone here?" he asked as he mounted the stairs to the second floor. No response.

"Where is that fool?" Suave mumbled as he approached the bedroom with hesitation where he saw Pat the night before. "Someone opened the gate and the door."

Suave stopped in front of Pat's bedroom door, baffled. The door was wide open too. "Pat? Where's my stuff?"

No response.

Suave took the gun from his waist and cautiously entered the bedroom, his heart hammering away in his chest. His mind flashed back to the nightmare he had the night before, and he tightened his grip on the gun.

"Wha . . . Wha . . . What the—" Suave stopped short. The gun fell from his hand to the wooden floor. Standing before him was Pat, as naked as a sensei fowl's behind.

Pat was posed with his right hip out, his hands rested on his waist, and his legs spread wide apart in a pair of black stilettos. Thick, glossy, ruby-red, pouting lips hinted at seduction and sexual stimulation.

"Heyyyy." Pat swiped his tongue lightly across his lips and winked. Suave almost choking him to death should have scared him away, but instead, had aroused a deep familiar yearning in Pat—Enough to take this risk.

For the life of him, Suave couldn't move or say a word. His mouth was opening and closing like a helpless barracuda as he watched Pat slither toward him.

Pat slid around Suave the statue to get to the door, shutting it. Without a word, he stood before Suave, his peppermint breath fanning Suave's face.

It was almost like Suave was hypnotized as he locked eyes with Pat, who had transformed into Pastor Ralph. With his heart somersaulting in his chest, and the occasional blinking of his eyes, Suave didn't move. The grown man had reverted to the scared twelve-year-old boy when he was first sexually molested by his uncle. Suave was helpless.

Pat smiled. This was even better than he had imagined. In no rush, Pat lowered himself to his knees, his face directly in line with Suave's groin. Reaching up, he unbuckled Suave's belt. The sound of Suave's pants unzipping was like a clap of thunder in the quiet room.

With his eyes now squeezed closed, tears leaked down Suave's face as Pat pleasured him orally. His body betrayed him again when it responded as it had done so many years ago, and the shame of it all came flooding back like a tsunami. Suave was being victimized all over again.

Suddenly, Suave felt sick to his stomach—literally. He coughed loudly, his body shaking—before vomiting his breakfast all over Pat.

Pat screeched and hollered, totally grossed out with barf all over his face and body, some even leaking into his mouth. He jumped to his feet and ran into the adjoining bathroom, slamming the door shut.

Suave hurriedly pulled up his pants, his hands trembling as he zipped it, leaving his unbuckled belt dangling. He rushed out of the bedroom, jumped down the steps two at a time from the second floor to the first floor, unlocked the front door, and rushed to his car.

He started the car and sped to the front gate. It was locked, but luckily, he knew that there was a manual switch on the gatepost. Suave was on the run.

Chapter Twenty-eight

The Benz screeched to a halt in front of a gas station. "Bobby, come here," Suave yelled through the open car window to the teenage son of the gas station owner who was standing in front of the store.

The boy ran over to the car. "Yes, Mr. Suave?"

"Here, go get me a few bags of ice. Make it quick." Suave avoided eye contact, his hand trembling when he handed the boy some money. "Hurry up," he shouted at Bobby's back.

With his head hanging low still in shame, Suave sat in the car as Bobby made a few trips from the store to the car trunk with huge bags of ice.

"I'm finished, Mr. Suave," Bobby remarked when he walked up to the driver-side window after closing the trunk.

"Thanks." Suave gave him a few bills before speeding off. He took a few shortcuts, weaving in and out of traffic, until soon, he was pulling into his garage at the hut. Suave knew he was in no frame of mind to go home and see Monica. He needed some alone time to get his head right because he was losing his mind.

After closing the garage door, Suave went back and forth from the car trunk to the bathroom, filling the tub with ice. Once finished, he stripped out of his clothes and lowered himself into the tub, ice cubes covering his entire naked body up to his chin.

"I'm not gay," Suave chanted over and over, his teeth rattling. "I love women. I'm no sissy." The tears poured from his eyes as he shivered uncontrollably. His knees were pulled up to his chest under the cold, melting ice. "*Grrrr,* I can't believe I let that fool touch me like that," Suave spat with distaste. "I should have killed him right there." He pounded his fists in front of him, sending ice and water splashing on the floor. "It's those punks playing with my head. I don't know how they're doing it, but I swear I'm going to stop them."

Suave sneezed and sniffled loudly. He couldn't feel his toes, and his fingers felt like popsicles. "I . . . I . . . I don't know what to do." Suave hiccupped, his head wobbling like a bobblehead doll.

"Come to me, my son," said a deep, thundering voice, ricocheting around the bathroom like a boomerang. *"Come to me, and I'll give you rest."*

Suave sat up straight in the bathtub, shots of needles pricking his numbed body. "Who are you?" He looked around the room frantically, shaking like a wet dog caught in a rainstorm.

"I am Alpha and Omega, the beginning and the end, the first and the last."

"Hahaha." Suave threw his head back and began to laugh like a madman. He coughed and sneezed. "Is that you, Lord?" Suave pulled himself to his frozen feet, stumbling, his hand grabbing the side of the bathtub, breaking his fall. "Aren't you a little too late, Big Man?"

Like an arthritic, elderly man, Suave dragged one foot out of the icy tub onto the bathroom floor, then the other. It felt like he was stepping on pins. His long, wet dreads hung heavily down his back. "Come to you, huh? Where were you when I called you to come to me all those years ago?"

Suave staggered like a drunk over to the towel rack, pulling off a fluffy, white towel. He coughed and hiccupped. "Where were you when that monster was . . ." Unable to continue, Suave fell to his knees, hid his face in the towel, and bawled. Deep, heart wrenching sobs shook his muscular body. "Why didn't you come before my father killed my mother, then himself? Why didn't you come and stop Pastor Ralph from messing with me?" Suave lifted his head and looked toward the heavens, snot and tears running down his face. "Why didn't you come before it was too late?"

Suave curled up like a baby on the bathroom floor for hours—crying, coughing, and sneezing—until he fell into a restless sleep.

It was the ringing of the doorbell that jerked Suave awake. He rolled his aching body into a sitting position on the tile floor, looking all around him, trying to figure out why he was asleep, naked, on the bathroom floor.

It didn't take long for an image of Pat on his knees to flash in his mind. The humiliation of what had transpired earlier that morning returned in full force. He ignored the doorbell that was still ringing at intervals and sneezed as he wearily rose to his feet.

Nude, walking on tiptoes, Suave entered the living room and cautiously peeked through the window. He saw the figures of Cobra and Daddy Lizard in the now darkened night.

He turned away without a sound, strolled in his bedroom, and threw himself on the king-sized bed. He wasn't in the mood for company.

It was two days later before Suave had any contact with the outside world. He stayed locked up in his house with a terrible cold, barely eating or sleeping, trying hard to fight the demons that tormented him. The voicemail for both his cell phones was full of messages from Monica, his other baby mommas, his kids, his men, and business colleagues.

"Suave! Suave! It's me," Cobra shouted from the front door. "I know you're in there and you better open this door right now!"

Suave lay curled up on the couch where he slept the night before and listened to his best friend.

"I gave you two days, but that's it. If you don't let me in, I swear I'm going to shoot out a window and come in," Cobra threatened.

Suave coughed and shook his head. He knew Cobra was crazy enough to do as he said. "I better let him in before he starts acting up," he muttered. He was wearing shorts and a T-shirt as he sluggishly ambled to the front door and opened it, squinting when the bright sun caught his eyes.

"So, you *are* alive." Cobra was livid.

Suave didn't answer. He struggled to open the door, then dragged his aching body back into the living room, leaving Cobra to follow.

"What's up, Boss? You disappear for days, not returning any calls. You do remember that you have a business to run, right?" Cobra was slouched on the couch across from Suave. "Monica keeps calling and crying, saying that you were kidnapped or dead. Joel threatened to go to the police if he doesn't hear from you by this evening. I mean, what's up, man?"

Suave was resting his head back against the couch, his eyes closed.

"You're sick." Cobra leaned forward and stared at his friend with concern. "It looks like you have the flu. I bet you didn't take anything for it." He took Suave's silence as a "no." "Okay, I'm going to get something at the pharmacy." Cobra stood, looking down at his friend. "I'll call Monica and Joel and let them know I've seen you. I'll also call Daddy Lizard and—"

"They just won't leave me alone, man," Suave mumbled.

"Who won't leave you alone?" Cobra leaned over so he could hear him better.

Suave raised himself and turned red eyes up to Cobra. "The darn ghosts. They are everywhere, trying to mess with my head." He tapped the side of his head with his fingers. "But I'm going to kill them again and again and again." Suave began a whooping cough.

Cobra's mouth popped open. He stared at his friend for a few seconds before rushing into the kitchen to get him some water. He returned moments later with a glass of tap water. "Here, drink this."

Suave's hand shook as he took the glass and sneezed before taking a long gulp, passing the glass back to Cobra. "They think they can defeat Smooth Suave? Huh?" Suave sneezed again, breathing deeply through his mouth. "I'm going to show them how I do."

Cobra peered at Suave as he continued his ghost-buster rant, noticing the madness in Suave's eyes. A superstitious man by nature, Cobra knew exactly what was going on here. "Good God, they obeah him," Cobra whispered under his breath. "Obeah" was a West Indies term for sorcery or witchcraft. "They're trying to make him crazy so they can take over his business." The anger boiled in Cobra's veins. He wasn't sure who was trying to hurt Suave, but he wouldn't let them succeed.

"You can't beat me." Suave weakly pounded on his chest, glancing around the room as if he were looking for someone. "Don't hide. Come out and face me, you little, nasty cowards."

Cobra took his cell phone out of his pants pocket, dialed a number, and put the phone to his ear, eyes glued on Suave. "Suave needs you now," he said when the phone was answered. He listened, nodding his head. "We'll be there in a few. Thanks, Prophet."

"Okay, let's go." Cobra stood up. "You have shoes by the garage door."

"Go where?" Suave coughed.

"To see Prophet." Cobra held up a hand when Suave opened his mouth again. "I know you don't believe in what he does, but please trust me on this. Okay?"

Suave sighed loudly. Prophet was Cobra's uncle, and he had heard tales about the man since they were kids, but Suave never met him. He was leery of Prophet as he was of God. Suave didn't need any of those jokers.

"Suave, you've always trusted me. Believe me when I say I know what's happening to you, and I'm sure Prophet can help. Just give it a try, man. What do you have to lose?"

He's probably right. I'll try anything right now to get rid of those two sissies. "All right, then. I'll go with you, but I'm not expecting much."

"That's cool. You know I always have your back, and I'm going to help you," Cobra replied with conviction.

Minutes later, Suave was riding shotgun beside Cobra in his truck as they headed to Bull Bay, a close-knit community that lies on the border of St. Andrew and St. Thomas. Many people associated Bull Bay with Rastafari as it had one of the largest settlements of Rastafarians in Jamaica.

Suave listened as Cobra called Daddy Lizard and informed him that Suave had the flu. The same was said to Monica, who demanded to know where Suave was before angrily hanging up the phone on Cobra.

"Joel is very happy I found you," Cobra informed Suave after he hung up the phone with Suave's oldest son. "He said to tell you that he's praying for you, and he believes God will make you better soon."

Suave nodded his head. Nadine, an English teacher at Jamaica College, was now married to the vice principal, who moonlighted as a deacon. Joel attended Sunday school and church service every Sunday, except when he spent the weekend with his father.

"We're almost there," Cobra said. "Just wait and see if Prophet won't free you."

Free me from what? Suave pondered, but said instead, "We'll see."

Chapter Twenty-nine

The truck rocked gently from side to side as it propelled over small, sharp rocks, maneuvering the narrow winding track that was laced with rich red dirt. Suave gazed out of the window at the small bamboo shacks painted red, green, and gold that lined this route. Small groups of Rastas sat outside their respective home or place of business, smoking marijuana, drinking, and conversing. Some had their dreadlocks piled high on top of their heads in hair wraps and rastacaps with their long beards skimming their chests, while others allowed their tangled mane to flow freely over their shoulders and backs.

"Blessed, my Lord."

"Heart of love, my brother."

These were some of the greetings directed at Suave, whom they identified as a brother because of his long locks. However, Suave's locks were more of a fashion statement and denouncement of Christ, with very little to do with the religion of Rastafarians. On occasion, Suave gave reverence to Haile Selassie as he had seen true Rastas do, but he knew very little about the Rastafarian religion that began in Jamaica in the 1930s and was inspired by the early nineteenth-century "Back to Africa Movement" of the powerful Jamaican leader, Marcus Garvey. Suave was ignorant of the significance of a culture that was respected and observed by approximately 265,000 Rastafarians worldwide. He wasn't the real-deal Rastafarian.

"Here we are." Cobra drove in and parked in a dirt yard. A small, wooden house sat on a pile of well-structured rocks, with two big, black water drums on top. High shrubs and numerous trees, including coconut, mango, and banana, surrounded it. A few chickens and roosters were scattered here and there, pecking at the ground, while four big mongrel dogs ran around crazily, baring their teeth and barking at the intruders.

"Sit!" The strong gravelly voice came from a tall, aged Rastafarian man who had just exited the house to stand at the top of the four small concrete steps smeared with red dirt.

Suave watched in amazement as the four dogs instantly quieted and sat, their long tails now wagging back and forth.

"Even the dogs obey the Prophet." Cobra chuckled as he opened his door and alighted from the vehicle. "You are coming?" he said to Suave, who was still sitting in the truck.

"Yeah." Suave hopped out and went to stand beside Cobra. He looked up at the man standing a few feet away, wearing a long, white dress like an African-style outfit, his gray locks hung down to his knees with his silver beard the same length.

Suave grew uncomfortable under the stare of deep, black, penetrating eyes. He glanced over at Cobra and said, "Listen, I'm feeling much better now. Let's just—"

Cobra stared pointedly at Suave. "You said you would give it a try. Come on. The prophet is waiting for us." Cobra walked toward his uncle, leaving Suave to follow him.

"Cobra," Prophet greeted his nephew before giving him a warm hug. "You look good," he said after he stepped back, looking Cobra up and down.

"Thanks, Prophet. You're looking well yourself." Cobra smiled at the man he respected. "This is Suave." He moved to the side so Suave could come forward. "He needs your help."

"What's up, Prophet?" Suave firmly shook the right hand offered.

Prophet released Suave's hand without a word, peering at him as if he were trying to read his mind. "Mercy mercy mercy." Prophet closed his eyes, shaking his head, and began groaning as if in pain.

Suave's mouth popped open, and his eyes widened in alarm. He glanced at Cobra, who was looking as cool as a glass of ice-cold lemonade, already familiar with his uncle's behavior. "Is he all right?" Suave whispered to Cobra.

"Oh, he's good. I think he just picked up on the blow they set for you," Cobra responded, referring to the obeah that he believed was affecting Suave.

"Man, there is no—"

"Follow me." Prophet hurriedly turned around and entered his house, followed by Cobra and Suave.

"Unbelievable," Suave muttered when he entered Prophet's small living room. The furniture was all wood. In the middle was a beautiful, flat, wooden coffee table sandwiched between two extra long wooden benches with red velvet cushions. An exquisitely crafted, humongous, wooden entertainment center lay bare except for the small, fourteen-inch, black-and-white television in the center. Pictures of Marcus Garvey, Haile Selassie, and other sculpted wooden plaques adorned the walls.

"He makes everything himself, including building this house," Cobra informed Suave. "My mother convinced him a few years ago to get electricity. The television which was my grandmother's and the cell phone I gave him are the only things in this house that use electricity."

"You guys coming?" Prophet yelled from somewhere in the back of the house.

Cobra and Suave followed the direction of the voice to a tiny bathroom. Prophet stood in front of a high vertical wooden box without a door masquerading as a shower. In a corner of the room was an inside latrine. There wasn't a face basin or any windows.

"He doesn't use running water," Cobra whispered in Suave's ear.

"Mr. Suave, please take off your clothes and get in the shower," Prophet instructed.

"I don't think so." Suave's face turned ugly in anger. "Man, you funny or something?"

Prophet chuckled deep down in his throat, and Cobra roared with laughter.

"He's going to give you a 'bath.'" Cobra wiped the tears from his eyes with the back of his hand. "Just relax. Prophet has been doing this for years. I've gotten a few baths myself."

Prophet weaved in and around Suave and Cobra in the cramped space, placing red candles all around the bathroom. "Cobra, please go back to the living room while I work." He exited the bathroom into another room.

"That's the kitchen. I think he's finishing up the stuff he boiled for your bath when I called him," Cobra explained. "Suave, please just do as Prophet says, and you will get better. Cool?"

Suave took a deep breath before he nodded. "But he better not try anything funny. I would really hate to kill the old man."

Cobra grinned and walked back out into the living room, leaving Suave to get undressed.

Suave left all his clothes in a heap on the floor and gingerly stepped into the shower that came to his shoulders, glancing around skeptically.

"I'll start in a minute, Mr. Suave," Prophet said upon his return, lowering a big, heavy-looking plastic bucket on the wooden floor by the shower. He then went around the room, lighting the candles. He flicked off the light switch by the door, plunging the bathroom into darkness with tiny flickers of candlelight.

Suave's heartbeat sped up. He hated to admit it, but things were getting creepy. "Hey, Prophet?"

"Not a word, Mr. Suave. I'm going to grab a chicken, and I'll be right back."

Why in heaven's name does he need a chicken? Suave looked over the top of the shower and watched as Prophet left to return shortly with one of the fluttering birds. Prophet lowered the chicken into a bucket and covered it with a broad piece of wood.

"I'm about to start my work, Mr. Suave." Prophet stood at the side of the shower, where Suave's naked body was unseen by him. "I don't want you to say or do anything that will disturb me or the spirits."

"The what? Man, I'm getting out of here." Suave began to tremble. It was bad enough that he had to deal with Pastor Ralph. Now Prophet was calling for more spirits. "Listen, Prophet, I don't deal with spirits. I don't like them, I don't talk to them, and I sure don't want anything to do with them. So, let's just call this whole thing off."

"Nothing to fear, my brother," Prophet assured him. "These spirits will be here to protect you and get rid of the evil ones that are tormenting you. Just let me help you."

Suave stared over the top at him with growing skepticism.

"I've been doing this since before you were born, Mr. Suave," Prophet continued. "I have people from all walks of life coming to me for deliverance. If you don't believe or trust me, then this thing won't work. What is it going to be?" Black eyes peered at Suave.

An image of Pastor Ralph and Pat chasing him popped up in Suave's mind. *I need help.* "All right, but please just make this quick."

Prophet nodded and said, "Please turn around with your back facing me and stoop down."

Suave did as directed, consciously crossing his hands over his groin.

"Hold your breath," Prophet warned before pouring some warm liquid that smelled like rotten eggs all over Suave's head. He began to chant in an unknown dialect as he splashed some of the nauseating mixture on Suave's back.

With his eyes closed, Suave bit his lips, while trying to hold his breath to keep from throwing up.

"Please repeat the Twenty-third Psalm and don't move." Prophet walked away.

Suave mumbled some gibberish under his breath. He didn't know Psalm One much less Twenty-three. If he wasn't dealing with God, why would he want to read some book about Him?

"Now we make a sacrifice to you, the dark one, asking for thy protection," Prophet's deep voice seemed to echo around the small bathroom.

Suave, frightened when he heard the word "sacrifice," jumped to his feet. He quickly spun around to see Prophet holding the flapping chicken by its neck, high into the air, with one hand, and a long, sharp knife in the other.

"*Acaramba, Cabaramba, Dacaramba, Ecaramba.*" The light from the candles reflected in Prophet's beady eyes, giving the impression they were shooting fire.

Suave stared in shock as Prophet recited his version of the alphabet as he called on the spirits. "No no no, don't—" Suave flinched and looked away when the knife sliced across the chicken's neck, sending its head to the floor, the body still quivering in Prophet's hand. Eyes closed tightly, Suave tried to swallow the bile that now filled his mouth.

"Spirit of the dark one, grant Mr. Suave thy protection! Protection!" Prophet yelled into Suave's ear.

Suave's eyes popped open, and he almost fainted when Prophet held the bleeding bird over his head, covering him in chicken blood.

"We need protection!" Prophet yelled, rubbing his hand that was smeared with chicken blood all over Suave's face.

That did it. Suave leaned over and vomited. The blood was stinging his eyes, the nasty odor from the bath was burning his nostrils, and Prophet's loud mumbo jumbo was giving him a headache. "Enough!" Suave shouted, causing Prophet to jump back a few steps. "Get away from me."

Suave used his hand to wipe across his eyes, making things worse instead of better. He stumbled over to his clothes in the semidark room, grabbed his T-shirt, and used it to wipe his face. With his back turned to Prophet, his body almost vibrating in fury, Suave pulled on his shorts.

His hand was on the door handle when Prophet's voice stopped him. "You can't run from your enemies, Mr. Suave. You have to beat the life out of them, or they will beat it out of you."

And that was probably the only positive thing that Suave took away from Prophet as Cobra drove him back home in silence, streaking chicken blood all over Cobra's nice leather seat. Suave took Prophet's words literally and embarked on a journey to beat the life out of his enemies, starting with the little sissy, Pat.

Chapter Thirty

Suave looked down at the ringing cell phone in his hand. "I wonder who this is?" he mumbled, not recognizing the number. Few people have his business number, and usually, he knew who was calling. "Hello?" his voice was stern when he answered.

"Hey, Suave."

Suave felt the hair stand up on his body at the sound of Pat's voice. "What do you want, fool, and how did you get this number?" No response.

Suave saw red. For the last two weeks since that horrible experience with Prophet, he had been gradually picking up the pieces of his life . . . or at least attempting to. He dove back into his business, spending as much time as possible with all his children, Monica, and his other honeys on the side, trying to forget that moment of temporary insanity with Pat.

"You there, baby?" Pat purred through the phone.

Suave leaned against his car, glanced around the mall where he was parked, his eyebrows almost touching in the middle. "You listen to me, sissy boy. I don't want you to call my phone again, you got it?" He lowered his voice as three girls walked by and said, "If you think I'm joking with you, keep messing with me and see what's going to happen."

Pat heard the threat, but instead of feeling scared, he felt excited. There was just something about an angry Suave that turned him on. "The only thing that's going to happen if you don't come to my house tonight is me telling my sister about our little 'special time' together."

The cell phone fell from Suave's hand. His eyes bugged out of his head, and his knees threatened to buckle under him. He braced his body against the car for support and felt faint with Pat's threat ricocheting in his head.

It would be better for Pat to kill Suave than to mention a word of what had transpired that day. Everyone knew Suave as a lady's man. He had six baby mommas, and he had been with more women than King David and King Solomon combined. To be labeled a homosexual was worse than death itself, especially in Jamaica where many people still upheld the Buggery Act 1533 and often ignorantly imposed violence against homosexuals.

I must kill him before he destroys me, Suave pondered, his breathing irregular and his heart pounding in his chest. He reached down with a trembling hand and picked up the phone. To his surprise, it was still intact. Suave lifted the phone to his ear, and Pat was there waiting patiently. "What's the address?" His voice was low and deadly. Suave listened as Pat excitedly told him where he lived. "Midnight." Suave flipped his phone closed.

It was final. Suave would have to kill again to survive. First, it was Pastor Ralph. Now it would be Pat. Tears stung his eyes as he got into his car and drove away. He wasn't gay, and he had only killed once to save his life. "I don't want to kill again, but I don't know what else to do," Suave said aloud as he drove.

"Yes, you do," said a loud voice in his ears. *"Come to me, and I'll help you."*

The car swerved a little into the other lane before Suave expertly steered it back on track, surprised but deeply annoyed at the intrusion. "Is that you again, Mr. So-called God? Why don't you leave me alone?"

"Come to me, my son, and I'll give you peace."

"I'm not your son! My daddy died many years ago, and I don't need another!" Suave's feet were getting heavier on the gas as he zoomed away to meet his workers for a meeting. He had more important things to do than waste time with God. Hopefully, if he ignored the Lord, He'd eventually go away.

Suave spent the day conducting business, trying to take his mind off what he had to do that night. In the evening, he picked up Joel, who would be spending the weekend with him, Monica, and their kids. Suave barely touched his food at dinner as everyone laughed and talked, enjoying the delicious meal of oxtail with butter beans and rice and peas that Monica had prepared.

"Daddy, are you okay?" Joel's face was filled with concern. At fifteen years old, Joel was almost as tall as his father. Once he learned what Suave did for a living, he asked him to stop.

"Please, Daddy. I know you have enough money to stop now," Joel had begged his father. "I don't want you to go to jail or get killed." Tears filled Joel's eyes as he pleaded.

Suave felt like an eel. For the first time, he felt ashamed of what he did for a living. "I'm going to stop soon, Joel," he had promised. "I'm going to buy a few more businesses and go legit. Okay? I'm going to do that for you and your brother and sisters."

"Babe?"

Suave blinked rapidly and turned toward Monica's voice. He glanced around the dining table, realizing everyone was staring at him.

Suave forced a smile. "I'm good. My mind just went for a walk." He scooped some rice on his fork and placed it into his mouth. Chewing dramatically, he winked at Monica, his dimples flashing. "Come on, you guys, eat up."

Joel and the kids laughed and resumed their eating, but Monica stared at him a little longer than necessary before she began to eat again.

After dinner, Suave took Joel, Raven, and Rayden to Devon House for their well-loved ice cream known as "I Scream." He left with the kids licking huge cones of the deliciously flavored ice cream, while he carried a few pints of takeout.

Suave pulled up in front of the house, the engine still running, dropping off the children. He watched as they walked into the house, carrying one of the ice creams for Monica. Once the door was closed behind their backs, he drove off.

Minutes later, Alissa and Janelle were squealing with excitement when Suave gave them ice cream and to the other kids living there. Darlene's and Charlene's bedroom invitations were turned down, to their surprise, but they didn't complain because Suave left each lady with a huge wad of cash.

Suave traveled over Kingston, paying visits to his three other kids and leaving money with their mothers. He was always a good father, but for some reason, he felt like he had to see all his children that night. He had this sinking feeling in his gut that after tonight, his life would never be the same.

***

The doorbell sang like a violin throughout the house. Pat eagerly rubbed his hands together, taking another quick glance around the semidark living room lit by a single tapered candle. The rest of the house was covered in darkness.

"I'm coming," Pat crooned when the doorbell sang again, sashaying toward the door in a white silk bathrobe and a pair of matching high heels.

Suave angrily pressed the doorbell again, thankful that Pat's veranda light was off but still uneasy by the streetlight close by. He tugged the baseball cap lower on his forehead, looking around warily. Luckily for him, it seemed as if all of Pat's neighbors were asleep because their houses were plunged into darkness.

Suave peered through dark sunglasses at the Rolex on his right wrist and saw that it was 12:04 a.m. He was growing angrier and angrier by the second. It was bad enough that this fool had blackmailed him to come to his house, but Pat even had the nerve to keep Suave waiting. He touched the 9 mm in his waist and kept his finger on the buzzer. He wanted to get this over and done with as soon as possible.

"My, my, aren't you anxious to come inside," Pat greeted Suave after he opened the front door. Smiling flirtatiously, he stepped aside for Suave to enter.

Suave stormed past Pat without a word and entered the living room. His hands folded into tight fists as he took in the seductive scene that Pat had created. But Suave, in fact, welcomed the lack of light for what he was going to do. A sinister smile worked its way onto his face as he backed against the wall and waited for Pat.

"Thank you for coming." Pat closed the door and stood in front of Suave. "I'm sorry about what I said earlier, but I just wanted to see you again."

Suave's cold eyes met and held Pat's, but he remained mute.

Pat shivered slightly. The last time Suave was like putty in his hands, but tonight, he looked like the devil from hell. Maybe this wasn't such a good idea. . . . "You know I won't say a word to anyone, right?" Pat nervously nibbled on his glossy lips.

Suave's nostrils opened up like a funnel, his eyes narrowing into slits. "You think you can threaten me and get away with it?" The temperature in the room felt like it had dropped to minus two degrees. "You think I'm going to allow you to molest me again, huh?" There was a very thin line separating Pat and Pastor Ralph, merging them as one in Suave's mind.

"I . . . I . . . Hmmm, see—"

"Shut up!" Suave backhanded Pat hard across his face.

Pat staggered back from the blow, rubbing his burning cheek, tears stinging his eyes. "I'm sorry." He stumbled over to a corner of the living room, his back facing Suave, cowering in fear.

Suave became empowered as he followed Pat. Now he was in control of the situation. "I was a child then, but I'm a grown man now," he hissed in Pat's ear. Just then, Prophet's words popped up in Suave's head. *"You can't run from your enemies, Mr. Suave. You have to beat the life out of them, or they will beat it out of you."*

"I couldn't agree more, Prophet," Suave said aloud, raising his foot to kick Pat in the behind, sending him to the floor. "I'm not gay." *Kick*. "Leave me the hell alone." *Kick*.

Pat curled his body into a protective ball as Suave rained blows all over him. It was painful . . . but in an exuberating kind of way.

Suave had his demon just where he wanted him, at his mercy. Huffing and puffing, now fully exhausted at whipping Pat's behind, Suave paused to catch his breath. "Next time, I'll kill you if you ever mess with me again." Suave leaned over, his gun pressed firmly against Pat's head. "Leave me alone. You got that?"

Pat didn't respond, his smile hidden in his hands.

"I asked if you got that!" Suave screamed, hitting Pat in the head with the butt of the gun.

"Yes," Pat mumbled, tucking his legs farther into his chest.

Suave stared down at Pat for a moment before he stood to his feet and marched toward the door. He peeked outside. He glanced up and down the street, but the upscale residential area remained void of any human activity. Throwing one last disgusted glance at Pat on the floor, Suave hurriedly left the house. With his head hanging low, he walked a few blocks to where he parked the old Honda Accord that he had borrowed from one of his workers.

Suave was smiling as he drove to his hideaway home. For the first time since he encountered Pat alone in that bedroom, he felt free. He was free from Pat and free from Pastor Ralph. That night, Suave slept like a baby. He had sweet dreams of his beautiful children and rendezvous with his women. There was no nightmare with the two sissies—Pat and Pastor Ralph. Suave was finally free.

But to remain free, Suave realized he had to beat the enemy over and over again, literally. So he kept going back to Pat, whipping his behind to keep his sanity, and Pat welcomed Suave to maintain his perverted sexual fantasy. It was a win-win situation for both men, a secret that ran into months, then into years.

Part Three

Chapter Thirty-one

Back to Current Day, 2003

"I have no idea what you're talking about." Suave readjusted himself on the bar stool, his arms folded across his chest, glaring at Detective Bird, who was seated on another stool beside him. "You come into my place of business to ask me about some murder over in Spanish Town? Man, are you crazy or something?"

Detective Bird smirked into his half-empty glass of brandy. He shook his head in amusement as he peered over his shoulder at Daddy Lizard and Cobra, who were positioned on either side of the bar's closed entrance door, their hands behind their backs. "You know I could have issued a warrant for your arrest, but I decided to come and talk to you, man to man, instead." Detective Bird was bluffing. He had no concrete evidence that Suave or his men were involved in the murder of Saddam's grandfather, Elder Bloom, but in his heart, the detective knew.

Suave smiled. He knew Detective Bird was fishing, but unfortunately for him, Suave wasn't biting. "So, that's how Jamaica is running now?" Suave reached for his cold Heineken and took a slow sip before he continued. "Warrants are being issued for innocent people? Huh?"

"Innocent? If you were so innocent, why did it take me three days to get ahold of you?"

"Detective, I'm a very busy man." Suave took another sip and then placed the bottle on the counter. Behind him at the door, Cobra and Daddy Lizard chuckled.

They were laughing at him. In fact, Suave and his men had been laughing at the police for years as they poisoned the country and got rich doing so.

"This is a joke to you, right?" Detective Bird was getting angrier by the second.

"Listen, you have nothing on my people or me. You know why?" Suave then answered his own question. "We didn't do anything. No disrespect, but you don't have a clue what you're doing."

"Oh, you think I don't know what's going on here?" Detective Bird threw his head back and roared with laughter. It took a minute for him to compose himself as Suave, Cobra, and Daddy Lizard scowled at him. "Let me tell you what I know so far, Suave. I know you and King Kong are at war. In fact, you two have been at it for years. I know that the grandfather of King Kong's right-hand man was killed three nights ago." Detective Bird's droopy eyes locked with Suave's. "I know that King Kong has been robbing you for a few months now. I also know that his partner, Danny, was kidnapped, beaten up, and released. How am I doing so far?"

Suave felt a cold chill run down his spine. Detective Bird seemed to be connecting the dots, and that wasn't a good thing. "So far, you are only talking nonsense." Suave kept his composure. "If you had anything on me, I would be in handcuffs right now."

"You will be soon, my friend. Don't worry."

"Are you threatening me, Detective?" Suave's face was now screwed up in fury. "You requested a meeting with me, and I closed my bar to the public so I could accommodate you. Then you come in here threatening me?" When Suave's voice raised a few octaves, Cobra and Daddy Lizard moved a little closer.

Detective Bird now swallowed nervously. He came to Rema by himself to meet Suave. He was a police officer locked inside Suave's bar with him and his two thugs. Detective Bird needed to do some damage control fast. "I-I'm not threatening no one, Suave. I'm just saying if you have anything to do with that old man's death, you will eventually be arrested."

The bar was held captive by a haunting silence.

Detective Bird jumped off the stool to his feet when Suave leaned back to take something out of his pocket. With his hand on the gun at his side, Detective Bird's eyes were filled with fear as he watched Suave, sneaking nervous glances at Cobra and Daddy Lizard, as well.

Suave laughed out loud. "Here you go, Detective." He held out a business card to the police officer. "That's my lawyer's information for the next time you have questions for my partners here or me."

Detective Bird hesitated before reaching for the card, relief plastered across his face. The next time he was going to make sure the meeting was at the police station where he had backup. "Thank you. I'll . . . leave you to your business." He nodded at Suave as he walked to the closed door guarded by Cobra and Daddy Lizard. "Gentlemen, if you would be so kind?"

Daddy Lizard reluctantly moved to the side, his nose turned up like he smelled something rotten. Cobra turned around and unbolted the door, pushing it open.

"Detective?" Suave yelled at Detective Bird's back.

Detective Bird turned around and met Suave's cold eyes.

"Just remember, the next time you threaten me . . . will be the last time." Suave raised his bottle in salute.

Detective Bird hurriedly exited the bar and walked out to the street. He noticed the dozens of men loitering, most of them on Suave's payroll, shooting daggers at him. If looks could kill, Detective Bird would be rotting in a grave. He hastened his steps to the old Maxima parked in front of the bar, quickly got in, and sped away.

Cobra watched until the car disappeared down the road, the same sickening feeling in his gut. It was the men he hired who had screwed everything up.

"Cobra, close the door and let's talk," Suave instructed.

Cobra did as he was told. Then he and Daddy Lizard joined Suave at the bar.

"We're in a tight spot." Suave stared solemnly at his two right-hand men. "What happened the other night shouldn't have gone down like that." It was the first time that Suave was talking to Cobra and Daddy Lizard about the shooting.

"Look, Suave. I'm sorry about—"

"No need to cry over spilled milk, Cobra." Suave looked from Cobra to Daddy Lizard. "The fact is crazy Saddam and King Kong are going to seek revenge against us. The question is, how do we prepare to fight them and avoid the police at the same time?"

"I say we hire more men and wipe out King Kong and his whole crew." Daddy Lizard locked eyes with Suave.

Suave shook his head, knowing that Daddy Lizard was the hotter tempered one. "We are not killers, Daddy Lizard."

"Okay, so we wait for them to kill us?" Daddy Lizard scanned his companions' faces. "I'm not going out without a fight, Boss. You know King Kong and Saddam will be coming at us hard."

Suave looked away. Daddy Lizard was right. Things were about to get crazy. "Let's think about—"

A hard knock sounded at the door. All three men stared at it, then at each other before pulling their guns. Everyone was on edge.

"Brother Suave, it's me," Reverend Stanford's voice came through the closed door. "I have an urgent message for you."

Suave fired off a few curse words. "I swear one day I'm going to hurt that pest."

"Ignore him," Daddy Lizard spat.

"He won't go away." Suave looked at the closed door again. "Cobra, let him in."

Cobra took a deep breath before unbolting and pushed open the door.

"Brother Cobra," Reverend Stanford greeted in a serious tone.

Cobra turned and walked back toward Suave, leaving Reverend Stanford to follow him.

Reverend Stanford entered the bar and nodded at Daddy Lizard, who was glaring at him before he approached Suave. "Brother Suave, I'm glad I caught you. I have a very important message for you." He sat on the stool that Detective Bird occupied earlier, facing Suave.

Suave stared at him without speaking.

"You guys are getting in over your heads," Reverend Stanford began. "I've been trying to get you to turn away from what you're doing, but you ignored me. Now you can't ignore the Lord."

Daddy Lizard rudely sucked his teeth loudly. Cobra, who was leaning against the bar counter, snorted. Suave remained silent, a pissed-off look on his face.

"There's going to be a war. People are going to die, others are going to prison, and innocent lives will be in danger. The Lord wants you gentlemen to put a stop to this now!" Reverend Stanford glanced from Suave, to Cobra, to Daddy Lizard, and back, his brows knitted in a frown. "I see lots of blood, I see . . ." Reverend Stanford groaned deep in his throat, got up off the stool, and started pacing the floor. "I see weeping and wailing. Oh Lord, have mercy! I see pain and God's people hurting." The reverend began speaking in tongues, his hands and eyes raised to the heavens, tears running down his dark, handsome face. "Lord, spare your people," he prayed aloud.

Cobra rolled his eyes in disgust, Daddy Lizard went behind the bar to fix the men some screwdriver cocktails, while Suave lit a joint, blowing a puff of smoke into the air, not the least bit concerned by the reverend's words.

Reverend Stanford concluded his prayer and looked around to see that his message had no impact whatsoever on the recipients. Suave, Cobra, and Daddy Lizard were drinking and smoking and looking at him as if he were crazy. This grieved the reverend very much. "Galatians 6:7 says, '*Be not deceived; God is not mocked: for whatsoever a man soweth, that shall he also reap.*'"

"Cheers, Rev." Daddy Lizard lifted his glass, chuckling, before taking a long sip.

"You better take heed of God's words before His words—"

"Enough!" Suave slowly got off the stool and closed the small gap between him and Reverend Stanford until they were face-to-face. "Get out of my place. Now." Suave hissed through closed teeth. The veins in his face were at attention.

Reverend Stanford opened his mouth to speak but closed it when he saw the anger shimmering in Suave's eyes. He felt some satisfaction inside. At least he had gotten some reaction from the cold kingpin. "You gentlemen know where to find me when it becomes too much for you to bear." With that said, Reverend Stanford turned on his heels and walked to the door. At the entrance, he paused and spun around to look at the three men sadly. "The Lord is always here waiting for you." He strode away with a heavy heart.

Daddy Lizard laughed and mimicked, "The Lord is always here waiting—"

"Stop it." Suave glared at Daddy Lizard. "I'm tired of all this crap."

Cobra and Daddy Lizard stared at him without another word.

Suave tried to hide it, but the reverend's words had hit a few nerves. Why, he wasn't sure because he had no dealing with that so-called God. Not only did he have to contend with that annoying voice that still plagued him from time to time, but now this. "Let's put together a plan to get the pigs, the gorilla, and his bulldogs off our backs."

But Suave soon found out that was easier said than done.

Chapter Thirty-two

Cobra's laughter filled the motel room as Bubbles nibbled on his earlobe. "You are a very naughty girl, you know that?" He lightly slapped her on her naked pear-shaped buttocks as she straddled him on the full-sized bed.

Bubbles giggled. "You know how I do, darling." She vertically stretched out her nude body on Cobra's, raining butterfly kisses all over his face and naked chest.

Cobra lost himself in her seduction as she kissed all over his body.

An hour earlier, Cobra was having a quick dinner at a restaurant on Molynes Road before making his runs, when the tempting Bubbles slid into the other unoccupied chair across from him. Surprised but very pleased, Cobra asked, "And you are . . .?"

"Bubbles." She winked at him, leaning farther over the table, her two large breasts struggling to break free of the tight, low cut blouse.

Cobra stared at them with lust. Being one of Suave's right-hand men had its perks, and sexy women like Bubbles throwing themselves at him was a regular thing. "Well, Bubbles, do you care to join me for dinner?"

"No. I'm not hungry."

"Okay, so you're just going to watch me eat?" Cobra popped a piece of fried chicken into his mouth and chewed on it, his eyes filled with amusement.

"Yes, and when you're finished, I'd like to invite you somewhere." Bubbles swiped her tongue across her full, glossy lips and winked at him.

Cobra's smile broadened. "Where are we going?"

"You'll see," Bubbles whispered mysteriously.

Thirty-five minutes later, Cobra was not only seeing but was feeling too. Led by his libido and not using his head, he found himself butt naked in a motel room with the strange, young lady.

Cobra, with a pleased grin on his face, his eyes closed in ecstasy, failed to hear the door softly opening and closing.

"Yeah, don't stop." Cobra protested when he felt Bubbles's weight lifting off him. "We're just getting— hey, what's this?" Cobra's eyes widened as he stared down the barrel of the .45 Magnum revolver.

"Don't say another word or make a move," the masked gunman leaning over Cobra warned. "Yo, Bubbles. Get dressed and get out of here."

From the corner of his eye, Cobra saw Bubbles hurriedly dressing as instructed. It was at that moment it hit him that he'd been set up. After everything that was going on with King Kong and crazy Saddam, he was caught slipping. But Cobra wasn't going out without a fight. "Who are you, man? What do you want?" he asked, inching his right hand over the pillow where his head lay.

"We want *you*, Cobra," said another rough voice from the doorway. Raising his head so he could see, Cobra's eyes locked with those of Danny, King Kong's business partner that they had kidnapped and beaten.

Danny laughed out loud when he saw the terrified look on Cobra's face. The "telephone" cut that ran from his ear to his mouth made him resemble the Joker. "My little sister came through for me, after all." Danny nodded at Bubbles who was strapping on her sandals in the corner of the room. "I really wanted your boss, but he was a little bit more slippery than you." Danny moved closer to the bed, smirking down on his captive. "So, we decided to set a trap for you instead, and look what we have caught . . ." He waved his arms wide open over Cobra as if he were a prize.

"All right, you got me, Danny. What do you want? Money? Drugs? What?" Cobra felt the edge of his fingers contact his gun. He shifted his body slightly, so his hand was now fully wrapped around the handle of the 9 mm under the pillow. A small detail that Bubbles missed.

"I said don't move," the masked gunman snapped before pulling the stocking cap off his face revealing his identity. "Make another move, and you're dead," said crazy Saddam.

Cobra felt like wetting himself. He wished it was anyone else except this psycho. Shucks, even the devil would have been a more welcome sight. Cobra knew his life was hanging by a thread. "What's this about, Saddam?"

"What's this about?" Saddam shouted. "You killed Dadda and ripped off our biggest loot, and you're asking what this is about?" Saddam used the gun and slapped Cobra hard across his face, sending blood flying out of his mouth.

Cobra groaned deep in his throat from the pain. "We didn't kill anybody, man," he said in desperation. "We've been feuding for years. Have you ever heard of us killing anyone for drugs and money?"

Danny and Saddam shared a quick look. Cobra had a point. While Suave was a ruthless drug dealer, he wasn't known as a killer.

"Okay, who did the job?" Saddam pressed the gun against Cobra's head. "I said, who did it?" he yelled, hitting Cobra across his face again. This time, a few teeth loosened.

"Listen, man, I'm not here for any Q and A game. This vulture kidnapped and almost killed me," Danny shouted. "You see this?" He pointed to the hideous scar on his face. "This was compliments of this fool. Smoke his behind, and let's get out of here." Danny knew he had a lot to lose as well. He was the one who gave Suave, Cobra, and Daddy Lizard the information about the stash house. If he killed Cobra, that would prove to King Kong that he had nothing to do with the murder and robbery. Danny's own life was depending on Cobra's death. "You want me to do the job or what?" Danny was getting impatient.

Bubbles gasped loudly, and all three men glanced over at her in surprise. They weren't aware she was still in the room.

"Get out of here!" Danny yelled.

This was the opportunity Cobra was waiting for. He knew it was now or never. He pulled his gun from under the pillow, but Saddam caught the move and rapidly fired two shots, one behind each other, into Cobra's chest.

Cobra screamed in agony, letting off a wild shot, his body twitching on the bed in the throes of death.

Bubbles shrieked from across the room before crumbling to the floor, a small hole in the middle of her forehead where Cobra's bullet found its mark.

"Bubbles!" Danny ran over to his sister. He knelt on the carpeted floor beside her body, staring down into her lifeless eyes. She was gone. Danny rested his head on her stomach and bawled. Of all his no-good sisters, Bubbles was his favorite. She did this to help him out and had paid with her life.

"Yeah, man, let's go before the cops come," Saddam said nervously, looking at the door. With all the commotion and shots that were fired, he was sure that someone must have called the police by now.

Danny rose slowly to his feet, tears pouring down his disfigured face. He pulled his gun from his waist and almost robotically he walked over to the bed where Cobra was still fighting against the claws of death.

"Plea . . . Plea . . . Please," Cobra begged a little above a whisper, froth and blood spurting from his mouth, his hands pressed against the bloody holes in his chest, his gun lying useless on the bed beside him.

"Let's get out of here before the cops come," Saddam repeated. "Look at him. He's as good as dead." He tucked his gun into his waist.

But that wasn't good enough for Danny. He leaned over and rested his gun in the middle of Cobra's forehead. "You killed my sister," he muttered before pulling the trigger, spraying Cobra's brains all over the pillow. "*Now,* he's dead." Danny slipped the gun into his waist.

Saddam grabbed Danny's arm and rushed to the door. "Let's go."

The two men dashed to a Nissan Sunny parked a few feet away.

As the getaway car lost itself in the flow of traffic, a lone figure raised himself from his hiding place behind the huge dumpster. The man reached for the cell phone in his pocket to make an urgent call, flicking his long dreadlocks over his shoulder. "Hello, Prophet?" he said when the phone was answered on the other end. "It's me."

Chapter Thirty-three

"I'm glad you're spending some time with the kids and me," Monica purred, nestling farther back into Suave's chest as they spooned on the long leather couch in the living room, his hands rubbing her huge stomach. The couple had less than five weeks to go before their third child was born.

The shouting and giggling of the kids playing in their room filtered into the living room.

"You know I always try to spend time with you guys." Suave's eyes were closed as he tried to relax his body. He had been on edge ever since that disastrous night in Spanish Town, and it was wearing him down.

"Uh-huh, and don't think you're going anywhere tonight," Monica warned.

Just then, Suave's personal cell phone that was on the coffee table beside them went off. And immediately, so did his business phone that was beside it.

Monica sucked her teeth loudly in frustration. "You better let them go to voicemail."

With his eyes still closed, Suave replied, "Do you see me moving? I'll call them back later." Both phones stopped ringing—before they started to ring again.

"It must be important." Suave gently pushed on Monica's back, and she raised her body so he could swing his legs off the couch. He reached over for his personal cell phone; it was an unknown number. "Yes?"

"From the grave cometh my grief and pain," Prophet responded in his gravelly voice. "My . . . my . . . soul is pierced by the agony and the evil deed of the devil." And the old man began sobbing.

Alarmed, Suave jumped to his feet, a sinking feeling in his gut. "What's wrong, Prophet?"

"Cobra."

"What's wrong with Cobra?" Suave whispered. *Please, God, say it is not so.*

"Murdered."

The cell phone fell from Suave's shaking hand, and he collapsed to his knees. Rolling himself into a ball on the floor, Suave howled like a tortured, caged jackal.

"Baby, what's wrong?" Monica sprang up and awkwardly kneeled beside her grieving man. "What's going on?"

But Suave continued to wail in excruciating pain.

Monica reached for the cell phone on the floor and brought it to her ear. Prophet was still on the line weeping. "Hello? Who is this?" She listened for a few seconds as Prophet told her of Cobra's death before she too started to cry. Cobra had been a huge part of Suave's life and, as such, a part of Monica's too. "We'll call you back," Monica mumbled before flipping the phone closed.

She drew Suave into her arms and held him as he mourned the demise of his best friend.

"Cheers, my brother." Later that night, Suave lifted the whiskey bottle into the air, spilling some of the whiskey on his chest. He was drunk. "Friends for life, Cobra." Suave burped loudly before taking a long sip, emptying the bottle before it slipped from his trembling fingers to the floor. With half of his buttock hanging off the bar stool, his back braced against the counter, Suave's glazed eyes peered unseeingly into the dark bar.

Immediately, his cell phone rang in his jeans. He fumbled, taking it out of his pocket. *Maybe it's Daddy Lizard.* Flipping the phone open, through half-closed eyes, Suave saw that it was Pat calling. Swearing aloud, he threw the phone against the wall, shattering it into pieces. "I should just go and kill that punk." His words slurred. He was a drunken mess.

Moments after hearing about Cobra's murder, Suave had found enough strength to pull himself off the floor, slipped on his sneakers, and fled the house ignoring Monica's protests. He drove aimlessly around Kingston City, the tears pouring down his face until he ended up in front of his bar in Rema.

Suave parked the car and dragged himself out before he paused. He glanced at the solemn faces of a group of his men standing on the sidewalk and knew the news of Cobra's death had already made its way to them.

The men nodded respectfully at him, but no one spoke. The look on their boss's face showed no conversation was welcomed.

Burke, one of Suave's bar managers, stepped forward. "I cleared everyone out after I heard and was just about to close up." He handed Suave a lit spliff. "There will be men on watch twenty-four, seven."

Suave took the spliff, nodded his thanks, and marched past his men into the bar, slamming the door shut. He went straight to the liquor wall, grabbed a flask of Wray & Nephew White Overproof Rum, unscrewed the top, and turned the bottle straight to his head. The burning sensation in his throat was appreciated as he gobbled down the liquor.

In record time, the bottle was empty, and Suave was feeling light-headed. Puffing away on the spliff, he reached for another bottle. This time, it was a bottle of whiskey. This too disappeared in record time before Suave grabbed something else to drink. He just wanted to end the pain he was feeling at the loss of Cobra.

The spliff long gone, Suave's throat and tongue burned like Scotch Bonnet pepper. His head felt like a helium balloon about to explode. Totally inebriated, Suave felt himself slipping off the bar stool but was unable to move a muscle.

"Oops, I got you, my brother." Reverend Stanford caught Suave just before he hit the floor. He wrapped his arm around the drunken man's waist and half-lifted, half-dragged Suave across the bar to the room in the back. He lowered Suave onto the small cot and adjusted him as best as he could with Suave's long legs hanging over the edge.

Reverend Stanford sighed as he straightened up his tall frame. As he stood looking down on Suave, who was now out cold, his heart was filled with grief. The reverend knew that disaster was coming as told to him by the Holy Spirit. It's declared in Matthew 24:35, *"Heaven and earth shall pass away, but my words shall not pass away."* However, Reverend Stanford was hoping he could have gotten through to Suave, Cobra, Daddy Lizard, and King Kong and his men before it was too late. Now, two young lives were wasted, and only God knows how many more to go.

"Father, please show me how I can help these young men." Reverend Stanford looked up to the heavens, his eyes filled with tears. "Please show mercy, Lord. I'm so tired of seeing so many lives wasted in this country due to drugs and violence. I know a war is about to get started now in retaliation of this young man's killing. Dear Lord, I don't want any more to die. Please use your servant, Lord, to keep the peace. In Jesus' name I pray. A—"

"Amen."

Surprised, Reverend Stanford spun around and came face-to-face with Daddy Lizard. Unlike Suave, Daddy Lizard seemed sober. In fact, he seemed too normal for someone who had just lost a very close friend and business partner.

"Praying for our souls again, Rev?" Daddy Lizard took a long drag from the spliff in his hand, turned his head upward, and blew the smoke into the air. "Or are you praying for the souls I'm getting ready to send to hell?" His smile didn't reach his cold eyes.

"Now, listen to me, young man." Reverend Stanford walked closer to Daddy Lizard. "That's not the way to go about this." He stopped a few inches in front of the hurting man. "Killing in retaliation will only make things worse. Look at him." Reverend pointed over his shoulder at Suave. "He's hurting so much right now that he drank himself into a stupor."

Daddy Lizard glanced over at Suave before looking back at Reverend Stanford. "He'll be all right. Come morning, he'll be back on his feet, and we'll get justice for Cobra."

Reverend Stanford closed his eyes, internally praying for strength and the right words to say to Daddy Lizard. He opened his eyes and said, "My dear brother, please let the police handle this. Please, I'm begging you."

"Thank you for looking in on the boss." Daddy Lizard waved him toward the door.

Reverend Stanford opened his mouth to speak but closed it when he looked into Daddy Lizard's deadly eyes. "Okay. I'll go." He left with a heavy heart.

Chapter Thirty-four

"They killed him like a dog." Prophet sucked on the tobacco pipe hanging from the corner of his mouth. He seemed to have aged even more since the nephew he loved liked a son was murdered the night before.

Suave and Daddy Lizard stared at him in silence as the men sat in a circle in Prophet's small, sparsely furnished living room.

"So, your people say they saw Saddam and Danny running from the motel room?" Suave asked after a moment of silence. Not that he needed confirmation. He knew it was King Kong and his men who killed Cobra.

"Yes. The gal that got killed in there too was Danny's sister."

Guilt flooded Suave's being. It took him most of the day to stop the hammering in his head, and even now, he still felt a little light-headed from all the liquor he had consumed the night before. Reasonably sober, he and Daddy Lizard had gathered as much information about Cobra's murder as possible. As soon as Suave heard about Bubbles's death, he knew Cobra was killed instead of him. He remembered the many times Bubbles had called him, but he had ignored her.

"Suave? You with us, man?" Daddy Lizard looked at Suave with concern. "We have a lot to do."

"I'm good." Suave glanced from Daddy Lizard to Prophet. "First, we lay Cobra to rest as soon as possible, and then we deal with Saddam and Danny."

"I'll take care of it," Daddy Lizard said. "My family will also help out. We'll bury him at Dovecot."

The three men continued planning Cobra's funeral, their hearts aching for their fallen loved one, trying hard to ignore the main thing on their minds—revenge.

It was a rainy, gloomy day. The large crowd wearing mostly black was symbolic of the mood of the mourners surrounding the white casket with gold-plated handles as it was lowered into the red dirt at Dovecot Memorial Park. Cobra's mother, his baby mothers, children, relatives, and friends sobbed uncontrollably, while Suave and Daddy Lizard, their red eyes hidden behind dark shades, stared at the expensive box that held the remains of their friend.

"*When the roll is called up yonder. . . .*" Reverend Stanford's deep voice broke out in a new song, and some of the mourners joined in.

Reverend Stanford was surprised but pleased when Suave had asked if he could preside over Cobra's funeral. He readily agreed and held the funeral service in his small church that was packed to capacity earlier that afternoon.

With the choir's soulful singing many heartfelt eulogies, worshipful praises, and Reverend Stanford giving the Word, Cobra's homecoming service was beautiful but tearful. Suave, flanked by Monica and all his children, sat motionless in the front row, his lips folded tight, trying to prevent the dam from bursting.

After the service, the big white hearse escorted by two police officers, followed by dozens of cars, drove down Spanish Town Road to the burial plot at Dovecot Memorial Park.

Security was tight. Suave hired extra men to keep watch just in case King Kong and his men decided to interrupt the funeral—or even worse. But so far, so good.

"It was a good turnout for my son." Prophet's voice interrupted Suave's thoughts. "Thank you for taking care of everything."

"No need to thank me. Cobra was my brother from another mother," Suave said softly. "A part of me is in that grave." He pointed to the casket that was being covered by dirt by the graveside workers.

"My people and I are going to roll out now."

Suave followed Prophet's gaze to where a group of silent Rastafarians stood at the back of the funeral crowd, dressed in their red, green, and gold. The men had not said a word since they had arrived at the church where they stayed outside.

"Okay, Prophet." Suave shook his right hand. "I'll come and check you soon so we can talk."

"I'm done talking," Prophet mumbled before turning abruptly on his feet and walked away toward his entourage. As silently as they came, the Rastafarians left.

Suave looked after Prophet with a perplexed look on his face. *I wonder what he meant by that? I hope he doesn't try to take on King Kong, Danny, and crazy Saddam by himself.*

After the burial, Suave's men and many of the funeral attendants went back to Suave's bar in Rema. Suave ordered the bar open to everyone, and liquor was flowing like Dunn's River Falls. Under the haze of the marijuana spliffs, the crowd that was mourning earlier was now laughing and chatting, enjoying the free liquor and the free food of jerk and fried chicken, rice and peas, and mannish water that was being catered at Suave's expense. It was a celebration of Cobra's life.

While across town in his hideaway house, Suave curled up alone on his couch, still wearing his stiff white shirt, black pants, and black socks. He was feeling extremely wiped out after burying Cobra. After dropping off his children and Monica following the funeral, Suave needed to be alone, so he escaped to his hut. It was here that the pain of losing his parents resurrected, along with the agony of losing his best friend, hammered away at his heart.

"I'm so sorry, Cobra," Suave sobbed. "I'm so sorry, man." He cried until there were no more tears. It wasn't long before exhaustion snatched him away into a hellish nightmare.

"One down, and you to go," Pastor Ralph mocked Suave. "That should have been you, but you are next." He was laughing like a jackass with tears running down his ugly face as he enjoyed Suave's pain.

"Leave my baby alone." Pat pouted his thick, red lips as he came to stand beside Pastor Ralph, his right hand resting on his narrow hip. "I don't want you to die, Suave. I just want you to live with me . . . in hell!"

The two men hooted with laughter, high fiving each other in victory.

"In fact, I want you to come with me now," Pat said after the laughter died down, moving closer to Suave.

"Stay away from me, you freak." Suave stepped back but stopped short by the wall behind him.

"Nowhere to run, nowhere to hide." Pastor Ralph also edged closer.

Fists folded, his heart pounding away in his chest, Suave glanced back and forth between the ghosts that were always haunting him. "I said, get back." Both Pastor Ralph and Pat reached for him, a menacing look on their faces. "No no no!" he screamed, kicking and punching in his sleep.

Suave fell off the couch onto the floor with a loud thud, still struggling against the invisible forces attacking him.

He took deep breaths as he scanned the room, realizing he was alone. There was no Pastor Ralph or Pat. A surge of anger overtook him. He jumped to his feet, marched over to the coffee table, grabbed his keys and cell phone, then strode out toward the garage. His shoes were at the top of the stairs where he had left them, and he slipped his feet into them.

As Suave backed his truck out of the garage on to the street, he reached for the cell phone on the seat beside him, but pulled back his hand, deciding against it. Suave, with a hard look plastered across his face, kept a heavy foot on the gas as the truck ate up the road all the way to Havendale. He parked two blocks away from Pat's house.

"I can't have any peace in my life, right?" Suave mumbled some curse words as he made his way toward Pat's house with his head hanging low, a baseball cap now covering most of his face. "I'm so tired of this crap." He walked through the gate and up to the veranda, but voices coming from inside the house halted his steps. His eyes grew big in fright. *No one can see me here!*

On tiptoes, Suave hurried off the veranda so he could make a hasty retreat. The front door popped open, and he dived into the thick shrubs by the gate.

"I'm glad we cleared everything up." Suave almost wet himself at the deep, familiar voice that made its way to him. "You know I don't want any misunderstanding between us."

Suave was flat on his stomach. He carefully lifted his head, peering through the bushes. Instantly, the blood rushed to his head, and Suave became dizzy and nauseated at the sight before him.

"As I said before, no one was supposed to get killed." Queen Bee took a puff on the lit cigarette in her hand. "Especially Cobra."

"It's that trigger-happy Danny." King Kong held Queen Bee's gaze, trying to look sincere. "I told those fools that we were only going to rob Suave for that stint in Spain Town, but Saddam just couldn't let the death of his grandfather go. I didn't want to kill Cobra," King Kong lied. "That's why I came to you for help in the first place."

"And I agreed to help you," Queen Bee snapped. "We were going to set up Suave, Cobra, and Daddy Lizard, make sure they go to prison for life, and then you and I would take everything Suave has. *That* was the plan!"

King Kong held up both hands as if he surrendered. "I know, and I'm sorry. But that's still the plan. Now we only need to get Suave and Daddy Lizard out of the race and take over the place," he sang.

"No, now we need to lie low for a while. You know you are their number one suspect. Plus, do you think Suave and Daddy Lizard are going to let Cobra's death go unavenged?"

"I'm not scared of those fools." King Kong's ugly face screwed up with distaste. "If they come at me, then I just might have to take them out too."

"Just don't call my name," Queen Bee warned. "I'll stay close to Suave as usual and will let you know when we'll make a move again. That's *if* any of you are still alive."

King Kong threw his head back and rumbled off a deep belly laugh that sounded just like the big gorilla.

While in the bushes, Suave's eyes were closed tight against the torture of Queen Bee's betrayal as he tried to control the tremor that took over his body. Even that little sissy, Pat, had betrayed him. *I'm sure he knows what King Kong and his sister had planned, but he never said a word.*

"I'll catch you later, Queen." King Kong strolled off the veranda with a big Kool-Aid grin on his face.

"Under no circumstances should you contact me. *I'll* call you."

King Kong paused right by the bushes where Suave hid. He turned around to face Queen Bee.

Suave held his breath. If he made even the slightest sound, King Kong would see or hear him.

"I'll wait for you to be in contact, Queen." The smile didn't reach the gorilla's rat eyes. "Then I'll kill you after getting rid of those two idiots," he muttered under his breath, loud enough for Suave to hear. Without another word, King Kong turned around and strolled out the gate to an old beat-up Nissan Sunny parked on the street.

Relieved, Suave watched until Queen Bee reentered the house, closing the door behind her. With his pounding head resting against the shrub, it took a few minutes before Suave dragged himself out of the bushes, still stooping low.

He crept away from the house back to his truck. Tonight changed everything. It was now a whole new game.

Chapter Thirty-five

"Get up, stand up: stand up for your right!" encouraged Bob Marley. Danny's head bobbed back and forth as the lyrics of the loud song wrapped itself around him in the parked car in his garage. "I know that's right, Bob." Danny took a big gulp from the bottle of vodka he held in his hand. "You killed my sister, fool." He sucked on the spliff and began to cough loudly. Soon, the coughing turned into sobs as the guilt ate away at him.

Tomorrow was the funeral of Bubbles, and Danny was dreading the whole thing. His alcoholic mother and scandalous sisters weren't talking to him after they found out he was involved with her death. His wife was nagging him to move to the country until everything died down. King Kong was acting even shadier than ever, pretending like they hadn't planned for Saddam to kill Cobra, and Danny just beat him to it.

"And for what?" Danny tucked the half-empty bottle of vodka between his legs. He leaned over on his side to dig into his pants pocket for his handkerchief to wipe his face. "They forgot that I was kidnapped and beaten." He blew his nose loudly into the handkerchief. "They forgot about this?" His index finger outlined the long, ugly scar on his face.

"Don't give up the fight!" Danny pounded his hand on the steering wheel. "I won't do that, Bob. Trust me. I'm not going down without a fight."

"Glad to hear that," said a coarse voice in Danny's right ear from the backseat of the car, drowning out Bob's conscious lyrics.

"Hey, who the—" A large, black-gloved hand clasped over Danny's mouth, pulling his head back against the car seat. The other hand was wrapped tightly around his throat, pressing hard against his trachea. Danny's eyes opened wide in fright.

"You talk too much, Danny boy." The tobacco breath fanned Danny's face. "Relax yourself!" the voice ordered when Danny began to struggle, flinging his hands wildly and aimlessly over his head to loosen himself from the hold on him.

Danny's screams were muffled. A sharp pain ran up his leg when his kicking foot connected with the car's dashboard. But Danny kept on kicking, twisting this way, and turning that way.

"You are really not going down without a fight, huh?" The hand around Danny's throat tightened, cutting into his neck, blocking the air from entering his starved lungs.

Little blue, yellow, and red lights danced before Danny's bulging eyes as he struggled against unconsciousness. *Good God almighty, I'm being strangled to death.* The deadly thought gave Danny a surge of energy, and he pushed his body up and away from the car seat, his right hand grabbing ahold of something over his head. It was the rough, matted coil of thick, interwoven hair—dreadlocks.

"This is for Cobra, scumbag." The hand around Danny's throat disappeared briefly and reappeared a few seconds later with a big, sharp butcher knife that sliced across Danny's throat, leaving a red trail from left to right, almost decapitating him.

"You live like a pig, and you die like one." The man eased back onto the backseat of the car, the knife in his hand dripping blood. He watched as Danny's lifeless body slumped over toward the passenger seat, his head at an awkward right angle. A smirk on his face, the man pulled a small, black towel from around his neck, wrapping the murder weapon in it like it was a gift. And as quietly as he appeared, he disappeared after alighting from the car.

On the car's stereo, Bob continued singing that now he saw the light.

"You heard the news?" Daddy Lizard asked Suave as he sat across from him on the couch in Suave's living room.

Suave nodded his head. "Yup. Someone took out Danny last night."

Daddy Lizard stared at him. "Any idea who?" He took a sip from the cup of strong, black Blue Mountain coffee he held in his hand.

Suave frowned as he returned Daddy Lizard's look. "We are partners in this. Our best friend was just murdered. You think I would make a move like that and not tell you about it?"

Daddy Lizard sighed deeply and ran a weary hand down his face. "My bad, Boss. This whole thing just has me on edge. But if it wasn't us, then who?"

Suave gazed at Daddy Lizard and watched as Daddy Lizard's eyes opened wide as it finally hit him. "And no, he never said anything to me. But . . ." He spread his hands wide as if to say, *who else could it be?*

Daddy Lizard smiled for the first time since hearing of Cobra's death. "One down and three more to go."

"Four."

"Huh?" Daddy Lizard leaned forward.

Suave took a deep breath. It had been a week since he overheard the conspiracy between King Kong and Queen Bee. It had taken him a few days to accept Queen Bee's betrayal, and enough time to plan what to say to Daddy Lizard without revealing his sick secret about Pat.

"You know, I went by Queen Bee's the other day to do some business," Suave lied. "Well, before I pulled up to her gate, I noticed a familiar car parked a few feet away from the house. I circled around, parked a few houses down, and doubled back on foot."

Daddy Lizard was staring at Suave's mouth as if he were lip reading.

"I almost wet myself when I heard King Kong and Queen Bee talking behind the big gate." Suave then told Daddy Lizard everything he had overheard at Pat's house, which was now at Queen Bee's house.

Daddy Lizard didn't speak for a while when Suave was finished. He took slow sips of his now lukewarm coffee as if it were scorching hot. "Queen Bee." It was a statement, not a question.

Suave nodded. "The one who has enough dirt on us to put us away for a lifetime."

Daddy Lizard chuckled, his eyes as cold as the Antarctic Ocean. "No. The one we have enough dirt on that *we* are going to send away for a lifetime."

A smile worked its way on Suave's face. "I like how you think, partner."

"It's kill or be killed, my friend. Queen Bee decided her fate when she joined forces with the gorilla. The same bastard who killed Cobra!" Daddy Lizard jumped to his feet, spilling a little coffee on the floor.

"She underestimates us," Suave remarked. "The little—" Just then, Suave's personal cell phone began to ring beside him on the couch. He held up a finger for Daddy Lizard to be quiet. "Suave." He listened a few seconds. "Cool. Thanks." He flipped the phone closed, ending the call.

"Who was that?" Daddy Lizard asked, lowering himself back onto the couch.

"One of our workers over at the bar. Detective Bird and two other detectives were there looking for us."

Daddy Lizard fired off some choice curse words.

"They've been trying to talk to us since Cobra was murdered. And now that Danny was killed last night, their search for us will only intensify."

"You know they're going to think we did it, right?" Daddy Lizard asked.

"I know. But last night I was with Monica and our kids, and you . . ."

"I was with my girl all night."

Suave nodded in approval. "There you have it. Let's head on down to the police station to hear what these pigs want. The sooner we get this done, the sooner we can deal with the rat and the gorilla."

"We'll take your ride," Daddy Lizard said as they walked out to the garage. "I'll come back and get mine later."

Suave nodded in agreement. Almost thirty minutes later, the two men were being escorted by Detective Bird to a small back room at the Half Way Tree Police Station.

"Gentlemen, please have a seat." Detective Bird waved toward two lopsided metal chairs on one side of the equally hideous, small, scratched up metal table, while he took a more comfortable chair on the other side facing Suave and Daddy Lizard. "Thank you for coming."

Suave and Daddy Lizard nodded.

"First, let me tell you how sorry I am to hear about the murder of Cobra."

Suave and Daddy Lizard nodded again.

"I'm the detective assigned to the case, and that's why I've been trying to get ahold of you two. I want you to help me find the person responsible for this and to get justice for your friend."

Suave chuckled at the baloney that the detective was spitting. You would think that after all this time the man would know who he was dealing with.

"Something funny, Suave?" Detective Bird asked in a cold voice, the pleasantries now forgotten.

"There he is." Suave smiled. "The *real* Detective Bird. Man, just cut out the crap and tell us why we're here."

Detective Bird looked from Daddy Lizard's cold face to Suave's. He had his work cut out for him. "Cobra was killed a little over a week ago. And I'm sure you've heard by now that last night Danny was also killed."

"My condolences to Danny's family." Daddy Lizard met the detective's eyes and held them. "I can just imagine the pain they are going through right now."

"Let's stop this nonsense!" Detective Bird jumped to his feet, pounding his hand on the rickety table that rocked unsteadily. "You two think this is a game?" The veins in his neck stood up as he leaned over the table toward Suave and Daddy Lizard.

"No, *you* think this is a game!" Suave jumped to his feet and leaned toward the detective. "Calling us down here, talking pure rubbish like we're stupid or something."

The two men squared off until Detective Bird moved his body upright and away from Suave. He reclaimed his seat and waited for Suave to do the same.

Suave felt Daddy Lizard's toe pressing down on his and slowly sat back down. "Get to the point, or we're out of here."

Detective Bird nodded. "Do you know who killed Cobra?"

The two men stared at him mutely.

"Which one of you killed Danny?"

"That's it!" Suave jumped to his feet, Daddy Lizard quickly doing the same. Suave reached into his pants pocket and took out a business card. "You should have this already, but just in case you need another one." He threw down his lawyer's business card on the table in front of Detective Bird. "He represents both of us."

"Let's get out of here," Daddy Lizard said and walked toward the door, Suave right on his heels.

"Where do you think you're going?" Detective Bird's voice halted their steps at the door. "I'm not through questioning you." He stood and took a few steps toward the men.

"Well, we're through talking to you," Suave said. "You either charge us with something now or speak to us with our lawyer present."

"Hiding something, Suave?"

"Fishing for something, Detective?"

A barrage of emotions played across Detective Bird's face—anger, disgust, and apprehension. He knew in his heart that King Kong was responsible for Cobra's death and that Danny was killed in retaliation. This meant Suave or Daddy Lizard killed Danny or, at the very least, ordered the hit on him. "Where were you last night?" He peered at Suave.

"At home with my fiancée and kids."

"All night?"

"All night," Suave remarked with a smirk on his face.

"And you?" Detective Bird turned his gaze on Daddy Lizard.

"At home all night with my wifey."

"Which one?"

Daddy Lizard laughed out loud. "Good question. But I have only one wifey. Natasha. The others are just side chicks. You want her number?"

Detective Bird nodded his head, and Daddy Lizard recited the number as the detective jotted it down on the notepad he held in his hand. But what was the use? He knew Natasha was going to confirm that Daddy Lizard was with her all night. No, what he needed was hard evidence against Suave and Daddy Lizard if he were going to charge them with murder. And by hook or crook, he was going to get it.

"Detective." Suave tapped the Rolex on his wrist when Detective Bird looked at him. "I'm a busy man. Are we through here?"

Detective Bird grinded his teeth. He glanced at Suave's watch and wished he could just snap the handcuffs on Suave's expensive wrists, but on what grounds? All he had now was suspicion. There was no evidence linking Suave to Danny's death. "For now. But both of you will be back here in no time, and when you are, you won't be leaving anytime soon."

Suave grinned, and Daddy Lizard winked. Without another word, they both swaggered out of the police station as if they didn't have a care in the world.

Chapter Thirty-six

"I need someone to tell me something right now," Suave yelled, his wild eyes running over the group of men standing before him in his bar. "Where is King Kong? Where is Saddam? Where is my son?"

Earlier that morning, Suave was awakened by Monica, shaking his shoulder. "Suave! Wake up!"

"What?" he asked groggily, his eyes still closed. "A man can't even get a little sleep," he complained.

"This is serious. Get up now."

The panic in Monica's voice was stronger than a jolt of caffeine. Suave popped up on the bed like a robot. "What's going on?" Fear filled his eyes when he saw tears rolling down Monica's face. Not again. "What, Monica?"

"It's Joel. Nadine just called."

Suave's two hands tightly grabbed the sheet on which he lay, and his body began to tremble as if he were about to faint. "Wha . . . What happened to Joel?"

"He was kidnapped."

The room began spinning around and around. Suave stared at Monica, noticing that she now had at least ten faces that were appearing and disappearing as if by magic, his mind consumed with a poisonous thought. *King Kong has my son*.

It was now hours later, and Joel was still missing.

Daddy Lizard moved closer to Suave and rested a hand on his shoulder. "Take it easy, man. We—"

"We have nothing!" Suave looked around the room in anger. "We've been searching for my son all morning. It's almost noon, and yet, we have nothing. Did King Kong disappear into thin air, huh? Did crazy Saddam vaporize?"

"Boss?" One worker hesitantly glanced up at Suave.

"What?"

"My people over in Jungle said King Kong's restaurant had been closed all day, and no one has seen him, Saddam, or Phil since yesterday."

"They're in hiding." Daddy Lizard made eye contact with Suave. "They knew once we got word about Joel that we'd be looking for them."

Suave shook his head in frustration. He was tired, hungry, and about to lose his mind. *Where is Joel? Would King Kong really kill my son?*

"Okay, everyone. I want you to head back out and continue the search." Suave's eyes implored his men not to give up. "Use *every* available source you have. Money is not a problem. Please find those vultures and my son by any means necessary."

As the men filed out to continue the search for Joel, Suave walked over to a bar stool and lowered himself onto it. "I don't know what else to do, man," Suave admitted to Daddy Lizard. "Time is of the essence to save my son."

"We'll find him, Suave."

"Yeah. But dead or alive?"

"Don't you dare think like that!" Daddy Lizard stabbed his finger at Suave. "King Kong knows if he hurts Joel, he's as good as dead."

Just then, Suave's cell phone rang. It was a private number. He gave Daddy Lizard a puzzled look.

"Answer it. Maybe it's that fool, King Kong."

Suave answered. "Suave."

"I know King Kong took your boy," said a very low, deep voice. It was clear the caller was trying to disguise his voice. "And he's going to kill him to teach you a lesson."

"Who is this?" Suave yelled. He jumped up off the stool and paced the floor. "Where is my son?"

Daddy Lizard stepped closer to Suave, his index finger over his lips. "Listen," he mouthed to Suave, tugging on his ear.

Suave took a deep breath, his chest rising and falling rhythmically as he tried to get ahold of himself.

"You ready to listen, or do you want me to hang up, and you never see your son alive again?" the man asked.

"Is my son okay?" Suave muttered through his teeth. Being at someone's mercy wasn't sitting too well with him.

"Not for long if Saddam and King Kong have anything to say about it."

With one hand holding the cell phone, Suave used the other to grip the bar counter. Perspiration washed his face as his legs began to tremble. "Please, don't let them hurt my boy." It was now dawning on Suave that he may very well need this person's help. Joel's life was at stake.

"I can save him, but for a price."

"Name it," Suave told him quickly. "You know I'm good for it."

"I know, and that's why I contacted you."

"Save my son's life, and I'll give you all the money I have." A few tears escaped down his face, and he used his fingers to wipe them away.

The man chuckled lightly. "I just want a little bit of it," he said, the extra bass still in his voice. "I have an overseas account number for you. Transfer $10,000 US in it by six o'clock today. I'll then call you and tell you where you can get your son."

"How do I know I can trust you?" Suave asked.

"How do you know you can't?" the man countered. "Your son is missing, and you've been searching for him all morning with no luck. Oh, and please don't get the police involved."

"Joel's mother already reported it to the police, and a detective was assigned to the case."

"You're talking about Detective Bird?" asked the man.

Suave had a shocked look on his face. "Yes. You know him?"

The man sighed loudly. "Listen, Detective Bird is on King Kong's payroll—and has been for years. I'm also a hundred percent sure that the good detective already knows who kidnapped your son and where he is."

Suave's eyes widened, his nostrils flared, and his headache just got worse. He knew there was something about Detective Bird he didn't like . . . but to be working for King Kong?

"I have to go now," the man whispered. "You want the account number or what?"

"Yes." Suave shook his head as if to clear it. He grabbed a pen that was on the bar counter. "Go ahead," he said, hastily writing on an old newspaper that was beside the pen. "Got it."

"I'll be in touch."

"Listen—" The phone went dead in Suave's hand. He kicked the stool and howled in pain, hopping on one leg, cursing up a storm.

"All right, try to take it easy," Daddy Lizard said. "Fill me in on what he said." He listened quietly as Suave told him everything the man had said. "Things are looking up."

"Looking up?" Suave stared at him like he were an octopus. "I'm about to transfer money into an unknown bank account, to an unknown person, who we are not sure will help us save Joel."

"It's a chance we have to take," Daddy Lizard replied. "But I have a feeling he will come through once the money hits his account. We have to do all that's possible."

Suave blew air through his dry lips. He felt like he were a hundred years old. "Yes. I'll do everything I can to make sure my son returns to me safe and sound."

"And once Joel is safe, we'll begin cleaning house." Daddy Lizard's voice was hard and cold. "Starting with that dirty cop."

Chapter Thirty-seven

"Meet me in thirty minutes at the end of the Causeway Bridge," the man informed Suave. "Your son and I will be standing beside a small blue fish stall."

"I'm on my way." Suave closed the cell phone and glanced over at Daddy Lizard, who was riding shotgun with him in the truck along Trafalgar Road. "Causeway Bridge in half an hour. He said he has Joel."

Daddy Lizard reached over and playfully punched Suave on the arm. "That's what I'm talking about. See? We're going to get Joel back safe."

But Suave nibbled on his bottom lip. He was nervous. Earlier that day, when his people still hadn't received any information on Joel's whereabouts, Suave had his bank transfer the money as instructed by the man. Still driving and searching all over Kingston and St. Catherine, touching base with every known friend and acquaintance, Suave had waited impatiently for the man to check his bank account and call him back. As the hours dragged on and night had fallen, Suave felt he had been tricked.

"He's not going to call back," Suave said to Daddy Lizard in despair as they filled up the truck at a gas station. "I bet he's just going to take the money and disappear."

Daddy Lizard shook his head. "I have a good feeling about this. I think he's waiting until it gets darker before making contact." And he was right.

It was close to midnight when Suave's cell phone rang. It was the Good Samaritan with instructions to get Joel. Suave was elated but still apprehensive. He would feel better when he sees Joel for himself. *Please be okay, Joel. Please.*

"Are you going to tell Nadine?" Daddy Lizard's voice interrupted Suave's thoughts.

"No. I want to wait until I get Joel back first. Just in case . . ." He didn't finish the sentence. Just the thought of it was too much for him to bear.

"We're on our way to get him back now," Daddy Lizard encouraged Suave. "Come to think of it, Nadine and her husband are probably still at church where they're holding a prayer meeting for Joel."

Suave snorted. "Fools! What can prayer do for Joel? What can their God do to help my son? If He was the big Savior that they think He is, then why didn't He prevent King Kong from taking Joel in the first place?" Suave was now getting worked up again. "God didn't help my son—I did! It was *me* who put that money in that man's bank account." He pounded his chest with his left hand, the right hand still navigating the truck toward the Causeway Bridge. "Me! Not some fictitious God!"

Daddy Lizard listened but remained quiet. He knew anything about church and God always upset Suave. He wasn't sure where it all came from, but Suave had been that way since he was a teenager living in Tivoli Gardens.

Suave continued to rant and curse for a few more minutes before he became quiet.

"We're almost there," Daddy Lizard said the obvious when the Causeway Bridge came into sight.

Suave's heart rate sped up as they joined the light flow of traffic over the bridge at that time of night. His hand on the steering wheel shook a little. Was this a hoax?

Moments later, the truck got to the other side of the bridge, and Suave pulled over to a dark, quiet area where a lengthy line of fish stalls stood. He parked the truck and shut it off. "Well, here we are," he said, looking over at Daddy Lizard.

Daddy Lizard nodded and pulled his gun from his waistband. "I think I see something up ahead." He pointed in front of him.

Suave leaned forward, squinting his eyes as he peered through the windshield into the darkness and the distance. He made out two figures. "That must be them," he said excitedly. "I'm going to get my son." Suave reached for the door handle but paused when Daddy Lizard rested his hand over his.

"Be careful," Daddy Lizard warned Suave. "We still don't know who that is. You have your piece?"

Suave patted his side. "You know I do. Any problems, I'll give you the signal." The man had commanded that only Suave should come and get Joel from him.

"Okay. Go and get your son." The men bumped fists, and Suave stepped out.

The sand felt soft and cushy under Suave's sneakers as he strode toward the two figures. A few vehicles passed on the road, their headlights illuminating the area for a few seconds, but Suave was still unable to see any faces. He breathed heavily as he kept his eyes trained on the taller of the two. Suave didn't feel any fear for himself. He was more concerned about seeing Joel alive and well.

"Daddy?"

Suave's heart almost stopped when he heard Joel's voice. "Joel. Yes, it's me, son." He broke into a little jog. He couldn't reach Joel fast enough. He ran until he was a few feet away from Joel and the man—then he stopped suddenly. Suave's mouth opened in surprise, his hand reaching for the gun on his waist.

"You don't need your gun," the man said, taking a few steps closer to Suave, one hand holding Joel's.

"You?" Suave was shocked. "But . . . but I don't understand."

"I'm guilty of a lot of things, but I don't hurt children," replied Phil. "This has gone too far, and I don't want anything to do with it."

Suave looked at King Kong's right-hand man and saw the sincerity in his eyes. "Thank you for saving my son."

Phil nodded and released Joel's hand.

Joel ran over to his father, and Suave grabbed him in a tight embrace. Tears filled his eyes as he felt Joel's heart beating against his.

Suave looked up at Phil. "Joel, go and get in the truck. I'll be right there." He rubbed a hand over his son's head and took a step back.

"Okay, Daddy." Joel walked over to Phil. "Thank you, sir." He held out his right hand to Phil, and he took it in a firm handshake.

Suave smiled, pride radiating from his body like rays from the sun. His son was such a respectful young man.

"I knew that the Lord would send somebody to save me," Joel told Phil. "Psalm 46:1 says, '*God is our refuge and strength, a very present help in trouble.*'"

The smile fell from Suave's face.

"Okay." Phil shifted uncomfortably, glancing over at Suave with raised eyebrows. "Well, uh, you take care of yourself now."

Joel nodded his head and walked away toward the truck.

"That's a special young man you have there," Phil said.

Suave looked at his former enemy. "I'm still not too sure why you did it."

"According to Joel, it was orchestrated by God." Phil chuckled, and Suave sucked his teeth.

"But as I said before, I don't hurt children. I have a son around Joel's age." Phil made eye contact with Suave. "King Kong and Saddam went too far this time. Plus, I'm tired of the game. It's time to get out."

"I hear you, man. Maximum respect for what you did."

"Once King Kong and Saddam realize what I did, they'll flip," Phil replied. "I'm supposed to be watching your son while they take care of business. But I knew it was the right thing to do."

"I transferred the money to your account."

"Yes, I know. That and what I have stashed away for a day like this should be enough for me to leave Jamaica and disappear for good."

"All the best," Suave told him. "If there's anything I can help you with in the future, let me know. I really mean that."

As Joel did earlier, Suave stretched out his right hand to Phil. Phil looked at it for a few seconds, chuckled, and then grasped it for a firm handshake. An unspoken understanding passed between the two unlikely allies.

"Oh, my baby is back! I love you so much." Nadine stood on tiptoes placing kisses all over Joel's face. "Thank you, Lord." Kisses kisses kisses. "I give you all the glory, Lord!" More kisses.

Suave rolled his eyes as he stood on the veranda, watching Nadine's reunion with their son. "Thank you,

Lord," he mimicked under his breath, disgusted that once again, God was getting credit for something He didn't do. "Makes me sick to my stomach."

As Nadine and her husband fawned over Joel, celebrating his return and giving God praise, Suave walked out to the truck parked in their driveway.

"Nadine is very happy." Daddy Lizard crossed his arms, his back braced against the truck, grinning at Suave.

"Yeah, and giving God all the thanks," Suave said dryly, his back turned toward the house. The men continued talking in hushed tones for a few minutes, making plans on how to get back at King Kong and Saddam for killing Cobra and kidnapping Joel.

"We have to teach them a lesson they will never forget," Suave said through his teeth.

"Hey, Nadine is coming our way, and she's not looking happy anymore," Daddy Lizard whispered.

Suave turned around to face Nadine and said, "So Joel is back home safe and sound."

"And I intend to keep it that way," she snapped. "I want you to stay away from my son!"

"Excuse me?" Suave looked at Nadine as if she had lost her mind. "*Your* son? He's *my* son too."

"I'll be in the truck," Daddy Lizard mumbled. He opened the door and hopped in, pulling it shut.

"You caused all this," Nadine yelled, spit spraying Suave's face. "You could have gotten Joel killed." Tears filled her eyes. "I don't want him around you and your dirty lifestyle."

Suave briefly closed his eyes in frustration, trying to curb his anger. "Listen, just calm down and take it easy, okay?"

"Don't tell me to calm down." Nadine pointed her finger into Suave's face. "My son was kidnapped by your drug-feuding enemies. Michael and I don't want you around Joel."

Suave stepped even closer, bending slightly until he was nose to nose with his son's irate mother. "If you think you and that bootlegged deacon boy can keep me away from my son, you better think again. You robbed me of the first four years of his life—wasn't that enough for you?"

Nadine's head snapped back like she had been slapped. She still felt guilty at times for having kept Joel away from his father for all those years. "That was then, and this is now." She refused to back down on her decision. "You are endangering Joel's life, and we have to protect him."

An ugly grin crept up on Suave's face, his eyes blazing fire. "We'll see about that. I dare you to try to keep my son away from me." With that said, he turned around and marched over to the passenger side of the truck. Suave tugged the door open, then paused to glare at Nadine one last time before he got in and slammed the door shut.

Daddy Lizard started the vehicle in silence and began reversing out of the driveway onto the street, the truck's headlights washing over a furious Nadine.

Chapter Thirty-eight

Suave stormed into the house he shared with Monica and their kids as Daddy Lizard drove off. It was almost 2:00 a.m., and he was mad, hungry, and . . . well, mad. An eerie quietness greeted him as he entered the living room. Certainly, Monica was only kidding when she said she was leaving . . . wasn't she?

He entered their bedroom, and the empty king-sized bed was neatly spread with one pillow in the middle. His heart racing, he moved to the closet and pulled it open. Only his clothes were hanging in there. Still unable to believe what he was seeing, Suave rushed into his son's room and began opening one dresser drawer after the other . . . to find them all empty. His daughter's room was the same. Monica had taken the kids and left him.

His chest rising and falling, Suave closed his eyes as he rubbed the center of his forehead. It felt like his head was about to split in two. "I can't do this," he muttered, his eyes filling with tears. "I really can't do this."

Suave walked like an old man to the master bedroom and threw himself facedown onto the bed. He had never felt so alone.

Unable to hold it back any longer, a small river began seeping from his eyes into the pillow. Soon, images of Cobra flashed into his mind like movie clips. There was a young Cobra when they were kids and going to high school. An excited Cobra when they were running drugs for Mason. A determined Cobra when he started working for Suave . . . and a dead Cobra as he lay still and powdery in his casket.

The pillow muffled the deep sobs. This wasn't Suave, the big wealthy drug lord but the wounded man who was facing one tribulation after another. And the images kept coming. Joel being kidnapped, Monica leaving with the children, Detective Bird questioning him about Danny's death, and Nadine vowing to keep Joel from him. Just then, the images were replaced by "The Voice." The one that Suave was now used to but least wanted to hear.

"I'm here for you, my son," said the Lord. *"Come to me."*

Suave's bawling increased, his body shaking at the intensity of his pain.

"You will find peace with me, my child. Come home, Suave."

Suave ignored Him as he usually did, crying himself into an exhausted sleep.

The sound seemed far off, but then it got louder and louder. Still sleepy and tired, Suave rolled over onto his back, yawning and stretching. The buzzer rang nonstop throughout the house. Puzzled, Suave glanced up at the clock mounted on the wall. It was 6:00 a.m. "Who the—"

The buzzer went on and on as if someone had their finger stuck on it.

Suave swore under his breath as he pushed himself off the bed, still in the clothes he wore the day before and his sneakers on his feet. He staggered a little when he stood up. His head hurt like crazy. "I'm coming!" he yelled when the buzzer continued singing. "This better be important!"

Suave marched into the living room and peeked around the curtain to see the veranda. His heart leaped in his chest when he saw that Detective Bird had the nerve to come to his house early in the morning and wake him up. "That two-faced rat."

Unclasping the lock on the front door, Suave pulled it opened and stepped out on the veranda, wrinkled clothes and all. "What do you want?" he yelled.

Detective Bird smiled cynically through the grill. "Good morning, Suave. I'm glad you're home." He looked off to the side and made a signal with his hand. Out of nowhere, four uniformed officers appeared at his side.

Suave's mouth opened wide when the officers pulled their guns on him. "What's this?" He looked at Detective Bird for an explanation.

"You're under arrest for the murder of Danny Moore."

"You're out of your mind." Suave took two steps back.

"Don't move," Detective Bird warned, his gun now pointed at Suave. "Please come and open the burglar bars right now and let us in. We don't want to hurt you, Suave." But the look on Detective Bird's face was almost begging Suave to move so he could take a shot at him.

"Detective Bird is on King Kong's payroll and has been for years." Phil's words filled Suave's head. He knew Detective Bird arresting him now was King Kong's doing. No doubt King Kong had now realized that Joel was rescued, and he wanted to put some pressure on Suave by using the dirty police officer.

"All right." Suave held up both hands in the air. "I don't want any trouble." *I need to play it cool and bide my time.*

"Wise decision." Detective Bird looked disappointed. He would have preferred to kill Suave and later justify his actions. But there were four other officers on the scene, meaning four witnesses. "Let us in now."

"The keys are inside." Suave still had his hands in the air. "I need to go get them," he said, anger and hatred spilling out of his eyes.

Detective Bird sucked his teeth loudly. "Go get them and come right back. We have the house surrounded, so don't even think about trying to run."

Suave nodded and walked backward, still facing the detective and the officers until he got to the door. He went inside and rushed into the kitchen. Peeping through the window into the backyard, he glimpsed two armed, uniformed officers. Detective Bird wasn't kidding. He did have the house surrounded.

Suave entered the bedroom and saw his cell phone on the bed. He grabbed it and noticed that the battery was almost dead. He quickly dialed Daddy Lizard's number. "I'm surrounded by pigs," he said when Daddy Lizard answered in a sluggish voice. "And the rat is heading the operation. Contact our lawyer and have him meet me at the station as soon as possible." Suave flipped the phone closed and threw it back down on the bed. He grabbed his keys off the dresser, then walked out the front door to the veranda, pulling it shut behind him.

"Took you long enough," Detective Bird snapped, a scowl on his face.

Suave ignored him and walked up to the grill. He unlocked it and pulled it open.

"Hands on your head!" Detective Bird yelled in total exaggeration. "Don't move! Turn around!"

Suave did as he was told. His hands were roughly twisted behind his back, pain shooting up his arm before the handcuffs were on him. But Suave said nothing as he was shoved down the steps and out onto the street.

"Watch your head," Detective Bird screamed as he jostled Suave into the back of his police car. "You comfy?" he asked before he closed the door.

"Like a king," Suave replied.

Detective Bird stared at him for a few seconds.

"I would like another officer to ride with us to the station, please," Suave said loudly through the opened window for the police officers close by to hear him. He didn't want to ride alone with Detective Bird.

Detective Bird chuckled a little nervously as he peered at Suave, trying to figure out why he made that request. However, Suave just looked straight-ahead, refusing to meet his stare.

As Suave requested, with a uniformed officer riding beside him, Detective Bird kept looking into the rearview mirror at Suave in the backseat. He noticed that Suave didn't seem nervous at all. The guy was just charged with murder, and he wasn't ranting and raving. *What's he up to?* Detective Bird pondered. *Did he find out about King Kong and me?* He shifted uncomfortably in his seat.

The handcuffs were almost cutting off the circulation in Suave's hands that were still crammed behind him. He felt Detective Bird stealing glances at him, but he kept his face turned toward the window. On the outside, he appeared calm, but on the inside, Suave was a little worried. He had been brought in for questioning on drug-related matters before, but never for murder. It was even stickier when the arresting officer was dirty and was being paid and directed by his worst enemy. *I have to be careful on this one. I can't let this dirty cop and King Kong frame me for murder.*

Upon arrival at the Half Way Tree Police Station, Suave was taken to the same dingy interrogation room that he and Daddy Lizard were questioned in before. Detective Bird removed the handcuffs and shoved Suave down into the rocky metal chair.

"Here we are again," Detective Bird said from his chair across the table. "I told you that you'd be back soon." He grinned at Suave.

Suave kept his head down, and his mouth shut.

"Oh, you're silent now." Detective Bird threw his head back and laughed. "The big rich, mighty Suave is scared."

Suave remained mute.

"Okay, let me start the conversation." He leaned forward, his gaze fixed on Suave. "As I stated before, you are under arrest for the murder of Danny Moore. And this time, we have enough evidence to put you away for life."

"What evidence?" Suave replied before he could stop himself.

"Now, he speaks." The detective smirked. "For starters, we found an engraved gold watch under the seat of Danny's car with your name on it. It broke when you were cutting his throat open."

"You're crazy." But Suave was getting a little nervous. King Kong may be hurting a little financially since that robbery in Spanish Town, but his pocket was still deep. And when combined with Queen Bee's, it was even deeper and big enough to fabricate evidence against him. "I didn't kill Danny, so that so-called watch isn't mine."

"Blood samples were collected at the murder scene and are being analyzed as we speak," Detective Bird continued as if Suave hadn't spoken. "I have a strong feeling we're going to find your blood as well."

Suave felt the perspiration on his face and down his back. Things were going from bad to worse.

"No more comments?" Detective Bird asked. "Why don't you just confess to the murder and make it easy for everyone?"

Suave glared at him. "I don't have anything else to say until I speak with my lawyer."

"Your lawyer? You think a lawyer can get you off this one?"

Suave shouted, "I know I don't have to speak with you if I request my lawyer."

Detective Bird's chest rose and fell in fury. Things were about to get very complicated, and he was caught in the middle. He knew the chance he was taking when he accepted King Kong's bribe so many years ago, but a brother had to live. His little meager police salary was a joke. He risked his life every day to serve and protect his country, but he could barely afford to pay his bills. On the other hand, the drug lords like Suave and King Kong broke the law every day, and they owned businesses, lived in mansions, drove luxury cars, and got richer and richer by the minute. Why shouldn't he get a slice of the pie too?

"I want my lawyer," Suave repeated, snapping back the detective's attention to him. "Are you going to deny me my rights too?" His eyes challenged Detective Bird.

Detective Bird's mind was running like a choo-choo train, Suave's words ringing in his ears: *Are you going to deny me my rights too?*

What did he mean by "too"? Does Suave know more than he's letting on? "I'm going to book you now and take you to the holding cell. We'll get you if and when your lawyer gets here."

Suave's Rolex watch, diamond-studded chain, and a few hundred dollars that he had in his pockets were taken and bagged, after which he was fingerprinted, and his mug shot taken. He was then led to a holding cell where eight other men were. The small room stank from the body odors, vomit, stale urine, and other unnamed substances littering the floor.

But Suave stepped inside the cell as if he were entering a five-star hotel. He went around the room, bumping fists with all the men. "Respect, my brother," he said to the big burly beast sitting on the floor. "How is it going, man?" he directed to the mean-looking man eyeing him with skepticism. This won over the men and before long, Suave got a space to sit on the bench and was conversing with the men like they were all old friends.

However, as the minutes ran into hours, Suave began to get impatient. What was taking his lawyer so long? He was certainly paying the overpriced man enough. "I'm going to fire his lazy behind," he muttered angrily.

"Suave Brown," a police officer called out, keys dangling from his hand.

Suave jumped up and hurried over to him.

"Your lawyer is here."

Suave felt relieved. "Finally." He waved to the other men.

"Turn around and put your hands behind your back." The officer opened the cell, handcuffed Suave, and led him back to the depressing room where his lawyer sat in the chair vacated by Detective Bird.

"I see you took your time," Suave said as the handcuffs were being removed, and he sat across from his lawyer.

"Hello, Suave," Mr. Gold replied as the officer exited the room, leaving him alone with his client. "I got here as soon as I could."

Suave breathed through his mouth. He had to remain cool so he could get out of here. "I'm being charged with murder. Do you know that?"

Mr. Gold waved his hand as if it were a minor traffic violation. "I spoke with Detective Bird. Anyone could buy a watch and engrave your name on it. That's not enough evidence to hold you for murder."

"What about my blood that was supposedly at the crime scene?"

"Now *that* may be a problem for you. But they haven't gotten back the results on that as yet. I can get you bail until then."

"*Until then?*" Suave snapped, leaning toward the lawyer. "I didn't kill Danny, so my blood cannot be at that crime scene. Someone is trying to frame me."

Mr. Gold gazed at him as if to say, *Yeah, right.*

"I didn't do it," Suave repeated adamantly.

"Okay, okay. We'll cross that bridge when we get there." Mr. Gold glanced down at his expensive gold watch on his left wrist. "I'm going to see if I can get a bail hearing for you tomorrow."

"*Tomorrow?* I have to stay here until tomorrow?" Suave looked at him like he was Big Foot.

Mr. Gold nodded. "And that's because I know the prosecutor and have a connection that I'm going to tap into. It usually takes between forty-eight to seventy-two hours for you to get a bail hearing."

Suave closed his eyes in frustration. He hadn't showered or had a decent meal in over twenty-four hours. And he was so tired that he felt like he would fall over any minute.

"Also, I assume money is not a problem?" Mr. Gold peered at Suave over the bifocals sitting on his little crooked nose. "A bail hearing doesn't guarantee you'll get bail."

"It always comes back to the almighty dollar, doesn't it?" Suave smiled cynically. "No, money is not an issue. Do what you have to so I can get out of here."

Mr. Gold clapped his hands in glee, a big grin now on his face, neon dollar signs flashing in his eyes. "You got it!"

Suave looked at him and shook his head. "Is Daddy Lizard here?"

"He's outside. They won't allow him back here to see you, though."

"Okay, ask him to call Monica at her parents and see if she and the kids are okay. Also, he should keep this thing on the down low."

Mr. Gold bobbed his head and jumped to his feet. "All right, let me see about getting you out of here."

Suave replied, "Cool. Listen . . ." But Mr. Gold was already rushing through the door without a backward glance at him. *I need another lawyer,* Suave brooded. *My life depends on it.*

"All you need is me."

Surprised, Suave spun around on the chair. But no one was there. He turned his head to the left, then the right, his eyes traveling all over the room, but he was the only person there. "This stress is getting to me." He shook his head and winced at the sharp pain that sprinted across his forehead.

"Come to me, my son, and I'll give you rest."

"Here we go again." Suave chuckled dryly. "You want to give me rest, huh?"

"In me you will find peace, my child."

Suave leaped to his feet, the unbalanced chair crashing to the dirty floor. "I'm *not* your child! Leave me alone!"

"What's going on in here?" a police officer asked as he entered the room, his hand on the gun on his waist. "Is there a problem, sir?"

Suave inhaled deeply and exhaled, unfolding his fists as he tried to get ahold of his anger. "No, there is no problem," he said, his voice shaking a little. But his nerves were still on edge. Whether or not he wanted it, "The Voice" was slowly but surely getting to him.

Chapter Thirty-nine

"Your Honor, the supposed evidence that the police have is a watch with my client's name on it," Mr. Gold informed the judge. "Anyone, including the real killer, could have bought that watch, engraved Mr. Brown's name on it, and dropped it at the crime scene."

"Your Honor, the police collected drops of blood from the backseat of the victim's car that we believe is from the killer," the prosecutor replied. "We believe that this will be a match with Mr. Brown."

"*We believe?* Your Honor, this man was arrested for first-degree murder. The police need hard cold facts for this serious charge."

"Your Honor—"

The judge held up a hand, cutting off the prosecutor. "Mr. Newman, did the blood analysis report note that it was Mr. Brown's blood in the victim's car?" He looked pointedly at the prosecutor.

"Well, hmmm, we haven't gotten back the report as yet, sir."

"Your Honor, in that case, I demand that my client be granted bail," Mr. Gold remarked.

"Sir, Mr. Brown is a very wealthy man. If he's granted bail, he can flee the country, and we will never see him again." Mr. Newman glanced over at Suave, sitting at the table.

"Mr. Brown is the father of eight children, all of whom are living here in Jamaica," Mr. Gold told the judge. "He also owns many businesses all over the country and has no intention of running anywhere. Sir, not only does my client have strong ties in this country, but he is innocent and is eager to have his day in court so he can clear his good name."

The judge glanced over at Suave. "I have to agree with the defense. The police don't have enough evidence to hold Mr. Brown for first-degree murder. Until the blood analysis report comes back and positively states that it is Mr. Brown's blood at the crime scene, I think he is entitled to bail."

Suave's heart flew to his throat, and his breathing became irregular as he gripped the edge of the table. He was getting bail!

"The defendant should hand over his passport to the court and be warned not to leave the country. Bail is granted in the amount of $200,000." The judge pounded his gavel.

Happiness filled Suave's eyes. He got bail.

"Congratulations, Mr. Brown. You got bail." Mr. Gold held out his right hand to Suave.

Suave stood to his feet and shook his lawyer's hand. "Thank you. Good job up there."

Mr. Gold smiled, glanced around the courtroom from the corners of his eyes, before leaning in close to Suave's ear. "We owe Mr. Newman $50,000," he whispered, "and the judge another $50,000."

"Mr. Newman?" Suave looked perplexed. "The man was fighting for me *not* to get bail."

Mr. Gold glanced around again, noticing that the courtroom was almost empty. "He had to make it look convincing," he told Suave in a very low voice. "But everything was already set before we came here." He winked with a big lopsided grin on his face.

Suave snickered, shaking his head. "I see. Get with Daddy Lizard, and he'll arrange everything with my accountant for the bail and the other fees."

"And remember mine too," Mr. Gold added quickly. "That will only be $50,000. I'm giving you a huge discount." He nudged Suave playfully with his elbow and chuckled.

"Of course." Suave's smile didn't reach his eyes. "I want out of this place today. It's Friday, and I don't want to spend the day here. Make it happen."

"Whoa, slow down, man." Daddy Lizard watched as Suave shoveled rice and peas and brown stew chicken into his mouth. "We don't want you to choke."

Suave ignored him, licking and smacking his lips, barely chewing as he brought one big spoonful of the delicious food after the other to his mouth. A brother was starved.

"Okay. At least you no longer smell like rotten eggs." Daddy Lizard looked at Suave's new red and white sweat suit and the brand-new white sneakers and white socks on his feet.

"I have to get a new lawyer." Concern etched across Suave's face. "I need the best, or I'll be going to prison for something I didn't do."

"Alwayne Clark is the best," Daddy Lizard replied. "But I don't think he's going to take your case."

"Uh-huh." Suave gazed out the window, deep in thought.

Alwayne Clark was one of Jamaica's top lawyers with a reputation for winning all his cases. Prosecutors feared him, and other defense lawyers respected him. With clients from all fourteen parishes seeking his representation, his calendar was always fully booked, and he was also very selective. As a result, many people got turned away, including Suave when he went to see him a few years ago. Alwayne had refused to represent drug dealers.

Suave was shocked. There was actually a lawyer who was turning him down. This was a first because he had lawyers competing for his business. But Suave wanted the best, and that was Alwayne Clark.

However, Alwayne had looked at Suave like he was a rodent peeing on his shiny gentleman's shoes.

"I doubt he'll change his mind," said Daddy Lizard, recapturing Suave's attention. "That brother is as straight as water bamboo."

"Gold can't handle a murder case, and the only thing he cares about is money." Suave turned in his seat to look at Daddy Lizard. "I tolerated him because we never had any serious legal issues. But this is do or die. King Kong and Queen Bee are trying to frame me for murder. I need Alwayne Clark at any cost."

"What are you going to do?" Daddy Lizard asked.

"I'm going to see him again," Suave announced, wiping his mouth with a paper napkin.

"Clark? Suave, you know you will *never* get an appointment with him."

Suave gulped down some of the D&G Ginger Beer, burping loudly. "I said I was going to *see* him, not make an appointment."

Daddy Lizard looked at him with apprehension. "I don't think that's a good idea. He might call the cops, and you don't need any more trouble."

"That's a chance I'm willing to take." Suave got up and walked into the kitchen with the empty food container and soft drink. He turned the bottle to its head, finishing off the drink, and then threw both items in the garbage bin.

"Let's go!" Suave moved toward the garage, leaving Daddy Lizard to follow him. Soon, they were on their way to Constant Spring Road, where Alwayne Clark's office was located.

Suave strolled toward the office. Desperate times called for desperate measures, and he was desperate. He walked up to the front door, peeped through the glass at the top, and saw a middle-aged lady tapping away on a computer keyboard. He turned the handle on the door, but it didn't budge.

"Hello," Suave tapped on the door.

The lady looked up and pointed at her watch and resumed typing on the computer.

Suave knocked again, a little harder this time, but not enough to create alarm.

Clearly frustrated at being interrupted, the woman stood and walked to the door. "We are closed, sir," she shouted through the glass.

Suave flashed his signature dimpled grin that always had a profound effect on the ladies. "I just want to ask you a question." He pointed to the lock on the door.

The woman hesitated for a few seconds. Then she unlocked the door. "How may I help you?"

"Hello, I'm Suave Brown. I was wondering if I could speak with Mr. Clark. I just need five minutes."

"I'm Evelyn, Mr. Clark's assistant. He doesn't have any more appointments for the day, sir. Please call Monday morning, and I'll check his availability."

"Is he here?" Suave asked, glancing over her head into the office.

Evelyn shook her head. "I'm sorry, you'll—hey!"

Suave moved around her and entered the office. With determined steps, he walked through the elegantly furnished reception area toward a deep voice coming from somewhere in the back. It was the voice that he wanted to represent him on this murder case.

"Mama, I'm wrapping up now, and I'll be there soon," said Alwayne Clark into the telephone he held to his ear. "As a matter of fact . . ." he paused as Suave entered his office.

"I'm so sorry, Mr. Clark." A flustered Evelyn rushed into the office behind Suave. "I told him you weren't available, but he forced himself in anyway."

"Mama, I have to go, but I'll see you soon." Alwayne glared at Suave. "I promise I won't be late. I love you." Alwayne hung up the phone, his eyes shooting daggers at Suave.

"Sir, do you want me to call the police?" Evelyn asked.

"Mr. Clark, that won't be necessary," Suave said respectfully. "I promise I just need a few minutes. Please." His eyes pleaded with Alwayne.

"Sir?" Evelyn stared at Alwayne for confirmation.

Alwayne took a deep breath, still locking eyes with Suave. "It's okay, Evelyn. He won't be staying long."

"I'll be right outside." Evelyn's remark was more directed to Suave than her boss. She gave Suave a dirty look before exiting the office, closing the door behind her.

"Thank you." Suave's voice was filled with gratitude. "I promise—"

"Don't you ever force your way into my office again." Alwayne was livid. "You may be able to intimidate other people, but not me."

This wasn't going too well for Suave. The last thing he wanted was to piss off Alwayne. "I'm sorry, but I knew there was no other way you would see me," Suave explained. "I'm in a lot of trouble, and I need your help."

"If I recall correctly, I had already told you that I don't want your business."

"This is different," Suave replied. He lowered himself into the chair across from Alwayne without an invitation. "I'm fighting for my life here."

"Don't even bother to sit down." Alwayne pointed his index finger at Suave. "I'm leaving in a minute." He stood up.

"I'm being charged with first-degree murder," Suave blurted out, standing to his feet as well.

Alwayne's eyebrows shot up. "Wow. You did it this time, huh?"

"I'm a lot of things, but I'm not a murderer." Just then, an image of Pastor Ralph dying popped up in Suave's mind. "Well, there was that one time—" He stopped when Alwayne held up his hand.

"I'm not your attorney, Mr. Brown. So be careful what you say to me."

"All I'm saying is that I didn't kill Danny Moore. I'm being set up, and I need your help," Suave begged. "I need someone like you to help me beat these charges."

"You may be innocent of these charges, but there is nothing innocent about your lifestyle. No, no." Alwayne put up his hand when Suave opened his mouth to speak. "I can't represent you. But what I'll do since you are so persistent is to give you the telephone number for a colleague of mine. She's very good."

Suave sighed in disappointment. "Fine, I'll give her a call. Can you do me a favor?"

"What is it?"

"Can you think about it?"

"And I want you to think about something," Alwayne said seriously. "If you ever beat these charges, get out of the drug-dealing business. You stated that you're a wealthy man, so get out before it kills you, or you end up in prison for the rest of your life." He held out a business card to Suave.

Suave took the card. "Thanks. But don't be surprised if I show up again." He walked out to the reception area, ignored Evelyn shooting daggers at him, and headed toward the front door.

As Suave pushed the door open and stepped outside, he collided with a young lady who stumbled but kept her balance.

"Sorry," Suave remarked as he looked at her.

"Sorry," she said at the same time as Suave, looking up at him.

"You?" they both exclaimed together.

"Well, if it isn't Mr. Smooth Suave," Dupree said lightly, a little smile flirting at the corner of her mouth.

Chapter Forty

Suave stared at the stunningly beautiful young woman, noticing the long, straight hair hanging down her exposed back like a satin curtain. Her dark, smooth, flawless complexion seemed to glow. Her tall, slim, toned body was wrapped in a tight-fitted flowery dress that flirted at her knees. Long, beautiful legs were tucked into a pair of espadrilles, showing off bright red pedicure toes. But to Suave, her best feature was the flashing megawatt smile sparkling through luscious, glossy lips. It was one thing he remembered clearly about the innocent young woman that he had betrayed in the worst possible way. Suave hung his head in shame.

Dupree peered at Suave's lowered head and felt compassion instead of anger. Seven years ago, this man had presented himself to Dupree as an educated, twenty-three-year-old sales representative who had graduated from the University of Technology, the same college she was attending at that time. Being the naïve country girl that she was, Dupree fell hard for Suave after he wined and dined her. But everything came crashing down one dreadful night when she had too much to drink, and Suave used the opportunity to rob her of her virginity. Dupree felt even more betrayed when Suave admitted that he was actually thirty-four years old, had eight children with six baby mommas, and the only thing he sold was illegal drugs. He didn't love Dupree. He only wanted to sleep with her.

It was a very tough time in Dupree's already-complicated personal life. For a long time, she was angry at the man who betrayed her. But just as she had learned to forgive the mother who abandoned her as a child, and the father who never acknowledged her most of her life, Dupree had also forgiven Suave. It took awhile, but standing here in front of him now confirmed what Dupree already knew in her heart.

"How are you?" Dupree asked brightly, displaying those pearly whites.

Suave's head snapped up, and he briefly glanced at her. She was actually smiling at him. "I'm . . . I'm . . . I'm, well, hanging in there," he mumbled. Feeling like a centipede crawling on its belly, Suave looked everywhere *but* at Dupree. This was the first woman Suave had ever felt like he had forced himself on. Something that had angered him after the incident but had quickly slipped his mind as he continued to build his drug empire.

"You look well," Dupree commented.

"Thank you." Suave took a deep breath before he finally made eye contact with her. "I'm sorry," he said. "I'm not sure why you're smiling instead of screaming at me, but I'm sorry. What I did to you was really messed up."

"Yes, it was," Dupree replied. "But I forgive you, and I've moved on with my life. God has been very good to me."

Suave shifted uncomfortably on his feet. This was something he remembered too. Dupree was a church girl, and obviously, she still was. "Hmmm . . . Did you go away to New York as you wanted?"

"Yes. I've completed my undergraduate and graduate studies at NYU. I'll be taking the CPA exam in a few weeks to become a certified public accountant. Isn't God amazing?"

Suave didn't respond.

"I'm here for my little brothers' fifth birthday party," Dupree continued happily. "They're twins."

Suave nodded politely but didn't say a word.

"So, you just had a meeting with Uncle Alwayne?" Dupree broke the uncomfortable silence.

"Yes."

"Didn't go well?" Dupree pressed.

"No, it didn't. But that's cool." Suave was ashamed to elaborate.

"It doesn't look 'cool' to me."

"I'm being charged with first-degree murder, and your uncle refused to take my case." Suave looked shocked that the words had actually left his mouth.

Dupree's mouth popped open, and her eyes widened in surprise. "Murder? That's very serious."

"I didn't do it. I know you'll probably find it hard to believe me, but I'm innocent of these charges."

Dupree nodded. "Suave, you need to turn this over to the Lord." She took a step closer, her eyes locked on his. "This is very serious, but I know God will see you through."

"I don't do God," Suave snapped. "If it's left to Him, I'll rot in prison for the rest of my life."

Dupree stepped back as if slapped. Her mouth opened, but no words came out.

Suave laughed at her expression. "God doesn't help people like me. He's more partial to those like you."

"That's not true at all," she finally spoke. "God loves all of us the same. He loves you just as much as He loves me, Suave."

"Listen, I don't mean any disrespect, but I have to go." Suave held out his right hand to Dupree. "Again, I'm sorry for the way I hurt you, and I'm glad you have forgiven me."

Dupree left Suave's hand hanging and said, "What if I talk to Uncle Alwayne for you?"

Now it was Suave's mouth that popped open. "You would do that for me?"

She nodded her head. "On one condition, though. No—hear me out," she said as Suave was about to speak. "Auntie Annette, Uncle Alwayne's wife, is at my mom's house. She was supposed to come and get Uncle Alwayne to take him to the party as she drove them into town today, but I volunteered." Dupree grinned. "Now, I know this was all a part of God's plan."

Suave mumbled under his breath, "His plan to ruin my life more than He's already done."

"I didn't hear that, and I'm going to ignore it. But here is what I propose—ready?" Dupree scrutinized him.

Suave shrugged his shoulders. "Let's hear it."

"I'll ask Uncle Alwayne to reconsider representing you on this case, if you, in turn, will attend Men's Fellowship and church with him for a few months."

"Oh no!" Suave was outraged. "Church? Me? I'd rather go to prison."

"Okay. At least I tried," Dupree replied chirpily. "Well, it was good seeing you again, Suave."

"'Seeing you again'?" Alwayne said as he exited the office to stand beside Dupree. "You know him?" He turned to glare at Suave before he even got the confirmation from his niece. Suave was bad news, and if Dupree knew him, then he must have tried to be fresh with her.

"Hi, Uncle Alwayne." Dupree reached out and hugged her adopted uncle. "Auntie Annette sent me to pick you up." She grinned at him.

"Hi, baby girl. Yes, she just called and told me." Alwayne returned the hug affectionately. "You know this man?" he repeated after he released her.

Suave felt the fear creep up on him. Not only because he feared any physical altercation with Alwayne, but he was still hoping Alwayne would change his mind and take his case. If Dupree told her uncle what he did, Suave could kiss that goodbye. In fact, Alwayne would probably make sure none of the reputable lawyers in Jamaica took his case.

"Yes, I do," Dupree replied. "I met Suave a few years ago when I attended UTECH, but we never kept in touch."

"Did he get fresh with you?" Alwayne observed Suave keenly.

Dupree laughed softly. "Suave will be Suave, but that's all water under the bridge. Come on, let's go." Dupree grabbed onto Alwayne's arm, tugging him a little. "Goodbye, Suave. I wish you all the best with everything."

Alwayne gave Suave another sharp look before he allowed Dupree to pull him toward the car parked a few feet away.

"Wait!"

Dupree and Alwayne turned around to look at Suave as he walked up to them. "I . . . I should probably, you know, give it a try."

"Suave, that's wonderful!" Dupree exclaimed. "Trust me. You have nothing to lose and everything to gain."

Suave wasn't too sure about that. But attending church for a few months versus going to prison for life? There wasn't much of a choice, although he had said differently moments before.

"What's going on?" Alwayne peered from Dupree to Suave.

Dupree took a deep breath and turned to face him. "Uncle Alwayne, you are going to represent Suave on his murder case, and, in return, Suave is going to be attending Men's Fellowship and church with you for a few months."

Alwayne looked at Dupree as if she were joking, but her face said otherwise. "I don't think so, sweetheart. Sorry, but I can't do that."

"Yes, you can," she persisted. "You are a child of God, and it's your responsibility to bring sinners to Christ. I know in my heart that God brought Suave to you so you could help change his life around."

"Oh, his life will change all right . . . when he goes to prison for life."

"Uncle Alwayne!"

"Okay." Alwayne held up his hands. "I guess I shouldn't have said that." He looked over at Suave. "Sorry, that was uncalled for."

"That's cool, man," Suave replied, feeling hopeful as Dupree went to bat for him. After everything he had done to her, she was still trying to help him. Wow.

"But I still don't think I'm the right person to take his case," Alwayne informed Dupree. "I gave him the number for a colleague of mine. She's a very good attorney."

"God didn't choose your colleague to bring Suave into His fold. He chose you, Uncle Alwayne." Dupree took ahold of Alwayne's hand. "Do you think it's a coincidence that I'm here now? Why Suave is so persistent that you represent him? Everything adds up. Don't you see?"

Alwayne took a deep breath, glancing back and forth between Dupree and Suave.

"Do you want me to run it by Aunt Madge and Mama Pearl for their opinion?" Dupree smiled too sweetly at Alwayne.

"What?" Alwayne gave Dupree a fake glare. "Little traitor," he said, smiling at her. "This Sunday, your aunt and I are going to a church rally in Westmoreland. How about I meet with Mr. Brown on Monday, 9:00 a.m. sharp, and we can go from there?"

"Yeah!" Dupree hugged her uncle again. "Thank you, Uncle Alwayne." She pulled back and looked him in the eyes. "If there is anyone who can introduce Suave to the true and living God, it's you."

"Ahem." Suave let his presence be known after being silent all this time. Both Dupree and Alwayne looked over at him. "I just want to thank you, Mr. Clark, for agreeing to meet with me. I have some hope now that you are on my case."

"You should be thanking Dupree. And don't forget, we have a deal. The minute you break it, our arrangement is done. Got it?"

"Got it." Suave nodded his head quickly. "Thanks, Dupree. You are really an amazing woman."

Suave's dimples were flashing like the siren on an ambulance. He stood and watched as Dupree reversed out of the parking spot, honked the horn, and drove away. "Yes! Yes!" Suave pumped his fists excitedly into the air. "I got Alwayne Clark."

"And I've got you too, my son. Right here in the palm of my hand."

"No no no." Suave shook his head. "I'm not doing this with you right now." He put his hands over his ears, shaking his head and walking around in circles. "This was all Dupree, not you."

"I assume things went well with Mr. Clark?" Daddy Lizard's face was filled with concern. "I saw you smiling. I thought . . ." he tapered off when he noticed the smug look on Suave's face. Gone was Crazy Suave, replaced by Smooth Suave.

"I'll be meeting with Mr. Clark at nine o'clock on Monday morning." Suave tugged on the collar of his blazer, straightening it up, his head held upright as if he were the man.

"What? You actually pulled it off?" Daddy Lizard laughed loudly and gave Suave a man hug. "You are one lucky devil."

Chapter Forty-one

"I-I-I didn't expect to see you," Pat stuttered after opening his front door to find Suave standing there. "Why didn't you call?" He peeped over Suave's shoulder into the yard. His eyes were wandering all over the place, avoiding contact with Suave's.

"I just left the gym and had to take care of something in the area," Suave responded casually, patting the gym bag he had over his shoulder. "I'm not staying. But it has been awhile since I've seen you, so I'm just touching base."

Pat laughed uneasily. "Okay, come on in. I'm running out myself in a minute." He moved aside so Suave could enter the house.

Suave strolled into the living room, sat on the couch, his bag at his feet, and crossed his legs. "How's my girl, Queen Bee?" he asked when Pat joined him, perching on the edge of the other couch like a pigeon.

"She's good." Pat's high-pitched voice sounded like a Chihuahua with a cold.

"I haven't checked in with her in a while because I had to take care of some personal issues." Suave smiled at Pat. "You know how it is."

Pat nodded his head. "Can I get you anything to drink?"

"No, I'll help myself." Suave quickly stood up and walked over to the wine rack in the corner of the room. He selected a quart of Appleton Jamaica Rum and headed to the kitchen before Pat could say a word.

Suave noticed a deep freezer beside the refrigerator. He opened the freezer, looked inside, and saw that it was packed with cold cuts of meat. *That little sissy surely loves to cook.* He closed the freezer and took out the orange juice from the bottom of the refrigerator.

Suave grabbed two glasses, practically filling one with rum and just a little touch of orange juice. The other glass was almost filled with orange juice and a tiny drop of rum.

"Here you go." Suave handed Pat his glass before he took a seat.

Pat took a big gulp of his drink, his eyes watering as the rum burned his throat. "Whoa, this is strong."

Suave took a sip of his orange juice, making a face and smacking his lips. "Yes, I did let the rum get away from me." He laughed out loud, and Pat joined in.

"Listen," Suave leaned forward on the couch, "I realized I hadn't been the nicest person to you over the years," sympathy filled Suave's eyes, "but I've been fighting some demons most of my life . . . and . . . and . . ." Suave choked up, lowering his head to the floor as if consumed by grief and shame. *Where was the Oscar Award for this performance?*

"It's all good, Suave," Pat responded. "You haven't done anything that I wasn't used to."

Suave felt sick to his stomach. While he was trying to exorcise his demons, Pat was fulfilling a sick fantasy. However, Suave had to keep the performance going. "Let me make us another round."

Pat finished off what was left in his glass, burping loudly. "Excuse me." He giggled, slouching on the couch.

Suave took the glass to the kitchen. Again, he prepared their drinks, dousing Pat's with the strong rum. This time, he added nothing but orange juice to his glass.

Pat almost emptied his glass in one gulp.

"So, how is business going with you and Queen Bee?" Suave asked as he relaxed back on the couch.

"Oh, we're balling." Pat was now practically lying on the couch. "In eight weeks, we're getting the biggest shipment of our lives. Hello!" He gave Suave a lopsided grin. "I call it OMG Thursday!" By now, his glassy eyes were glazed over.

"You guys aren't joking." Suave sat up straight. "I may as well just get out of the business. I can't compete with you shot callers."

Pat drunkenly laughed. "I know that's right. This deal has been in the works for a loooong time, and this is going to put us at the top!" He began to sing, *"Higher level, oh, higher level."* He had his hands in the air, waving them as high as he dared.

"Let me get us another drink," Suave remarked excitedly. This was going really well. Queen Bee is getting a big shipment in a few weeks.

After the fourth drink, Suave had all the information he needed from Pat, who was now passed out on the couch. His bladder full of all the orange juice he consumed, Suave threw his gym bag over his shoulder and went to use the bathroom.

Minutes later, Suave left Pat's house and drove off toward New Kingston with the reggae music blaring. He was now feeling better about his unfortunate circumstances. Alwayne Clark was his lawyer, and he'd gotten everything he wanted from Pat. However, he still had two big sharks and a barracuda to catch—King Kong, Queen Bee, and Detective Bird.

Suave pulled into the parking lot of the Pegasus Hotel. He glanced at his watch as he swiftly walked to the suite he had reserved.

After a quick shower and a change of clothes, he was ready for his guest. He poured himself a glass of wine while he waited. Moments later, someone knocked on the door. "Okay. Here we go," Suave muttered as he placed his drink on the small, glass table in the sitting area and went to answer the door. "Detective Stone, thank you for coming." Suave's smile wasn't returned. "Please, come inside." He stepped aside so the police officer could enter.

"I'm still not sure why I'm here," replied Detective Stone, entering the hotel suite. "However, you said you have information on a dirty cop, and that piqued my interest."

Suave closed the door. "Please have a seat." He pointed to the sitting area where two soft velvet couches faced each other.

Detective Stone sat on one of the couches.

"Can I get you a drink?" Suave asked.

"No, thanks. I'm still on duty."

"Okay. I hope you don't mind me finishing mine." Suave took his seat across from the detective, reached for his drink, and took a sip. "I know you are stationed in Spanish Town, but I'm sure you heard I was charged with the murder of Danny Moore, King Kong's business partner," Suave began.

Detective Stone nodded. "I also heard about the killing of your friend as well. My condolences to you and his family."

"Thank you. Cobra's death was a huge blow to me. He was like a brother."

"Mr. Brown, so that you know, your reputation is legendary on the streets." Detective Stone observed Suave. "I'm on one side of the law, and you are on the other side. I work twenty-four seven to put away guys like you. So not for one minute should you think that anything you are about to tell me will immune you from the law."

Suave's dimples flashed. "Whatever you have heard of me, Detective, I'm sure you have never heard that I go around killing people."

"That's true. And that's one of the reasons I'm here," Detective Stone replied. "I'm a fourth-generation cop in my family, and my badge and oath mean everything to me. It pisses me off that some police officers get greedy and go over on the other side. So, who are we talking about, and what evidence do you have to back this up?"

Suave placed the half-empty glass on the coffee table. "Well," he leaned toward the detective, "it's a very long story."

Chapter Forty-two

The next day, Suave drove to his different baby mommas' houses, picked up his six children, and little Mr. Chin, and loaded them into his truck. Missing were Raven and Rayden, who Monica took to the Bahamas. Also absent was Joel, who Nadine had forbidden to go with his father.

Suave took the children to the Hope Zoo. They started by looking at the different exotic animals, which included the zebra, spider monkey, ring-tailed coati, and the collared peccary.

"Daddy, look at the husband and wife tigers!" Alissa exclaimed, jumping up and down in excitement.

Suave laughed out loud. "Those are the African lion and lioness, sweetheart."

"Lions don't get married," Janelle informed her sister.

"Yes, they do," Alissa responded. "I saw it on TV."

Suave watched in fascination as the children debated the marriage status of the lions. "Okay, who wants a hot dog?"

"Me!" They all shouted, the debate now forgotten.

After eating tons of junk food, they all played hide-and-seek. Suave did most of the seeking, dramatically looking behind trees, bushes, benches, and flowers, pretending he couldn't find the kids even in plain sight. The children's laughter was like a song to his ears.

Later that day, with everyone safely secured in the van, Suave began dropping off the children at their various homes. At each house, he left a wad of money with the mother for his children. By the time the van was empty, Suave was exhausted but happy for the enjoyable day he had with his children.

"Great job, today," Suave said into his cell phone, looking through his rearview mirror at a black Toyota Corolla parked a few feet away with three men inside. Suave was parked outside Darlene's house after dropping off their daughter, Janelle. "You guys take a break, and make sure your replacements are at their posts."

"Yes, Boss," responded the driver of the Corolla.

Ever since Joel's kidnapping, Suave had a few of his soldiers watching each of his children around the clock. "I'm not going to let that gorilla get his hands on any more of my kids," he had told Daddy Lizard, who had agreed wholeheartedly.

As he drove home, Suave thought hard about the call that he was going to make. This would help him take care of King Kong once and for all. This could give Suave his life back. This call could change everything.

Once home, Suave called Daddy Lizard, and they talked business for a while. "I'm going to make that link now," Suave informed him. "Stop by later, and I'll bring you up to date."

"Cool. I'm going to make a few runs, then come by."

Suave hung up the phone and took out a small piece of paper from his pants pocket. It was 7:06 p.m. "So, it's actually 8:06 p.m. over there," he muttered. "Perfect timing." He started dialing the telephone number that was written on the paper.

"*Qui parle?*" asked the gruff Haitian drawl that answered the telephone. "Who speaks?"

"This is Suave in Jamaica. May I speak to Mr. Dapper?"

The line went silent, and Suave heard some mumblings in the background. Anxiously, he waited, hoping to speak to the man.

"Mr. Smooth Suave. To what do I owe this honor?" asked Toussaint Grand Jean, a.k.a. Mr. Dapper, when he came to the phone.

"The honor is all mine." Suave smiled, relieved now that he was talking to Mr. Dapper. "I'm sure you're surprised to hear from me, but I have a business proposal for you."

Mr. Dapper was silent for a few seconds. "Take this number and call me back." He rapidly recited a telephone number as Suave wrote it down, before hanging up the telephone.

Suave immediately dialed the number he was given.

"Now we can talk," Mr. Dapper said with a thick Haitian accent. "This is a very secure line. I must say I was very surprised to hear from you, my brother."

Mr. Dapper was one of Haiti's biggest drug lords, if not the biggest. He was also King Kong's and Queen Bee's main supplier. Suave knew that King Kong owed him a lot of money because of the huge stash of drugs and money that Suave had stolen from King Kong.

"As I said before, I have a business proposal for you," Suave repeated. "This will be very beneficial to both of us."

"Really now?"

"Word on the street is that a certain someone owes you a lot of money. I'm sure you are not too pleased with that."

"Word on the street is that the person who benefited from my loss is you. However, I had no dealings with you and only want what's mine."

"You know you can't believe everything you hear. But I'm in a situation."

"Yeah, I heard. Your best friend was murdered, your son was kidnapped, and you were charged with murder. That's a lot, my friend."

"And we both know who's responsible for all of that. I have a proposal that will give me back my life and you your money with a huge bonus."

"I do need my money back, which is why your friend is still alive. A dead man can't repay, right? Talk to me." Mr. Dapper was all about his money.

"Okay, so this is what I have in mind." Suave laid the business proposal on the table.

"This time, Mr. Clark is expecting you and is waiting for you in his office." Evelyn still had an attitude from the last time Suave forced his way into the office.

"Good morning, beautiful." Suave's dimples winked at Evelyn. And against her will, she blushed, rolling her eyes at him.

"You better not keep him waiting," she said in a more pleasant tone. "His schedule is tighter today because I had to squeeze you in."

"I appreciate that." Suave walked through the open door into Alwayne's office. "Good morning, Mr. Clark."

Alwayne looked up from the *Jamaica Gleaner* he was reading. "Good morning. Please close the door and have a seat." He folded the newspaper and placed it on his desk.

"How was the birthday party?" Suave asked after he took his seat.

"Wonderful. Those little boys are going to need a few more days to open all their gifts," Alwayne replied. "Their paternal grandparents, the Humphreys, took up most of the living room with just their gifts."

Suave smiled. "First grandchildren, I bet?"

"Yup. I'm telling you that Eve Humphrey is something else. But it's always great to spend time with family and friends."

"When this is over, I'm going to take all my kids on a wonderful vacation."

"How many you said you got?" Alwayne asked Suave.

"Eight. Probably nine by now." Suave sighed loudly. He had tried to call Monica repeatedly, but no one answered the telephone. He had a feeling they took the phone off the hook to avoid his calls because it just kept ringing and ringing.

"Remember what I said about getting out of the game. If not for you, then do it for your kids."

Suave nodded. "You're probably right."

"We have a lot of work to do, Mr. Brown. As you are aware, I never lose a case, and I don't intend to smear my record. First, Evelyn will be bringing you some papers to sign to seal our attorney-client relationship. She will also be going over my fee and payment schedule," Alwayne informed Suave.

"Money is not a problem," Suave assured him. "I'll pay whatever you charge to keep me from going to prison for murder."

"You'll pay the same as all my clients, Mr. Brown. Just—"

"You can call me Suave."

"All right. So that you know, I'm doing this because of our agreement which requires you to attend church with me for a few months. You break our agreement, I walk. That will be in the contract you'll be signing today." Alwayne stared pointedly at Suave.

Suave shifted uncomfortably in his chair. "Fine. I'll come to church, but so that you know, I don't want anything to do with your so-called God. I'm doing this to stay out of prison."

Alwayne chuckled lightly. "We'll see about that, Saul. Oops, I meant Suave."

Suave had no idea who Saul was, and quite frankly, he didn't care. He would show up at church so that Alwayne would show up at court. But once Suave was free, he was gone.

Someone knocked on the door. "Come in, Evelyn," Alwayne responded.

Evelyn entered with a pile of papers in her hands. She sat in the chair beside Suave. "I have a few things for you to sign, Mr. Brown." Evelyn went on to explain each document in detail.

"Do you have any questions, Suave?" Alwayne asked when Evelyn was finished.

"No, let me have those." Suave had a big smile on his face as he signed all the documents. Alwayne Clark was now officially his lawyer.

"Thanks, Evelyn," Alwayne said as she exited the room. "Now, Suave, I want you to tell me everything that you know about Danny Moore, and why the police think you murdered him." Alwayne rested back in his chair, a very serious look on his face. "And please don't leave anything out. I can't help you if you hold anything back."

Suave looked away when an image of Pat popped up in his mind. *I certainly can't tell him everything. He'll think I'm gay or some sort of freak.*

"Suave?" Alwayne leaned forward. "Why would someone frame you for murder?"

Suave swallowed loudly. "The feud between King Kong and me goes back to our childhood." Suave gave him a brief synopsis of his parents' demise, living with Pastor Ralph—but omitting the sexual abuse—and Pastor Ralph's murder. He spoke about moving in with Mason, Miss Pam, and King Kong, and being a dope boy. Suave also told Alwayne of him launching out on his own, later joined by Cobra and Daddy Lizard and of Mason's murder. "I know you don't approve of what I do, but it was all I knew."

Alwayne's heart was filled with sympathy for the young Suave. He had a feeling that Suave left out a lot of things that were probably too horrific to talk about. "You and King Kong have been feuding all this time?"

"Yeah. But things escalated when Danny and Saddam, King Kong's men, killed my best friend and right-hand man, Cobra. Then someone took out Danny, after which my oldest son, Joel, was kidnapped." Suave omitted the robberies and the fact that Saddam's grandfather was also killed.

Alwayne looked at Suave in amazement. If Suave didn't look so serious, Alwayne would have thought he was making everything up. It was like some gangster movie. "For real?"

"I know it's crazy, and I'm certainly not innocent in all this. But I swear to you I didn't kill Danny."

Alwayne didn't say anything for a few seconds. "Suave, I'm sorry for what you went through as a child. I see how this life you are now living started."

The two men talked some more about the watch and blood that were found at the crime scene.

"The watch is not an issue," Alwayne informed him. "As you said, anyone could have bought that watch, but who would have access to your DNA who is associated with King Kong? Any body fluid could be used to frame you."

Again, an image of Pat flashed before Suave. He didn't see how Pat could have gotten his DNA. They had never had sex, kissed, or exchanged body fluids. But knowing that conniving sissy, anything was possible.

"Why don't you think about it and let me know Thursday night?"

"Thursday night?"

"Yes. Men's Fellowship is at seven o'clock," Alwayne informed him. "Don't be late."

Suave uttered a curse word under his breath. "Fine," he said through gritted teeth.

"You're going to need a Bible." Alwayne saw the horror flash across Suave's face. "Also, I'll be filing a motion today with the court to exclude the watch from evidence and informing the prosecutor that I'm now your lawyer."

"Thank you."

"I'll see you Thursday night." Alwayne stood and shook Suave's hand.

Chapter Forty-three

"I thought you weren't coming," Alwayne said as Suave walked up to him at the top of the church steps. "You're five minutes late."

"I'm not late. I was sitting in my car," Suave pointed to a BMW parked a few feet away, "trying to decide which was worse—church or prison."

Alwayne smiled. "Here's your Bible."

Suave looked at the big Bible like it were a two-headed dragon. "Is that really necessary?"

"If you'll be attending church with me . . . as agreed, yes, it is."

Suave sighed and took the Bible from him. "I hope I won't have to read all this bull—"

"As a matter of fact, you will." Alwayne gave Suave a firm look. "Let's go take our seats." He walked into the church, with Suave lagging behind.

"Hey." Suave touched Alwayne on his shoulder. Alwayne stopped in the church aisle and turned around to face him. "Do we have to go to the front?" he whispered.

"We're going just a few more rows up. Come on." Alwayne continued down the aisle until he got to the third row from the front. He slipped into the bench beside another man, making room for Suave at the end.

Suave sat and rested the Bible on his lap. Uncomfortable, he glanced around the church at the men in attendance . . . from teenagers to elders. He noticed that several men were dressed casually like him in jeans, T-shirt, and sneakers, including Alwayne.

"Relax," Alwayne whispered in his ear. "Bishop Hudson will be starting service soon."

But Suave only grew more uneasy when Bishop Hudson took the pulpit. He was a powerful-looking man with salt-and-pepper hair, wearing a pair of blue jeans, a white, long sleeved shirt, and white Nike sneakers. The seemingly pleasant pastor greeted the men with a big smile. "It's great to be in the house of the Lord," Bishop Hudson said loudly. "And great to have all you men here tonight. Give God some praise!"

"Praise the Lord," "Amen," and "Hallelujah" rang out in the church. A few men stood up, lifted their hands to the heavens, and praised God. Suave glanced over at Alwayne and saw that his eyes were closed, and his right hand was lifted as he gave praises to the Lord.

Suave tugged restlessly at the neck of his T-shirt. The thing felt like it was choking him.

"Everyone please stand to your feet for the reading of God's Word," Bishop Hudson said when the church quieted down. "Please turn your Bibles with me to Romans 6:23."

The men stood with their Bibles in their hands, except Suave. Alwayne reached over, touched his arm, and used his fingers to indicate that Suave should stand.

Suave reluctantly stood with his new Bible but kept it closed. He didn't have a clue where Romans was in the Bible, and he wasn't going to embarrass himself trying to find it either. It wasn't like he wanted to read Romans anyway, so whatever . . .

But Alwayne wasn't making it so easy for Suave. He pushed his Bible over to share with Suave and used his finger to tap the page where the scripture was.

"For the wages of sin is death; but the gift of God is eternal life through Jesus Christ our Lord," read Bishop Hudson. "That's the passage we will be discussing tonight. First, let's pray. Heavenly Father, we give you thanks to be in your presence one more time. We thank you for your blessings to our families and us and ask for your continued mercy and grace. Lord, forgive us for our sins and create a clean heart within us. . . ."

Suave looked around the church and saw that everyone's eyes were closed. He peered intently at Bishop Hudson and remembered how Pastor Ralph used to pray like that. Suave took a deep breath, willing the memories away as the bishop prayed.

". . . As we gather here tonight in Men's Fellowship, Lord, I pray that you will touch each and every brother in this church," Bishop continued. "Heal, deliver, and set free, dear Lord. Let your words penetrate their hearts and change their lives. Hallelujah! Make them law-abiding men of God who will serve you and give you the honor and the glory. In Jesus' name we pray. Amen."

The men responded, "Amen." Alwayne lowered himself to his seat, and Suave followed. Light perspiration was now gathered on Suave's face. He shifted uncomfortably, his breathing labored, his chest rising and falling as he ignored Alwayne who was staring at him with concern.

"You okay, man?" Alwayne asked softly.

Suave nodded, coughed into his hands, and looked up at Bishop Hudson, who was saying, "Our sins separate us from God, our creator. This verse is contrasting the spiritual death with eternal life. If your work is sin, you will receive a payment of spiritual death. This is ultimately eternal separation from God in hell."

"Death," "Hell," these words began hammering into Suave's head. He had to kill Pastor Ralph—death. Danny murdered Cobra—death. Someone killed Danny—death. Does that mean he was going to hell? Was Pastor Ralph in hell? Was there even a hell? Suave lowered his head until it was almost touching his lap. He felt Alwayne's hand on his shoulder, but it was like Suave was underwater struggling to breathe. "Death," "Hell," "Death." He covered his ears with his hands as he rocked from side to side. "No!" Suave screamed, jumping to his feet, his wild eyes scanning the church as if he were looking for the devil.

Bishop Hudson and all the other men turned to look at Suave. The room was arrested in silence.

Suave peered at Bishop Hudson but only saw Pastor Ralph looking at him. "You're a fraud!" Suave yelled, pointing at the bishop. Alwayne and the men gasped loudly, but Bishop Hudson stared at Suave with compassion. "You're nothing but a child molester and deserve to die and go to hell!"

"Suave, stop it!" Alwayne hissed, tugging on Suave's T-shirt. "Sit down."

Suave flicked off Alwayne's hand and ran out of the church, astonished eyes following him. Once outside, he ran to where his car was parked. With his two hands resting on the hood, he hyperventilated, tears running down his face. "I hate pastors. I hate church. I hate God," he muttered over and over.

"Suave, you okay?" Alwayne asked from behind him, lingering a few feet away.

"Are you okay, my son?" Bishop Hudson inquired as well. He had followed Suave and Alwayne out of the church, after instructing the men inside to start praying and interceding on behalf of the "troubled young man."

Suave took his handkerchief out of his pants pocket, blew his nose, and wiped his face, his back still turned to Alwayne and Bishop Hudson.

"Son?" Bishop Hudson stepped closer to Suave. "May I pray for you?"

Suave spun around and glared at the bishop. "You better stay away from me."

"I'm not your enemy," Bishop Hudson replied in a meek voice. "It's the devil that has been tormenting you. But the Lord can set you free. Please, let me help you."

"Help me, huh?" Suave began to laugh crazily. "See why I don't do church?" He looked over at Alwayne after the laughter tapered off. "These no-good, low-life pastors are always trying to mess with me. You kill one, another just pops right back up. Why can't they all just die, man?"

Bishop Hudson took another step closer to Suave, but Alwayne put his hand on the bishop's arm to stop him. "I'll take it from here, Bishop," Alwayne informed him. "Please go back inside, and I'll contact you later or tomorrow."

Bishop Hudson stared at Suave for a moment before he lightly slapped Alwayne on the back and walked back up the steps into the church.

"Suave, you need some help." Alwayne moved closer to him until they were standing face-to-face.

"More help, right?" Suave sucked his teeth. "You are really the Good Samaritan."

"Hey, I thought you said you didn't do church or the Bible," Alwayne joked. "Look at you talk about the Good Samaritan and all."

Suave rolled his eyes. "My mother used to take me to church before she died."

"Listen, Suave, my wife is a psychiatrist and works with Kingston Public Hospital. I think it's a good idea for you to meet with her."

"Do I look like I'm crazy to you?" Suave nostrils opened and closed in anger.

Alwayne held his hands up. "You don't have to have a mental illness to see her. She also does psychotherapy and counseling. No, don't say anything yet. I can tell you have some stuff going on inside here." He pointed to his head. "You just called my pastor a child molester, Suave. It's obvious he wasn't really the one you were talking to. Am I right?"

Suave lowered his head in shame.

"There is nothing to be ashamed of," Alwayne told him. "If you were a victim, you can get help. As your doctor, my wife is required to be confidential. She won't even speak to me about your sessions."

"Really? No one will know?"

"No, it will be between you and her." Alwayne almost held his breath as he looked at Suave anxiously. "I'll speak to her when I get home and have her call you."

Suave took a deep breath and locked eyes with Alwayne. He saw the care in Alwayne's eyes and almost teared up again. Boy, he was really getting soft. "I guess I can meet with her, especially if she's fine." Suave's dimples twinkled in his handsome face.

"Man, I'm trying to get you off a murder rap, and you're trying to let a brother get charged with one."

Alwayne and Suave shared a hearty laugh, lessening the tension that was in the air.

"Oh, before I forget, service begins at 11:00 a.m. on Sunday," Alwayne informed Suave. "Please don't be late."

"Hello?" King Kong answered his ringing cell phone. He was sitting on the couch in the back of his restaurant.

"You know who this is," Mr. Dapper said. "Can you talk?"

"Yes, yes, of course," King Kong replied nervously. "How are you?"

"I have a business proposal for you that should get us back on track." Mr. Dapper wasn't in the mood for pleasantries. "Are you interested, or what?"

King Kong started to beam from ear to ear. He owed Mr. Dapper a lot of money, thanks to Smooth Suave. He had been hustling hard to pay up but was still behind. "Yes, I am," he answered eagerly.

"I'll be sending you a huge shipment on consignment in eight weeks. I want you to turn this around, and split it fifty-fifty between us. This will square us off."

King Kong almost wet his white linen pants. He looked up at the heavens as if he expected to see some angels playing on their trumpets. Hallelujah! "You ain't said nothing but a word, Mr. Dapper. I promise I won't disappoint you."

"I hope not. This is your last chance."

"Thank y—" The dial tone rang in King Kong's ear, but he was too happy to care. King Kong stood and walked to the front. "Yo, Saddam," he waved to get Saddam's attention as he sat drinking a bowl of red pea soup, "come to the back."

Saddam got up with the soup bowl in his hand and followed King Kong to the back room.

"You won't believe this." King Kong then relayed his conversation with Mr. Dapper.

Saddam rested the soup bowl on a small table in the corner before he gave his boss a man hug. "This is good news." Saddam's eyes were sparkling. "I bet he heard that our little friend is facing a murder rap, so he wanted to get us on top."

King Kong nodded in agreement. "I'm glad he didn't ask about that traitor Phil." His ugly face screwed up, just mentioning Phil's name. "We had everything planned out, and that fool betrayed us and gave Suave his son back."

"Don't worry. We'll catch him soon." Saddam had been actually looking forward to sending pieces of Suave's son to his father, little by little. "I bet he went to the country to hide."

"Anyway, that's his bad luck because you and I are about to take over Jamaica." King Kong was back in the groove. "Not even that fat pig can test us now," he said in reference to Queen Bee.

"We're going to slaughter the pig anyway," Saddam reminded his boss. "So, oink oink oink." King Kong and Saddam fell out laughing. They laughed so hard that tears ran down their faces.

Chapter Forty-four

"Hello, Mr. Brown. I'm Annette Clark," said the tall, light-skinned, strikingly beautiful woman who greeted Suave at the door. "Please come in." She waved her hand toward her office.

Suave swallowed and stepped into the professional, elegantly decorated office. He flinched when Annette closed the door behind him, still unsure if he were actually doing the right thing.

"You're already here, so you might as well just give me a few minutes," Annette said as if she had read Suave's mind. She walked over to the beige, leather, La-Z-Boy chair and lowered herself into it. "Please have a seat." Annette pointed to the matching couch that faced her.

Suave perched on the edge of the couch and looked at Alwayne's wife's pleasant face and found himself relaxing.

"I'm glad you decided to come." Annette smiled at him. "I promise you that I'm only here to help you, and anything said in this room is strictly between us." She was now all business, her expression seriously conveying her message.

"That's what your husband told me. You know he's representing me on a murder charge."

"Yes, he mentioned it, but never went into detail. He also has a level of confidentiality to maintain."

"Yeah, he is the best, and I have faith that he will help me," Suave noted.

Annette bobbed her head in agreement. "He's very good at what he does," she said proudly. "I'm not too bad in my field, either." She winked at Suave.

"I don't encounter many people like you and your husband."

This was the opening Annette was waiting for. "What kind of people do you usually deal with, Mr. Brown?"

"You can call me Suave. People who want to use or abuse me," he informed Annette. "Except for my children, and my boys, Daddy Lizard and Cobra, most people only want what they can get from me."

"And how does this make you feel?"

Suave relaxed back into the couch and crossed his legs. "I'm not a fool. I'm in control of my own destiny, and I don't allow anyone to play me. It's kill or be killed."

"Powerful statement. Are we talking about killing in the physical sense of the word or are you speaking in general?"

"A very wise man once told me when I was very young that if you cut off the head off the snake, you'll kill the body. I've been living by that principle ever since, and he was right."

"Seems as if you really respect this man's opinion," Annette noted. "Care to tell me some more about him?"

A smile appeared on Suave's face as he reflected on Mason Sr. Surprisingly, without much prompting, he began to tell Annette about his parents' death, how he went to live with his uncle who got killed, and Mason took him in. "I don't care what people say about Mason, he was there for me when I needed him, and I'll always be grateful. Doesn't matter that he eventually turned his back on me. I still love and respect him," Suave said with conviction.

"I understand. And I'm sorry about your uncle getting killed," Annette said with sympathy. "To lose your parents, and then your uncle must have been very hard on you."

Suave burst out laughing. "You're sorry for good old Pastor Ralph? He was a pig!" Suave spat angrily. "He lived like one, and I killed him like one." Suave's eyes widened when those words came out of his mouth.

Annette gasped but quickly regained her composure. "You killed your uncle? Why?"

Suave paused, wondering if he had said too much. No one knew that he was the one who had killed Pastor Ralph, and within minutes he was confessing to this shrink. It was because her soothing voice sounded so much like his mother's. Come to think of it, she even resembled Gloria. Was that why he was so open? Was he about to face *two* murder charges?

"It's okay, Suave. That's why you're here," Annette assured him. "Was your uncle hurting you?"

Tears filled his eyes, and he quickly wiped them away with the back of his hand. "Hurting me? He was molesting me," Suave yelled and jumped to his feet. He began pacing the floor, walking from one end of the office to the other as he spoke. "Night after night, that vulture would . . . would . . ." Suave's legs suddenly felt too weak to hold up his body, and he fell to his knees and bawled. His shoulders shook as the grown man was reduced to a child by the secret and the pain he had kept locked inside him all these years. Despite all the wealth Suave had accumulated over the years by building his drug empire, it still wasn't enough to eradicate the sexual abuse he suffered as a child.

As a mother, Annette's heart was breaking, but right now, she had to be professional. *Please, help me, Lord.* Annette prayed silently. *I know you didn't send Suave here for me to fail him. Please help me so that I can help him.*

"Talk to me, Suave. What did that pig do to you?" Annette prompted, getting in agreement with Suave so he would know she was on his side.

"He would pull down my pants . . . and . . . and . . . put his mouth on me." Suave curled himself into a ball on the floor as if he were protecting his private parts. "Then he'd beat me when I resisted." His loud crying filled the room. "I tried to stop him, but he was too strong."

Annette replied above the sobbing. "He was a grown man, and you were a child."

Whether or not Suave wanted to believe it, he was no longer in control of the situation. It was time for him to heal. "He told me that if I told anyone, they would say we were gay and kill us both." Snot ran down his face as he poured everything out. "I begged God for help, but He never came. He let that nasty piece of trash suck on me night after night."

Help me, Lord. "I'm so sorry, Suave." Annette now understood Suave's resentment of God and pastors.

Alwayne had told her about the incident in church the night before. "What made you finally decide to stop Pastor Ralph's abuse?"

Suave didn't respond. He cried for a few more minutes, and Annette allowed him the space. Soon, the crying faded, and Suave pulled himself up into a sitting position on the carpeted floor. He fished his handkerchief out of his jeans pocket, blew his nose, and wiped his face. Surprisingly, he didn't feel ashamed for displaying so much emotion.

"Suave? Why did you kill the pig?"

Suave turned red eyes to Annette. "He told me he was about to turn me into a man," he replied. "Said I was ready and slapped me on my behind. I knew he was going to rape me next time."

Annette felt sick to her stomach. She got up and walked over to a small table in the corner of the room. On it was a pitcher of ice water and two glasses. She filled both glasses with water and took one over to Suave.

"Here." She handed him his glass, where he sat on the floor.

Suave gratefully took the glass, turned it to his head, and greedily drank.

Annette waited for him to continue as she sipped her water. "So, you felt you had to kill him?" Annette finally asked when Suave remained silent.

"I couldn't tell anyone what was happening. They would say I was a punk and probably kill me. Mason and his men always talked about killing gays." Suave leaned back on his elbows and gazed at the ceiling. "I couldn't let him rape me either. Then the answer came to me, and I knew what I had to do." Suave told Annette about the pig he saw being slaughtered. "I knew it was a sign. Pastor Ralph was a pig too, so I decided to do him the same."

"You carefully planned it out?"

Suave smiled nastily and related everything he did in preparation for Pastor Ralph's death. "'Take it like a man' he always told me when he was molesting me. And you know what? I told him the same thing after I cut his throat, and he was dying. Then he was gone, and I was free."

"Are you really free, Suave?" Annette leaned forward, her eyes locked on his face. "Are you free from Pastor Ralph?"

Suave looked away from her. How could he tell her about the nightmares that sometimes seemed like they were strangling him to death? Would she understand his will to survive Pastor Ralph by torturing another homosexual man for so many years? Would she think he was sick . . . or even worse, that he was gay?

"I won't judge you, Suave. I want you to talk to me so I can help you to help yourself."

"I'm feeling tired," Suave said, shutting down. He staggered a little when he rose to his feet. "I think we should call it a wrap."

Annette didn't push. In fact, she was amazed that they had made so much progress in their first session. God certainly had a part in this. "Okay. I just want to thank you for trusting me."

"To be honest, I'm not even sure what just happened." Suave went and sat on the couch. "I never talked to anyone about that before. I don't even like to cry in front of people like that." Suave shook his head in amazement. What's going on?

"So, when is our next session?"

Suave shook his head, a little smile pulling at his mouth. Annette Clark reminded him so much of his mother. "You know you're just as pushy as your husband, right?"

"Yup, we're like two peas in a pod." Annette and Suave shared a laugh.

Chapter Forty-five

Suave stood in front of his wardrobe mirror, examining himself head to toe. His long, freshly washed and waxed dreads were pulled back in a ponytail that hung luxuriously down his back. A huge diamond earring, the size of a marble, glittered in his left earlobe. The Boss three-piece, black suit with a white silk shirt and black tie fit his tall, muscular frame to perfection. On his feet, black silk Armani socks were enclosed by his shiny Salvatore Ferragamo patent leather shoes. It was Sunday morning, and Suave was ready for church.

"Okay, let's get this over with," Suave said to his handsome reflection in the mirror. "I just need to suffer through this until that murder charge is dropped. Then I'll be a free man."

Suave noted the time on the diamond Rolex on his right wrist, then strolled over to get his wallet and cell phone resting on the bed. The phone rang as soon as he touched it. He was pleasantly surprised when he looked at the caller ID. "Monica? Baby, is that you?"

"Hello, Suave. It's Mother Lambert," replied Monica's mother. "How are you, son?"

"I'm okay, ma'am. Is Monica okay? Did she have the baby? How are they doing?"

"Slow down, my dear." Mother Lambert laughed lightly. "Let's take one question at a time. Yes, Monica gave birth to your son last night. They are both doing all right."

Suave sat down on the edge of the bed, a big grin on his face. "Thank you for calling and letting me know."

Mother Lambert always liked Suave, unlike her husband. She often told Suave that she didn't like his lifestyle and what he did for a living, but he had a good heart. "One day, God is going to turn you around and use you for His kingdom," she had often said.

"Now, Monica is still pretty upset about Joel's kidnapping. She forbade me to call you, but I think you should know what's going on with your family."

"I appreciate it, ma'am. I hope Monica will come home as soon as the doctor says it's okay so I can see my son."

"Why don't you come for a visit, son? I haven't seen you in a while."

Suave's eyes widened in alarm. How could he tell her that he couldn't leave the country because he was on bail for a murder? "Umm, well, I . . . I have a personal matter I'm taking care of right now. I won't be able to get away for a while."

Mother Lambert was silent for a few seconds. "Suave, are you in trouble? Or, should I say, *serious* trouble? God knows with what you do, you're always in trouble. Son?"

"Not really, just a few issues that I have to take care of," Suave informed her. "I have everything under control."

Mother Lambert sucked her teeth. "The only person who has things under control is God. You know I've been praying for you since you got my daughter pregnant, and she moved out to shack up with you? It may have taken a long time for a change, but God does things in His own time."

Suave tugged on the tie around his neck. His air conditioner was on full blast, but all this "God" talk was really getting to him. He hadn't even gone to church yet. "May I please speak to Raven and Rayden?"

"I know you're changing the subject. Anyway, they are not here right now," Mother Lambert told him. "Their grandfather took them to visit their baby brother in the hospital. I'll make sure they call you as soon as they return."

"I'm on my way to church, so—"

"Church? Hallelujah! Thank you, Lord! You are a God of miracles! Is there anything too hard for you, Lord?"

Suave silently mimicked Mother Lambert, thankful she couldn't see him, as she gave God thanks for Suave going to church. *Why didn't I just keep my big mouth shut?* Suave pondered. *If she only knew the reason I was going.* Suave had yet to realize that the Lord would get his attention one way or the other.

"Mother Lambert? Ma'am? Hello?" Suave tried to interrupt the praise session, knowing it had the potential to go on all morning. "Ma'am, I am running late."

That did the trick. Mother Lambert quickly settled down, breathing heavily into the phone. "Okay. I won't keep you, dear. You go on and give God the glory and the honor due unto His name. Just wait until Monica and Mr. Lambert hear about this."

"Great," Suave responded sarcastically. "I'll call the kids when I get back. Thanks for calling." He quickly hung up the phone before Mother Lambert started up again.

Suddenly, Suave felt a pressure in the middle of his forehead and bent over slightly, his face toward the carpeted floor. "I don't think I'm going to make it to church after all," he mumbled, rubbing his forehead. His head was hurting and feeling light.

"That's because you're scared," said a mocking, sing-songy voice. *"You were always a little coward."*

Suave closed his eyes and didn't say a word. He knew he wasn't sleeping, so it wasn't a nightmare. Therefore, he must be losing his mind. Taking deep breaths in and exhaling out, Suave pulled off his tie and threw it behind him on the bed. The room now seemed to be swaying a little. He was feeling dizzy.

"You can ignore me as much as you want, but I'm not going anywhere." Pastor Ralph laughed loudly, dancing around on the back of his heels like a jackrabbit.

Suave began to shake uncontrollably, beads of perspiration appearing on his face. His phone rang.

"Yeah?" Suave said into his cell phone.

"You don't sound too good, Suave," Alwayne said with concern. "You all right, man? Annette and I are outside church waiting for you."

"I'm a little under the weather." Suave's tongue felt heavy in his mouth.

"That's the devil speaking. Hold on a sec. Annette wants to talk to you."

Annette came on the phone. "Suave, listen to me. Do you feel well enough to drive over here to church?" she asked.

"I'm not coming to church. I'm sick."

"Alwayne and I will come and pick you up," Annette assured him. She lowered her voice. "It's just the devil trying to prevent you from coming to church so that he can torture you in that house. Don't let him win, Suave."

Suave moved the phone from his ear to look at it, a puzzled look plastered over his face.

Unbeknownst to Suave, while he was hallucinating about a ghost from the past, Annette was manifesting in the Holy Ghost.

"Suave? You there?"

Suave heard Annette when he put the phone back to his ear. "Pastor Ralph was here," he whispered, scanning the room to see if his tormentor was still lurking around.

"Satan, I rebuke you in the name of Jesus!" Annette began speaking in tongues.

Suave listened with his eyes closed. He was so relieved that he could finally share this with somebody who wanted to help him. "I'm on my way," Suave said with determination. "I'll be there in twenty minutes."

Suave hung up the phone, rested it on the bed, and walked into the bathroom.

He was going to church, and Pastor Ralph could stay in hell.

"I'm so glad you could make it." Annette hugged Suave like a long lost brother.

Suave returned the hug awkwardly. The Clarks were treating him like family, and he wasn't used to it. "Well, I don't want to lose my lawyer," he joked.

At the church's door, Suave paused and said, "I think I'm going to sit in the back. You guys can go up front."

"Okay," Annette replied without hesitation. "After church, I would like you to meet our family." She took ahold of her husband's hand, and they all entered the church where service was already underway.

While Annette and Alwayne went down the aisle for a seat closer to the front, Suave noticed one in the last row and slipped into it before the usher could even acknowledge him. Almost sitting on the edge of his seat, Suave looked up at the podium and saw that Bishop Hudson was about to give the word. "Just great," he muttered.

"Pardon me?" responded the lady sitting beside Suave. "Did you say something?"

"Oh no. Sorry." Suave focused his attention back on Bishop Hudson. He was determined to listen and not compare the man to the ghost that was haunting him.

"Today, I want to talk to you about redemption," Bishop Hudson began. "Ephesians 1:7 says, '*In whom we have redemption through his blood, the forgiveness of sins, according to the riches of his grace.*' Amen. Redemption is possible through the blood of Jesus! Hello, somebody? I said that you can be delivered from the bondage of sin and find peace with God. Am I speaking to somebody?"

"Amen, Pastor," a member shouted from the front.

"You better speak to me, Bishop," a young lady in the choir yelled.

Bishop Hudson paused, took off his jacket, and handed it to his assistant. He grabbed the microphone out of the stand and paced the pulpit. "We all need redemption. You know why? Because we all have sinned and have fallen short of the glory of God."

Hmmm, interesting, Suave thought. *Even Christians need redemption too.*

As if he read Suave's mind, Bishop Hudson remarked, "So you can act like you were born holy, pure, and righteous all you want, but that's not the case. We were able to become a child of God because Jesus paid the price for our sins on the cross. His death was in exchange for our life."

"Praise the Lord," "Thank you, Jesus," and "Hallelujah" rang throughout the church.

"Do you want to be free from the burden of guilt?" Bishop Hudson asked, looking out at the congregation.

Suave shifted in his seat, wondering why the bishop was looking at him.

"Do you want to be free from curses and bondage?" Bishop Hudson stepped down from the pulpit into the aisle. "God already purchased our freedom," he said, his eyes wandering from one face to the other as he moved closer to the back.

He better stop picking on me, or else I'm stepping. Suave defiantly stared at the bishop as he got closer, his arms folded, and his face screwed up like a dried apple. *I'm no punk.*

"I said, you can go from being a sinner to a saint if you accept God's gift of eternal life." Bishop Hudson was now at Suave's bench, where he paused.

Suave glanced at the bishop through the corner of his eyes, and his head held straight. He didn't acknowledge the bishop, and for the bishop's sake, Suave was hoping he wouldn't acknowledge him.

"I'm glad to see you this morning, my brother." Bishop Hudson looked down at Suave, who still wasn't looking at him.

All eyes in the church turned toward the back where Suave sat. Alwayne and Annette held hands and nervously looked on. Bishop Hudson was known to prophesize to his members, revealing things that no one else knew but God. He would also predict certain happenings that always came true. This usually made some members excited about receiving a blessing, and others nervous when they hadn't been walking on the "right" side.

"God is going to give you a second chance." Bishop Hudson rested his hand on Suave's shoulder. "Those demons that are haunting you are leading you down a narrow road."

Suave's heart began to gallop in his chest. He wanted to brush off the preacher's hand, but he felt compelled to hear what the man had to say.

"Your mind gets so mixed up at times that you find it hard to differentiate between the real thing and your imagination. But God says to tell you that He is going to give you the victory."

Some people were now standing on their feet, clapping, some praying, and others speaking in tongues.

"Deliver him, Lord," an elderly man shouted.

"Set your son free, Father Jesus," screamed another member.

"God is going to right the wrong that was done to you, so you can be free to serve Him and His people." Tears filled Bishop Hudson's eyes as he leaned over to Suave, his face only inches away from Suave's.

On a will of its own, Suave's neck turned, and he locked eyes with the bishop. Suave's tears betrayed him and seeped down his face.

"Like He did for the Egyptians, God is going to deliver you from your enemies. In return, you must give Him thanks by giving Him your life," Bishop Hudson said, then whispered for Suave's ear only. "I know you don't trust pastors, but not all of us are the same. There is no sin too hard for God to forgive, you hear me?" He moved his head back to look in Suave's eyes. "Accept God's forgiveness now and be free. I'm here if you ever need to talk to someone."

Bishop Hudson straightened himself up, patted Suave on the back, and walked back toward the front of the church. *"Would you be free from the burden of sin?*

There's power in the blood," he began to sing. The musicians playing the guitars, drums, and organ picked it up, and soon, everyone was one their feet, singing and dancing.

Suave wiped his face with his handkerchief. It took him a moment to compose himself and stand to his feet. Remarkably, he didn't feel upset at all that the bishop had called him out. He was more intrigued that the man didn't know him personally, but yet, knew so much. First, it was Annette, now the bishop. *Let me find out these church people are up in here working obeah . . .* Soon, Suave was bobbing his head a little to the music. No, it wasn't a Bounty Killa reggae hit, but it didn't sound too bad at all for a church song.

Chapter Forty-six

Pacing the hotel room, Suave glanced down at his watch one more time. His face was etched with concern. "Come on, come on," he muttered, looking at the door for the umpteenth time. "Where are you?"

It was 3:45 p.m., and Suave had an appointment with Annette Clark at 4:00 p.m. This would be their fourth meeting in less than two weeks, and Suave was looking forward to it. But first, he had to take care of this other important meeting, and he had been waiting for thirty minutes.

"He has to come," Suave said aloud. "Nothing can go wrong now." Then the knock came at the door. "Finally."

Suave hurried over to the door and looked through the peephole before unlocking it. "Boy, I was getting a little nervous that you weren't coming."

"It's been a crazy day today," Detective Stone replied, stepping into the room. "I have been to four murder scenes so far," he shook his head, "and I have to run to another right now. People feel like they have to kill each other to make a point these days. It's just ridiculous."

"Still, I'm glad you found the time to come," Suave replied quickly. Detective Stone's words had struck a chord in him. He had killed in self-defense, and his actions had resulted in someone getting killed as well. A few weeks ago, this wouldn't have affected Suave so much.

However, since his counseling sessions with Annette and attending church with Alwayne, he was beginning to look at his life in a whole new light. "I just want to give you an update on everything." Suave still had business to take care of.

"Yes. Let's go over this in detail. I don't want there to be any mistakes."

Detective Stone and Suave didn't bother to sit as they both had places to be. They talked in hushed tones for a few minutes.

"All right. I'll be meeting with my team tomorrow, and we'll be going over everything," Detective Stone said to Suave.

"No one should know I'm involved in this." Suave stared pointedly at the detective. "That was our agreement."

"Relax, man. I refer to you as my confidential informant," the lawman assured him. "I hope when all this is over, you'll get on the straight and narrow. As we agreed, you will get no pass from me if you continue to break the law."

Suave grinned and winked at Detective Stone. "So, we're still in agreement." He looked at his watch and saw that he was already five minutes late to meet Annette Clark. "I have to run, but we'll link again next Wednesday." He walked to the door and unlocked it for the detective to exit.

Suave waited another ten minutes before he left the room, exiting the hotel through a side entrance. He sped out of the hotel's parking lot in his truck, maneuvering around the thick traffic in New Kingston as he fought his way to Cross Roads.

Ten minutes later, Suave screeched into an available parking spot in front of Annette's office.

"I see you made it," Annette said when she opened the door. She wasn't smiling as usual.

Suave felt like an eel. "I'm sorry. I had an important meeting that took more time than I thought."

Annette stepped aside so he could enter the office. "That's why we have telephones, Suave." She closed the door and walked over to her chair.

Suave sat on the couch. It never occurred to him to call Annette and let her know he was running late. Annette was helping him get his life in order, and he didn't want her to think he wasn't grateful. Even though they were close in age, Annette reminded him so much of his mother. Suave absolutely respected her. "Sorry, it won't happen again. I also appreciate all the help you have been giving me."

Annette saw the sincerity in his eyes. She knew a man like Suave rarely apologized and was glad he was also making progress in that regard. "I accept your apology. I'm invested in helping you, Suave. I want the same commitment from you as well."

He nodded his agreement. "You got it."

"In our last session, we spoke about your father killing your mother, and then himself. It was a very emotional session. I'm so glad you spoke to me about it and how you feel about everything."

It was the first time Suave ever talked to anyone about his parents' death in detail. He spoke of the anger he had toward his father and the fact that he still hadn't forgiven him. "If he hadn't taken my mother from me, I never would have gone to live with Pastor Ralph. He wouldn't have molested me, and I wouldn't have to kill him in self-defense. I wouldn't be so freaking messed up in here!" Suave angrily pointed to his head. "Who knows? Maybe I wouldn't have started to deal drugs. Don't get me wrong. I love being a wealthy man, but now the price is getting too high. You know what I mean?"

"That's a lot of 'wouldn't.' We can't change the past, so I want us to focus on changing now, so we can change the future," Annette informed him. "This will start with you forgiving your father. Remembering the good things that he had done for you, and the love you once had for him."

Suave had spent the last few days doing just that. He reminisced on the good times with his parents. They had little, but he always felt loved.

"Today, I want us to talk some more about Pastor Ralph and him molesting you."

"I'm not gay," Suave blurted out. "I only got involved with that sissy to punish his behind for what Pastor Ralph did to me."

"What sissy?"

Suave's eyes bugged out of his head. Good God, he had said too much again. "Huh? I . . . I . . . I was just . . . hmmm, speaking in general." He hung his head in embarrassment.

"Suave, please look at me." Annette waited until he glanced at her, his eyes flicking on and off her face. "We have come too far to shut down now. Please, talk to me. This might actually be the key we need to unlock everything."

Suave pursed his lips as he stared off into space. No one knew this secret he had kept for so many years. Should he reveal it now? "His name is Pat, and he's gay," Suave began softly. He got up and walked over to the window. He peered through the open blinds, watched as vehicles zipped up and down the street, with people scurrying in every direction. "He's a business associate's brother. It all started one day when I went by Queen Bee's to do some business."

Suave told Annette everything about his twisted relationship with Pat. He walked her through every scene—Pat dressing in drag, the merciless whippings, his ice baths to cleanse himself, and his addiction to go back time after time to punish the man who had molested him.

Through it all, Annette didn't say a word. With Suave's back turned toward her, she listened and silently prayed for him.

"I haven't been back to . . . you know, see him like that since Cobra was murdered," Suave concluded the story, holding onto the wall to support his body weight. He felt drained and emotionally exhausted as he waited for Annette's comment.

"Why don't you come and rest your legs?" Annette's kind eyes met Suave's when he spun around. "Come on," she pointed to the couch. "I'll pour you something to drink."

Suave did as requested. "Thank you," he said when Annette handed him a glass of water. He drank thirstily, watching her over the rim of the glass as she reclaimed her seat. "I'm not gay," he said forcefully after he drank.

"No, you are not," Annette responded.

Suave was surprised that she agreed with him. "I . . . I thought you would judge me. I told myself that if anyone ever found out, I would kill myself."

"You are not going to do any such thing," Annette said sternly. "You also won't have any need to go back to that man again. You are getting to a better place, Suave. Don't you see that?"

"Why did I keep going back time after time?" Suave wanted to know. "I hated it, but I just couldn't seem to stop."

"Firstly, I don't think you are gay because you never had sex with Pat. You also never engaged in any sexual activity with him, except for your first meeting, and you got sick to your stomach. See, this was little Suave's first encounter again with his molester. Pat became Pastor Ralph, and you reverted to that helpless child that you once were. You kept going back to Pat, back to Pastor Ralph, and beating him mercilessly, because in your mind, you were conquering him. You killed Pastor Ralph, but he came back. This was your way of defeating him again and protecting yourself."

"Man, I am really messed up." Suave shook his head, tears swimming in his eyes.

"No, you *were* really messed up, but not anymore. Don't be too hard on yourself," Annette told him. "What you had gone through as a child, only the Lord could have kept you."

"Kept me? Why didn't He prevent it in the first place?"

"Suave, bad things happen to good people. It's even more painful when it's helpless children." Annette reached over and grasped his hand, and her voice shook a little. "God didn't say we wouldn't suffer, but He promised He would be there with us through it all. Revelation 21:4 says, '*And God shall wipe away all tears from their eyes; and there shall be no more death, neither sorrow, nor crying, neither shall there be any more pain: for the former things are passed away.'* God is helping you now."

Suave looked at her intently. He was confused, but what's new? When it came to God and the Bible, he didn't know much.

"I know it all sounds baffling, but you'll get it." Annette squeezed his hand and let go. "We're going to stop here today. You did well, Suave."

"Thank you." Suave did feel lighter now that he had gotten that dark secret off his chest. "I'll see you on Friday?"

Annette smiled. Yup, they were certainly making a lot of progress.

Over the next few weeks, Suave's life was like a roller coaster. He met with Annette twice per week for counseling, attended Men's Fellowship on Thursdays and church on Sundays. He was also running back and forth between his businesses as time allowed, dealing with his soldiers, attending to his children, and working on "The Plan" with Detective Stone. It was just chaos—physically and mentally.

"What's really going on with you?" Daddy Lizard finally asked Suave one afternoon when he stopped by the bar. "I know you have to do the church thing with that lawyer, but there are some days you just disappear without a word."

Suave knew Daddy Lizard was overwhelmed with Cobra gone and him slacking off. While Daddy Lizard knew about the agreement with Alwayne, he didn't know about Suave's counseling sessions with Annette. Suave decided to come clean about some things. "I've been going for some therapy too."

"Huh? Say that again? You mean like a shrink?"

Suave nodded and held Daddy Lizard's stare. He wasn't ashamed anymore. "She's my lawyer's wife. You know that my father killed my mother and himself when

I was a child. That thing had always been on my mind, man. I'm just now talking to someone about it, so I can let it go. You know what I mean?" Daddy Lizard didn't know about Pastor Ralph or Pat, and Suave decided to leave it at that. Some things were better left unsaid.

"That's cool. I didn't know it bothered you like that," Daddy Lizard replied. "Is that all, though? Maybe it's just me, but you don't seem that interested in business like you used to."

Daddy Lizard was right. Suave was rethinking his life. He was even reading the Bible scriptures assigned in Men's Fellowship and was actually looking forward to going to church. "I've been thinking about that too. To be honest, I'm getting to that place where I want to make some changes in my life."

"It's that church thing getting to you, Suave. We're at the top of our game. We can't give that up now." Daddy Lizard looked at Suave like he was crazy. "You're just getting nervous because of that murder rap hanging over your head."

"My lawyer is on top of that, so it's all good," Suave replied. "I'm wondering if it isn't time for us to go fully legit. We already lost Cobra, and I almost lost my son. We're getting too old for the game."

Daddy Lizard eyeballed Suave and saw that he was serious. "What about me?" Daddy Lizard had money in the bank, but to him, it wasn't enough for the rest of his life.

"I'm offended you asked me that. You, Cobra, and I built all of this. I'd split up everything between us and make sure you get your fair share. We're wealthy men, my friend."

"And our soldiers? That would be a big move," Daddy Lizard said. "I bet King Kong and Queen Bee will celebrate if we do that."

"We'd make sure all our workers get a good piece of change. The businesses we can sell, or you can decide which ones you want to keep." The more Suave talked about it, the more he was feeling compelled to quit dealing drugs. "I know the cops are watching all of us like hawks with all the killings that have been going on. The 'bee' may lose her sting, and the gorilla may be caged. I'm only thinking about you and me right now. I want us to quit while we're ahead."

"Hmmm, I think a lot of this is the church getting to you," Daddy Lizard responded. "No," he held up a finger when Suave opened his mouth, "you have changed since you started hanging with your lawyer friend. I think that's good, Suave. You used to get so mad whenever anyone talked about God. Now you know I'm no Holy Roller, but a brother believes in the Almighty."

"I was going to tell you that you're right," Suave replied, grinning. "I'm trying to figure out God, although it seems as if He already figured me out. What a thing, huh?"

The men shared a hearty laugh . . . one signifying changes to come. Would it be according to their plans . . . or those of their nemeses?

Chapter Forty-seven

"World dance a done by di kings an queens," King Kong sang along with Beenie Man blasting on the CD player, kicking out one leg in front of him, then the other, his potbelly jiggling side to side. *"Brand new dance run di scene."* He flung one flabby arm to the right, the other to the left, dipped his big head, and shook his fat behind.

Saddam roared with laughter. "Give us the Bogle dance now, Boss," he yelled, taking a gulp of his Courvoisier and a puff on the marijuana spliff in his hand.

King Kong obliged him, pushing his head all the way back, sweat pouring down his face, with his hands rotating at his sides like mufflers. Then he started to dip forward, but King Kong's back couldn't cooperate from that angle, bearing all the weight it had. Like Humpty Dumpty, King Kong collapsed backward, his two short, stubby legs up in the air.

Saddam spat the drink out of his mouth, hooting with laughter. King Kong joined in as he lay on his back. It was a celebratory night for the men. Two hours ago, they had met Mr. Dapper's men down at the wharf for a huge shipment of cocaine.

The drugs were taken to Saddam's grandparents' house in Spanish Town. After Elder Bloom's death, Mother Bloom was so distraught she moved to St. Mary to live with her sister. The house was left in Saddam's care, and he and King Kong officially converted it to one of their stash houses.

Once the drugs were safe and sound in the hidden compartment, the men turned on some reggae music, lit some spliffs, and got their drinking on. King Kong was really on top of the world now. Smooth Suave who? Queen Bee what?

Boom! The loud sound ricocheted around the living room. The house shook a little as the front door was knocked off its hinges, plummeting to the floor.

"What the—?" King Kong rolled over on his big gut, his beady eyes bulging out of his head in alarm.

Saddam grabbed his gun beside him on the couch, jumped up, and dashed toward the back of the house.

"Police! Police! Police!" Ten DEA agents burst into the living room, their guns drawn and pointed at King Kong. "Don't move," the task force leader screamed, his gun a few inches away from King Kong's head. "Search the house for the other one," he instructed. Some of the other agents ran off to various rooms in the house.

King Kong scanned the cops surrounding him, groaned, and lowered his head in defeat. What happened to the two men standing guard outside?

"Where's Saddam?" the agent barked at King Kong. He got no response.

Saddam hid under the bed in a back bedroom, his heart galloping in his chest as hurried footsteps approached. He waited, perspiring profusely, his breathing irregular and his finger on the trigger of his gun.

Two DEA agents cautiously entered the bedroom, their eyes and guns scouring the room. They searched in the closet and behind the dresser but found no one. The agents shared a look. Then one nodded toward the bed before they slowly backed out of the room, pulling the door closed.

Back in the living room, King Kong was handcuffed, read his rights, and was sitting on the couch shaking. He had enough drugs hidden in the kitchen cellar that could send him to prison for the rest of his life.

"He's hiding in a bedroom," King Kong overheard someone telling the taskforce leader.

"Okay. Take this worthless piece of trash to the car," the leader said of King Kong to two agents. "The house is surrounded, so Saddam has nowhere to run." He walked toward the bedroom where Saddam was hiding.

"Saddam!" said a loud voice outside the bedroom door. "Come out now with your hands in the air. You're surrounded by the police."

Saddam's head began to throb. The strong weed and alcohol he drank earlier only intensified the craziness going on inside his head. "I'm not going to prison." Saddam shook his head. He peeked out from under the bed, and realizing he was alone in the room, he crawled out. Down on all four, he moved to the window and sneaked a quick look outside. There were at least three agents in the backyard.

"I'm giving you another chance to come out before we come in," threatened the menacing voice. "Surrender yourself now!"

Saddam stood to his feet. He kept glancing from the bedroom door to the yard, over and over.

"Okay, we're coming in!"

As the bedroom door was kicked in, Saddam opened fire at the police, yelling and screaming obscenities, firing off one bullet after the other.

The DEA agents returned fire, unloading a massive amount of lead into Saddam.

Saddam's now empty gun fell from his hand, his body following it to the floor. As the life slipped out of his bullet-riddled body, Saddam's blood leaked out, staining the beautiful beige carpet. Taking one last deep breath, his eyes wide open, staring up into the heavens, Saddam died.

One of the sinful angels slipped out of her bikini top, dropped it on the floor, then strutted her nude bootylicious body across the living room floor. Sprawled out on the long couch looking like a stuffed chicken, Queen Bee moaned and groaned as two naked girls kissed on her. They were at Lizzy's, Queen Bee's right-hand lady's house in Norbrook.

Ninety minutes ago, Queen Bee, Lizzy, and five sinful angels had entered the house with large suitcases containing bricks of cocaine. The ladies disappeared into the basement for about an hour before they came back to the living room to celebrate and party.

Drinking and smoking joints, with the sinful angels wearing only their birthday suits, the women kissed and fondled each other, giggling and frolicking in a big orgy fest. Queen Bee was in her own heaven—or was it an undercover hell?

Suddenly, a loud explosion reverberated around the room as the front door fell in. "Police! Police! Nobody move!" A dozen DEA agents rushed into the room, waving their guns at the occupants.

The sinful angels screamed and scrambled behind the couch for cover. Lizzy leaped for her gun on the coffee table. "Touch it, and you're dead." The cold butt of the M16 Magnum was resting on Lizzy's forehead. She looked up, and her eyes met and held those of the DEA agent. Lizzy lay down on the floor and put her hands behind her back.

Queen Bee remained seated on the couch, looking as cool as VapoRub. However, her heart was hammering away in her chest. The largest shipment of cocaine she had ever bought was hidden in the basement with her present in the house.

"Hello, Queen Bee." Detective Stone had a smirk on his face. "I'm sorry to interrupt your party, but I have a search warrant for this house." He waved a piece of paper in her face.

Queen Bee hung her head.

"You have the right to remain silent. Anything you say can and will be used against you in a court of law. You have the right to—What in heaven! We need an ambulance!" Detective Stone shouted.

Queen Bee had fallen off the couch, landing facedown on the floor, shaking the house. Lying as still as a log, the queen was out cold . . . fainted at the reality of her demise.

Pat was curled up on his couch, feeling sexy in a short black negligee. His thick lips were painted a bright red, his long eyelashes were down as he dozed. Tomorrow would be a long day, and Pat needed his beauty rest. He and Queen Bee had a lot to do with the shipment that was about to solidify their position at the top of Jamaica's drug empire.

Suddenly, a loud pounding came at the door. "Police! Open up!" Pat jumped up, shivering as if he were doused with a bucket of ice water. "Police! Open the door, or we'll kick it in!"

Pat glanced around the living room. He had a gun in the bedroom, but did he really need it? The police hadn't kicked their way in, so they obviously didn't think he was a threat. Also, he didn't have any drugs in the house. Thank God they were safe at Lizzy's.

"Last chance! Open the door now!"

Pat sprinted to the door, unlocking the locks as he pulled it open, raising his hands in the air. "Don't shoot," he said in a low, squeaky voice.

"What the . . .?" Six DEA agents stared at Pat, flabbergasted, their mouths wide opened, and their eyes bugged out.

Pat was standing before them partially naked in the negligee. The agents were taken aback from the made-up face, to the exposed penis, down to the long, smooth shaven legs.

"What kind of drug man is this?" one agent muttered, looking away from Pat's nakedness.

"What is this, dear Father?" Another agent lowered his gun, staring at Pat in shock.

"Hmmm . . . put . . . put your hands behind your back?" the taskforce leader asked instead of commanding.

Pat quickly spun around. Smooth, high butt cheeks came face-to-face with the agents. Placing his hands behind his back, he waited to be cuffed.

"Okay, people, we have a job to do." Four agents rushed into the house. "We have a search warrant for this house," the agent informed Pat. "We're going to take you inside so you can put some clothes on."

As Pat got dressed in the bedroom with two agents standing watch, the others were turning the house upside down, looking for drugs.

"I have something here in the freezer," one agent shouted from the kitchen.

"Found some white lady here in the bathroom tank," another yelled.

"What are they talking about?" Pat asked, now dressed in a pair of jeans and a T-shirt. "I don't have anything illegal in my house."

"Uh-huh. Turn around."

As Pat was handcuffed and dragged out into the living room, he noticed the DEA agents with large packages of cocaine in their hands. "Wait a minute!" Pat yelled, "Those aren't mine. You're trying to frame me."

"You have a right to remain silent. . . ."

Pat blocked out everyone in the room, the blood running to his head. He breathed heavily through his mouth, his mind trying to comprehend what was happening. How in heaven's name did those drugs get in his house?

That was a question that Pat would have to try to answer in his jail cell. He was marched out of the house and carted off to jail.

Chapter Forty-eight

"Early this morning, the Drug Enforcement Agency seized the largest amount of cocaine ever in Jamaica's history," the pretty reporter remarked. "Two of the country's biggest drug lords were arrested in two raids simultaneously. One is in jail, and the other is at the University Hospital recovering from a heart attack."

Suave and Daddy Lizard watched as mug shots of King Kong and Queen Bee flashed across Suave's television screen. The men were at his hideaway house.

"Also killed in the raid was Saddam Bloom. Police said he opened fire on them, and it was returned. Mr. Bloom died on the spot." The reporter also noted that Lizzy, Pat, and the five sinful angels were all arrested and charged with possession and intent to distribute narcotics.

"Unbelievable." Daddy Lizard gazed at the television in amazement. "How did the police pull that off? This is some . . . wait a minute." He looked over at Suave.

Suave silently regarded Daddy Lizard. "It's kill or be killed."

"Not even a word to me, huh?"

"It was a risky move that could have blown up in my face or gone the other way," Suave told him. "You had to stay isolated, just in case you had to pick up the pieces."

Daddy Lizard nodded. "So, we're still packing up shop? I mean, we have it all to ourselves now, Suave."

"We're sticking with the plan. Today, we're going to meet with our accountant and go over some stuff. All right?"

"That's cool," Daddy Lizard said. "I wish Cobra was here with us."

"Yeah, me too. That's why I want us to do this. Let's honor his memory by staying alive and keeping our families safe."

Over the next three weeks, Suave and Daddy Lizard worked with their lawyers and accountant as they put some of their businesses up for sale, including the bar in Rema. Suave met with all his soldiers, giving each of them a generous sum of money before he terminated their services permanently. He was cleaning house and making positive changes.

"What? You get here before me?" Alwayne asked when he saw Suave waiting for him at the top of the church steps that Thursday night.

"You're late." Suave grinned. He had really been enjoying church.

"That's because I was wrapping up a few things on your case."

"My case? What's going on?" Suave peered at him anxiously.

"Okay, I was going to tell you to come by the office tomorrow." Alwayne glanced around and saw that only he and Suave were outside. "I have some news."

Suave shifted nervously from one foot to the other. "What news?"

"The DA called me this afternoon. He's dropping all charges against you." Alwayne punched Suave playfully on the arm.

Suave's mouth opened, but he was unable to speak.

"He said there wasn't enough evidence to take this to court," Alwayne said. "The blood analysis report came back, and only Danny's blood was at the crime scene. I wonder why that detective thought yours was there too."

Because they didn't get a chance to get my blood to put there, Suave thought.

"The Lord really worked it out for you, my brother," Alwayne said. "Your enemies fighting against you are dead or in jail, and you are a free man. I hope you don't stop coming to church or meeting with my wife, though. I see some great changes in you, Suave."

"I've been changed, and I can't thank you enough," Suave replied. "No, I have no intention to stop coming to church. I think I'm beginning to understand a few things." Suave almost seemed embarrassed to admit that. He still had some issues to work out with God, but He didn't seem as bad as Suave had thought. "I'll also be continuing my sessions with Annette. She is really a lifesaver. Both of you are."

The men exchanged a man hug. "Come on, let's go inside before Bishop Hudson comes out to find us," Suave remarked.

"Let's give God the praise that's due unto Him," Bishop Hudson said into the microphone as the two made their way to the front of the church. "Praise the Lord with all your heart! Praise Him because He's worthy!"

Suave sat with his head bowed, a river flowing down his face. "It looks like it's over," Suave mumbled. To him, he was just talking aloud, but he knew in his heart he was talking to God. "I'm getting out of the game, and it's not in a body bag or locked away in prison."

As the men continued to worship, the Holy Ghost took over the service, and a revival broke out. Praises echoed off the walls. Wailing, clapping, and stomping of feet created a soulful harmony. Unknown tongues permeated the air. Tears freely flowed, broken hearts were mending, and lost souls were regenerating.

"I think I'm going to call it a night," Suave whispered moments later. The men were still getting on their praise and singing.

"Okay, "Alwayne responded. "Stop by the office tomorrow, and we'll finalize everything."

Suave quietly exited the church.

"Listen, I'm not sure what's going on here, but I'm sort of changing my mind about you," Suave spoke to the Lord as he walked to his car in the parking lot. "I'm still working through some stuff. Know what I mean?" Taking his car keys out of his pocket, Suave pressed the button unlocking his Benz. "I'm trying to do better. I'm—"

"Speaking to yourself, Smooth Suave?"

Suave's head jerked up, and his eyes opened wide as a lone figure came from behind his car to stand in front of him.

"No, no, don't do it," the person warned, pointing a gun at Suave, who had his finger on the panic button on his key chain. "Do it and you won't live long enough for them to get out here."

The harmonizing of male voices in the church singing "Jesus Dropped the Charges" by Grace Thrillers filtered into the parking lot. *"I was guilty of all the charges, doomed and disgraced, but Jesus with His special love . . ."*

Suave stood paralyzed, caught between a rock and a hard place. "What do you want?" he asked, glancing at his car where his gun was hidden under his car seat.

"Where's your piece, man?" Daddy Lizard had asked Suave two days ago as they left Suave's house.

"Oh, it's in the car," Suave had responded. "With those fools in jail, it's all good."

"Is that the only reason?" Daddy Lizard gave Suave a knowing look.

Suave had waved off Daddy Lizard's comment, but they both knew it was that subtle change that was taking root in Suave. He was becoming less dependent on his gun.

Until now . . . when Suave was caught slipping. Who was going to help him now?

"Now that's a good question." The person stepped closer, the gun still pointed at Suave's chest. "I want you to die." The evil grin was spread from ear to ear, but the eyes remained cold. "How does it feel knowing that you are seconds away from death, Suave? I hope you repented in there," the person said, nodding toward the church. "Because—"

"Noooo!" Suave screamed, throwing himself at his attacker. His fist landed on the jaw but seemed to have little or no impact. As if in slow motion, Suave watched as the gun was raised and fired. Seconds later, it felt like burning hot metal was running through his body. Suave was knocked back, his body crumbling to the ground.

As the blood seeped from his body, Suave's eyes stared up into the heavens. Grasping for breath, he muttered, "Lo . . . Lord," blood poured from his mouth, "for . . . for . . . forgive . . . me," inhaling deeply, "and . . . have . . . have . . . mercy." His chest fell as he exhaled, welcoming the black blanket that came down over him, taking the excruciating pain away.

Inside the church, the men were still singing, *"Jesus dropped the charges, Jesus dropped the charges . . ."*

Epilogue

Tears filled Monica's eyes as she stood in front of the dresser mirror, gazing at her reflection. She adjusted the black-and-white wraparound dress that was draped seductively around her body, then dabbed her wet eyes with a tissue. "Lord, please help me to get through this day," she prayed.

A knock came at the door. "Come in," Monica said softly. She turned around to face her mother as she entered the bedroom with the baby, who was kicking and screaming.

"I don't know what's wrong with him." Mother Lambert's face was filled with concern. "I fed him, changed his diaper, and I don't think he wants to sleep."

Monica reached for her son. "What's wrong, baby?" She kissed his chubby cheek. "You miss Daddy, huh?" She rocked the baby back and forth in her arms. "It's okay, Rayan," Monica said soothingly, pacing the bedroom floor as she gently swayed him. Soon Rayan's crying tapered off, and he closed his eyes.

"Is he sleeping?" Mother Lambert whispered from where she sat on the edge of the bed.

Monica nodded. "He's fussy with everything that's happening today."

"Today is going to change your lives." Mother Lambert peered at her daughter affectionately. "Remember, my daughter, this is the day that the Lord has made. No matter what, we're still going to rejoice and be glad in it."

"What if something happens to—?"

"Hello." Mr. Lambert entered the open bedroom door. "We're running late for the church. Your sister went ahead with the kids, except for Joel. He wants to ride with us." Mr. Lambert strolled over to Monica and took the sleeping baby from her arms. "I'll put him in his car seat. Come on, ladies, let's go. People are waiting for us at the church." Mr. Lambert left the bedroom with the baby.

"Ready?" Mother Lambert asked Monica as she stood to her feet.

Monica took a deep breath. "As I'll ever be," she replied, slipping her feet into a pair of black high heel pumps. Next, Monica scooped up off the bed a big, black hat with white ribbons around it and slipped it on her head. "Okay," she said, taking a deep breath. "Let's go."

Mother Lambert took her daughter's hand in her own, and the ladies walked outside where Mr. Lambert and Joel were waiting by the SUV.

Joel walked up to Monica, wrapped his arms around her, and said in a trembling voice, "It's going to be all right, Miss Monica. God has got him now."

Monica squeezed Joel gently, then pulled back to look at him. Tears filled her eyes as she took in the distinguished-looking young man decked out in his black-and-white suit. "You look so much like your father," she said, straightening Joel's black tie. "Okay. I guess we should go."

Minutes later, with everyone loaded in the van, Mr. Lambert drove out of the driveway onto the main street. Monica was wringing her hands and breathing nervously through her mouth as she gazed through the window deep in thought.

"Seems like we have a great turnout today," Mr. Lambert noted as he pulled into the church's crowded parking lot. "All the spots are gone," he complained, driving around and searching for somewhere to park. There was nothing available. "Okay, I'm going to let you guys off here. I'll drive around to the back and see if I can find a space." Mr. Lambert unlocked the doors, got out, then helped his wife with the baby out of the van.

Joel hopped out as well. "Miss Monica?" He looked up at her anxiously. "Come." He held out his hand to Monica, who was still sitting in the van.

Monica took a deep breath and released it. She took ahold of Joel's hand and stepped out of the van. Up ahead, the small church appeared like Mount Everest. *Suave is in that church,* Monica thought. *Lord, I never thought I'd see this day.*

"I have the baby. Come on." Mother Lambert walked toward the church with the baby over her shoulder, leaving Monica and Joel to follow.

As they slowly walked down the aisle to their seats at the front, Monica noticed that the church was packed to capacity. The organist was playing a somber rendition of "Amazing Grace," which only intensified Monica's anxiety.

Monica sat at the end of the long bench in the front that was reserved for the family. She looked over at her sister and Suave's children—Raven, Rayden, Janelle, Alissa, Angel, Tiana, and Natasaja, and also little Mr. Chin. Joel was seated in the second row beside Mother Lambert, now holding his sleeping brother in his arms.

"Praise the Lord, brethren," Associate Pastor Reverend Deeks said loudly into the microphone. The organist stopped playing, and everyone grew quiet. "Thank you all for coming out this morning. Romans 6:4 declares, '*Therefore we are buried with him by baptism into death: that like as Christ was raised up from the dead by the glory of the Father, even so, we also should walk in newness of life.*' Glory be to God."

"Hallelujah," "Glory," "Amen" filled the church.

"Everyone, please stand to your feet."

With a loud sigh, Monica stood. She looked up at the pulpit, noticing that a black curtain blocked off most of it from the congregation.

"Firstly, we welcome the Father, Son, and Holy Ghost in our midst today." The curtain was pulled back to reveal a glass pool in the middle of the pulpit. Standing in the water was the senior pastor, Reverend Harper. Beside him was a tall man wearing a white shirt and white pants, his long dreads pulled back in a ponytail hanging down his back.

Monica burst into tears, and the children screamed. Mother Lambert began speaking in tongues, waking up the baby, and Mr. Lambert yelled from the back of the church, "Won't He do it!"

The congregation clapped and cheered excitedly.

Suave lifted his hand and waved, a stream of water running down his face. Through his tears, Suave saw the blurry images of his family and cried harder. Sixteen months ago, he never thought he would ever see their faces again when he was shot and left for dead.

"Suave!" Alwayne screamed, jumping the steps two at a time to get to the body lying on the ground. "Someone call 119! Hurry!"

At least four church brothers were on their cell phones calling for help for Suave.

Alwayne knelt beside Suave, unaware that Suave's blood was seeping into his pants. He grabbed Suave's hand and felt for a pulse . . . but nothing. "Suave," Alwayne repeated over and over. He pressed his finger to Suave's neck, but he still didn't feel a pulse.

"Gather around and pray!" Bishop Hudson instructed, and everyone complied, beating on heaven's door on Suave's behalf as they waited on the ambulance.

Alwayne sobbed openly. "You have come such a long way, Suave. Fight! You hear me, Suave? Fight for your life, my friend."

A few minutes later, an ambulance screeched into the church's parking lot, siren blaring and lights flashing. Two paramedics jumped out with a gurney and ran over to Suave. "Out of the way, sir," one said to Alwayne. He quickly felt for a pulse, looked up at his colleague, and shook his head. As one paramedic began CPR on Suave, the other paramedic applied pressure to the bullet hole in Suave's stomach.

"Keep praying, brethren." Bishop Hudson was speaking in an unknown language, walking in a circle around Suave and the two paramedics, waving his hand over Suave's body.

The long, desperate seconds ticked away. "I'm getting a faint pulse," said the paramedic who was performing CPR and hastily put the oxygen mask over Suave's nose.

The other paramedic hooked up IVs to Suave and yelled, "We have to go. He has lost a lot of blood."

Suave was lifted onto the gurney. A cervical collar was put on him, and his head secured with towel rolls and tape. He was then loaded into the ambulance, which peeled out of the parking lot at record speed, lights flashing, loud siren crying.

Alwayne watched the ambulance until it disappeared. He knew in his heart that only one person could save Suave now—the God that he had resented all these years but was getting to know over the last few weeks. Would Suave get a chance to experience God's redeeming mercy?

At the University Hospital, Suave was immediately rushed into surgery. He had lost a lot of blood and was in critical condition. It was touch and go a few times, but the dedicated doctors and nurses worked feverishly to save his life. By the wee hours that Friday morning, Suave was finally stabilized and placed in intensive care under strict supervision.

His heart rate dropped a few times over the next forty-eight hours, but he recovered. By the fourth day after being shot, Suave was moved to a regular room for recovery.

"Who did it?" Daddy Lizard angrily asked Suave when he was finally allowed visitors. "I'll mobilize a few soldiers and head out now."

Suave looked at his friend, his brother from another mother, and gave him a weak smile. "There's no need for that. It's over now."

Daddy Lizard stared at Suave like he had lost his mind. "I think something got messed up in here." He pointed to his head. "I'm going to ask the doctor to run a few scans and stuff." He walked toward the door.

"Man, come back here." Suave coughed and winced at the sharp pain in his stomach.

Daddy Lizard walked back over to the bed. "Well, stop talking rubbish and tell me who tried to kill you."

Suave glanced down at his hand, a few emotions flicked on and off his face before he met Daddy Lizard's eyes. "I didn't see their face," Suave lied again. This was the same thing he told the detectives who had visited him earlier. "He was wearing a mask." *God forgive me, but it ends right here.*

"Mask?" Daddy Lizard spat in disgust. "The coward came at you in a mask?"

"Knock, knock," Alwayne said from the doorway before he, Annette, Bishop Hudson, and eight other church brothers entered Suave's hospital room.

Daddy Lizard gawked at the visitors in surprise, while Suave beamed with gratitude.

"Brother Suave," Bishop Hudson greeted, and Suave grimaced at being called a "brother" as if he were a member of the church.

"It's great to see you on the road to recovery." Bishop Hudson grabbed Suave's hand and shook it passionately.

"My turn." Annette moved closer to the bed, a big vase of white roses in her hands. Without asking, Annette sat down on the edge of the bed facing Suave. "These are for you," she told him, her eyes filled with tears. "They express respect, pay homage to new beginnings, and signify hope for the future. That's what I want for you, Suave Brown. I want you to start over brand new with Jesus Christ at the center of your life."

Suave lost it then. He lowered his head and cried. *These people actually care about him, and it felt good.*

As Annette got up to place the roses on a small table in the room, Alwayne walked over to Suave, handing him his handkerchief. "I spoke with your doctor a few days ago," Alwayne said after Suave wiped his face and looked at him. "He was surprised you didn't die in that parking lot after losing so much blood."

Suave used his finger to beckon Alwayne closer. "You know I prayed before I passed out," he whispered in Alwayne's ear, glancing out of the corner of his eye at the others. "For the first time, I felt that this time, He would help me. I actually believed it, man."

Alwayne gleamed like a proud father. "He did help you, my friend. God gave you a second chance. The question is, what are you going to do about it?"

"Trust me. I got it." Suave winked at Alwayne and said to everyone, "Thank you all for coming."

"We know you're still weak, so we won't be staying long," Bishop Hudson remarked. "Let's hold hands and pray."

Daddy Lizard silently tiptoed toward the door.

"Don't take another step, son." Bishop Hudson stopped Daddy Lizard in his tracks. "Come on and join us." He held out his hand to Daddy Lizard.

Daddy Lizard glanced from the bishop's hand to Suave, then back. He sighed loudly before he took it, feeling a little embarrassed. It had been many moons since Daddy Lizard had prayed. Maybe this was the beginning of something different for him too.

The group held hands, formed a circle around Suave's bed, and prayed. Suave lay in the middle and closed his eyes in reverence, with a heart full of thanksgiving for the Lord.

Suave was released from the hospital two weeks after being admitted. Monica flew back to Jamaica with the kids to take care of him in their home. Suave met his new son, Rayan, for the first time. This was an extra boost for Suave to implement the changes he intended.

Joel also packed a suitcase and told his mother that his father needed him, and he would be staying with Suave for a while. Nadine readily agreed, although she doubted she could have stopped him. Almost losing Suave was a very traumatic experience for Joel. Nadine now realized that Joel needed his father, as much as Suave needed him.

Over the next few weeks, Suave's five-bedroom house was filled to capacity. At any given time, there were at least five of his nine children there, with all the children wanting to be with their father. Monica forbade the baby mommas from even stepping foot in the driveway. However, drop-offs and pickups were allowed on the sidewalk.

Suave's business lawyer, his accountant, and Daddy Lizard were also frequent visitors to the house as Suave liquidated his assets, giving Daddy Lizard his fair share. Suave was officially legit and completely out of the illegal drug business.

"I'm going to make a move and just want to run it by you," Daddy Lizard informed Suave one evening as the men sat on Suave's veranda chilling. It had been seven months since Suave was shot, and he had recuperated nicely. "I'm planning on building a plaza and opening up a small movie theater. The rest of the space I'll rent out." Daddy Lizard peered at Suave and then added, "In Trinidad."

"Trinidad?" Suave was surprised. "Who's in Trinidad?"

"You remember Natasha, right?"

Suave bobbed his head. Natasha was the mother of Daddy Lizard's first daughter, Krystal.

"She got a job and moved there with Krystal about six months ago."

"And you didn't tell me?" Suave asked, frowning.

"You had a lot on your plate. Anyway, we've been talking and getting close again. I want to see where this can go." Daddy Lizard's eyes locked with Suave's. "I want to start over fresh, Suave. I want to settle down with a good woman, be a good father to my children, and just live life and love God."

With a big grin on his face, Suave reached over and shared a man hug with Daddy Lizard. "Go and be happy, my friend. You deserve it." Suave reached into his pocket and took out a little black box. He peered through the open door inside the house, then opened the box and showed Daddy Lizard the big oval diamond ring inside. "I'm making a fresh start as well."

Daddy Lizard whistled. "All right now. Who's that for?"

Suave cut his eyes at him. "You better stop playing. You know a brother has been straight and plans to stay that way. I'm finally going to do the right thing and marry that wonderful woman God gave me."

"Okay, Brother Suave." Daddy Lizard laughed out loud when Suave rolled his eyes at him. "Congratulations, man."

"I'm also planning on leaving this place," Suave said seriously. "I'm going to marry Monica, and we're moving to the Bahamas. I want the same fresh start in a new environment, a new country. I'm glad you and I are getting a chance to do that."

"We are a few of the lucky ones," Daddy Lizard replied.

"Thank you, Lord," Suave said sincerely.

***

Suave and Monica's wedding took place in a private ceremony on the East Lawn at Devon House, two months later. Surrounded by luscious green trees, a variety of scented, exotic flowers, with the magnificent nine-teenth-century Devon House Mansion in the background, the couple exchanged vows by a water pond filled with colorful fish and water lilies.

In attendance were Monica's parents, who flew down from the Bahamas, Daddy Lizard, Alwayne and Annette, Bishop Hudson and First Lady Hudson, Nadine and her husband, Suave's nine children, and little Mr. Chin. Reverend Stanford officiated the ceremony.

Three months later, true to his word, Suave sold the house in Jacks Hill and his hideaway hut in Belgrade Heights. The luxury cars and trucks were also sold as Suave and Monica got ready for their permanent move to the Bahamas.

"What's this letter?" Monica asked, waving an envelope in her hand as she walked into the living room where Suave was lying on the couch.

"Oh, Alwayne gave it to me last night at church, and I completely forgot about it." Suave took the letter, and Monica went back to her packing.

I wonder who would send a letter to me at my lawyer's address, Suave pondered as he opened the envelope and took out the letter. He sat up straight as he began to read.

Hello, Smooth Suave. I hope when this letter reaches you, you will be fully recovered (smile). I also hope that you have learned your lesson. You betrayed me, and for that, you had to pay. I checked around, and while there is a warrant out for my

arrest, it's not for attempted murder. I guess you
never told the police who shot you, huh? Too many
secrets, boo? Anyway, I'm back where I am freeee
to be meeee! Big Apple, baby! Aren't you glad I'm
such a poor shot? Or maybe it was actually my in-
tention for you to live? After all, I had the gun right
at your heart but aimed instead at your stomach.
And I only fired one shot. Hmmm, that's something
for you to think about. Anyway, I'm good now. I
showed you that I'm a sissy only when I choose to
be. I'm no punk, Mr. Funk. Cheers, darling! Pat.

Suave quickly folded the letter and stuffed it in his
pants pocket. After he had gotten home from the hospital,
Suave had contacted Detective Stone and was informed
that Pat was released on bail the day before Suave was
shot. "It wasn't that large an amount of cocaine, so the
judge granted him bail," Detective Stone had said.

"I hope you stay in New York," Suave mumbled. "I'm
done with all this crap."

"Say something, baby?" Monica went and sat beside
her husband.

"I'm ready to get up out of here." Suave reached over
and kissed her passionately. Two days later, he, Monica,
and their kids were off to the Bahamas.

In the Bahamas, Suave continued attending church
with Monica and the children. Monica got saved and was
baptized within weeks of them being there. Something
she had wanted to do for years.

Suave, however, needed some more time to sort out a
few things. He continued his counseling with Annette by
phone and had long talks with Alwayne discussing the
Bible and God.

Suave also closely followed Queen Bee's trial. Lizzy and the sinful angels who were arrested each took a plea deal of five years in prison in exchange for their testimonies against their madam. Queen Bee was found guilty of possession and distribution of cocaine, prostitution, and money laundering. She received fifteen to twenty years in prison.

King Kong cut a deal with the district attorney and received ten years for the possession and distribution of cocaine. This was in exchange for his testimony against Detective Bird, who was stripped of his badge and sentenced to ten years in prison.

As reported in the *Jamaica Gleaner,* a warrant was issued for Patrick Walters, the brother of the notorious drug dealer, Queen Bee, who had jumped bail, and was feared to have left the country.

"It's over," Suave had said aloud, and sixteen months after almost losing his life, he was ready to give his life to God.

So here Suave was today in the baptism pool, about to take that next phase in his walk with the Lord.

"I now baptize you in the name of the Father, and the Son, and the Holy Spirit." Reverend Harper, assisted by a church brother, pushed Suave back and under the water.

Suave came back up soaking wet, his dimples flashing like shooting stars, and shouted, "Lord, I accept your final deal!"

The church erupted in praise. While in heaven, the angels rejoiced. Smooth Suave had finally come home to where he belonged—a part of the family of God. It was a done deal.

Discussion Questions

1. What are your feelings about what happened to Suave's parents? Have you or any child you know gone through a similar experience as Suave? How did it change people's lives?

2. Pastor Ralph was someone you could probably refer to as a "wolf in sheep's clothing." Was Suave justified for the way he "handled" the situation? Were you appalled? Would you have done the same if it were you?

3. Mason Dyke Sr. became Suave's savior and role model. Was this a good thing for Suave? Why? Why not? Do you think Mason was responsible for Suave's career choice? How?

4. King Kong made an enemy of Suave since childhood, and this was carried over into adulthood. Was this pure jealousy? If so, what was King Kong jealous of? Were his feelings justified?

5. Daddy Lizard seemed to be a fierce and loyal friend to Suave and Cobra. Would you agree? Were you satisfied with the decision he made in the end? What predictions do you have for Daddy Lizard's future?

6. Did you support Nadine's decision concerning Joel's birth? Was it right to keep Joel from his

father? What would you have done if you were Nadine?

7. What do you think about Pat? Were you surprised about the "special" relationship between Pat and Suave? Was this unnatural? How? Did it help or make things worse for Suave? State specific reasons for your answer.

8. Monica was Suave's "wifey" who stayed with him even after he had many children with different women throughout their relationship. Was this love? Did it pay off for Monica in the end? How? What would you have done if you were in a similar situation?

9. What was your impression of Prophet? Do you believe in witchcraft/obeah? State the reason for your answer.

10. Suave struggled with his own demons from his past. Were you sympathetic toward him? Did this explain some of his bizarre behavior? Why? Why not?

11. What are your thoughts about Saddam? Did he deserve what happened to him in the end? How do you feel about Phil? Were you shocked by what he did for Suave?

12. Was Danny's kidnapping and what had been done to him validated? What about what Danny did to Cobra? Who do you think is responsible for Danny's demise?

13. Suave's motto was, "I don't do God." Could you understand his reason for this? Have you ever felt like God had forsaken you? How did this affect your relationship with Him? What advice would you give to someone who has the same motto now?

14. Dupree from *Are You There, God?* and *God Has Spoken* made a brief appearance in this story. Did you see the relevance? If so, what was it?

15. Were you astonished at Dupree's reaction to Suave, and what she did for him? Would you have done the same? Did this give you an update on Dupree's life? If so, were you happy about it?

16. Alwayne Clark played an integral role in Suave's personal and spiritual life. Did you think God orchestrated this? If so, please explain.

17. King Kong would have done anything to get rid of Suave and to become the biggest drug lord in Jamaica. Did he go too far? Did you agree with Suave's deal pertaining to King Kong? Was it a wise decision? What are your feelings about the way things worked out for King Kong?

18. Even though Suave cursed at Him and wanted nothing to do with Him, God still showed up in Suave's situations again and again. Why was this? Do you believe God will do what's necessary to get your attention? Was that what He had done to Suave?

19. Suave came face-to-face with his dark past that fateful night in the church parking lot. Were you horrified by what was done to him? Did Suave deserve this? Why? Why not? Were you surprised by who did it?

20. Do you agree with Suave's "final deal"? Are you happy with the way the story ended? Why? Why not?

About the Author

Theresa A. Campbell is the author of the soul-ful-filling, entertaining novels *Are You There, God?* and its sequel, *God Has Spoken*. Her first novel, *Are You There God?* was selected as a Must-Read HEA romance in 2015 by *USA Today*. She hails from Jamaica, West Indies.

Growing up in rural Jamaica without electricity until she was about eleven years old made Theresa read a lot. The lack of modern amenities did not detract from her creativity. In a sense, it improved her ability to see the ending of a story from a different perspective.

Theresa's sense of purpose is entrenched in the belief that God is always there for us, and she knows in her heart that she has to share this with her readers. It's Theresa's objective to keep it real in her books always so everyone can relate to her characters. Visit her online at www.theresaacampbell.com.